UNTIL I FALL
THE SEMIDEUS CHRONICLES

T.M. Ford

"The spark is lit. The storm is near. Hope grows faint beneath the fear. Rise again - do not stall. The darkness waits for you to fall."

Sign up for T.M. Ford's newsletter at tmford.com

To the doubters, both **loud** and *quiet*, **spoken** and *silent*.

This is what happens when belief outlasts their absence.

You **absolutely** can. You **absolutely** should.

Meridian
Prophetic Cave
Sulu's Keep
The Oasis
Silas' House
Rialtu
Welderan
Rekesh's Path
Calistia
Mystic Barrier
Temple of Amun
The Respite
The Dreadway
The Barrens
Davensclaw

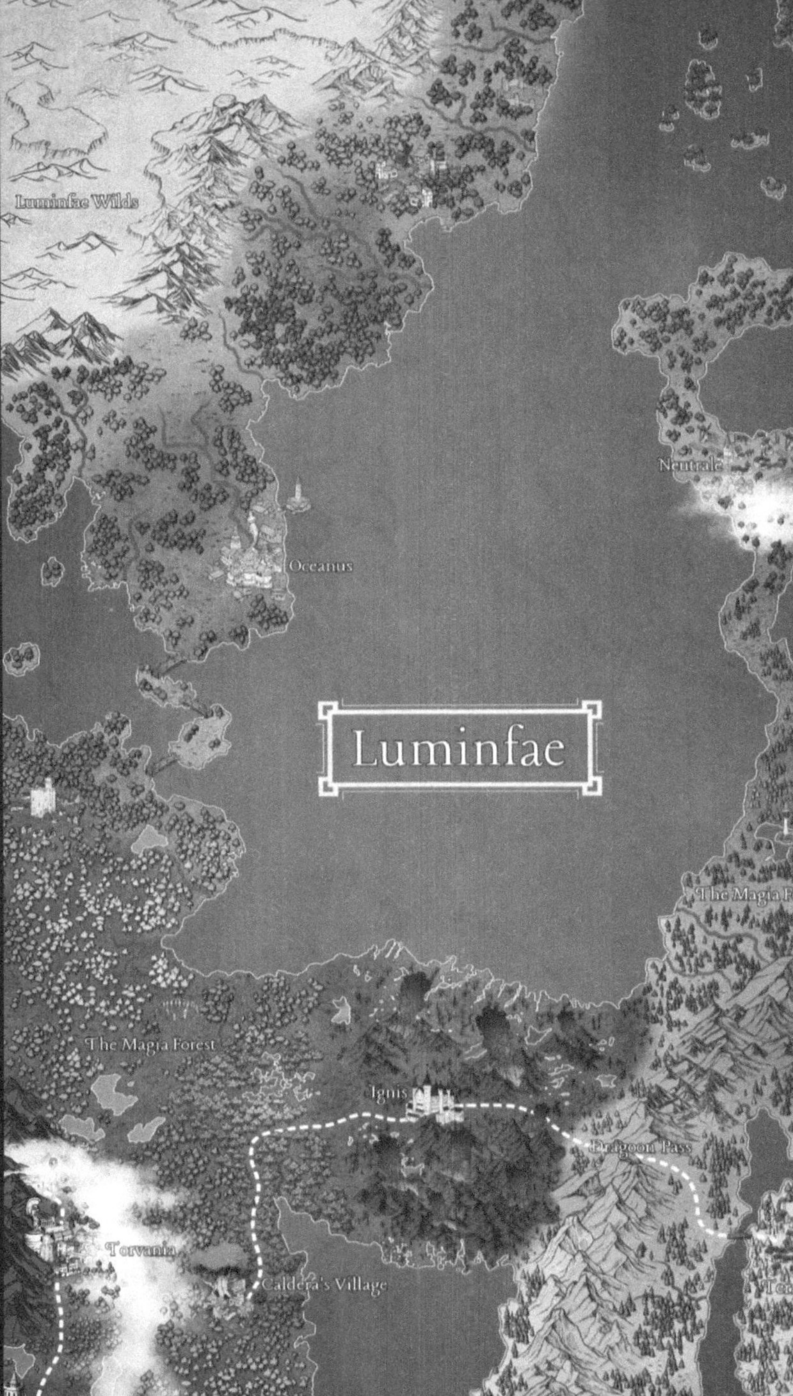

Luminfae Wilds
Oceanus
Neutrale
Luminfae
The Magia
The Magia Forest
Ignis
Dragoon Pass
Torvania
Caldera's Village

Pronunciation Guide

Semideus – Sim I Deuce

Tah'quhal – Taa Q Hall

Sarika – Sarah Kaa

Caldera – Call Dare Ahh

Nidalle – Nigh Doll

Luminfae – Lou Men Fae

Oceanus – Oh Shee An Us

Ignis – Ig Niece

Magia – Madge E Ah

Calistia – Kal Ist E Ah

Neutrale – Newt Trolly

Orgí (Οργή) – Or Yee

Contents

Chapter 1

The Fickle Fae

Derek adjusted the strap of his pack as he neared the Fickle Fae, the weight on his shoulders heavier than it should have been. A month. A month since everything changed, and still, the world was unraveling. "I wonder who all will be here today?" Derek thought to himself.

Walking through the doors of the tavern, Derek's nose was greeted by the charming notes of the nectar being poured. Two scents battled for Derek's attention: crisp, smoky sharpness against creamy citrus with a honeyed depth. It was sweet and fiery, fresh and warm, and exactly what Derek wanted. But it was far too early in the day for that.

Around the large table in the middle of the room, Mia, Johnathan, and Mr. Monton were looking at a large map of Luminfae.

"Ahh, Derek! Glad you are here, my boy. We were just talking about where everyone is." Mr. Monton joyfully quirked.

"So everyone once again didn't show up?" Derek asked, his forehead angled towards the ground.

Mia stepped up to him, warmth in her touch as she took his hands. "Hey. Look at me. We'll figure this out. Everyone will be together again."

Derek met Mia's gaze and wanted to force out a smile, but he did not need to. Something about staring into her forest green eyes always brought one to his face anyway. Even if the world was ending.

"Well, give me the updates then."

Derek and Mia strolled over to the table and glanced down at the map as Mr. Monton and Johnathan began pointing out all the points of interest.

"Well, Chieftain Tah'quhal is in Terra still meeting with all the other leaders," Johnathan started, "Most of them agree that the rifts that are appearing are from Malum's plan and believe what you have told from your vision, but..."

"But what?" Derek asked with one eyebrow raised.

Mia chimed in, "But because of Barry's intel from Ignis, some of the Chieftains now want to find a diplomatic solution... as if diplomacy could settle literal rifts in the fabric of space."

Derek rubbed his forehead and let out a huff, "The voice in the void told me we are on the right path. I may have ended him, but Malum's plan had already been set in motion."

"Presumably ended him." Mr. Monton cut in, "His body, along with Trey and Sarika's, was never found.

"Yea, thank ya for that one, Pops." Jonathan blurted out.

"Okay, is there any update on David's coma? Are we going to at least get Barry out of Ignis soon?" Derek asked.

Mia and Johnathan glanced at one another, neither wanting to answer. After a few moments, Mia finally broke the silence, "Nidalle has the best healers in Neutrale watching over him, but no new updates yet."

Derek stared at the map, but the lines blurred. Another dead end. Another thing he couldn't fix. He had led a large army into the depths of Oblivion and snuffed out Malum. While his death was questionable, at least he had defeated him in that battle. He was whisked away into some blindingly white void where he could hear a booming voice praise him for what he had done, only to then be told his fight was far from over.

Mia noticed him getting lost in thought. She squeezed his hand, hoping to bring him back to the conversation.

"Okay, where is Caldera?" Derek asked through a deep breath.

"She left Ortug and Tae in charge of the Magia Forest in her absence." Mr. Monton said.

Johnathan added, "Caldera is in the Wilds. Ya know she was down right pissed that Barry agreed to serve in Ignis while David was still in a coma."

"But the information Barry has been able to give us on Talissa's mindset has been invaluable. We wouldn't have known she was considering swearing allegiance to Malum's cause if Barry had not been there." Mia reminded Johnathan.

"Fine, but why the Wilds?" Derek wondered aloud.

Johnathan shook his head, frustration laced in his voice. "She couldn't just sit around and wait for somethin' to happen, Diamond. That ain't her. She's a warrior Fae, through and through. But between Barry bein' stuck in Ignis and Codi's death... she needed to get away." His expression darkened. "The Wilds ain't a place you go wanderin' for fun. She's hopin' to find somethin'—someone—who can stop Malum's plan or keep Talissa from draggin' more people into her rebellion." He let out a slow breath. "I just hope she ain't bitin' off more than she can chew."

Mr. Monton placed his hand on his son's shoulder, "Calm down, John." He turned back towards Derek, "When you vanished, can you recall anything more, anything that might give us some more insight?"

Derek's brow furrowed, his eyes shut as he probed his mind for any new information... but he came up short. Warmth followed Mia's touch as she ran her hand up his arm. He tried to find the words to say, but each passing second the silence seemed to linger. Then he was back, back in the void, hearing the booming voice once again.

"Derek Stratum. You have achieved the unimaginable. You have bested Malum."

A cold weight settled in Derek's chest. He wasn't just remembering—he was reliving it all over again.

The air felt heavy, pressing against him, the voice curling through the white nothingness like a phantom's whisper, "Wh ... who is there?"

"Don't be scared, young Semidues. I only brought you here to open your eyes."

"Where exactly is here?" Derek whispered.

The ancient voice brushed off his question, as if Derek hadn't even asked, "You defeated Malum, but his shell seems to have disappeared. Do not be so quick to think you have bested his plans." The echo paused for a moment before continuing, "Do not think one battle with Malum is all it will take. Even now the dimensions are..."

Derek could feel Mia stroking his arm, it was enough to keep him calm, to bring him back from inside his mind. Finally breaking the silence, "It told me that while we are on the right path, Malum's plans have not been foiled."

Clasping her hand tightly in Derek's, Mia spoke up, "I wish I could have heard everything with you. Maybe I could have helped you remember."

"Tah'quhal said both of ya'll disappeared," Johnathan blurted out, "I still ain't understandin' where exactly you went, Mia."

The corners of Mia's mouth turned down. "I used the bracelet Nidalle gave us. It definitely took me somewhere... somewhere close to Derek. I... I could feel him, like his presence. But I couldn't see him or hear him or hear the voice. Before I could panic, I was back at his side, standing in front of all of you in Oblivion."

"There is no need to go over what we already know, kids." Mr. Monton spoke up, drawing a glance from the three around him,

"Err, hardly kids, I guess, with everything you have been through. Either way, we need to focus on the present, unless Derek can remember anything else."

A knot formed in Derek's stomach, he took a deep breath and said, "The voice... it told me, in a fallen world we now stand, come with me, I'll guide your hand. Listen close, or you will fall, soon you will heed the Lonesome Call."

Silence stretched between them. The words hung in the air, ancient and unshakable. Mr. Monton exhaled sharply. "Where have I heard that before?

Johnathan chirped up, "That sounds awfully close to what the warriors say before battle here in Luminfae. Still I stand, Until I fall, I will heed the Lonesome call."

"You're right, son, but what does that mean in *this context?*" The elder Monton rebutted.

Derek glanced at a large, blank piece of parchment on the wall. Almost as if instincts took over, marched to it, grabbed a quill, dipped it in ink, and started writing. At first, his hand moved with purpose. S. U. L. Again. And again. But the letters wouldn't align, the meaning slipping through his grasp. His grip tightened on the quill. Faster. Harder. Ink blotched across the parchment until his strokes became nothing but frantic scratches.

As she walked to Derek, Mia placed her hand on the small of Derek's back. Mia frowned at the scribbled letters, her eyes flicking between the mess Derek had made and the symbol forming in her mind. "That's not right," she muttered.

Before she even knew what she was doing, she took the quill and traced the letters again—but not in the common script. The shapes curved, flowed, transforming into something ancient. Greek.

The moment she lifted the quill, Derek's lightning markings flared to life.

He fumbled around in his satchel, finally finding the vial of soil from the Start that Nidalle had given him. Pulling it out, he flipped it upside down and looked at the bottom of it. The very same sigil was there, etched into the glass.

"Mia! This. You just drew this!" He shouted, showing her the underside of the glass.

Mia glanced back and forth from the sigil she had drawn and the one on the vial. "Have you seen it before?" He asked, hoping it would lead to answers.

"No. No, I haven't, but watching you scribble S,U, and L over and over again, it just kinda came to me." She answered with wide eyes.

Mr. Monton arched an eyebrow quizzically, "Nidalle gave you that. Right, Derek?"

Derek nodded in agreement.

"Perhaps she would know more about it then. Maybe we should travel to Neutrale and see what she may know."

"Not Neutrale, Dad," Johnathan interrupted, "All of the Chieftains are in Terra for the summit with Tah'quhal."

Derek turned to Mia. Staring deeply into the lush forest that was her eyes, he was silently waiting for her approval. Or at least her agreement. After she gave him a nod, he turned back to Johnathan and Mr. Monton, "Well, it looks like we are heading to Terra then."

Johnathan and Mr. Monton both agreed to stay in Torvania in case any of the other members of the Enchanted Ensemble showed up. It wasn't likely that they would, but if not, it would give them a chance to continue poring through the history books that were discovered in a secret chamber of the Cressidia library.

As Derek and Mia turned to leave the Fickle Fae, Mr. Monton reached out and placed his hand on Derek's shoulder. "I know you haven't been able to see them much, but your parents want you to know how proud they are of you." He took a deep breath before he continued, "They want to be here with you ... they want to help you, but they are doing a phenomenal job back home keeping the community calm with the rifts appearing and everything that happened at the school."

Derek swallowed hard, staring at the door. He wanted to say something—to acknowledge his parents, to reassure Mr. Monton that he understood. But the words wouldn't come. Instead, he just nodded and reached out for Mia, who was already reaching for him. He took her hand. The warmth of her skin met the crackle of his magic, and his markings flared to life.

A sharp crack split the air. A flash of blue lightning. And then, they were gone.

Chapter 2

The Summit

The sky split open with a crack of thunder as Derek and Mia materialized in the heart of Terra. The air trembled from their arrival, charged with static, but Derek barely noticed. His feet touched the worn cobblestone, and a wave of unease crashed over him.

His chest tightened. Something happened here.

He didn't know how, but the pain was stitched into the ground itself. An echo of suffering, lingering just beneath the surface.

Mia's fingers brushed against his. "Everything okay?" she asked, her voice quiet, careful.

Derek blinked, realizing his hands had curled into fists. A single tear burned at the corner of his eye, but he refused to let it fall. He had no memories of this place, but the sorrow was woven into the very air.

"I can feel pain here," he murmured. "Something happened."

Mia squeezed his hand, grounding him. "Then let's find Nidalle and head back as soon as we can."

They walked the streets of Terra, hand in hand, the city's gentle hum of life a stark contrast to the weight pressing on Derek's chest. For a fleeting moment, it almost felt normal—like they were just two teenagers on a date, not warriors in a crumbling world.

Fae and humans bustled around them, laughter spilling from street vendors, the scent of baked honey tarts drifting through the air. A child chased a floating ember sprite, its golden wings flickering in the late afternoon light. Peace. Stability. A world untouched by rifts and war.

Mia smiled, tilting her head toward him. "This almost reminds me of shopping on the square back home."

Derek forced a smile back. *Home.*

The word felt heavy, like an echo from another lifetime.

Seven months. That's how long it had been since he last stepped foot on Earth. Time moved differently when he'd been trapped in Mythos with Sarika, six months had passed in a blink. Then, another month since the battle in Oblivion. Everything had changed.

He stole a glance at Mia, wondering if she felt the same ache he did. None of them had gone back, not really. Except Johnathan, and even then, it was only to deliver the impossible truth.

But this wasn't the place or time to think of that. Right now, they needed to get to the Chieftain summit, figure out how to get everyone on the same page, and have Nidalle explain the sigil.

As Derek and Mia approached Serene's home, they could hear muffled arguing from outside. Derek eased the front door open, listening to Tah'quhal and Talissa argue back and forth.

"How could you ever support any plan that was devised by a vile creature such as Malum?" Tah'quhal shouted.

"Listen, young chieftain. All I'm saying is, we have no idea what Malum's true plan was. You and your little human playthings raised an army and took the fight to him before any of us had time to really question what was going on." Talissa hissed as she spoke, "Maybe Malum wants what is best for Luminfae? Maybe we can find him, since your precious human let his body disappear along with his cronies, and find a diplomatic solution to all of this."

The moment Derek stepped through the doorway, the air felt charged, not just from the rising argument but from the crackling energy gathering beneath his skin. He took in the scene. Tah'quhal, fists clenched, fury written across his face. Talissa, standing in effortless defiance, a smirk dancing at the edges of her lips. Serene and Nidalle both watched silently, waiting for anything to happen. Karrent disregarded the commotion as soon as he saw Derek and Mia walk in. The others in the room did not move.

Something in him snapped.

A sharp crack split the air as lightning flickered across his arms. "Talissa of Ignis," he thundered, his voice thick with fury. "Do as you damn well please, but if you support Malum, you are an enemy of Luminfae!"

Talissa glided toward Derek, every step deliberate, calculated. Her tail traced a slow, teasing line against his neck, sending an involuntary shiver down his spine. She leaned in just enough for him to feel the warmth of her breath as she purred,

"Oh, sweetie." Her voice dripped with mock affection. "Who died and made you king?" She trailed a single claw down his arm, stopping just before his crackling energy could bite at her skin.

"Last I checked, each Chieftain controls their own lands," she continued, turning her gaze back to Tah'quhal as if Derek had already ceased to be interesting. "Ignis has never bowed to Torvania. And your predecessor certainly never wanted his people to know about the outside world."

Derek could see the anger bubbling up inside Tah'quhal, but he couldn't react to stop him. Talissa wasn't necessarily wrong, and he knew that. He *was* just an outsider here. Luckily, he didn't need to step in.

Mia's touch pressed against Derek's back—steady, grounding. Her voice rang through the room, smooth as steel.

"Back off, Talissa."

The succubus turned her gaze toward Mia, her smirk widening. But Mia didn't flinch. She met Talissa's eyes and tilted her head slightly, as if already unimpressed with whatever game the succubus thought she was playing.

"You think humans are just playthings?" Mia continued, her fingers curling slightly against Derek's back. "Funny. Humans are the reason Malum is gone. And if you keep pushing, we'll show you just how much stronger than you we really are."

Talissa laughed, sharp and cruel. "Stronger?" She tilted her head, eyes flickering with amusement. "You humans are all the same."

She snapped her fingers. A burst of flame ignited beside her, heat rippling through the room as Barry materialized. His shoulders were stiff, his expression carefully blank, but Derek could see the tension in his clenched jaw.

Talissa grinned, pleased with herself. "Even this one. He refuses the blessing of Ignis, refuses to become our Keeper."

Barry's voice was steady, but Derek could hear the weight pressing against it. "Because I am not your Keeper. Not yet, anyways. Not while David still breathes."

Talissa closed the distance between them in an instant, moving like a shadow slipping through candlelight.

Her fingers trailed along Barry's exposed arms, slow and deliberate. "How sweet you are," she purred. "You do not even need to be here, yet... here you are. By my side."

Barry's body remained rigid, but the slight twitch in his throat betrayed him.

Derek had heard enough. His pulse thundered in his ears, his skin buzzing with the charge of his growing magic. He knew the truth—Barry had no choice. He was trapped. Talissa was dangling David's life over his head like a puppet string.

And she had the audacity to act like he was here willingly?

Lightning flickered up Derek's arms, the scent of ozone thickening in the air. His eyes burned white and blue as the energy coiled inside him, aching for release.

"Talissa!" His voice shook the walls, the very air vibrating with his fury. "You think humans are weak? Mia is right. We stalled Malum's plans. And do not forget... I am not just human. I am Semideus."

Talissa's laughter split the air like shattering glass. She tilted her head, lips curling into a wicked smile.

"Semideus?" she echoed, mocking. "Oh, child... you do not even comprehend what that means."

Derek's anger swelled, heat rising under his skin. His palms dripped with sweat, fingers twitching with barely restrained energy. He was ready to show her just how much he understood what it meant to be a Semideus.

But before he could even open his mouth, screams tore through the air.

The room erupted into chaos. Every attendee of the summit surged toward the door, Tah'quhal leading the charge. Derek moved to follow, but his eyes locked on the chieftain's back as he reached for the sword slung over his shoulder.

A lot had changed in the past month. Tah'quhal wasn't just a warrior anymore, he was a leader. And as a symbol of that, the citizens of Torvania had gifted him a blade unlike any other.

Derek hadn't got a good look at it before, but now, as Tah'quhal unsheathed it, time seemed to slow.

The blade itself was slender, curved like a katana, but its edge shimmered with something unnatural. Intricate runes had been carved into the steel, each one pulsing faintly as it slid free from its sheath. One by one, they ignited. Deep, burning purple, like ancient power waking from slumber.

Derek swallowed hard. He hadn't asked much about it yet, but he would. Immense magic emanated from that sword. It was clear how much energy was put into crafting it.

Then, they were outside and Derek understood why the city was screaming.

Suspended in the air, ripping through the very fabric of reality, was a rift. A tear in the sky, swirling violently, its edges pulsing like a fresh wound and stemming all the way to the ground. Inside, shades of blue twisted and churned, flickering between dark abyss and ethereal glow, as if it were shifting between realms.

Derek's breath caught in his throat, "Another one."

And this time, it was in the middle of Terra.

"Oh, how fun this looks!" Talissa's voice dripped with amusement as she sauntered toward the rift, utterly unfazed by the raw energy pulsing from its surface. The vortex twisted and churned, tendrils of blue light crackling outward, distorting the air around it like heat on pavement.

She reached out, fingers hovering just above the swirling abyss, her expression one of playful curiosity. But at the last second, she curled her fingers into a snap.

Fire exploded beside her and Barry appeared in a burst of flame, shoulders tense, eyes immediately darting toward the rift.

He let out a frustrated sigh. "What? What do you want me to do, Talissa?"

A wicked grin curled across her lips. "Well, Barry dear," she mused, tilting her head, drawing out the pause like she was savoring a secret. Then, with a slow, deliberate wink at Derek, she purred, "Seeing as you are my... Interim Keeper ... I would like you to step through this rift and tell me what is on the other side."

Derek's pulse spiked.

"I don't think so!" he snapped, stepping forward, his body already crackling with energy. "No one touches that thing, we don't even know what it is!" But when he turned to Barry, his breath caught.

Barry stood frozen, his fists clenched so tight his knuckles had gone white. He wasn't looking at Talissa anymore. He was looking at Derek. And in that single glance, Derek understood.

Barry didn't want to go. Every part of him was screaming against it, but he was going to.

Derek swallowed, his chest tightening. "Barry..."

Barry forced a weak smile, but the pain in his voice betrayed him. "It's fine, Derek. I'll be fine."

Derek turned to Tah'quhal, hoping– no, praying– for some way to stop this. The chieftain met his gaze, then gave a slow, reassuring nod.

Derek exhaled sharply, his hands shaking with barely restrained magic. "Fine, Barry. In and out. If you're not back in a minute, we're coming in after you."

Barry hesitated for only a second before nodding. He turned toward the rift, his entire body rigid.

Then, with a shaking hand, he reached out. His fingers brushed against the swirling vortex—and in an instant, it swallowed him whole.

Derek, Mia, and Tah'quhal stood frozen, their eyes locked on the swirling rift. Each passing second felt like an eternity, the air thick with unspoken dread.

Derek clenched his fists, forcing himself to stay still. One. Two. Three. Every muscle in his body screamed to do something, but all they could do was wait.

Then, the rift shuddered.

A figure burst through, stumbling onto the ground.

Derek moved first, grabbing Barry's arm, steadying him. His friend's breathing was ragged, his hands shaking. His clothes were intact, no visible wounds, but something was off.

Mia stepped closer, her voice urgent. "Barry! What was it? What did you see?"

Barry exhaled sharply, running a hand through his hair. "I ... " He hesitated. His brows furrowed, like he was trying to piece something together that didn't make sense. "I don't know. I couldn't see anything. It was pitch black, and all I could smell was ..." He swallowed. "Sulfur."

The word sent a cold chill down Derek's spine. A murmur spread through the gathered Chieftains. Some took cautious steps forward, their curiosity outweighing their fear.

Derek's instincts flared. He could only think of one place that resembled Barry's description.

He stepped between them and the rift, his voice sharp. "Wait!"

The urgency in his tone stopped them in their tracks. He turned to Barry, searching his face. "How long were you in there?"

Barry frowned. "I dunno… I explored a little, but I never went too far from the rift. Probably ten minutes or so."

Derek's stomach dropped. His fingers curled at his sides. "Barry… you were gone for a minute. Tops."

Silence crashed over them.

Barry blinked, his breathing uneven. "What?"

Derek's pulse pounded in his ears. He could see it now, the way Barry swayed just slightly, the unfocused look in his eyes. It wasn't just disorientation. It was wrong.

"You said it was dark," Derek pressed. "And you're sure it smelled like sulfur?"

Barry gave a stiff nod, the unease in his expression deepening.

Derek turned back to the others, his voice low but firm. "No one goes near it." He forced himself to say the words, to name it. "That's a rift to Mythos."

A ripple of unease swept through the summit.

Serene didn't hesitate. She yanked the whistle from around her neck and blew a sharp, commanding note. Within moments, five Fae appeared at her side. "Lock it down," she ordered. "A full containment barrier, no one touches that rift until I say so."

They nodded, immediately moving into position, essence flowing from their hands as they wove a magical shield around the rift.

Barry took a shaky step forward. "Wait, the Hellfire Brigade!"

Serene turned to him, her expression softening just slightly. "Do not worry, Barry." Her voice was steady, reassuring. "They have not returned since you helped put a stop to them last time. The Terrian fae have been practicing magic ever since. Helian and his goons have not been able to touch us.

Derek glanced at Barry and caught the briefest flicker of relief in his expression, but it was short-lived.

The gathered chieftains erupted into debate, their voices clashing in a storm of worry and urgency. The decision came swiftly: they needed to return to their lands, in case another rift appeared. It was a brief and almost dismissive farewell, but they all agreed to remain in contact through the torquewhirlers to coordinate their next steps.

As the leaders dispersed, Derek's pulse quickened. Now was his chance.

He hurried toward Nidalle, the chieftain of Neutrale. "Wait, one second, Nidalle, I need to ask–"

She barely slowed her stride. "Make it quick. If a rift opens in Neutrale, I need to be there."

Derek pulled the vial from his satchel, flipping it upside down to reveal the etched symbol. "Do you know what this is?"

Nidalle's eyes narrowed. "I have no idea. It was already there when the vial was delivered to me. I do not think now is the time to worry about silly designs."

Mia stepped in. "Do you know when or where it was found? Maybe that could help us figure out what it means."

Nidalle's gaze flicked toward Derek, a slow, knowing smile creeping onto her lips. "That, I do know." She folded her arms. "That vial was discovered next to the prophecy that supposedly speaks of you. It was found in a cave on the edge of the Luminfae Wilds."

A heavy silence fell between them.

Derek turned to Mia, their eyes meeting in immediate understanding. The Wilds. That's where Caldera was.

No one outside the Enchanted Ensemble knew she was there. And they couldn't just mention sending her to investigate, not without risking her, or the Magia Forest's, safety.

Before Derek could think of a response, Tah'quhal approached. "I am sorry to interrupt," he said, his voice steady but laced with urgency, "but I need to get back to Torvania. I am hoping that you two..." he gestured toward Derek and Mia "... are heading there as well." He hesitated for a moment before adding, "Selfishly, I am hoping you have enough energy to take me back with you, Derek."

Derek let out a tired but amused breath. "Yeah, I think I can manage that." He glanced around. "Just let me say goodbye to Bar..."

His words cut off. His stomach dropped.

Barry and Talissa were gone. Derek's eyes darted around the square, searching for any sign of them, until he caught the last wisps of a fading vortex of embers. His fists clenched, but he forced himself to exhale slowly. He just wanted to say goodbye to his friend.

Turning back to Tah'quhal, he nodded. "Alright. I think I can muster up enough for all three of us, but after this, I'm done for a while."

Tah'quhal placed a firm hand on Derek's shoulder. Derek reached for Mia's hand, her fingers slipping into his with effortless familiarity.

Electricity hummed along his forearms, pulsing like a living thing. The energy built, filling the air with static, and with a crack of thunder... all three of them vanished.

Chapter 3

Dreams

"Tah'quhal… your sword," he said, excitement buzzing in his voice. "How did the Fae here make it?"

Tah'quhal barely glanced over his shoulder. "I do not know how to answer that, Derek Stratum."

Derek frowned, ready to argue, but then he caught the slight twitch at the corner of Tah'quhal's mouth. The chieftain was hiding a smirk.

"Oh," Derek muttered, crossing his arms. "Very funny, Chieftain."

Tah'quhal let out a quiet chuckle before continuing toward the Fickle Fae, his pace steady. "When the Torvanians gave me this blade, it was unfinished. No hilt, no runes, nothing of what you see now." His voice grew more thoughtful. "They told me to take the ethereal blades from Torviid, along with this one, and place them within Torviid's shrine. Then, I was to leave them there for a week."

Derek walked alongside him, eyes locked on the sword strapped to his back. "And you just… left it there?"

"I will admit, I was skeptical," Tah'quhal said, his fingers grazing the hilt. "But the elders told me that when I looked upon the blade again, I would know its name."

With practiced ease, he drew the sword from his back, the deep purple runes shimmering in the dim Torvanian light.

"When I returned to the shrine, the chamber was filled with light. A brilliant, blinding purple. As it faded, I saw the sword." He paused, his voice lowering. "And I knew."

Tah'quhal stopped walking. Turning to Derek, he held the sword out, laying it across his hands as though presenting something sacred. His gaze was unreadable.

"Orgí."

Derek's brow furrowed. "What does that mean?"

Mia's breath hitched.

"Wrath," she whispered.

Tah'quhal's expression flickered with something, not quite surprise, but something close. He turned toward her. "I did not know that. But that is all I could hear in my mind when I laid eyes on the blade." His grip on the hilt tightened slightly. "I took that as its name." He studied her carefully. "What language does the word hail from?"

Mia hesitated, then exhaled. "It's... Greek." She looked at Derek, her voice even quieter now. "Just like the symbol we're trying to figure out."

Tah'quhal exhaled sharply, sliding Orgí back into its sheath. "It seems I have missed quite a bit." He gestured toward the Fickle Fae ahead. "Come. Let us sit, and you two can catch me up. I will pour us some nectar.

Laughter was becoming a rare and precious thing in Luminfae. But inside the Fickle Fae, for the first time in what felt like forever, there was nothing but warmth and mirth.

Johnathan and Mr. Monton sat with Derek and Mia, helping to catch Tah'quhal up on everything he had missed. But after the weight of their conversation, Johnathan decided enough was enough. It was time for something lighter, something that reminded them of who they were before all of this.

"And then..." Johnathan snorted mid-sentence, barely able to breathe through his own laughter. "And then Barry's tall ass came runnin' outta the barn... covered in cow shit!"

A collective burst of laughter shook the table. Even Tah'quhal, the ever-stoic warrior, let a rare grin slip through. But then, with the utmost sincerity, he tilted his head and asked,

"But... why would Barry have feces on him?"

Mia chuckled, shaking her head. "Tah'quhal, Barry wasn't used to working on a farm. He had no clue not to wear tennis shoes in the barn. Cow poo is slippery, and tennis shoes didn't help. So he fell. Face-first."

"Oh..." Tah'quhal's expression remained neutral. Until, suddenly, his mouth widened, revealing perfectly white teeth. Then, to everyone's shock, something came that none of them had ever heard.

The warrior laughed.

Not just a polite chuckle. A full-on, deep, belly-shaking laugh.

Derek blinked, looking around the table. He took in the wide smiles, the tears of laughter in Johnathan's eyes, the relaxed ease in Mr. Monton's shoulders. The weight of war, of rifts, of what lay ahead... for just a few hours, it didn't exist.

He let his gaze linger on each of them. Mia. He thought back to that day in school, the first time she ever placed her hand on his knee, the silent reassurance she had given him even before he understood how much she would mean to him.

Looking at Johnathan and Mr. Monton, he thought of the first time he stayed over at their house, how Mr. Monton had made no-bake chocolate oatmeal cookies and jokingly called them cow patties to mess with them.

Tah'quhal. A true warrior. A true friend. And someone who, apparently, had the goofiest laugh he had ever heard.

Derek yawned, stretching his arms. As he did, he caught a glimpse of his lightning-marked skin. The glow was already starting to fade. He exhaled, letting exhaustion settle over him.

"Well, guys," he said, rubbing his face. "Tonight was a much-needed break. But tomorrow..." He turned to Mia, his voice quieter. "We have to get to Oceanus. And then it's a long ride into the Wilds."

He reached for her hand. "And I need to sleep."

Mia laced her fingers through his, squeezing gently. "I'll follow you anywhere."

Her smile was soft, full of understanding and quiet promise.

With that, the two bid their goodnights, slipping away to their room above the tavern.

Derek stretched out in the soft, yet unfamiliar bed, letting out a slow breath. These beds were clearly made for the Fae. Even with his above-average height for a human, his feet didn't even come close to the edge. For once, there was space.

But, right now, he wasn't thinking about that.

Mia curled up beside him, tucking herself into his side, her head resting against his chest. Derek's arm instinctively wrapped around her, pulling her close. The warmth of her body seeped into him, grounding him in a way nothing else could. He leaned down, pressing a lingering kiss to the top of her head.

"Thank you," he murmured.

Mia shifted, tilting her head up to meet his gaze, her green eyes glistening softly in the dim light. "For what?"

"For being here." His voice was quiet, almost reverent. "For being by my side. I don't think I could do any of this without you."

Mia opened her mouth to respond, but Derek wasn't finished. A small, almost hesitant smile tugged at his lips. "Earlier, you knew. You knew I was about to lose myself. I could feel it coming... the panic, the weight of everything... and you just knew what to do." His grip on her tightened ever so slightly. "And I..."

Before he could finish, Mia propped herself up and pressed her lips to his.

The kiss was slow, deep, and full of unspoken promises.

Derek melted into it, his fingers curling gently against her back as he let himself forget, just for a moment, all the battles waiting for him outside this room.

When Mia finally pulled away, she simply nestled her head back against his chest. Her breath warm and soothing against his skin.

"I'll always be here for you, Derek," she whispered.

Derek's chest rose and fell in a slow, steady rhythm as sleep claimed him.

He had gone a full month without dreaming. A month of silence in his mind. But tonight, that changed.

A voice called out to him. Familiar. Unrelenting.

"Why won't you tell them?"

Derek's eyes snapped open, but he wasn't in his room with Mia. He was back in the void.

Nothing but endless white stretched in every direction. A weight pressed against his chest, thick and suffocating.

"Why are you not telling them everything, Derek?" The voice echoed from everywhere and nowhere at once.

Derek clenched his fists. "Because there has to be more. There has to be another way."

"NO!" The voice thundered through the void, shaking the very air around him. *"The path you walk, the path you revealed, the path you chose... is the only path forward."*

Derek opened his mouth, but before he could speak, the voice rang out again.

"What is done CANNOT be undone. Everything has a purpose now. Everything must happen."

Lightning crackled across his arms, the brilliant blue glow a beacon in the constant white void. "I can't do it this way," he pleaded. "Too many people will be hurt. Please, help me change this..."

Silence was his only response. Seconds stretched into minutes. Minutes into eternity.

Then, a sound. A sound that he felt he'd heard before, but he couldn't quite place it. A faint, high-pitched trill, followed by a series of chirps.

Derek turned sharply, scanning the void, but there was nothing. His eyes darted back and forth, his head snapping in every direction, but all he could hear was,

"Derek! Derek, wake up!"

His body lurched forward as his eyes flew open.

Sweat drenched his skin, his heart slamming against his ribs. His breath came in ragged, uneven gasps.

To his left, Mia sat up, her hands gripping his shoulders. Worry lined her face.

"You... you were screaming in your sleep," she whispered. "And you've never sweat like that before."

Derek let out a shaky breath, forcing his body to still. He placed a reassuring hand on Mia's leg. "It was just a nightmare. I slept well until it started. I'm sorry."

The first light of dawn bled through the window. A new day. A new excuse to pretend nothing had changed.

Sliding out of bed, he grabbed a towel, wiping the sweat from his face before pulling on his robes. "I'm going to grab breakfast before we head to Oceanus."

Mia shot up, reaching for his hand before he could walk away. Her fingers wrapped around his wrist, firm but gentle.

"Derek. I told you last night, I will always be here for you. Tell me about the nightmare."

He hesitated.

"It was nothing," he lied. "I just saw the battlefield in Oblivion."

The crease in Mia's brow deepened. "Derek... You've had dreams that meant something before. What if this is like that?"

Derek forced a smile. He leaned in, brushing a quick kiss against her lips.

"Get dressed and join me for breakfast," he said softly. "I promise, if it happens again, we'll figure it out. But for now... I think it was just a nightmare."

Reluctantly, Mia nodded.

Derek turned away before she could see the lingering fear in his eyes.

Downstairs, Johnathan, Mr. Monton, and Tah'quhal were already waiting. Derek took his seat at the large table, where plates of food had already been set out for him and Mia.

Johnathan leaned in. "Everything okay, buddy?"

Derek forced a grin. "Yeah, man. Just didn't get enough sleep."

Johnathan smirked. "Ohhh, Mia keeping ya up all night, huh?" He cackled mid-bite.

Derek rolled his eyes, grinning. "Nothing like that, John."

Before Johnathan could throw another jab, Derek's gaze drifted toward the staircase. Mia was descending, each step unhurried, graceful. Something in the way she moved, the quiet confidence, the light in her eyes, it wrecked him.

She wasn't just his friend, his girlfriend. She was *his* anchor. Ever since this chaos started, she had been his constant.

Mia slid into the seat beside him, arching a brow. "What's with that goofy grin?"

Derek coughed, looking away. "Uh... oh, nothing. We were just going over our plan."

The group shared a knowing glance. Johnathan opened his mouth to press further, but his father nudged him subtly, a silent warning to let it go.

A few moments went by when Johnathan couldn't take it anymore and broke the silence.

"So, you two are gunna use Derek's magic to teleport to Oceanus and get help from Karrent to reach the Wilds, right?" He asked.

Derek nodded. "That's the plan."

"I've already sent a torquewhirler ahead to inform Mr. Karrent," Mr. Monton added.

Tah'quhal folded his arms. "I will be visiting the rifts on Earth, attempting to decipher where they lead."

Mia's expression darkened. "Aren't you worried about a rift opening up here?"

Tah'quhal placed a reassuring hand on Johnathan's shoulder. "The Keeper of Torvania will alert me if anything happens. I have the utmost faith in him."

Johnathan puffed his chest slightly, smirking. "I got it covered."

Derek hesitated for a moment before turning to Tah'quhal. "My... parents. Will you check on them for me?"

Tah'quhal's gaze softened. "Of course. Mr. Monton has already informed them of my likely visit. I am also meeting with Isabella's parents to offer my condolences."

A heavy silence fell over the table.

Derek and Johnathan both lowered their heads. They should be there. They wanted to be there. But there were bigger battles ahead.

Finally, Derek straightened his back. "It's settled then. Mia and I will head to Oceanus, then the Wilds, and try to uncover whatever we can."

The group rose, exchanging goodbyes.

For once, the farewell didn't feel final.

Derek and Mia stepped out of the Fickle Fae's front door. The sky had darkened. Then—BOOM. A loud clap of thunder shook the air.

Johnathan watched them go, then murmured, "I hope they find what we need out there."

Mr. Monton's expression remained unreadable, his gaze lingering on the door, the thunder still echoing.

"I hope they do, too," he said quietly. "I hope they find it fast."

Chapter 4

I'm Sorry

The thunder still echoed as Derek and Mia arrived in the sea breeze city. Before them, the massive gates stood tall, gleaming in the soft morning light. Perched on the cliffs of Luminfae's ocean, Oceanus was a marvel—elegant, powerful, timeless.

Derek let out a slow breath. "I didn't really get a good look around the last time we were here."

Mia chuckled beside him. "We were kinda in a hurry."

The full splendor of the city unfolded as they stepped through the gates. The sun danced along white stone facades laced with golden veins, while sandstone towers soared toward the sky, their swirling engravings mimicking the waves crashing below. Canals of crystalline water wove through the streets, reflecting the city in a dance of endless hues. Golden lilies floated lazily on their surface, glowing faintly even in daylight.

From the steps of a grand library, Karrent emerged, his sapphire-blue robes rippling in the salty breeze.

"Ahh, Derek, my boy!" Karrent's smile was as warm as the city's sun-warmed stone. "Mr. Monton sent word of your arrival. I have arranged two *Steeds* for you and our lovely Keeper."

"*Steeds*?" Derek raised an eyebrow. "You mean horses?"

Mia stifled another chuckle. "Kinda. Just wait and see."

As Karrent led them toward the stables, he noticed Derek still looking around, taking in every detail.

"Art is the soul of Oceanus," the elder Natare mused. "Every building is a masterpiece, adorned with sweeping murals that shift under the moonlight, telling stories of wars won, lovers lost, and the legends of my people."

Derek's gaze lingered on one such mural—a massive painting across the side of a domed building. It seemed almost alive, waves cresting and falling, figures moving in the foam, a battle frozen in time.

"What do you love most about this place?" Derek asked.

Karrent's eyes gleamed. "A difficult question, my boy. Perhaps the sculptures, flowing figures half-translucent, as if made of seafoam, their voices whispering secrets to those who truly listen." He inhaled deeply. "Or maybe it's the air... thick with salt and parchment, paint and polished steel."

They walked on, Karrent pointing out more wonders as they passed. The Great Halls of Knowledge stood proudly at the city's heart, their stained-glass ceilings depicting forgotten constellations.

Inside, endless shelves held books crackling with enchantments, their words eternally preserved. Scholars and artists roamed within, either debating in hushed tones or lost in their craft.

As they exited the city walls, Karrent gestured toward the towers along the sea wall and the border of the Wilds.

"You've seen firsthand how well-equipped our military is," he said.

Derek followed his gaze. The golden fortresses stood like eternal sentinels, their towers crowned with watch-fires that never died. The warriors of Oceanus, clad in flowing white and deep ocean blue, moved like dancers on the battlefield. Their sea-glass and enchanted steel weapons shimmered with the fury of the tides. The Natare fought like the ocean itself—unpredictable, relentless, and impossible to contain.

Derek's gaze dropped to the ground, his voice quiet. "Your warriors were some of the best when we went to Oblivion... I only wish more of them had come home."

Karrent's smile softened, though a hint of sorrow flickered in his silver-blue eyes. "No need to dwell on the past, my boy. There is much to look forward to."

Mia squeezed Derek's hand, pulling him forward gently. "Look, we're here."

The stables were right ahead, the scent of fresh hay and saltwater mingling in the air. The echo of faint whinnies came from within.

Derek smirked. "Sounds like horses to me."

As if in response, the stable doors swung open with a soft rush of magic. Two magnificent creatures emerged, their hooves barely making a sound against the stone.

They had the shape of horses, and yet they were anything but ordinary. Their deep-blue coats shimmered, the color of the ocean just before a storm. Their manes and tails flowed like living water, cascading endlessly but never spilling. With every step, small droplets trailed from their hooves, sinking into the ground like ripples fading on a pond.

Karrent spread his arms, pride gleaming in his eyes. "These are Steeds, Derek. Magic-born, swift, and just as powerful in the sea as they are on land."

Derek eyed the creatures warily. "Right. But our clothes are gunna be soaked."

Mia grinned, eyes bright with mischief. "Nope. The rider only gets wet if it's necessary."

Karrent chuckled. "Magic, my boy." He stepped closer, running a hand through one's watery mane. "Steeds bond deeply with their riders. Call, and they will come. Trust them, and they will carry you where you need to go."

Derek hesitated before approaching the nearest creature. The beast tilted its head, studying him with silver-blue eyes, ancient and knowing.

"Easy, boy," Derek murmured.

A soft snort.

Mia stifled a laugh. "That's a girl."

Derek huffed, patting its neck. "Easy, girl."

The Steed whickered softly before bending its front legs, inviting him to mount. Derek swung himself onto its back, half-expecting the cold rush of water to soak through his clothes. Instead, the magic felt like a passing breeze—cool against his skin, then gone. He ran his fingers through the creature's ever-flowing mane, watching the water slip between his fingers without leaving a trace.

His grin widened. "Okay. That's actually pretty cool."

Mia settled onto her own Steed with practiced ease. "To the Wilds?"

Derek glanced at her, excitement flickering in his chest. "To the Wilds."

Just as they turned to leave, Karrent's voice cut through the moment.

"One last thing, lovebirds."

Derek sighed. "Here we go."

Karrent's usual humor dimmed, replaced by something heavier. "The Wilds are just that... for a reason."

A long pause. A hesitation that said more than his words.

Derek frowned. "Karrent, what..."

Before he could ask, the elder Natare simply smiled and said, "Be careful."

The sandstorm howled around them, grains stinging their skin as Derek and Mia reached the jagged border of the Wilds. The towering sand-covered mountains ahead stood like silent sentinels, their peaks lost in the swirling winds.

Derek squinted, shielding his eyes. A dark void yawned at the base of one of the peaks. "There." He pointed ahead, his voice raised over the wind. "I see the cave!"

Mia nodded, guiding her Steed forward. Their mounts moved fluidly over the shifting dunes, hooves barely sinking before stepping onto solid ground.

As they reached the cave entrance, the wind died as if something unseen had swallowed the sound. Dismounting, they stepped inside, where the air was dense and charged, heavy with something Derek couldn't name.

Then it hit him.

A rush of power, not warm or cold, but electric. It shot through his veins, making his skin prickle. His breath hitched. This place was alive.

"I wonder how long it's been since anyone's set foot in here?" Derek asked, voice quieter now.

Mia barely heard him. She had started to smile, about to say something about Caldera, when her words faltered. Her eyes widened.

"Derek..." Her voice held a strange note, hovering between awe and concern. She lifted a finger and pointed at his arms.

They were glowing.

A brilliant white radiance pulsed from his skin, spilling into the cave like a rising sun trapped in stone. Shadows fled, leaving no corner untouched.

Derek's stomach twisted. He flexed his fingers, panic creeping into his voice. "I'm not doing this.

Mia was at his side in an instant, grabbing his hands. Her fingertips interlaced with his, grounding him. "Breathe," she whispered.

Derek inhaled, forcing his pulse to steady. "I'm fine..."

But before the words fully left his lips, his vision bled into white. Nothing. Endless, suffocating nothingness.

His heart pounded. He knew this place. The void. Silence stretched, thick and absolute, before a voice, *that* voice, pierced the emptiness.

"Share the truth, Derek!"

Derek's chest heaved as he searched the blank expanse above, if there even were an above. His fists clenched. "That's your truth. I'm looking for another way."

The void shuddered around him.

"THERE IS NO OTHER WAY!"

Derek flinched but held his ground. "Says you! Show your face! Tell me who you are!"

The voice softened, as if exhausted.

"Time is running out. I've told you before, the path you walk is now the only way forward. You need your friends... and they need the truth."

Derek exhaled sharply. "At least you're not screaming now."

For a moment, there was only silence, until there came another familiar sound. A faint, high-pitched trill and a series of chirps that followed.

The voice returned, calm but unyielding.

"Malum's plan is already in motion. The rifts will widen. The dimensions will collapse into one another. He will rule that land."

Derek's brow began to sweat. "No. There has to be a way to stop it."

There was another beat of silence, but no trill this time.

"I know that's what you want, but it's not possible." The voice finally echoed.

A cold certainty settled into Derek's bones.

"I will give you one last gift." The voice's tone shifted, finality lacing each word. "Use it to find the Trinity. Decipher it. Prepare Luminfae to become home to all realms."

There was the trill again. The trill and the chirps. Derek knew he had heard that sound before all of this, but he still couldn't quite place what it was.

"Derek! Wake up!"

Mia's comforting voice pulled him from the void like a hook dragging him back to reality.

His eyes fluttered open, the cave coming into focus—Mia's panicked face inches from his, her hands clutching his arms.

"I—I'm okay," he rasped.

Mia let out a breath of relief before helping him into a sitting position. "Don't do that again," she scolded, but her hands still trembled where they touched him.

Derek's gaze drifted past her and then froze...

Etched into the cave wall, glowing softly, was the symbol, its intricate design eerily similar to what Mia had drawn at the Fickle Fae.

He lifted a shaking hand, pointing. "Do you see that?"

Mia turned, brow furrowing. "See what?"

Derek's pulse pounded in his ears. "The symbol."

Mia turned, watching him cautiously. "It's just a wall, Derek." Her teasing tone was gone. "Did you hit your head?"

He didn't answer. His gaze stayed locked on the symbol as he whispered, "Trinity."

Mia blinked. "What's a Trinity?"

"The voice in the void..." Derek started.

Mia cut him off, voice sharp and certain. "I knew there was more to it. Tell me everything, Derek."

His breath hitched.

Then, without a word, he reached for her hand.

At his touch, a blue glow bloomed, spreading from his skin to hers. It wasn't just light, it was knowledge, memory, truth. Mia gasped as her eyes shifted from their deep forest green to a brilliant cerulean.

And suddenly, she saw it. The symbol, now clear and undeniable, etched in light.

Her voice came in a whisper. "What does it mean?"

Derek swallowed hard. "There's more." Guilt threaded into his softened tone. "I'm sorry I didn't tell you before."

The glow intensified, and Mia's vision was now waves of blue.

Then, the voice in the void. The warnings. The fate of the realms. She heard everything and when the vision ended, she staggered, her hands trembling in his grip. Tears clung to her lashes but never fell.

Derek held his breath. Then, voice barely above a whisper, he said it again.

"I'm sorry."

Chapter 5

Earth

Tah'quhal stepped through the Anchor and onto the Monton family farm. The moment his feet touched the earth, he took a deep breath, expecting the crisp, sun-kissed scent of the country-side. Instead, the air was thick with the acrid tang of smoke, clinging to his throat like a warning.

Rows of tattered tents stretched endlessly across the once-green fields, their faded fabric fluttering like wounded birds. The land was turned into a refuge, or a graveyard of hope, depending on one's perspective.

His jaw tightened. "This is what they don't want the others to know," he whispered to himself.

Rustling ahead made him turn. Two figures approached, their pace uneven. The woman strode forward with urgency, the man trailing behind her like a cautious shadow. Tah'quhal had never met them, but he recognized them instantly. Derek's parents.

The man bore a striking resemblance to his son, same strong build, same unruly dark hair. But the similarities ended at the eyes, which were a deep, weary brown, and the long, unkempt beard that obscured much of his face.

The woman was shorter, but there was no mistaking those ice-blue eyes. Derek's eyes. The intensity in them was almost unnerving, like staring into a mirror of the boy's determination.

Before they could speak, Tah'quhal inclined his head in greeting. "Ah, you must be the Stratum's." He hesitated for a fraction of a second before adding, "Derek has made it very clear to me that humans do not like being addressed by their full names. I am Tah'quhal. What may I call you?"

The man stepped forward first, extending a rough, calloused hand. "Phillip, but you can call me Phil."

Tah'quhal accepted the handshake, though his brow arched slightly. The human custom still felt odd to him, so much unspoken meaning in a simple grasp.

The woman let out an exasperated sigh. "Oh, Phil, stop it. You're going to confuse the poor man." She turned to Tah'quhal with a small, tired smile. "I'm Missy."

"It is my pleasure to meet you both," Tah'quhal said, dipping his head slightly. "Forgive me if I am blunt or stubborn with anything I see today. I have only recently become Chieftain, and I am still unsure if this role suits me."

Missy's lips quirked into a small smirk. "Easy there, Chieftain. You're starting to sound a little more human than you realize."

"Come on, we'll take you to the main tent," Phillip added, already stepping forward.

As they wove through the labyrinth of tents sprawled across the Monton family farm, the weight of the situation pressed heavily on Tah'quhal's chest. He had known Earth's crisis was dire, but this, the sheer scale of displacement, the despair woven into every whispered conversation, this was worse than he had imagined.

He caught fragments of voices as he passed.

"When can we go home, Daddy?" a child's voice drifted from one tent, small and hopeful.

"How could any of this be real?" an older man muttered, his tone hollow.

Eyes turned toward him as they passed. Faces, gaunt and exhausted, peered out from behind canvas flaps. Fingers pointed. Questions whispered. Some expressions held curiosity, others suspicion, but most were simply tired.

Then, a gentle tug at the side of his britches made him pause.

He looked down to find a boy no older than six, maybe seven, standing before him. The child's wide eyes locked onto his, unblinking. There was no fear in them, only sorrow. The kind of sorrow no child should have to carry. It was not the pain of scraped knees or scoldings. It was of loss. Of leaving behind a home that might never exist again.

The boy swallowed hard. "What are you?"

Before Tah'quhal could respond, a man, his father judging by the resemblance, rushed forward and scooped the boy up. His movements were frantic, apologetic. "I ... I am so sorry for him. He's just confused, that's all."

Tah'quhal held up a hand, a silent reassurance, then motioned for the father to set the boy down. When the man hesitated, Tah'quhal softened his gaze. "Please," he said quietly.

With a nod, the father lowered the child back to the ground.

Tah'quhal knelt so they were at eye level. "My name is Tah'quhal," he said, his voice calm, steady. "And what is yours?"

The boy flicked his gaze toward his father, waiting for some unspoken approval. When he got it, he answered, "Zachary."

"Well, Zachary," Tah'quhal said, folding his hands over his knee, "I come from a place that is both very far away and yet not so far at all. I am the Chieftain of Torvania, a city in Luminfae—the land of the Fae. And that is what I am. A Fae."

He reached into his pocket and pulled out a small whittled carving, its edges sharp and fresh. "This," he continued, holding it between his fingers, "is a Tourqewhirler. They're like birds, but much, much faster." He turned it over in his palm, remembering the feel of the branch before it became this. "I carved it from a tree that grows by my ancestor's graves. It has always brought me good luck." He extended it toward the boy with a small smile. "And now, I want you to have it."

Zachary hesitated, but reached out, his tiny fingers curling around the carving. He held it to his chest as if it were the most valuable thing in the world. "Thank you, mister Taahuel!"

A rare, genuine smile spread across Tah'quhal's face. He opened his mouth to correct the boy's pronunciation, but before he could, Zachary spun on his heel and darted toward his tent, clutching the carving to his chest. His father trailed behind him, pausing just long enough to glance back at Tah'quhal.

No words were spoken, but the gratitude in the man's eyes was unmistakable.

Tah'quhal simply nodded. As he rose to his feet, he exhaled, slow and deep. He had always believed strength was measured by battle prowess, by leadership in war, by standing against one's enemies.

But today, he realized true strength might be measured by something much smaller. Something as simple as kneeling beside a child who had lost his home and offering him a piece of hope.

Tah'quhal took a step toward the center tent as Phillip's hand gripped his shoulder.

"You might have this Chieftain thing down better than you thought," he murmured, a flicker of admiration in his tone.

Tah'quhal offered a half-cocked smile and pushed through the heavy canvas flaps into the massive tent. The air inside was thick with the scent of parchment and ink, the room a chaotic sprawl of desks, tables, and scattered maps. Some papers were stacked in neat piles, others hastily scribbled with notes, as if their writers had been too frantic to organize.

He took it all in, his voice cutting through the tense atmosphere. "Tell me exactly what is going on here."

Missy didn't hesitate. She gestured for him to follow as she led him to a desk near the back, speaking as she walked. "After Riverrun ... after everything fell apart, Mr. Monton gathered the parents of Johnathan's friends." She eased into her chair and motioned for Tah'quhal to sit. When he did, she continued, her voice tight with frustration. "He told us about magic, about the attack, and how it was only a matter of time before the government got involved." A humorless chuckle left her lips. "Of course, none of us believed him. We thought he'd lost his damn mind. The news called it an earthquake. Text alerts backed up the story. It was easier to believe that than the truth."

Phillip hovered behind his wife, one hand resting on her shoulder. "Some of us wanted to believe him ..."

"Not now, Phil."

He rolled his eyes, pressing on. "Anyway, once he started showing us magic, real magic, and shared the information coming from Luminfae about what Derek and his friends," he gestured at Tah'quhal, "and you were dealing with, well ... there was no denying it anymore."

Missy placed her hand over Phillip's, grounding herself. "Then the black SUVs came. Military vehicles. They put the town under quarantine, claimed the 'earthquake' had caused a sulfur leak."

Phillip's voice dropped, his jaw tightening. "Then the phone calls started. People from outside the quarantine, from all over the world. They were seeing things. Things like what happened in Riverrun."

Tah'quhal watched them carefully. The way they clung to each other's words, the way their eyes darted, uncertain. There was more, something they hesitated to say. He leaned forward, his voice quiet but firm. "And then the rifts started opening?"

Missy exhaled the breath she had been holding. "Exactly." Her voice barely carried.

"That's when Mr. Monton made the call," she continued. "He knew we couldn't wait any longer. He had to find Derek and his 'Enchanted Ensemble.' He had to find all of you and figure out what the hell was coming next."

Phillip's beard twitched as his lips pressed into a straight line. "When John Sr. returned, he gathered most of us here. Used magic to create this place, the tents, the wards, all of it. As more people escaped the quarantine or fled whatever nightmare crawled out of that rift, he kept expanding it."

Tah'quhal swept his gaze over the tent, imagining the fear and desperation that had driven people here. "Is there enough room for everyone?"

Phillip spread his arms wide. "The farm is massive. But it doesn't matter. No one's come in weeks."

Tah'quhal's brows knit together. "Why not? Is everyone already here?"

Missy hesitated. "John Sr. didn't tell you?"

Tah'quhal shook his head.

Her voice dropped to a whisper. "The rift at Riverrun ... it's grown so large, it's almost swallowed the town."

A heavy silence settled between them.

Phillip broke it, his voice grim. "We got a call two days ago. Some family members had been on vacation when this all started. They were in Rome." He paused, as if saying it aloud would make it real. "A rift opened at the Vatican." He swallowed hard. "It's gone now. The whole damn thing."

Tah'quhal exhaled slowly, trying to process the weight of it.

"The creatures coming out of these rifts are bad enough," Phillip continued, voice raw. "But now, it's not just creatures. The rifts are consuming everything. And we don't know how to stop it. We were hoping you, Derek, and the others had this figured out by now."

Tah'quhal pinched the bridge of his nose before rubbing two fingers against his temple. "The rifts in Luminfae aren't growing. More are appearing, yes, but they aren't expanding. That's a difference worth noting." His eyes lifted. "Can you see anything through the rift?"

The Stratums shook their heads in unison.

"Barry stepped through one in Terra. It led him to Mythos. I wonder if they all lead there?"

Missy and Phillip's eyes widened in unison. She quickly hushed him, her voice low but urgent. "Woah, keep it down. Glorinda and Davis are right over there." She nodded toward Tah'quhal's right shoulder. "They don't know exactly what Barry has been up to. They just know he's safe from the rift while he's there."

Tah'quhal's expression hardened as a shadow of concern crossed his face. "So not everyone here knows the whole truth?"

Phillip shook his head. "No."

Tah'quhal exhaled slowly. His voice dropped, the weight of experience pressing into every syllable. "I knew a great leader once." He paused, reflecting for a moment before continuing. "The downfall of his reign was his inability to be honest with his people. When the situation got worse... I do not wish to follow in his footsteps."

Phillip's voice was softer, but no less firm. "Sometimes, hiding the whole truth keeps people calm. And calm people are safe people."

THUD!

Tah'quhal's palms slammed against the table, rattling the maps and papers. Conversations in the tent died instantly, all eyes locking on him. His gaze swept across the room, steady, unreadable. Only when the moment had fully settled did he sit back down, fixing his attention on the Stratums.

"I apologize," he said evenly, though the fire in his voice remained. "I do not mean to cause an uproar. But this is a point we will not agree on. If information exists, it should be given. When people are kept in the dark, bad things happen."

He drew in a slow, deliberate breath.

"I am not the Chieftain here. I will not tell you how to inform your people. What I will do is step into the rift outside this farm."

Missy's breath hitched. "Why would you do such a thing?"

Phillip answered before Tah'quhal could. "Honey, he just told us. Information."

Tah'quhal inclined his head. "Your mate is correct, Missy. I need to know where it leads. If all rifts go to Mythos, then maybe the key to stopping them is there."

The air was heavier as he rose once more, his movements deliberate. Phillip and Missy exchanged a glance before silently following him out of the tent. They walked in silence through the winding paths of makeshift camps and worried faces. Over a hill, the rift loomed into view, a gaping wound in the world, swirling with violent hues of molten orange and deep, bleeding red. It pulsed, alive in a way that sent a shiver down the spine.

As they neared its lowest point, Missy finally spoke. "How is Derek?"

Tah'quhal reached a hand toward the rift, fingers grazing the strange energy, feeling the unnatural hum in his bones.

"He's doing the best he can," he answered, voice heavy. "But all of this weighs on his shoulders more than he lets on."

Phillip and Missy held each other, fear and longing intertwining in their embrace.

Tah'quhal looked at them for a long moment, then turned to the rift. Just before he leapt through, he spoke one final truth.

"He wants to see you. He wants everyone together again. And he is going to make that happen."

The vortex's glow reflected in his eyes.

"He just needs our help along the way."

Chapter 6

Where is Here?

The portal vibrated violently as Tah'quhal stepped through, its swirling reds and oranges collapsing behind him like a dying ember. He braced himself for the expected time dilation, for the bone-chilling cold and the suffocating black void of Mythos. Derek had warned him, had spoken of the Harpy and the Minotaur, of battles fought in an abyss with no sky and no mercy. But this was not that place.

Heat pressed against his skin, thick and cloying, the air itself humming with a molten pulse. Shadows danced in the flickering glow of the lava pits surrounding him, their sluggish rivers of molten rock carving paths along the jagged ground. Though dim, the light casting everything in an eerie, shifting orange, just enough to see.

He turned, expecting to find the rift still pulsing behind him, but there was nothing. No shimmering portal, no way back. The rift in

Riverrun had swallowed him whole and spat him out here—wherever here was.

His sharp gaze swept the landscape. The lava pits flanked him on both sides, their currents flowing away from where he stood, sloping downward ever so slightly. The rock formations around him were immense, serrated walls of blackened stone that stretched impossibly high. Yet, when he tilted his head back, he found no ceiling. Just an empty expanse stretching into darkness, an abyss above rather than below.

He closed his eyes, steadying his breath. A familiar tingle ran along his skin as his stigmata responded, glowing faintly. Blue essence flickered to life, coiling around him in delicate wisps. "This feels familiar," he whispered, the words barely more than a breath.

Keeping his hand firm on the hilt of Orgí, he took his first step forward, following the path of the lava's flow. One foot in front of the other, he moved with quiet precision, his pointed ears twitching at the slightest sound. This place was not Mythos, but something told him it was just as dangerous.

He walked for what felt like an eternity, each step blending into the last. The path remained unchanging, twin rivers of lava flowing endlessly beside him. Their molten currents casted rippling shadows on the jagged stone walls. The oppressive heat never waned, clinging to him like a second skin, yet the monotony of the journey was more unnerving than the suffocating air.

Then, finally, something new. A massive stone door loomed ahead, its surface weathered but unmarred with time. Carved into its center was a symbol, a large, intricate circle. His stomach twisted as recognition flickered in his mind. He knew this symbol. Mia had told him about this. About how she drew it back at the Fickle Fae.

As he moved closer, the blue essence swirling around him trembled. At first, it was a faint vibration, like the plucking of a harp string, but with every step, the intensity grew. The essence writhed and hummed, faster, wilder, until it was nearly unbearable. Still, he pressed forward.

His outstretched fingers met the bottom of the engraved circle, and the moment they did, the essence stilled. It was unnatural, like the sudden silence before a storm. His breath hitched as the magic that had always been an extension of himself disobeyed. It peeled away from him in thin, glowing tendrils, moving of its own accord, slithering toward the door as though answering an unspoken command.

The deep grooves of the carving drank in the blue essence, veins of magic crawling through every crack and crevice. The glow intensified, brighter and brighter, until the entire engraving pulsed like a living thing. It swelled to a near-blinding radiance, forcing him to squint. Then, just as suddenly as it had come to life, everything went dark.

Not just the essence. Not just the engraving. The lava pits that had been his only source of light flickered and died, their molten glow snuffed out like candle flames in the wind. An unnatural, suffocating blackness swallowed the corridor whole.

Suddenly, A low, grinding noise, deep and ancient, filled the cavern. The circle on the door moved, rotating slowly, impossibly, as though the stone itself had been set into motion. It completed a full turn, and then,

"Click."

The door eased open with a low groan, revealing a vast circular chamber. The walls were adorned with intricate engravings, their patterns twisting like ancient script lost to time. Three hallways branched off. One behind him, the path he had come from, and two before him, one veering left, the other right.

Tah'quhal stepped cautiously to the center of the room, his ears sharpening for any sound. At first, there was only the distant crackle of unseen torches, the faint whisper of air moving through unseen cracks. Then, voices.

From the left corridor, hushed words drifted toward him, too muffled to understand. He adjusted his grip on Orgí and inched forward, careful to keep his steps soundless.

As he approached, the words sharpened.

"If I do this... what will I get in return?" A woman's voice, smooth, deliberate.

Another woman replied, her tone rich with certainty. "You get to live in luxury under his reign."

Silence stretched between them.

Tah'quhal crept closer, the flickering glow of candlelight bleeding through the cracks of a doorway at the corridor's end. The pause in conversation stretched just long enough to make his skin prickle.

Then, a low, amused giggle.

"I will live no matter what happens next," the first woman said, her voice dripping with self-assurance. "I have ruled Ignis for far too long for anyone—especially the likes of you three—to change that."

Tah'quhal's breath caught in his throat.

"Talissa?" he whispered.

The air stiffened.

"What was that?" a man's voice snapped.

A second male voice, colder, more certain, replied, "We are not alone."

A chill shot through Tah'quhal's spine. His grip on Orgí tightened, instincts screaming at him to move. His feet were already pivoting, muscles coiling to flee. He turned and then—

Thud.

He crashed into something, or rather, someone, and they both went sprawling to the ground. He scrambled to his feet, weapon poised, but then he saw the wide-eyed human staring up at him.

"Barry?"

Barry pushed himself up with a grunt, his breaths coming fast and panicked. "Dammit, dude..." he wheezed, barely keeping his voice down. "You've been made, and we need to get the hell out of here. Now. Follow me!"

The two sprinted down the corridor, their footfalls echoing like war drums against the stone. Behind them, boots thundered, gaining ground. They were being hunted.

Barry skidded to a stop as they burst back into the circular chamber.

Tah'quhal wheeled toward him. "What now?"

"Through here, trust me!" Barry hissed, bolting straight for the wall.

Tah'quhal's breath caught. He'd lost it. But before he could shout a warning, Barry vanished, swallowed by the stone.

The footsteps were too close. There was no time to question it. Tah'quhal grit his teeth and charged, bracing for impact, but the wall wasn't solid. He slipped through as if plunging into water, stumbling into another dimly lit passage.

"I don't know if Talissa knows about this way. Keep running!" Barry's voice echoed ahead.

"You better tell me everything you know, Barry," Tah'quhal grunted, matching his pace.

They wove through the tunnels, zigzagging through twists and turns, their breaths harsh and ragged. The sounds of pursuit faded, but Barry wasn't slowing down. Finally, they emerged into a massive cavern.

A narrow stone bridge arched over a lake of roiling lava, leading to a raised circular platform. Several paths converged on the far side, but all Tah'quhal could see was the portal at the platform's center—its swirling energy casting eerie purple light over the molten landscape.

"Barry, what is going on?" Tah'quhal demanded.

Barry doubled over, hands on his knees, gasping for air. "I can't ... explain ... everything right now, man. You blew our cover."

Tah'quhal clenched his fists. "Who was Talissa talking to?"

Barry swallowed hard. "I don't know for certain. I've been sneaking down here for weeks, trying to figure that out."

"And where is here?"

Barry straightened, dragging in a final deep breath. "This ..." he gestured around them "... is the heart of the volcano of Ignis. Talissa's fortress has tunnels that lead here." He pointed toward the portal. "I saw that the first time I came down. No clue where it leads. No clue why it's here. I just knew I had to find out what Talissa was up to."

A voice rang out from one of the side tunnels. "I think they're in here!"

Barry spun, cursing under his breath. "Look, we don't have time. If they catch us, I need deniability." He pointed at the portal. "You go through that." Then, at the tunnel they came from. "I'll double back and hide until it's safe."

He turned to run, but Tah'quhal snatched his arm. "Wait, what if they *do* catch you?"

Barry smirked. "I'm a runner, baby." Then his face sobered. "Seriously. Tell Derek that Talissa is up to something." A pause. A weight settled over his voice. "And you're thinking the same thing I am, right? That was Malum and Sarika she was talking to."

Tah'quhal's breath hitched.

Barry looked away before adding, "Tell Derek it's time to get me out of here."

Then, he was gone, vanishing into the tunnels.

Tah'quhal stood frozen. Malum and Sarika? No. It couldn't be. They were dead. Weren't they? But doubt curled in his gut like smoke.

He turned to the portal, its violet vortex spinning like an unblinking eye. There was no time to hesitate. He lunged through. Just as the world wrenched around him, he heard a familiar voice.

"Dammit!"

Chapter 7

Between

The ground was wrong. Solid, yet shifting beneath him. Hard, but humming with an unnatural warmth. Tah'quhal groaned, pressing a hand to his pounding head as he pried his eyes open.

Blinding light. Too bright. He winced, squeezing his eyelids shut again before slowly cracking them open. The horizon blurred in waves of heat, the landscape stretching out in endless cracked stone. No landmarks. No movement. Just a vast, empty wasteland that felt neither alive nor dead.

Yet, in the distance, something was there. A shimmer. Gold light, twisting like molten sunlight trapped in the air. He squinted against the glare, his body already moving toward it.

His lungs burned as he inhaled. The air carried a scent that was familiar, yet otherworldly, like a forgotten memory teasing the edges of his mind.

"I've heard of this place."

The words tumbled from his lips, unbidden. His voice sounded strange here, too loud and distant at the same time. He swallowed hard, eyes darting toward the sky.

"I am Between."

The realization settled into his bones like an iron weight. But how? The last thing he remembered was diving headfirst into the portal beneath Ignis.

"Why is there a portal to the Between in the volcano of Ignis?"

The flickering portal ahead was the only answer, its golden light pulsing in time with his heartbeat.

A sudden sound broke the silence. A single chirp. A soft trill. Then... the flutter of wings. His pulse spiked.

Tah'quhal turned sharply, scanning the endless expanse. Nothing. No movement. No birds. No life at all. And yet, the sound lingered, echoing in a space that should not have carried them.

He pressed forward, keeping his voice low. "The hummingbird, huh? The sign of spiritual awakening. What are you trying to show me?"

The portal loomed before him now. Unlike others he had seen, this one didn't swirl chaotically, it shimmered, fluid but strangely solid. Like a wall of captured light. He hesitated only a moment before reaching for it. But before his fingers could make contact, a voice tore through the air.

"Tah'quhal. Once again, I am permitted to speak to you. Once again, I do not have much time."

He knew that voice. He spun on his heels, eyes wide as he scanned the empty horizon.

"Torviid?"

"I must be brief. I apologize. I wish I could stay with you."

Tah'quhal's heart clenched. "Then stay!" The words came out desperate, raw. "Let me ask you questions! I can sit right here for as long as it takes!"

He tried to drop to the ground, to force himself into stillness, but the portal reacted. Flakes of gold peeled from its surface, swirling around him, holding him upright.

His breath came faster now. The air pressed in on him, thick and electric with unseen energy.

"That is not how this works," Torviid's voice echoed. "You must know...the forces that pull the strings are not always truthful. The Forest of Life has many that tend to its trees."

Tah'quhal's fingers curled into fists. "What the hell does any of this mean?!"

Silence.

"Don't leave me with another cryptic message!" His voice cracked.

Nothing.

"Where does this portal even lead?"

This time, an answer. Not words, but sound. The chirp. The trill. The flutter.

And suddenly, he knew.

The knowledge slammed into him like a memory he hadn't lived. This portal could take him anywhere. He had been here before. He had stood in this place before. Hadn't he?

Should he go to Derek, warn him that Barry needed to get out? Should he go to Oceanus, seek out Karrent and the scholars?

No.

He knew where he needed to be.

"Home."

Torvania. He had to gather the city guard, march on Ignis. He had to free Barry. Eriene. She was in the stables in Torvania. She would be ready, willing to fly.

His resolve hardened. He stepped forward and the moment his fingers touched the golden surface, the portal responded.

It lunged for him, swallowing him whole. The last thing he heard was the flutter of wings.

Tah'quhal groaned as consciousness clawed him back to the waking world. His body ached, his limbs heavy as if weighed down by stone.

He pressed his palms to the ground…it was solid, familiar. The right kind of solid. He was in Torvania.

Relief flooded through him, but it was short-lived. He wasn't at the Anchor. He was sprawled in the middle of the street. *Damn it*, he thought to himself.

Pushing himself upright, he scanned the area. No curious eyes. No guards demanding an explanation. Good. He had no time to waste explaining how he'd come crashing out of a portal in the middle of town.

He needed his guard. He needed Eriene. He needed to march on Ignis, but first, he needed Derek and Johnathan.

The Fickle Fae was his best bet. At this time of day, the Enchanted Ensemble wouldn't be far. He made his way through the winding streets, barely sparing a glance at the passersby. His head still pounded, but urgency drove him forward.

The moment he stepped inside the tavern, his eyes locked onto Johnathan and Mr. Monton, hunched over a map of Luminfae's rifts.

"Gentlemen," he said, striding toward them. "Where is Derek? It is time we retrieve Barry from Ignis."

Johnathan lifted his head, exchanging a glance with his father before answering. "Well, I reckon he's still in the wilds."

Tah'quhal's jaw tightened. *Damn it all.* "Fine. Come with me, Johnathan. We need Eriene, she will trust you more than she does me. I am getting Barry out of there. Now."

Mr. Monton folded his arms. "Might I ask what's invoking these emotions, Tah'quhal?"

He turned sharply, already heading for the door. "I will explain on the way to Ignis. We must leave now."

Johnathan and Mr. Monton moved to follow, but as they stepped outside, a brilliant violet light erupted in front of them, flooding the front of the tavern in unnatural radiance.

Tah'quhal's instincts took over. In an instant, Orgí was in his hands, its edge gleaming with a cold readiness. Beside him, Johnathan brandished his Keeper staff, his stance firm.

The light faded, revealing two figures within its dissipating glow. It was Nidalle and...

"David?" Tah'quhal's grip on Orgí tightened. His voice was edged with suspicion. "Nidalle. Perfect timing, especially with your guest. I was just heading to free Barry." Tah'quhal's nostrils flared.

David took a step forward, his face set with quiet resolve. "You may want to hear what I have to say before you do that."

Tah'quhal's muscles coiled. "And why should your words have any bearing on my plans? Are you not now the rightful Keeper of Ignis?"

David hesitated, but Nidalle placed a steadying hand on his chest, guiding him a step back. She turned to Tah'quhal with measured calm.

"Chieftain Tah'quhal," she said, voice deliberate, "David has...well, he has been awake for a few days now."

Tah'quhal's eyes narrowed. "And you are just now bringing him here?"

Nidalle sighed. "When he woke, he could not manifest his magic. Even his Keeper items seemed to have gone dormant. We gave it time, assuming it might be an effect of the coma, but I no longer believe that is the case."

With a sharp snap of her fingers, two objects materialized at their feet—a gun and a large knife.

Johnathan peered at them, muttering under his breath, "Now, why'd that fella get actual weapons, but I got a wooden staff?"

"Now is not the time, son," Mr. Monton murmured back.

Nidalle pressed on. "Once David realized it seemed like Talissa was abandoning him, he started talking. I promised him my protection in exchange for his *knowledge*."

Tah'quhal's gaze flicked to David. His silence was telling.

"What manner of secrets are we talking about?" Tah'quhal asked, voice sharp.

Nidalle's expression darkened. She glanced toward the street, eyes sweeping the area with a touch of exaggeration before lowering her voice. "Perhaps we should continue this conversation inside, away from curious ears and prying eyes."

A muscle twitched in Tah'quhal's jaw, but he gave a single nod and turned back toward the Fickle Fae.

One by one, they stepped inside.

As Johnathan entered last, he spun his staff and a pulse of blue essence radiated outward. The energy surged toward the door, sealing it in a crackling glow. For a brief moment, the wood shimmered, settling into a strange stillness.

Johnathan smirked, tapping the staff against his palm. "Ain't nobody getting through that door unless we want 'em to." Another flick, another rush of essence. "And now ain't nobody listenin', either."

The air inside the tavern shifted. It was heavier, quieter. Tah'quhal turned, his gaze settling back on David.

"Talk."

Chapter 8

The Wilds

"Why would you hide this from us, Derek?!" Mia's voice cracked, echoing through the cave's hollow expanse.

Derek flinched. She never yelled at him.

"I thought..."

"You thought you knew best?" She cut him off, her tone sharp. "How could you make that decision without asking any of us?"

Derek swallowed hard. He thought he could find another way, but saying that wouldn't change anything.

"I didn't want this path to be our only choice," he said instead, his voice barely above a whisper.

He reached for her hand, but the second his fingers brushed her skin, she pulled away. His chest tightened. She had never pulled away from him before, not even when Johnathan shoved him down in front of her back at school.

His lip quivered, and the sting of unshed tears burned behind his eyes.

"I'm sorry," he whispered, eyes squeezing shut.

Then...warmth. Arms wrapped around him, her head pressing against his chest.

Derek let out a shaky breath, relief crashing over him like a wave.

"Derek, I'm not going anywhere," Mia murmured. "I told you, I will always be here. But you should have told us about this. Told me."

He nodded, guilt twisting in his gut. She was right.

"I just... I couldn't accept that the only way forward was to let everything fall apart."

Mia pulled back slightly, just enough to look up at him. "There might be another way. I... we... the Enchanted Ensemble, maybe we can find a path the voice hasn't foreseen."

Before Derek could answer, the ground beneath them shuddered.

A low rumble built deep within the earth, vibrating up his legs. Cracks splintered through the cave walls. Dust rained down, tiny shards of stone pelting his shoulders. Then, a voice, everywhere and nowhere at once, ripped through the space.

"THIS IS THE ONLY PATH."

Mia jerked back, eyes wide.

Derek met her gaze, and in that instant, he saw it—the quiet, sinking realization that maybe the voice wasn't lying. His throat tightened.

"I don't think so, Mia." His voice came out hoarse. "I think we need to press forward. The voice wanted me to find this symbol and show it to you."

Mia inhaled deeply, her expression unreadable. She nodded. "Then let's keep moving. But we keep our eyes and ears open for any other possible solution."

Derek gave a small nod, but doubt still gnawed at the back of his mind.

"I don't feel anything else here. I think the symbol is all we were meant to see. Should we go further into the Wilds?"

Mia didn't hesitate this time. She grabbed his hand, lacing her fingers through his.

As they walked toward the cave mouth, she glanced at him. "I'm assuming you heard it, too—since I was watching your memory—but what was that fluttering and chirping sound?"

Derek frowned.

"I know it sounds familiar... but I just can't place it."

Once they emerged from the cave and mounted their Steeds, Derek and Mia ventured deeper into the Wilds. The desert stretched before them, endless and ever-shifting, but this was no ordinary wasteland. The sand shimmered like crushed gemstones, its hues flickering between molten gold, burning amber, and eerie silver as the fractured sky shifted above. Every step of their Steeds sent up wisps of glowing dust, as if the ground itself exhaled in slow, enchanted breaths.

Hours passed in silence, the only thing keeping Derek grounded being the rhythmic sound of hooves on strange terrain. He wasn't sure if he should apologize again or let Mia process everything. The longer they rode, the more this journey felt like a cruel illusion. There was nothing ahead but rolling dunes and jagged, crystal formations that jutted from the sand like fractured blades of glass.

The rocks hummed softly in the heat, their facets refracting slivers of light in mesmerizing patterns. The air carried an unnatural scent—ozone laced with spice, tinged with something sweet, like burnt sugar dissolving into the wind. Strange, twisted trees, their bark smooth as obsidian, clung stubbornly to life. Their translucent leaves shimmered, scattering flecks of iridescent light with every shift of the breeze.

Above them, the sky rippled in unnatural waves, as though the very air was fluid. Wisps of violet lightning crackled between sparse, swirling clouds. The horizon wavered like a mirage, teasing glimpses of something just beyond reach—structures, shapes, figures that vanished the moment one tried to focus on them.

The Wilds were alive. Watching. Breathing. The deeper they rode, the stronger that presence became, pressing against Derek's skin like an unseen force.

Finally, he spoke. "The sun will be going down soon. Should we make camp?"

Before Mia could answer, a desperate voice cut through the thick desert air.

"RUN! Derek! Mia! RUN!"

Sprinting over a dune to the North, Caldera was moving at full speed toward them, her stigmata flaring with a brilliant blue glow.

Derek barely had time to process what was happening before she zipped past them in a blur.

"Dammit, I said RUN!" she shouted over her shoulder.

The ground shuddered beneath them, the sand shifting in unnatural waves. A tremor climbed up Derek's legs, and his Steed whinnied, muscles tensing beneath him as it tore off behind Caldera.

Mia's eyes darted to him. "Earthquake?"

"I wish," Caldera panted. "I'll explain in a minu—"

The words died in her throat.

The ground ahead convulsed, and the sand exploded outward in a violent eruption.

A monstrous head burst from the dunes, its elongated snout lined with jagged, needle-like teeth. each fang slick with a thick, oozing acid that hissed as it dripped onto the sand, scorching deep holes into the earth. Its maw gaped wide enough to swallow them whole, a guttural, ear-splitting shriek rattling the air.

The rest of its serpentine body surged upward, impossibly long, covered in thick, overlapping scales that emitted a faint glow with a sickly, amber sheen. The beast had no front limbs—only ruined, tattered wings, their shredded membranes flaring out like a grotesque mockery of a dragon's grace.

With a powerful lunge, its massive hind legs dug into the sand, propelling its sleek, muscular body forward with terrifying speed. Its battered wings snapped once, sending out a brutal gust that kicked up a blinding storm of sand.

Derek's heart pounded against his ribs. "What the hell is that?!"

Caldera's breath hitched.

Her voice wavered as she answered, "Sand Drake. And a pissed off one at that."

Its guttural snarl shook the desert, and slitted eyes locked onto them with an ancient, predatory hunger. Its massive body coiled, hind legs tensing, muscles flexing beneath shimmering amber scales.

The beast launched itself toward them once again, its jaws gaping wider, its saliva slinging from its fangs like a sick wolf. Another piercing screech sent a cold chill down his spine, but Derek reacted first.

Lightning crackled to life in his hands, blue arcs dancing along his fingertips before he hurled a bolt directly at the Drake's head. The magic shot forward, illuminating the battlefield in a blinding flash, but the beast was fast.

With a violent twist, its head jerked sideways, the bolt seared its thick scales but didn't slow its momentum.

"Scatter!" Caldera shouted.

Derek barely had time to yank his Steed to the side before the drake crashed down where he had been a second before. Its massive claws carved deep trenches into the sand.

Mia had already dismounted, her hands moving in fluid motions. Water shimmered between her fingers, forming two jagged daggers of glistening blue. She darted in, slicing at the drake's flank. They cut deep, but the wounds closed almost instantly, the beast's scales knitting together as if the magic-infused sand was healing it.

Mia's eyes widened. "It's regenerating!"

Caldera didn't hesitate. She sprinted forward, her long spear spinning in her grip, the weapon pulsing as the blue essence around her shifted to a green glow. Vines erupted from the sand, lashing around the drake's limbs, trying to hold it in place.

The beast let out a furious roar. Its tattered wings snapped outward, sending a violent gust of sand into the air. The sheer force shattered the vines and sent Mia skidding backward, barely able to shield herself with her magic.

Derek gritted his teeth. They couldn't keep fighting like this; they needed to hit harder.

Lightning surged through his body, crackling up his arms. He clenched his fists, the air around him electrified. Dark ominous clouds appeared above, and he raised his hands to the sky. A massive bolt ripped downward from the storm-ridden clouds, striking him directly. Channeling it through his body, he turned, unleashing it all at once.

A storm of blue lightning exploded from his hands, slamming into the Sand Drake's chest. The creature screeched in pain, its body convulsing as the energy surged through it. This time, the impact wasn't so easily shrugged off. The scent of scorched scales filled the air.

"Mia, now!" Derek shouted.

Mia was already moving. She thrust her hands forward, her watery daggers shifting, elongating into twin spears of ice. With a fierce cry, she hurled them at the drake's eyes.

The beast reared back, one spear slamming into its left iris. The other missed by inches, but the damage was done. The creature thrashed, its roar shaking the ground.

Caldera saw her opening. With an explosive burst of speed, she leapt, her spear glowing vivid green, infused with the life force of the Magia Forest itself. She landed on the Drake's back, balancing on its shifting scales as she plunged her weapon deep into the base of its skull.

The beast let out one final, ear-splitting screech. Then, it collapsed.

For a moment, all that remained was the crackle of fading magic, the distant roll of thunder from Derek's summoned storm, and the heavy breathing of three warriors standing victorious over a slain legend.

Derek wiped his brow, exhaling shakily.

Caldera pulled her spear free and jumped down. "I hate Sand Drakes," she muttered.

Mia let out a breathless laugh. "Yeah? Same."

Derek's eyes lingered on the slowly dissolving body of the beast, its remains sinking back into the enchanted sands. The faint shimmer of magic clung to the air, flickering like embers before vanishing into the desert wind. He exhaled, trying to steady his breath, but the weight of exhaustion pressed heavy against his chest.

"Why was that thing chasing you?" His voice came out hoarse, barely above a whisper.

Caldera dragged her spear through the sand, using it for balance as she glanced toward the distant horizon. Sweat clung to her brow, her usually sharp gaze softened by fatigue. "Best I can tell? It's one of the guardians of the barrier." She swept her hand through her hair, her stigmata still faintly glowing.

Derek swayed where he stood. His pulse hammered against his skull, each heartbeat echoing in his ears like distant thunder. His limbs felt distant, sluggish, a marionette with its strings cut. "Wh at...barrier?" The words barely made it out between ragged breaths. The world tilted.

His knee hit the sand hard, his vision swimming as the strength drained from his body.

"Derek!"

Mia was beside him in an instant, sliding through the sand. Her hands pressed firmly against his chest, trying to steady him. War mth...no, a tingling sensation spread from her palms, but it wasn't enough to stop the crushing weight dragging him down.

"He used too much magic," she breathed, her voice tight with concern. "Malum warned him... he has been careful... but he had to, he needed to use it just now, right?" The faint shimmer of watery magic clung to her fingers, but she was no healer.

Derek's vision flickered. His thoughts scattered, slipping through his grasp like grains of sand in the wind. The battlefield blurred, Mia's face the only thing in focus, her green eyes wide, desperate.

Somewhere in the haze, Caldera's voice cut through. "Damn what Malum said. He just needs to rest. There's an oasis not far from here. We'll be safe there."

Mia's hands tightened on his shoulders as tears welled in her eyes. "Derek, stay with me."

But the darkness surged forward, swallowing everything whole. The last thing he felt was the faint pressure of Mia's grip before the darkness took him.

Chapter 9

Oasis

The first thing Derek felt was the coolness. Not the blistering heat of the desert pressing against his skin, but something softer—damp, fine sand clinging to his fingertips like silk. A faint mist curled around his arms, cool and delicate. His breath came slow, heavy, as his mind clawed its way out of unconsciousness.

A floral sweetness drifted through the air, threaded with the crisp, earthy scent of fresh water. Somewhere close, palm leaves rustled in a breeze that carried none of the desert's suffocating weight.

"That is bullshit, Mia!"

Caldera's sharp voice cut through the quiet, shocking Derek's senses. His body still felt sluggish, but he kept his eyes shut, focusing on the conversation unraveling near him.

"I'm just telling you what I saw," Mia said, her voice even but edged with something unshaken. "What Derek finally let me see. If you don't believe me, ask him for yourself when he wakes up."

A frustrated huff. The sound of shifting sand as Caldera crossed her arms. "So why is this 'voice in the void' even telling Derek to do things if we're supposed to just let Malum's plan happen?"

Mia sighed. "Just wait for Derek. He's had more time to process all of this. Let him explain."

His lashes fluttered. The golden light of morning filtered through swaying palm fronds, casting dappled shadows across his face. The sky above wasn't the unrelenting, burnt expanse of the Wilds but a soft watercolor of blues and golds, the air charged with something unseen—alive, ancient.

He swallowed, his throat dry. "Ahem..."

Mia and Caldera whirled around.

"Finally!" Mia scrambled to her feet, the tension in her body vanishing as she threw herself forward. "Don't ever scare me like that again!"

Derek exhaled, a hoarse chuckle slipping from his lips. He pushed himself onto his elbows, wincing as soreness rippled through his muscles, then pulled himself onto his knees.

The sand beneath him was cool, kissed by the mist rolling off the water. The oasis stretched before them like something out of a dream, a crystalline pool shifting to create impossible colors, trees swaying in a breeze that never touched their skin.

His gaze flickered to Mia, who was watching him as if he might disappear if she looked away.

Without thinking, he reached up, his fingers grazing her hand against his chest. A quiet moment, an unspoken reassurance.

"I'm okay," he murmured.

Mia didn't answer right away. Her fingers twitched slightly beneath his. Finally, she exhaled, her shoulders easing. "You scared me," she admitted, voice quieter now.

Caldera scoffed, arms still crossed. "Scared is an understatement. She thought you might have … "

Mia shot her a sharp look. "Not the time, Caldera."

"Not to ruin a moment or anything," Caldera's voice cut through the quiet, her usual sharpness laced with something else—something uneasy, "but I need to know exactly what you heard in the void, Derek."

Derek exhaled, nodding. He knew this moment would come. There was no running from it anymore.

He raised his hand to the sky, fingers splayed. The magic came naturally now, answering his call without hesitation. A ball of pure white light flared to life in his palm, illuminating the misty air. This wasn't like when he had shown Mia—then, she had lived it with him. This time, it played like a recording.

The voice spilled into the space around them, low and resonant, like something speaking from the bones of the world itself.

"Derek. You have done well. You always knew something was amiss but could never put your finger on it. I thought letting the Seer Stone

reveal your name might speed things along, but it seems as if it sped up other things in the process..."

The words echoed in the oasis, shifting in tone like a tide pulling away from shore.

Caldera's eyes narrowed. "This is what you heard?"

Derek nodded.

The voice resumed.

"You will not enjoy what I have to tell you, but it is a truth you must accept. Your life has been a series of choices. Your friends' lives have been a series of choices. Your enemies' lives have been a series of choices. A series of choices that have led you to strike a mighty blow against the one called Malum."

Derek closed his eyes, bracing himself. He knew what was coming next.

A small, warm pressure settled against his free hand. Mia. Her fingers interlaced with his, a silent tether pulling him back before the weight of it all could drag him under.

"Those choices, while well-intended and brave, have consequences. Even a being such as myself is not free of consequence, as you will soon find out."

Caldera crossed her arms, shifting her weight. "Okay, but what exactly is this voice?"

Derek's shoulders tensed. "I don't know. But whatever it is... it isn't done yet."

The light pulsed.

"*I put the prophecy in the mind of a young Fae boy so many years ago. All in hopes that one day it would be found, and keep my tree standing tall in the forest of existence. I foresaw the threats of Malum, Helian, and many others, but in my hubris, I did not extinguish the correct flames.*"

Caldera's brow arched, the one on the shaved side of her head lifting in skeptical curiosity. "What others?"

Derek shook his head, eyes flickering downward as the voice carried on.

"*When you began your journey, there was hope. A rainshower moving toward the wildfire. You succeeded where many would have failed. But it is not done yet. The path you walk now must be completed. There is no other avenue for success. The rain will not fall if you stray from your walk. Malum's grand plan is already in motion, and cannot be stopped.*"

Caldera's fists clenched. "There has to be some way!"

Derek's fingers curled slightly, and the glow in his palm dimmed. His voice was quiet, but heavy.

"Caldera. I have been searching. Every single time I try to find another way, the voice comes back to me. Tells me I'm straying from the path."

Caldera's expression cracked. Her breath hitched, and tears swelled in her eyes, but she held her ground.

Derek managed a knowing smile, despite the weight in his chest. He stretched his palm outward again, and the voice continued.

"Just because it cannot be stopped does not mean all is lost. There is still hope, but in order to extinguish the flame, we must make sacrifices. Change must happen. Part of my tree must burn, but life will remain. You will fall, but rise again. I will prepare you the best I can, but I am limited in my interference in your life. I can unlock some of the dormant power inside you, but to completely prepare for what is coming, you need your friends. Take them and seek out the Trinity. You MUST learn how to stop the fire at its source. You cannot undo what was started, cannot unburn that which was burned. But you can put the fire out, and let the grounds be reborn. When you return, you will be changed... and not all for the better. But I can only do so much."

The light flickered once, then, with a whisper of energy, it vanished.

Derek turned his gaze to Mia. Her green eyes shone, rimmed with unshed tears. But she held firm.

Caldera, however, made no attempt to hide her emotions. Tears traced silent paths down her face. She sniffed, and then forced a laugh.

"That is why you came back with a frown on your face and lightning on your arm." Her voice was thick but steady. "Whatever that voice belongs to... it is not of this world."

Derek let out a breath, shaking his head. "I don't know where they're from. But they know more than any of us do."

Mia didn't hesitate. She turned into him, wrapping her arms around his torso. Her grip was strong, like she could anchor him to something steady.

"We can figure this out," she whispered.

Caldera sniffed and wiped her face with the sleeve of her coat. "We find the Trinity."

Derek raised an eyebrow. Mia turned, equally confused.

Caldera's lips pressed into a thin line. "We find the Trinity, whatever that is, and we do what the voice said. If we cannot stop the plan, then we walk the path."

Derek studied her. "Me and Mia thought the same thing. I just wasn't sure you'd be on board."

Caldera ran a hand through her hair, exhaling a breath that almost sounded like a laugh. "It's not like we have much of a choice."

Then her expression darkened. "There is only one problem."

Mia frowned. "What's that?"

Caldera tilted her head, gaze flickering to the distance. "I have never heard of anything called the Trinity before. And I have not had much luck breaking past the barrier in the Wilds to see what is out there." She exhaled sharply. "But I have a feeling... whatever the Trinity is, it is hidden somewhere deep in them."

"That's right, you mentioned the drake being a 'guardian of the barrier' right before I passed out," Derek said.

The corner of Caldera's lip quirked up. "Right before you fainted."

Mia snorted before clapping a hand over her mouth, her shoulders shaking with suppressed laughter. Derek shot her an incredulous look.

"Haha, very funny. I passed out, not fainted. I don't faint!" he insisted.

Caldera giggled, then crouched, using her finger to trace a large circle in the sand. She dragged a deep line through the middle, splitting it in two. "This is Luminfae," she said, tapping one half, "and this is the Wilds." She jabbed a finger at the line dividing them. "This barrier, whatever it is, will not let me through. Every time I get close, my skin tingles, and if I linger too long, something comes hunting me. That is where the Sand Drake came from."

Mia paled at the memory. "I don't want to go up against anything else like that," she admitted, her voice laced with unease. Her green eyes flickered toward Derek.

Derek gave her a reassuring nod, though his mind was elsewhere. Fighting another beast like that didn't scare him. What scared him was what happened when he fought, what happened when he let go. He could still feel the raw burn of magic in his veins, the exhaustion that had nearly broken him afterward. Malum had warned him about what lurked inside him, and though Derek hated to admit it, the warning lingered in his thoughts. But the voice in the void had never mentioned it. Why?

"Okay, Caldera, what do you think this barrier is?" he asked, pushing the thought aside.

Caldera rocked back on her heels, arms crossing. "I have seen something like this before... the barrier that kept Torvania hidden from the rest of Luminfae."

Mia's brow furrowed. "So, then you know how to take it down?"

"Not exactly." Caldera sighed, uncrossing her arms. "Torvania's barrier was more of a glamour... it was meant to conceal, not keep people out." She scowled, frustration curling her fingers into fists. "But this damned thing will not even let me get close."

Derek mulled it over for a moment before meeting her gaze. "Take me to it."

Mia and Caldera exchanged glances before Mia asked, "What are you going to do?"

Derek's jaw tightened as his gaze drifted toward the horizon. Lightning crackled along his forearms, dancing over his skin like restless spirits. The thought of using his magic in a large capacity again made him nervous, but he knew they needed to get on the other side of the barrier. He could feel it in his gut. He clenched his fists, blue sparks flashing between his fingers.

"If what we need is on the other side of this barrier... then I'm going to destroy it."

Chapter 10

The Barrier

The desert of the Wilds stretched out before them, an endless expanse of golden dunes shimmering beneath the merciless sun. They left the Oasis hours ago, but Mia's grip on Derek's hand remained unyielding. He wasn't sure why. He wasn't nervous, he wasn't anxious. He knew exactly what needed to be done. The only question was how he would do it.

A sharp hiss of pain broke his focus.

"Ugh." Caldera winced, her body tensing as if a current had passed through her.

Derek turned toward her. "What's wron... ugh!" His sentence died as a sudden jolt shot through him. He ripped his hand from Mia's, fingers curling into fists as electricity crackled wildly around his wrists. A sharp, stinging sensation coiled through his veins, forcing a grunt from his throat. "What... what is that?"

Mia's gaze darted between them, panic creeping into her voice. "What's happening?"

Caldera exhaled sharply, scanning the desert. "It's the tingle. It doesn't hurt, but it's... strange. Happens every time I get too close to the barrier... and then a guardian shows up to fight me away."

Derek's breath hitched as the lightning on his arms lunged outward, striking at the invisible wall before him like a living thing. The energy rebounded, arcing in violent flashes. His muscles locked. "Caldera... this is more than a tingle."

"I don't feel anything. Maybe I can walk through?" Mia didn't wait for an answer. She stepped toward the barrier, reaching out...

The instant her fingertips brushed the unseen force, a pulse of energy exploded outward.

Mia was launched backward.

"Mia!" Derek dropped to his knees beside her, sliding through the sand. Sparks still snapped along his arms, forcing him to keep his distance.

Mia groaned but smirked up at him. "I'm fine, Lavender. No need to go all sparky."

Derek's cheeks burned hotter than the desert sun. "I was already going all..." He exhaled sharply, shaking his head. "Never mind."

Mia shifted to stand, but the ground rumbled. A sickening, all-too-familiar vibration rolled beneath them. The dunes shifted, trembling as grains of sand danced along the surface. Caldera went rigid. She knew exactly what was coming next.

"Derek, whatever you're going to do, do it now!" she shouted.

A flicker of light ignited behind Derek's eyes. He exhaled and rose to his feet. Every step toward the barrier made the lightning around him snarl, its tendrils lashing out, growing wilder, more erratic.

The sand beneath them churned like a whirlpool, spiraling faster. The tremors deepened.

"Hurry, Derek!" Mia pleaded, scrambling to her feet.

But Derek was already moving.

His hands were glowing. That familiar, pure white light pulsed from his fingertips, spilling over his knuckles like liquid fire. Overhead, the sky darkened and thunder rumbled in the distance. He was calling another storm.

Mia and Caldera stared in awed silence as his power swelled. The air around them became electric, heavy. The first bolt of lightning didn't come from Derek's hands, it came from the sky, splintering down into the dunes with an ear splitting crack.

And then Derek struck. His palms met the barrier...

BOOM!

A shockwave erupted outward, shaking the desert. Lightning ripped along the barrier's surface, stretching to the horizon in both directions. The force sent Mia and Caldera stumbling backward.

Time slowed to a snail's pace. Derek was swallowed by light. A sphere of pure, blinding energy engulfed him, crackling and pulsating like a living star. A final bolt of lightning speared downward from the sky.

Mia stumbled backwards. The electrical energy inched down from the clouds like a pane of glass shattering in slow motion. It struck the ground near Derek's feet, and the following thunder shattered the air.

When the light began to fade, the world stilled. Caldera inhaled sharply. The tingling sensation? Gone.

The clouds above? Parting.

The oppressive charge of magic? Dissipating.

Derek had done it. Derek had destroyed the barrier. Derek...

Derek lay sprawled in the sand, unmoving.

Mia dropped to her knees beside Derek, pressing her ear to his chest. The wind howled around them, kicking up sand, making it impossible to hear anything, but she felt the faint rise and fall of his chest. He was breathing. He was alive.

"Caldera! Get over here!" she shouted, desperation laced in her voice.

Caldera froze. For a split second, the scene before her blurred... Derek's unconscious body was replaced with a memory. Codi. Lying still, unmoving. The Keeper of the Magia Forest. Her friend.

She forced the memory away and ran to Mia's side.

"Come on, get him to his feet," Caldera grunted, grabbing Derek's arm.

Mia slung his other arm over her shoulders, and together, they heaved him upright.

Then, they saw it. Beyond where the barrier had once stood, atop a distant dune, a lone figure loomed against the shifting sands.

Mia's breath hitched. "Who... who is that?"

Before Caldera could answer, the figure melted. Darkness bled from its form, slithering into the sand. The shadows raced toward them, moving like a living thing, silent and relentless.

"Derek! Derek, wake up!" Mia shoved his side, her voice breaking.

"Come on, Derek. We are going to need you." Caldera's tone was firm, but edged with urgency.

The shadows closed in. Ten feet. Eight.

"Mia, you have to hold him. I can not fight while keeping him upright."

Mia tightened her grip, bracing her legs against the shifting sand as Derek's weight threatened to pull her down. "I've got him."

Caldera rolled her shoulders, drawing the spear from her back. A pulse of magic rippled through the air as the spear's tip forged itself from pure essence, glowing with dangerous intent. She stepped forward, muscles taut, stance unwavering.

"Show yourself!" she commanded.

The shadows halted just ahead of her, writhing and twisting, before rising.

Tendrils of darkness pulled together, coiling and shifting until they formed the shape of a man. A fae.

He was tall, with lean muscle wrapped in black leather and a tattered white tunic. A bandolier of daggers was slung across his chest, hilts gleaming under the harsh desert sun. His skin, darkened from the unforgiving heat, seemed to drink in the light. But it was his eyes that sent a chill through Caldera's core.

Pitch-black. Endless. Two voids, each pierced by a single pinpoint of white light at its center. His lips curled into a playful smile, but the glint of razor-sharp canines twisted it into something far more menacing.

Caldera gripped her spear tighter. "Who are you?"

The Fae tilted his head, that wicked smile widening, "Silas."

"And what do you want, Silas?" Caldera's grip tightened around her spear, though she forced her breathing to stay steady.

Silas barely acknowledged her, lifting a hand and pointing a single finger at Derek. Shadows bled from his fingertips like liquid smoke, curling and dissipating into the air. "To meet the Semideus who just shattered a millennia-old barrier between our lands."

Caldera glanced back at Mia, who took a defensive step forward, her arms bracing Derek's weight.

"How the hell do you know what he is?" Mia demanded.

Silas' lips curled into a knowing smirk. He stepped forward, slow and deliberate, his bare feet making no sound against the sand.

Caldera immediately blocked his path with her spear. "I did not permit you to come closer."

Silas paused, his gaze flicking down to the weapon. His smirk never faded. "I do not need your permission, Chieftain." He stepped closer anyway, the movement so casual it was infuriating.

Caldera's stomach twisted. "How do you know anything about us?"

Silas' solid black eyes flickered, just for a moment, before shifting into a stunning, unnatural shade of blue. "Because I have been watching." His voice was smooth, his words careful, almost soothing. "Listening. I am not your enemy. If I were, you would have never known my name."

Mia tensed, holding Derek closer. "What... what are you?"

Silas' expression softened just enough. "A friend." Another step.

Caldera hesitated. Just for a second. And in that second, the shadows moved.

They didn't lash out, didn't strike... they simply rose. Like a heavy fog creeping in from the sea, they curled around their feet, thick and cloying.

Mia inhaled sharply. "What are you..."

The darkness swallowed them whole. For a moment, there was nothing. No ground beneath their feet. No sky above them. Just an endless, soundless void. The air felt dense, pressing in on their chests, stealing their breath before the world snapped back into place.

The sand was gone. The desert heat vanished. And as their vision adjusted, it was clear. Silas had taken them somewhere else.

Chapter 11

Power

Derek's eyes fluttered open, and a jolt of cold shot through him. The hard bite of wood against his back felt like ice. For a heartbeat, his mind stumbled through fog—scrambling to remember. Sand. Heat. The Wilds. Blistering sun against his skin.

Now... this. Cold wood. Clawing shadows.

Not again. "This is becoming a nightmare," Derek rasped, his throat dry as dust. He barely recognized his own voice. Waking up in strange places had become far too familiar, but this time felt worse, much worse.

"Derek!" Mia's voice cracked through the shadows, shrill and trembling.

His heart kicked. He lurched toward her, but iron chains snapped taut around his legs and chest, yanking him back. "Mia?! Mia, where are you? What's happening?!"

"The barrier... when you brought it down..." Mia's voice quavered, breath hitching.

"Some bastard came out of nowhere," Caldera growled, her voice tight with frustration. "Shadow magic dragged us under before we could fight back."

Derek's pulse hammered in his ears. He wrestled with the chains, his skin scraping raw against the cold iron. "Where are we? Why am I shackled?!"

"We do not know," Caldera snapped. "We have not seen him again. But..."

Mia's breath quickened into shallow gasps. "Derek..." Her voice shrank to a fragile whisper. "Derek, please... get us out of here. I can't..." Her words fractured. "I can't be tied up like this again."

There was raw fear in her voice now, fear that twisted Derek's insides. He could almost see her. Her fists clenched, back pressed to the wall, reliving horrors she thought were behind her.

"I'm coming, Mia. I swear." His voice was hoarse but resolute.

He pushed, desperate to summon his magic, to feel even a flicker of lightning or light. His palms sparked with a faint white glow, then guttered out like dying embers.

"No, no, come on!" He forced harder, teeth gritted, sweat prickling at his brow, but the chains seemed to leech the strength from him.

"Ugh! Why isn't this working?!"

"I tried," Caldera grunted. "Before either of you woke. Nothing."

Heavy, deliberate footsteps echoed on the wooden floorboards, growing closer.

"Derek..." Mia's voice cracked into panic, raw and fraying. "He's coming."

Derek's heart slammed against his ribs. Even without magic, he braced himself. He would not let Mia go through this again. He would tear the chains from the wall if he had to. His eyes locked on the door, every muscle coiled tight.

The heavy door creaked open, and the shadows peeled away from the corners of the room, rushing like liquid ink to pool at the feet of the figure standing in the doorway.

"Ahh. Good." The man's voice slithered into the room, smooth and sharp all at once. "You're all awake." His gaze swept over them, sharp as a blade. "Now, who wants to explain to me why you thought it was a brilliant idea to destroy a barrier that's stood for millennia?"

Mia forced herself to her feet, though her hands trembled. Her glare was fierce, even through her fear. "You... Silas, right?" she spat. "You said you were a friend. Friends don't lock their friends in chains and shadows."

Silas offered a thin, almost amused smile. "I could not risk our Semideus friend waking in panic and losing control," he purred, inclining his head toward Derek.

Derek's breath caught. "You know what I am?" His voice was taut, sharp with confusion and growing fury. "And my magic... why can't I use it?!"

"So many questions," Silas mused, stepping closer. His eyes gleamed in the dim light, as if enjoying their helplessness. "Tell you what. If you promise to behave, I will release your chains and answer all your questions..."

A cruel smirk twisted his lips.

"Afterward, I will ask a few of my own."

Derek's eyes narrowed, but a glimpse of Mia's face stopped him cold. Fear etched her features, raw and barely restrained. His heart twisted. He just wanted to get her out of this place, away from the chains, the dark, the shadows.

Before he could speak, a sharp twinge pulsed through his body. Then, that voice... low, ancient, and laced with warning, rattled in his skull like a bell in a storm.

"Do not trust the shadow caster."

Derek's thoughts surged forward, trying to speak, to ask, but the voice overpowered him.

"Stay on this path. But DO NOT TRUST THE SHADOW CASTER."

Frustrated, Derek roared back in his own mind, *"TELL ME WHY!"*

There was a pause, so brief it made his breath catch.

Silas's smooth voice cut through the air around him. "Do we have a deal, Semideus?"

Derek's eyes locked onto him, silent, searching. Every instinct screamed at him to stay on edge. Silas looked calm. Too calm. Derek couldn't read a thing on his face, and that scared him more than if he'd seen malice.

At last, the voice whispered one final time.

"Find the Trinity. Stay on the path. Do not trust the shadow caster. Do this... and I will reveal everything you seek."

The pain in Derek's body ebbed away. The voice went quiet, vanishing into the corners of his mind.

That was new. It didn't even need the void anymore. It could just... speak. Whenever it wanted.

A chill coiled down Derek's spine.

He looked from Mia to Silas, heart thudding, and gave a single, stiff nod. "Question for question, then."

Silas's grin widened, and with a lazy snap of his fingers, the shadows writhed forward, slithering across the floor like snakes before unshackling their limbs.

"Before you get any clever ideas," Silas said, voice syrupy smooth, "the elixir I gave you will keep your magic dormant a while longer. Just a precaution. Now... come along."

Mia wasted no time. She bolted toward Derek, practically launching into his arms. He caught her, holding her tightly and pressing his face into her shoulder.

"You okay?" he murmured, his voice barely audible.

"I am now, Lavender," she whispered, her breath warm against his neck.

He gently ran his hand over the back of her head, fingers sliding through her brunette hair. The once-vibrant pink highlights had started to fade, dulling into dusty rose. He hated that. It felt like something else slipping away.

"Now is not the time to be romantic, Derek," Caldera grumbled behind them. "I do not trust this fae, but we are not in a position to fight. So we should hear him out."

Mia stepped back, her hand still on Derek's arm as she turned to Caldera. "She's right. I hate this... but, she's right."

Derek nodded, jaw tight, and turned toward the open doorway Silas had left through. He stepped cautiously into the hall beyond.

It was... disarmingly beautiful.

Polished wooden floors stretched ahead, warm and honey-toned, gleaming under lanterns that floated midair– no hooks, no wires, just soft orbs of light. The walls were curved, made from rich desert cedar, forming a cozy, nest-like structure.

Shelves were carved directly into the walls, each one cluttered with strange and fascinating things. Old leather-bound tomes, jars of glowing sand, dried flowers, and glittering herbs that shimmered in the low light. A cast-iron teapot let out a gentle hiss from across the room, steam curling from its spout. No flame beneath it, just a glowing ember of magic that flickered like a spirit.

At the center sat a low, circular table made from cactus wood, its surface carved with swirling, ancient runes. Mismatched chairs surrounded it. And there sat Silas, casually waiting, one leg crossed over the other, fingers steepled beneath his chin.

He smiled as they approached, like a man who had all the time in the world.

Chapter 12

Answers

"Let us start with an easy one," Silas said, his voice almost too calm. He waved a hand through the air, and across the room, the teapot and several cups lifted, drifting toward them like obedient ghosts, carried on tendrils of shadow. "What brought you to the Wilds?"

Derek took his cup without a word, but didn't drink. He placed it on the table, just as Mia and Caldera did.

"We're searching for something," Derek answered flatly.

Silas raised an eyebrow, unimpressed. "If you are going to be cryptic, we will get nowhere. Let me ask again... what are you doing in the Wilds?"

Derek grunted, frustrated, but Mia and Caldera both gave him subtle nods of encouragement. He sighed. "Fine. We're looking for something called the Trinity."

That seemed to satisfy Silas. His expression smoothed. "Hmm. And why would you think you would find it here?"

Derek leaned forward. "No. I said question for question. My turn. How do you know I'm a Semideus?"

Silas grinned like he'd been waiting for that one. "I thought you might start simple as well, but fair enough," he said, sipping from his cup. "I know because... *I* am Semideus. I can feel it in you. Your aura, your presence. And besides... the power it took to destroy that barrier? That was not ordinary magic."

Derek's jaw dropped. Mia elbowed him sharply, and he blinked, snapping back to the moment.

"If you're Semideus," Derek said breathlessly, "then tell me what that means. We haven't found anything written about it."

"That's another question before my turn, but..." Silas smirked, swirling the tea in his cup, "I will allow it. Being Semideus means the blood in our veins descends from beings in the Sacred Dimension."

Derek's mind reeled. Thoughts crashed into each other like waves. *Sacred Dimension? That's not possible. My parents... no, they would've told me. Wouldn't they?*

The words slipped out before he could stop them. "My parents would've told me if I wasn't theirs!"

Silas chuckled. "Calm down. The blood can lie dormant for generations. It awakens under two conditions. Either the blood is on the verge of extinction, it being too diluted to hold power anymore... or the host becomes aware of the truth."

Mia gently took Derek's hand, threading her fingers into his. "You were having nightmares... maybe Malum was forcing the blood to awaken?"

Silas bolted to his feet. "Nightmares? Tell me about them. How did Malum cause them?"

Caldera rose, too, wary now. "Wait a second... Malum wielded shadows, didn't he?"

The shadows around Silas began to stir again, pooling at his feet like ink. "Of course he did. He drew power from Oblivion, a corrupted offshoot of shadow magic. Oblivion was forged by Erebus, the Father of Shadows, but twisted by Maulum's influence."

He turned back to Derek, arms folded tight. "That is not the point. I need to know how Malum caused those nightmares."

"I... I'm not sure he did. But it was definitely his voice I heard in them," Derek admitted.

Silas leaned forward. "And what did his voice say?"

Mia crossed her arms, annoyed. "For someone who knows so much, you sure ask a lot of questions."

Silas snapped, voice sharp as glass. "Listen, human. This is important..."

"Do not talk to her like that!" Derek shouted, his voice rising with a crackle of energy. His fists clenched, and the faint snap of lightning lit his knuckles.

"I will do damn well as I please..." Shadows surged up around Silas's shoulders like wings of smoke.

Derek tensed, fists glowing now. "Back off."

Silas froze. He closed his eyes, exhaled slowly. The shadows crept back, reluctantly sinking to the floor.

"My apologies," he said, voice more composed. "I did not mean to lose my temper. But this...this detail matters. Please. Tell me what exactly was said in the nightmare."

Derek's shoulders relaxed slightly. He opened his palm, letting the lightning fade. "To bridge the gap, unite the world's divide. With courage, he'll mend what's torn inside. The realms tremble as the battle draws near. In his hands, the fate of all appears."

Silas's eyes widened, the whites overtaking the black for a split second. "You killed him, right? You made sure he was dead?"

"Y-yeah. I think so?" Derek stammered.

Silas stepped closer. "No. I need to know. Did you burn his body?"

"Well, about that..." Derek hesitated.

"The body vanished," Caldera said flatly. "So did Trey and Sarika."

Silas swore under his breath. "Shit. We do not have time. I need to get you to the High Court."

"The what now?" Mia asked.

Silas gave her a baffled look. "The High Court. You do not know? Have they forgotten all our traditions in Luminfae?" He sighed. "No matter. I promise I will explain everything later. But for now, we leave. The King needs to hear this."

Silas turned toward the door, but Caldera's voice cut through the air like a blade. "Why would we follow you anywhere else? You promised answers if we gave you ours. So far, all you have done is give us more questions."

"You do not understand." Silas spun on his heel, his eyes sharper now, darker. "If Malum was behind those dreams... if he was the one reciting the prophecy to you... and now you're searching for the Trinity..." He hesitated, just for a breath. "Then the Culling is near."

Derek's brow furrowed. "What the heck is a Culling?"

Silas stepped closer, urgency vibrating in his voice. "The prophecy you recited... it is meant to stop the Culling. We found it carved into stone long before our own recorded history, before Luminfae and Welderan split into two lands."

"Welderan?" Mia echoed softly.

"The true name of the Wilds." Silas waved it off like dust. "I know very little about the Culling, and even less about the Trinity. Some say the Culling is a cosmic reset. Others, the final end. But everyone agrees on one thing...it is catastrophic for anyone still drawing breath when it happens."

Derek swallowed. "And this High Court... they'll know more?"

Silas nodded once. "They... he will know. But we must move quickly. I can not shadow-whisk us there. It is warded against my kind of magic. And we can not afford to be caught by the other courts. Especially not the Murder."

Mia's eyes narrowed. "What the hell is the Murder?"

Silas hesitated, then said grimly, "No one we need to face right now. In Meridian, the capital, the home of the High Court... you will get your answers. All of them. I know you barely know me, but I need you to trust me."

There it was. That word again. Trust. The voice from the void had warned him. *Don't trust the shadow caster*. But how could he trust a disembodied whisper any more than a stranger who bared just enough truth to sound convincing? Both offered answers. Both held secrets. But only one offered a tangible path.

Derek looked to Mia and Caldera.

"I'll go with whatever you decide," Mia said gently, leaning into him, her head resting on his chest. "I trust you."

"I do not understand any of this," Caldera added, "but I will follow you, Derek Stratum. And then we will return to Luminfae with whatever information we can gather." She paused for a moment as her eyes watered ever so slightly, "Then we will get Barry away from Talissa."

Derek stood there a moment longer, torn between fear and purpose. He listened for the voice again, for a whisper from the void, but there was only silence.

"If we go with you..." he said finally, "will you answer our questions along the way?"

Silas offered only a nod.

Derek took a breath. "Then I guess we're going to Meridian."

Silas opened the door. Blinding sunlight poured into the room, cutting through the dim interior like a sword. Heat clung to them instantly. A dry, stinging wind rushed inside, carrying the scent of scorched sand. The desert stretched beyond the doorway, endless and rippling, alive with mirage and menace.

Derek squinted into the glare, already feeling the first grains of sand nestling into his clothes, like the land itself was welcoming him with a thousand tiny irritations. He didn't know why this felt like the right decision. Only that it did.

Chapter 13

Demands

Mr. Monton poured the Nectar with deliberate care, each drop hitting the cups like a countdown. He passed the drinks around, but the gesture did nothing to loosen the noose of silence tightening around the table.

Tah'quhal looked straight past his cup. He stared daggers through David, unblinking, unyielding, making the air heavier with every breath.

The others sipped. Tah'quhal downed his in a single gulp.

He wiped his mouth and finally spoke, each word as sharp as a blade. "Someone I consider a friend is trapped in Ignis. He is there because of a gamble... a bargain that balances on your life. You said you had secrets worth sharing. Five minutes. That is all you get before I drag you back to Talissa in chains."

David gave a lazy smirk and raised his palms in mock surrender. "Easy there, big guy. Look... Talissa's been scheming since before you were born. I've been her Keeper for twenty years, and most of her moves? Political. Petty. Power grabs. Nothing world-ending."

He took a sip of Nectar like they were chatting about the weather.

Tah'quhal ripped David's cup from his hands and slammed it down, the ceramic shattering into splinters and honeyed liquid. "We do not have time for your casual drinking, you damned fool! What has the temptress done?!"

David flinched and Nectar soaked into his shirt. He blinked once, then chuckled under his breath. "Alright. You want the truth?" He leaned in, voice low but not shy. "Talissa's been working with Malum since the start."

The room went still. Mr. Monton and Johnathan exchanged a look of pure dread.

Nidalle's voice was barely a whisper. "If that is true... it would explain why Malum's body and the others disappeared almost immediately after the battle... Talissa must have helped them."

"Why are you whispering, Nidalle?" Tah'quhal barked.

Nidalle flinched, her eyes flicking toward the tavern windows. "Because if what David says is true, we can not trust anyone. He has told me... Talissa has spies in every city. Even here, even *before* the barrier fell."

There was a shift in the air, it was subtle, but it was there. A prickle on the skin. A taste of something off. Tah'quhal's instincts growled in the back of his mind.

"Do you feel that?" he asked.

"Yeah, buddy," Johnathan replied, his grip tightening on his staff. "Feels like somethin' just changed. Want me to drop the wards?"

"Slowly," Tah'quhal said, not taking his eyes off the windows.

Johnathan twirled his staff counterclockwise. The silence spell began to fade, and suddenly the tavern filled with the muffled hum of city life outside.

"What is going on?" Nidalle asked, her voice tight.

But before anyone could answer, a voice rang out above the street noise.

"JOHN! TAH'QUHAL! Where are y'all, man?!"

Tah'quhal's heart seized mid-beat.

"Is that..." he began.

"Barry!" Johnathan was already running, the Keeper staff thudding against the tavern floor as he dropped the last spell and burst through the doors.

Tah'quhal was right behind him. The others followed in a blur of movement and rising hope.

There, in the middle of the dusty street, stood Barry. One shoe missing. Shirt torn nearly to ribbons. Dirt streaked down his arms and legs, and his hair looked like he'd run through half of Luminfae... but he was smiling.

He looked exhausted, sun-worn, and utterly alive.

"Barry!" Johnathan shouted again, his voice thick with disbelief and something close to relief.

Barry threw his arms wide, panting between words. "Finally! Dammit, man, I've been looking all over this gods-forsaken town for you!"

Johnathan didn't stop running. He slammed into Barry with a fierce hug that lifted them both off the ground.

Tah'quhal slowed, watching the reunion. His hands curled into fists, but not from rage this time. Relief, sharp and sudden, bloomed in his chest, and for the first time in what felt like hours, he exhaled.

"You stubborn, lucky idiot," he muttered under his breath.

Barry looked over Johnathan's shoulder and grinned at Tah'quhal. "What? No hug from you?"

Tah'quhal rolled his eyes, but a ghost of a smile tugged at the corner of his mouth. "Don't push it."

They stood in the street, still catching their breath, still smiling.

Johnathan clapped Barry on the back. "Buddy, ya look like hell, but it's damn good to see ya."

Barry laughed, short and breathless. "You don't know the half of it, my guy."

Even Nidalle let out a small laugh. The tension from the tavern had cracked just enough to let some light in. For the first time in what felt like forever, it almost felt safe. But then, everything stilled.

The air around them shifted like a breath caught in the throat. The breeze, once playful, vanished. No laughter echoed from the market stalls. No footsteps tapped against the cobbled streets. It was as if the whole city had paused mid-sentence. Even the sunlight seemed to dull.

Barry's smile faltered. His eyes lost their spark, distant now. His face went rigid, brows stitching into a single unbroken line across his forehead. The shift was so stark that even Johnathan, still half in hug-mode, felt his stomach drop.

Tah'quhal noticed it too. "Barry?" he said, his voice low.

Barry pulled back from Johnathan's embrace, slowly, like something inside him had turned cold. When he spoke, his voice was quiet, but it carried like thunder.

"I think..." He looked each of them in the eyes, pausing at Tah'quhal. "I think Malum is alive."

Chapter 14

Revelations

"Tah'quhal, you already know I'd been snooping around," Barry said as he sat at the warped wooden table inside the Fickle Fae. "Following Talissa when she'd vanish without a trace."

Tah'quhal nodded slowly, eyes sharp. "I have not had the chance to tell the others about our... encounter. Not before you showed up."

Barry raised an eyebrow. "Damn, man. You left from under that volcano, what, two days ago? Where the hell have you been?"

Everyone's attention shifted to Tah'quhal. The warrior's silence was heavy. Finally, he spoke, "The portal beneath the volcano did not lead me here." He glanced toward the floor, as if staring through the boards. "I ended up in..."

"Mythos," Johnathan cut in. "Reckon I would've bet on it. A random portal in Ignis's belly? You're lucky it didn't spit ya out into Oblivion."

Barry winced. "Bro... I swear I didn't know it would toss you there. That's on me."

Tah'quhal debated saying more. But the truth wouldn't help, not right now. He turned his gaze to Barry. "Go on."

Barry hesitated, rubbing the back of his neck, then nodded. His smile faded like a ghost.

"I followed Talissa again. She went deeper this time, into another part of the tunnels. A new chamber. I swear, it was built like the first one we found... circular, ringed with portals. But this one had ten arches instead of just one. Six were active, swirling with color. The other four looked dead. Empty."

The room went still as Barry paused. He took a long breath and cracked his knuckles against the table. He knew he needed to go on, but his stomach was in knots. He gathered himself.

"And in the center," Barry continued, voice quieter now, "there was a hollowed-out pit. She descended into it. I couldn't see what she was doing. Not right away."

He paused again. His eyes flicked to each of them.

"Then, the first portal shimmered. Someone stepped through." Barry's breath hitched. "It was Sarika."

Gasps broke out. Johnathan cursed under his breath.

"She's alive?" Nidalle whispered.

"Her hair's different, fiery red now. But it was her. Her walk, her voice, her smirk. I'd bet my damn soul on it." Barry's hands balled into fists as he continued, "Then, the second figure came through. A fae. Sickly. Gaunt. His skin looked stretched thin, like it was barely holding on. I couldn't tell who he was at first. But when the light caught his face..." Barry looked up, and the tremble in his voice cracked through. "I saw his eyes."

There was complete silence in the tavern, not even the scurry of a mouse across the floor. Every ear that could hear was on the edge of their seat, waiting for Barry to finish.

"Swirling red and black rings around the pupils. The same ones we have all seen."

He looked at Tah'quhal, then Johnathan.

"It was Malum. Alive."

Johnathan shot out of his chair. "Horseshit. That's horseshit, Barry. Derek killed him. We all saw it. Derek literally obliterated him, and Trey went down before that. And you..." he pointed at Tah'quhal, "you drove your dadgum blade through Sarika. They're gone. That was the end!"

Barry's eyes dropped to the floor. His next words were barely more than breath. "John..."

He looked up, locking eyes with his oldest friend. Voice shaking, he said, "The third figure who stepped through that portal..."

A beat of silence. A *heartbeat.*

"...was Trey."

Johnathan stumbled back like he'd been shoved by an invisible force. His mouth opened, but no words came out, just a raw, strangled sound as he turned and paced away from the group. Then, the curses started.

At first, they were thrown at the situation in furious disbelief, but they shifted, aimed squarely at Barry. "You couldn't've seen that," he snapped. "You couldn't've! He was dead, Barry. We saw it. Derek eviscerated him. All that was left was a blast shadow!"

Tah'quhal moved fast, stepping between them as Johnathan's voice cracked under the weight.

Johnathan's words faltered again. His chest heaved. "I ain't...dammit, I ain't mad at you, Barry. I just..."

He gritted his teeth, tears shining in his eyes, but refusing to fall. "How the hell are they still alive? Derek nearly died ending that fight. He still ain't okay. Izzy...she died, and somehow came back to help us win. And now you're tellin me it wasn't enough? That it didn't matter?"

Barry didn't speak. He just stood there, guilt pooling in his expression. Quietly, Johnathan turned away again, and after a long moment, Tah'quhal gently asked, "Barry... what did they talk about?"

Barry's voice was low, roughened by dust and disbelief. "They weren't the only ones who showed up."

That made everyone look up.

"One of the dormant archways suddenly flared to life. Two fae stepped out... hooded, robed, real secretive. Only reason I know they were fae is 'cause their ears were poking through their hoods."

Mr. Monton crossed his arms. "The portal just... turned on?"

Barry nodded slowly. "And it wasn't the only one."

Nidalle leaned forward. "Please. Go on."

Barry's hands moved as he spoke, like he needed to shape the memory in the air to believe it himself. "After the two newcomers stepped into the center chamber, another arch lit up. But this one...it was different. It shimmered in gold and silver, like starlight spinning in water. Lit the whole place up."

He exhaled sharply, rubbing the back of his neck. "And the woman who stepped out... was the second most beautiful woman I've ever seen."

Johnathan jumped in, his voice cracking with forced humor, desperately trying to dismiss his earlier outburst. "Ahh, somebody misses Caldera."

Every face in the room snapped toward him with a silent "Not now."

"What?" he said, lifting his hands. "We're getting trauma bombed. Just trying to...ya know...cope."

Barry blinked. "Speaking of Caldera... where is she?"

Tah'quhal stepped up and laid a hand on Barry's shoulder. "She is in the Wilds. Same as Derek and Mia."

Barry's head jerked up. "Why? Why the hell is she there?"

"I promise we will explain soon," Tah'quhal said calmly. "But first... finish your story. This woman, what else do you remember?"

Barry sat back down slowly. "She was in red. A robe, I guess, if you could call it that. Barely covered anything. Her hair was gold, real gold, and it reached past her knees. She moved like... like royalty. Like fire that knew it could burn you."

Nidalle shook her head. "That does not sound like any fae I recall."

Barry hesitated. "Her eyes... they were green. Bright green. Not normal, almost like hellfire green. Same color as Helian's magic back in Terra."

Johnathan visibly flinched. His hand reached instinctively to his shoulder, rotating it slowly. No one had forgotten what Codi's arrow did to him at Helian's command that day.

Barry's voice dropped to a near whisper.

"And then... right before the woman stepped forward, another portal opened."

He looked around the room, meeting their eyes one at a time.

"And Helian walked out of it."

The silence that followed was crushing.

Johnathan slammed his hand on the table. "What the hell?! What's next, huh? Dracula shows up? Maybe my dead mamaw's plotting against us, too? Every dadgum villain we've ever faced is now having tea in a lava cave?!"

Barry chuckled dryly. "That's everyone, John. Sarika. Malum. Trey. The hooded fae. The golden woman. Helian. All of 'em. They all met in the hollowed-out center." He leaned forward. "So I snuck closer. Close enough to hear what they were saying."

"Well, what did they say?" Tah'quhal asked, his face unreadable.

Barry shook his head. "I couldn't stay long, but I caught a few words. One of them mentioned something about a culling... and then Malum laughed. Said not to worry about anything like that."

"A culling?" Johnathan echoed, eyes narrowing.

"I don't know, man." Barry rubbed the back of his neck. "But the golden-haired lady, at least I think it was her... it didn't sound like Talissa or Sarika... she said something about how if the merger isn't completed soon, the culling would definitely happen."

Nidalle leaned forward. "What next, Barry?"

Barry hesitated. His hands trembled slightly in his lap before he raised them, palms up. "Then... I felt this burning pain rush through my hands. And this happened."

A red flame flickered to life in each palm, dancing and spitting with unstable heat. Barry winced as it flared, the sting on his skin almost nothing compared to the deeper memory, the hellfire from Terra, roaring and cruel.

Johnathan sprang to his side. "Barry, you're attuned!"

From the far corner of the room, David, silent until now, let out a dark chuckle. "That's why I can't use my damn magic."

All eyes turned to him, confused and wary.

Mr. Monton took a careful step forward. "Please... elaborate."

David slowly looked around the room before gesturing to Johnathan and Mr. Monton. "You two. You passed your Keeper title on to your son. Your staff, your position... but you kept your magic. That's how it usually works in Luminfae, right?"

Johnathan nodded. "Well, yeah. That's tradition."

David gave a bitter smile, eyes dropping to the floor. "Not in Ignis. When Talissa names a new Keeper... the old one begins to fade. The magic drains out of you. And when it's gone... so are you."

Barry leapt up, fire extinguished, panic flooding his voice. "Hell no! I don't want to be the Keeper! You can keep all of this! I don't need any magic. I didn't ask for this!"

David gave him a sad look. "But you did ask for this, bud. Talissa must've started the transfer while I was still in that coma. The process has already begun. It won't be long now... until I'm gone. And the bargain you made with her will be complete."

Barry shook his head, voice cracking. "No. No way. I won't have your blood on my hands, I won't let her win."

"You'll be the Keeper of Ignis," David said softly. "Until she gets bored of you."

Tah'quhal moved to Barry and locked eyes with him. "We will not let that happen."

"No, we won't, buddy," Johnathan said, placing a firm hand on Barry's shoulder.

Nidalle stepped in close, her hand steady on Barry's back. "Talissa will not get away with this."

Silence stretched, thick with unspoken fear.

Then Mr. Monton cleared his throat, his voice steady and low.

"I think it's time we found a way to bring Derek, Mia, and Caldera back home."

Chapter 15

We Only Need One

The inside of the Fickle Fae had never been busier, not with customers, but with movement, worry, and desperate searching.

Tah'quhal and Barry stood over the large map of Luminfae, the former filling the latter in on everything Derek, Mia, and Caldera were doing and pointing out the known rift locations. Barry, meanwhile, frowned and asked why there was no map of the Wilds.

Johnathan and Mr. Monton sat at a table buried in scrolls and ancient tomes brought from the Cressida Library, hunting for any mention of a culling, the Keeper transfer in Ignis, or anything that might help them locate Derek and the others.

Near the window, Nidalle and Abhaya were focusing their essence, trying to sense any change in David's aura. The latter had arrived not too long ago. They weren't sure if they could save his magic, but if they could at least save his life, it would be worth it. Every ally counted now.

"Okay, Taco, look... Oceanus is right on the edge of the Wilds, right?" Barry asked, tracing the coastline.

Tah'quhal raised an eyebrow. "When will you learn to pronounce my name correctly? But yes, Oceanus is the closest city."

"I can say your name, man. I just like giving you shit. You're way too serious, way too often."

Tah'quhal crossed his arms. "I am not too seriou..." He stopped himself with a sigh. "Nevermind."

Barry smirked. "Anyway. If Oceanus is that close, that's where I'm headed. It'll be the first place Caldera comes back to."

"You might be right... if Derek does not just transport them here directly."

Barry blinked. "Wait, what? When did he learn how to do that? Or is that from that fancy necklace those two gave him?" He nodded toward Nidalle and Abhaya.

"It is a new power," Tah'quhal replied. "He discovered it shortly after Talissa summoned you to Ignis."

Barry opened his mouth to respond, but nothing came. He couldn't find the words.

He'd missed so much, missed it because of one stupid deal with Talissa. His friends had changed, grown, gained new powers... and he hadn't been there. Sure, some of them were back now. But their glue wasn't. And neither was his heart.

"I think I need some air," Barry muttered, turning for the door.

Tah'quhal watched him go. "Of course…" he whispered.

Barry could hear the recognition in his voice. The hint of acceptance. He knew Tah'quhal read the pain on his face.

Outside, Barry breathed in the fresh Torvanian air. The city looked so calm, so happy. People walked by smiling, unaware of the storm rising around them. He wanted to scream, to warn them… but it would only cause panic.

Johnathan stepped out behind him and sat beside him on the ground. "You doin' alright, buddy?"

"No, man," Barry said simply.

"Well," Johnathan said, "you can tell me about it. We could take a walk, see if we find any of them magical mosquitos again." He gave a crooked grin.

A ghost of a smile crossed Barry's lips. "Look, dude. I know me and Derek aren't as close as you two are… but after everything I've been through, it'd be good just to hang with him again. Like the old days."

"The old days?" Johnathan laughed. "Ya mean last year?"

Barry blinked, then laughed too. "Damn. It really has only been a year since all of this started."

He paused, now quieter, "Dude… I'm in love with a girl. A fae. One I've known for like… less than a year."

"Caldera?" Johnathan asked, nudging him with a grin on his face.

"No, man. Sarika, of course," Barry deadpanned. "Of course it's Caldera. You know what they say… absence makes the heart grow fonder… or some crap like that."

Johnathan beamed. "Well, does she know that?"

"I haven't told her, but I think the vibes are there."

Johnathan's smile faded. "You should tell her, Barry. The way things are going... tomorrow ain't promised, ya know?"

"I know, man. I know." Barry looked down, quiet for a moment. "Hey, John... can I ask you something?"

"Go ahead, buddy."

Barry looked over. "Do you think Trey and Izzy would've worked things out if none of this ever happened?"

Johnathan's expression fell. He didn't answer, just looked at his friend with a deep sadness.

Barry went on. "I don't know. I just... when I used to think about the future, before all of this, I always imagined me and Derek going to the same college. Him playing baseball, me on the football team. I figured you'd take over the family farm, but we'd all come back once a month to hang out. And I always saw Trey and Izzy as endgame. Like they'd get married. Grow old together."

Johnathan wiped a tear from his cheek. "I didn't know you thought about stuff like that, man."

Barry looked away, and for a moment, the world was still.

Black clouds rolled in above them, fast, silent, and wrong. The air went dead stale. It felt eerily familiar... too much like the moment when Barry arrived in Torvania.

Johnathan stood. "We never did ask," he said, voice tight. "How'd you get away from Ignis anyhow?"

Barry frowned. "I'm not really sure. My hands started burning, and I gasped, it was loud enough for them to hear me. I ran, but I could hear someone behind me, gaining fast. I tripped over something and thought that was it... but when I got up, I was here. In Torvania. I figured I fell through a portal or something. The place was covered in them."

Johnathan's face turned cold. Hard. More serious than Barry had ever seen.

"Shit," he muttered. "You didn't fall through no portal. They sent ya here. And I think they're coming now."

He turned back toward the tavern and shouted at the top of his lungs.

"EVERYONE GET OUT HERE NOW!"

The group inside the tavern came busting out the front door, Tah'quhal leading the way, Orgí already in his hand. Mr. Monton and Nidalle were right behind him, the latter's hand pulsing with purple essence. Abhaya and David brought up the rear.

"What is going on?" Tah'quhal asked, scanning the sky.

Johnathan pointed upward. "The clouds... they got dark again. Just like when Barry got here."

"And?" Nidalle asked, her essence already starting to dissipate.

"Barry didn't run here. He got teleported." Johnathan said, voice heavy. "I reckon they sent him... and now they're coming."

Tah'quhal's grip tightened on his sword's hilt. "Let them come. We can end this now."

As if answering his challenge, the air thickened. Red essence boiled around them, swirling into a violent vortex behind Johnathan and Barry. A figure took shape inside the blood-colored mist.

"Barry," the figure said, voice layered in sorrow and venom. "I told them to leave you out of this. I told them you'd just try to snoop, but Talissa was adamant about the deal she made with you."

Barry stared into the mist, his heart clenching. He knew that voice. "Trey? Why are you doing this?"

Johnathan took a cautious step forward. "Trey, come home, buddy. Help us stop all of thi—"

"STOP IT?" Trey's voice cracked into a furious shout, cutting him off. His whole body shook as he pointed a trembling, accusing finger at Johnathan. "You... you don't get to say that."

Johnathan flinched but held his ground. Trey's words tumbled out, bitter and broken.

"I fought this. I fought it every single day, every single hour. I tried to stop it, John. I begged, I bled, I sold pieces of myself trying to change what was coming." His voice cracked again, but he pushed forward, louder now. "And where were you?"

Johnathan opened his mouth to answer, but Trey wasn't done.

"You were there, Johnathan," Trey spat. "You were there when Izzy—"

He choked on her name. A raw sound escaped him, somewhere between a sob and a snarl.

"You let her die."

Johnathan's eyes widened, horror creeping across his face. "Trey... I... there ain't no way I could've saved Izzy."

"You could have told Derek to just go with Tarik!" Trey roared, voice shaking the ground. "You could have let him go! I would have found him. I would have brought him back!"

Red tears streaked Trey's face, the mist around him swirling wilder. His fists clenched so tight blood welled from his palms.

"But you didn't. You just watched," Trey seethed, voice fraying apart. "You all tried to play hero while she screamed for help... while I... while I..."

He couldn't finish. His face crumpled for just a heartbeat, the old Trey, their friend, still buried beneath the rage. Then, it hardened, twisting into a brittle, cruel smile.

"And now look at us," Trey said, his voice low and vicious. "A bunch of fools. Broken and bleeding. You have no idea what's coming."

He straightened, hellfire sparking in his eyes. "But you will. You all will."

Barry took a trembling step back, trying to pull Johnathan with him. "Trey... whatever they promised you, we can fix it. We can fix you."

Trey only laughed, a bitter, hollow sound.

"Fix me? Barry, you may not want the gift Talissa's bestowing," he said, voice dripping with mockery, "but we only need one Keeper."

"Gift?" David scoffed from the back. "More like a curse. Talissa only poisons those around her."

Trey's gaze snapped to him like a striking snake. His arms tensed, the red vortex calming to a deadly stillness. When he spoke, it was not to David, it was to Johnathan and Barry.

"Like I told Derek, in this very same spot... we stand on opposing sides now. You may have won the first battle," Trey said, voice low and vibrating with fury, "but make no mistake..."

He raised his hands, hellfire green and red essence swirling together like a living storm.

"...this is war. And in war, people will die."

"I didn't kill her, Trey!" Spit flew from Johnathan's mouth as his voice cracked, his head shaking in desperate denial.

Trey's answer didn't come in the form of words. Hellfire surged from him, ripping across the clearing. It slammed into David before he could react.

A haunting scream tore from David's mouth, not just pain, but terror, disbelief, agony. The group watched in horror, frozen, as David's body convulsed once, then crumpled to the ground. Still. Silent.

Nidalle and Abhaya screamed, shattering the silence. Tah'quhal spun toward them, but the damage was already done. Barry turned to grab Johnathan, but Johnathan wasn't there.

A whisper of red mist lingered where he'd stood.

"I told you..." Trey's voice echoed, already distant.

"We only need one Keeper."

The red essence laced vortex spun up again, faster, fiercer, then shot into the sky, carrying Trey with it.

Barry stood, stunned, trying to make sense of it, until the absence hit him like a blade to the gut.

"John?" Barry spun to the others. "Where is John?!"

Mr. Monton dropped to his knees, silent.

"John... JOHN!" Barry shouted at the sky, voice breaking, pleading for his friend, but the only answer was the roaring wind.

Chapter 16

A Whole New World

The salty taste in the air made Derek's mouth dry and raw. Sweat rolled down his forehead, stinging his eyes. He hadn't sweat like this since the championship baseball game his junior year, but that had been a crisp autumn afternoon. This was different. This was punishment.

The sand stretched forever in every direction, the ground alive and shifting beneath his boots. Cracks spider-webbed between dunes, each breath carrying a metallic tang. Grit stung his skin with every gust of wind. Even the sky looked exhausted, a muted blue burning under a relentless sun.

Their trek to Meridian was brutal, and they were barely halfway.

"Are you paying attention, Semideus?" Silas called, grinning as he walked backwards with maddening ease, his bare feet barely sinking into the dunes.

Mia gave Derek's hand a soft squeeze. He realized he'd been some-where else entirely. His mind kept circling the voice from the void.

"Do not trust the shadow caster."

It haunted him, gnawed at him. Why? What did the voice know that he didn't? He should tell Mia. He *wanted* to tell her. He hated keeping things from her again, but he needed to understand first. He needed to see.

"Yeah," Derek said finally, clearing his throat. "You said there are four courts in Welderan, right?" He frowned, digging through the fog in his brain. "The High Court in Meridian, The Shimmering Court in Calistia, The Bloodsport in Davensclaw, and... The Mur-der in the Barrens?"

"Mm-hmm." Silas grunted approvingly. "Just making sure you were not melting that brain of yours."

He spun on his heel, kicking up a little spray of red sand, and con-tinued walking forward, his voice carrying easily on the dry breeze. "The High Court's the only one we need to worry about for now. They hold the most power, although The Murder's not far behind these days."

"The Murder?" Mia asked, wrinkling her nose. "Why such a creepy name?"

Silas chuckled, a rough sound that somehow blended into the whistling wind. "Well, dear, what else would you call a group of crows?"

"Crows?" Caldera echoed, squinting against the sun.

Silas grinned. "Each member of The Murder has a patron crow. A spirit bound to them. They can see through its eyes, speak with it, even act through it." He paused, eyes flicking up to the white-hot sky. "Before Luminfae cut ties with us, they actually went by a different name. The Last Court."

"What made them change it?" Derek asked, shifting his pack higher on his shoulders. A fine sheen of magic in the sand made the pack feel heavier than it should.

Silas jabbed a finger skyward. "They claim the stars spoke to them. Showed them the 'true path' of this world. Whether that is madness or prophecy..." he shrugged. "Depends on who you ask."

They trudged on in silence, the sand crunching underfoot.

Then, Caldera spoke up, brushing grains of sand from her tunic. "Were there courts in Luminfae before the split?"

Silas gave her a sly look over his shoulder. "Thought you would never ask."

He turned to Mia, wagging a finger at her. "Your favorite Chieftain, good ole Karrent, should know all about this."

Mia raised an inquisitorial brow but said nothing.

"There were four courts in Luminfae once," Silas went on, voice low and almost reverent. "Earth, Water, Fire, and Air. Each ruled by a fae who mastered an element's set."

"Was it... different then?" Mia asked, her voice almost lost in the dry wind.

"Very different." Silas nodded. "Elemental magic was everything. It was forbidden for a Luminfaeian to study outside their birth court. Earth did not touch fire. Water did not dare learn air. Magic was rigid, bloodbound. Archaic times."

He kicked a stone, sending it skittering across the cracked sand.

"Now," he said, glancing back at Derek with a gleam in his eye, "the rules are gone. Chaos reigns. Power's up for grabs."

And somewhere, deep inside Derek's chest, that cold warning from the void pulsed again.

"Do not trust the shadow caster."

They walked for what felt like hours, but Derek wasn't quite sure how long it had really been. His mind was not at ease, but he still managed to listen to everything Silas had to say.

Silas went on and on about how Luminfae should have never hidden behind the barrier. He told them that, even though Welderan had not agreed with the decision, they eventually came to accept that their siblings to the east no longer wanted anything to do with them.

Then, his tone shifted. Bitter.

He spoke of creatures that once thrived only because of the bond between the lands. Dragons that chased the warmer skies, drakes that followed blooming storms, serpents that swam up river through freshwater channels stretching into Luminfae. They all once moved freely, guided by the shifting seasons. But when Luminfae stopped allowing passage, the migrations ceased. Trapped in Welderan's harsher terrain, the creatures began to die out. Some starved, others turned feral. The few who endured became leaner, meaner, twisted echoes of what they used to be. What once were awe-inspiring beasts of myth had become territorial monsters, their old grace burned out by isolation.

"Just over this last dune," Silas whispered as they started the ascent of the sandy hill.

"Finally—" Mia blurted out, but abruptly stopped when Derek tugged her arm.

Derek pointed with his other hand to the sky, "Are those crows?"

Overhead, hundreds of black birds began to block out the sun. They formed a flowing circle, letting the light shine through in rhythmic pulses like a heartbeat.

Shadows coiled around Silas. "Shit," he muttered. He balled his hands into fists, shadows lashing out in the form of twin daggers. "The Murder. This could go bad."

Derek asked, "What do we do?"

"Let me do the talking," Silas answered.

From the swirling halo of crows above, three began to descend.

"CAW!"

The largest of the three shrieked before it exploded into a flurry of feathers. A tall, bony man with translucent skin stretched over too-prominent bones stood where the bird had been. His long, dark purple hair fell straight to his shoulders, and a jet-black beard ended in a split fork.

"Caw."

"Caw."

The other two crows followed suit. One became a short, stubby man with skin just as pale and glassy. The other mirrored the tallness and eerie build of the first.

The first man swept his unsettling gaze over the group. Mia shivered and pressed into Derek's side. Even he felt a chill crawl beneath his skin as the man's unnatural purple eyes locked with his.

A fragile voice rasped from the man. "Silas. Tsk tsk tsk." He clicked his tongue. "Why are you moving toward Meridian?"

"Well, Gregory," Silas replied, his voice carefully drained of emotion, "I was just going to take my new friends here to see the jewel of the desert."

Gregory inhaled slowly, almost as if savoring the tension. "I do believe you know better. If there are newcomers in Welderan, that can only mean one thing... the barrier has fallen."

"About tha—" Silas tried to continue in his monotone cadence.

"We brought it down," Caldera interrupted confidently.

Her words landed like a thunderclap. The three crow-men jerked their heads in unison, twisting them at unnatural angles. Thick veins pulsed visibly beneath their skin, and violet liquid oozed from their eyes, slick and slow like poison tears. It was like something out of a horror film.

Mia pushed herself harder into Derek's arms, and Caldera, even with her bravado, took a cautious step back.

Silas didn't raise his voice. He didn't twitch. "I said to let me speak. If you can, show no emotion. Their magic feeds off of it.

"Listen to your new friend, strangers," Gregory hissed through clenched teeth. His mouth twitched unnaturally with each word, like it hurt him to speak them. "I would hate for something to…take over."

"We will be going now, Gregory," Silas said, voice steady as he took a step toward Meridian.

Gregory tilted his head, his cracked lips curling into a sharp grin. "Will you?"

The sand beneath Derek's boots shifted subtly. Shadows, like oil slicks, snaked silently across the ground. He caught just a flicker of them at the edge of his vision, writhing, creeping from Silas's feet toward his own. They slithered up his back, cold and whispering, curling into his ears like smoke.

"When I run, unleash your power into the sky. Trust me."

The voice was low, urgent. Not in his head, but inside him. Derek's heartbeat thundered in his ears. Trust him? He didn't know who to listen to. The faceless voice from the void? The shadow-wielding fae he'd barely known for a day?

The crows above circled like vultures sensing a final breath. The sky pulsed with their wings. A dark wind scraped across the dunes. His muscles locked, his stomach churned. He wanted to run. He wanted to scream.

He looked toward the distant gates of Meridian. They were so close. Maybe… just maybe, he could play both sides. If he could grab Mia and Caldera and get to Silas fast enough, they could ride the lightning all the way there.

But he needed a distraction.

"Silas," Derek whispered, barely audible. "Is Gregory the leader of the Murder?"

Silas turned slowly. "No. That would be Everan."

Derek nodded once. "Then I'd like to speak with Everan before we go any further."

Silas flinched. "What!?" The word slipped with more emotion than he'd meant to show.

Instantly, the veins in Gregory and his two companions bulged and pulsed. The violet ooze weeped again from their eyes.

Silas took a breath and re-centered himself. "Why would you want to do that?"

"Because I don't think we're getting the full story," Derek said, raising an eyebrow. "You haven't told us anything we couldn't have learned from anyone in Welderan."

"I promise you," Silas said, darkly. "You do not want to meet that vile creature."

Derek took a step toward Gregory. "I think I do."

Mia's hand tightened around his. Caldera's brow was furrowed, uncertain, but her eyes never left Derek. He reached out his other hand.

"Wouldn't both of you agree we need all the information before making a choice?"

A tiny bolt of lightning cracked down his arm as his fingers brushed Caldera's. She blinked at it, then gave a single nod.

The three of them stepped closer. The electricity around Derek sparked brighter now, arcing from finger to elbow. The storm was building.

Silas hesitated, then let the shadows peel away from his arms. "Fine. Do what you want."

Gregory's grin widened. "Now, now, Silas. Do not take it personally. These are clearly clever little things. They just wish to know." He tilted his head, and his eyes locked onto Derek. "But you have miscalculated, boy."

The wind stilled.

Gregory's voice turned into a rasp that scraped at Derek's bones. "You see, it's not just emotion in your voice that feeds us. I can feel it in your skin. Your veins. Every ounce of fear boiling inside you." He licked his teeth. "And I will drink it."

Suddenly, wings erupted from all three crows, massive, ink-black and lined with jagged purple feathers. The force of them kicked up waves of sand. The sky shuddered with their caws. Their bodies twisted, veins bulging, purple ichor spilling like tears.

Gregory drew a long, curved obsidian blade from his waist, and lunged.

Derek reacted on instinct. He shoved Mia toward Silas, who had already shifted to the side. With his other hand, he yanked Caldera forward and dropped to one knee.

Caldera leapt, flipping over Derek's head in a blur of motion and sprinted toward Mia and Silas. Silas turned to run, but Mia clutched his arm, yanking him back.

Gregory's wing tore across Derek's cheek… just a scratch, but it burned like acid.

Derek snarled, twisted his hand, and released a blast of lightning straight into Gregory's torso. The bolt cracked like a whip, lighting the entire dune in a burst of blinding white. The crow screamed as he was hurled backward, his companions flung like rag dolls into the sand. Smoke rose from his cloak.

It wouldn't kill him, but it bought Derek a heartbeat. He sprang to his feet, storm clouds now rolling overhead. Not shadows. Not crows. Real storm. His storm.

He lunged, grabbing Mia's hand. Then pulling in Caldera, they fell into Silas.

And the moment they all touched, BOOM, the lightning struck.

They vanished in a thunderclap.

They reappeared just outside Meridian's gates, wind whipping around them, the air buzzing with static. Behind them, the dunes trembled. Above, the crows were already coming, fast and furious.

"We just made a very powerful enemy," Silas whispered, eyes wide.

"It would not be the first," Caldera muttered, drawing her weapon.

Derek turned toward the approaching shadows, lightning still humming at his fingertips.

"I don't think it'll be the last either."

Chapter 17

City of Silver

The gates of Meridian swung open just as the crows came to a screeching halt outside the city. Derek and Mia rushed through first, followed closely by Caldera and Silas.

Silas glanced back at the Murder. The flock hovered in place, wings flapping hard but unmoving, as if some invisible force kept them from crossing.

Inside the city, the High Court Guard stood ready, their formation precise and gleaming beneath the sun. They met the group just inside the towering silver gates, polished so perfectly they mirrored the world behind them.

"They always come close," said the tallest guard. "But they never cross."

He stepped forward. "I am Darren, Captain of the High Court Guard, Champion of Meridian, and the Stone of Welderan."

"I'm Derek—" Derek began.

Darren cut him off. "No need. You travel with Silas, and Silas only brings trouble. State your business."

Silas moved to the front, his shadows writhing lazily around him like a serpent sizing up prey.

"My friend here would like to speak with the High Court," he said, calm and confident. "He's a Semideus."

Darren's eyes flicked to Derek's hands, where faint crackles of lightning still danced across his fingers.

"The Court's not taking visitors," he muttered. "Hasn't for a month..."

He paused, sizing them up. "But two Semideus in Meridian? Hell. Dallis will want to know. Follow me."

Darren turned on his heel and strode toward the palace at the city's center. The rest of the guard formed a half-circle around them, only leaving the front open.

"I've never seen a place like this," Derek whispered to Mia.

She brushed his shoulder lightly. "It's beautiful, isn't it?"

"Too beautiful. Oceanus is home, but it has its rough spots. This place... it's flawless." Derek's eyes took in every inch of the city. Something just didn't feel right.

Everything sparkled. The guards' armor was spotless, no dust, no smudges. The buildings looked freshly washed, their stone exteriors shining with a coat of silver. Even the spacing between the doors and windows on shops and homes were perfectly symmetrical. No dirt kicked up as they walked; the streets felt... sterile.

The citizens they passed were just as immaculate. Fae with pearly smiles and pristine clothing, not a wrinkle or hair out of place. They moved gracefully, mechanically, like actors playing a role too well.

Mia leaned closer and whispered, "You're right... that is strange."

As they neared the palace, it seemed to grow considerably larger with every step. Derek was pretty sure it could swallow the entire Oceanus library, palace, and Torvania's library without breaking a sweat.

At the palace doors, Darren raised two fingers. Two guards broke formation and rushed ahead to open them. Inside was even more breathtaking.

Silver-painted marble floors stretched forward, their polish so pristine they reflected the party like ghosts beneath their feet. The walls were carved stone, etched with unfamiliar glyphs, and washed in white and silver hues that shimmered faintly under the magical light.

They walked the length of a vast hallway until it opened into the throne room.

There, at its center, spun a barefoot man in silver robes, whistling an off-key tune as he danced in slow, uneven circles. He stopped every few rotations to cast a glance at them, eyes flickering with curiosity, but said nothing.

"Dallis, I have brought guests," Darren announced.

The man didn't respond—just kept spinning and whistling.

"Ehem," Darren cleared his throat. "Sir?"

Dallis halted mid-spin. He turned, eyes too wide, a smile stretched too far. "If I am split in two, do I gain a twin... or lose myself?" he asked, voice twitching with laughter.

Darren remained stone-faced. No reaction. No visible emotion. Derek imagined that's why they called him the Stone of Welderan.

"Sir. I do not know."

Dallis threw his arms skyward. "Ah, it doesn't matter! I am the only one!"

He twirled dramatically before locking eyes with the group. "Now this is interesting. I sense power... so much of it! Two Semideus? Oh, how my halls hunger for excitement."

His eyes fluttered unnaturally, as if zooming in on each of them.

"Silas! My old friend! And who have you brought me this time?" His grin widened, just a hair too far for comfort.

"This is the Semideus who brought down the barrier, Dallis. His name is Derek," Silas said, his tone cautious.

Dallis spun on one foot, a full circle of silver and bare feet. "Wonderful! So very wonderful! And what may I do for you..."

He snapped his fingers.

In an instant, he was behind Derek, whispering into his ear, "Semideus?" Another snap and he was back where he began, dancing in lazy circles as if nothing had happened.

Derek flinched at the sudden whisper, but steadied himself by reaching for Mia's hand. Her fingers curled tightly around his.

"We're looking for the Trinity," Derek said. "Short version."

The dancing stopped.

Dallis turned slowly, too slowly. His eyes somehow widened further, his grin twitching at the corners until it exploded into wild, echoing laughter.

Derek glanced at Silas, raising a brow.

"I have no idea," Silas whispered. "I have never seen him like this."

The laughter rang through the vast marble room, bouncing off silver pillars and polished floors. Dallis finally drew a breath, grinning like a madman.

"The Trinity," he said, still chuckling. "Oh, the Trinity is not real. It is a myth..." He twirled again, his robe flaring at his heels. "A legend!"

He vanished in a shimmer and reappeared behind Mia this time, gently twirling a lock of her hair between two fingers.

"A story told to children before bed," he cooed.

Then, mist-like, he returned to the center of the room, standing in front of his silver throne.

"It is real," Derek said, his voice steady and firm.

The grin vanished. Dallis's mouth flattened into a thin line.

From the edge of the room, a woman in flowing silver robes approached. Her hood cast a deep shadow over her face. She leaned close and whispered something into Dallis's ear. He nodded, then she glided away without a word or glance at the others.

"Who was that?" Mia finally spoke up to ask.

Dallis's smile returned, as if flipped on by a switch. "Oh, her? Just family. She prefers to stay quiet. Do not mind her." He did a little shimmy, "Well then... it sounds to me like you have a story to tell. The long version."

He clapped his hands once, the sound ringing like a bell. "You must stay for dinner and for the night! I will have rooms prepared for you. Three, I assume? Unless..."

His eyes flicked back and forth between Caldera and Silas, gleaming with mischief.

"No," Caldera said immediately, her tone flat.

Dallis grinned wider. "Is that a no to dinner... or a no to sharing a room with the lovely Silas?"

Silas smirked faintly, but said nothing.

Derek exchanged a quick glance with Mia, then looked at Caldera and Silas. Silent agreement passed between them. None of them wanted to linger in this unsettling palace. Something was wrong here. Deeply wrong.

A lively servant with bright silver eyes and a joyful smile led them down a labyrinth of twisting hallways, the walls glowing faintly with enchantments woven into their silver stone. Their footsteps echoed, soft and rhythmic, muffled by velvet carpet runners. The deeper into the palace they went, the more Derek felt the air grow still. Too still, as if the place were holding its breath.

The servant stopped abruptly at a fork in the corridor and turned to Silas. Without a word, she pointed to a door on the left, then gestured for the rest to keep moving.

But before Derek could take another step, Silas's hand shot out and grabbed his arm.

"Wait."

Derek turned, surprised by the edge in his voice.

"You ignored my plan," Silas said quietly. "Back in the sands, you did not trust me."

It wasn't an accusation… not exactly. But there was weight behind the words. A wound. A question in disguise.

Derek's eyes dropped to the marble floor, his voice low. "I panicked. I wasn't sure what was going to happen, so I just… did what I thought would work."

It wasn't the truth. Not all of it. He had hesitated, because part of him hadn't trusted Silas at that moment. Not fully. And that realization sat like a stone in his gut.

Silas studied him, long enough that Derek dared a glance up and something flickered behind his eyes. But when Silas noticed the others waiting, he released Derek's arm and stepped back.

"If we are going to do this," Silas said quietly, "we have to be on the same page. No more guessing, no more secrets. Trust has to go both ways, Semideus."

Derek nodded once, but the guilt still clung to his ribs like wet fabric.

Derek caught up with the group. The servant gave no sign that she'd noticed the exchange, though her eyes had flicked back just once, sharper than before.

She led them further down the corridor and stopped at another door, this one polished so bright it reflected Caldera's face like a mirror. Without a word, she opened it and motioned her inside.

"I will try not to touch anything expensive," Caldera muttered under her breath as she stepped in, casting a wary glance at the perfect walls.

Finally, the servant led Derek and Mia to the room at the very end of the corridor. The handle was shaped like a rose in bloom, silver petals cold under Derek's fingers. She opened the door for them and offered a graceful bow before vanishing back the way they came, her footsteps silent as smoke.

As soon as the door clicked shut, the silence of the room pressed in on them. No wind. No humming magic. Not even the distant echo of footsteps.

Then... a whisper of motion. A folded note slid under the door. Derek froze, exchanging a tense look with Mia. She gave a single nod.

He bent down slowly and picked it up. The parchment was soft, expensive, imbued with a faint trace of magic that made the ink shimmer faintly under the dim lighting.

He unfolded it, holding it where they could both see:

"You are not safe here.

He speaks in riddles to hide truth, not wisdom.

The quiet one is Dallis's sister. Katalynn wants to help you.

Meet her in the east courtyard after the feast. Come alone."

157

Chapter 18

Truths

"If something is wrong, why wouldn't she just say something when we arrived?" Derek asked, his voice low, cautious.

Mia took the note from his hands, studying the scrawl. Her eyes narrowed slightly as she folded it back up with care and tucked it into his pocket. "It must be something she doesn't want Dallis to hear," she said. "If he's watching... or listening..."

Derek nodded, his eyes drifting across the room as if he were trying to see past its walls. "Then we keep our guard up."

But the words felt brittle as they left his mouth.

He was tired of keeping his guard up. Tired of flinching at every sound, every shadow. Of feeling like the truth had to be hidden, even from the people who mattered most. He'd made so many choices with half-truths and silent prayers and every time, the weight grew heavier. He was tired. So damn tired.

Mia must have sensed it. She tried for levity. "So," she said with a faint smirk, "we're definitely in someone's trap, right?"

"Probably." Derek's answering smile was crooked, hollow. "But at least the accommodations are nice?"

Mia stepped across the room and opened a carved oak door. Steam ghosted into the air as the glow of the washroom spilled out. Clean stone, warm light, and a crystal spout pouring water in an endless fall.

"Okay. Wow," she murmured. "Is that... a real shower?"

Derek peered in behind her. The gentle hiss of falling water echoed like a lullaby. For a second, he thought he might actually cry.

"A hot shower sounds illegal," he said with a shaky laugh.

She turned, smirking. "We both smell like burnt leather boots."

Mia leaned in slightly and mock-sniffed before crinkling her nose in faux horror. "You first."

Derek nodded, grateful for the excuse to retreat. He grabbed a towel from the shelf and disappeared into the steam.

The heat hit him like a wall, scalding and raw. It burned in a way that was almost cleansing, as if pain could undo the choices he was forced to live with.

He pressed both hands against the cool stone and let the water slam against his shoulders. Dirt washed away. As did blood. But the guilt... the guilt clung to him like a second skin.

"Do not trust the Shadow Wielder."

The voice's echo twisted in his mind like smoke under his ribs. Was it a warning... or manipulation? Was it trying to protect him, or isolate him?

He clenched his fists against the wall until his knuckles ached.

Silas hadn't given him any reason not to trust him. Sure, their meeting was a little shaky, but that aside, Silas had proven to be a decent ally. Fought beside him. Stood by him. But the moment the voice returned, Derek's instinct was to shut him out. To change the plan. To lie. Was that fear? Or something darker?

The doubt curled in his chest like a slow poison. *What if I'm already being pulled apart? What if that voice is inside me now, wearing my face and my decisions, and no one, not even Mia, can see it?*

He scrubbed at his skin harder, as if he could scrape away the feeling. Should he tell her? He wanted to. God, he wanted to.

But, he was afraid... afraid that if he said the words out loud, they'd take root between them. And he'd lose her the moment he needed her the most.

He shut the water off, his breathing shallow. The silence in the washroom was too heavy.

Wrapping the towel around his waist, he stepped back into the room, carrying a weight no one else could see.

He didn't dress. He just sat at the edge of the bed, dripping, unmoving, staring at nothing.

When Mia stepped out of the bathroom, her hair damp, cheeks flushed from the steam, she froze mid-step.

Derek's towel still clung to his waist, but he was hunched forward, hands slack between his knees. His eyes weren't focused on anything in the room. They looked through it, like he was somewhere else entirely.

"Hey," she said gently, drying the ends of her hair with a towel. "What's going on?"

He blinked, startled, like surfacing from deep water. "It's nothing."

"Derek," she said, more firmly now, crossing the room, "you know I can tell when you're lying."

He gave a weak smile that didn't touch his eyes. "Using magic on me, huh?"

"Maybe." Her arms folded, voice quiet but sharp. "Or maybe it's just that you've been acting weird ever since Silas's house. You spaced out. You shut down. And now, you're doing it again."

His smile faded. His throat worked once. Then, finally, he said, "The voice... the one from the void. It talked to me again."

Mia's eyes darkened. Her hands stopped moving.

"It told me not to trust Silas," he said. "In the desert, when we met the Murder, Silas had his shadows whisper a plan to me. A way to end things quickly. I didn't go through with it. I couldn't risk it."

A long silence stretched between them. It wasn't just shock; It was betrayal, blooming slowly across her face.

Her jaw set. "So you thought it best to keep that to yourself."

"I didn't know what to do—"

"No, Derek." Her voice cracked, anger surging to the surface. "No. You don't get to do that again."

He shot up, the towel slipping dangerously low. "I wasn't trying to hurt anyone… I just… I didn't want to make things worse."

"But you did." Her voice rose, and her hands trembled at her sides. "You always think you have to carry everything on your own, and it's exhausting. For you. For us. I'm not just here to be your backup plan when things fall apart. I'm here, Derek. I'm in this with you."

She stepped forward, something hot and heavy welling in her eyes.

"Derek, I can't love you in the dark."

The words sliced through the room.

He flinched, like she'd physically struck him. "Wh… what?"

"You keep shutting us out. Not telling us everything. We're supposed to be fighting side by side, and you're still holding the map upside down. We need all the pieces to finish the puzzle."

Her voice softened now, but only just, grief pressing down on every word.

"I want to be here. I want to always be here for you. But if you keep pushing me away, if you keep hiding, how am I supposed to be?"

Silence. The kind that pressed against his ribs and clawed at the back of his throat.

He stared at her, his heart pounding. "No… Mia. What did you just say?"

She blinked. "What?"

"You... you said you love me." His voice was barely audible. "Did you mean that?"

She hesitated. For a second, she looked like she might backtrack. But then, her jaw clenched. Familiar and fierce. She stepped even closer.

"Dammit, Lavender," she whispered, "of course I love you."

The words cracked something open inside him. They didn't float gently into his heart. They crashed into it, shocking, radiant, undeniable.

His breath caught. "I love you, too."

No hesitation. No fear this time. He reached for her like a lifeline, and she met him halfway.

Their kiss wasn't soft. It was a collision. Raw, aching, desperate. The kind that said I missed you, even when they hadn't been apart.

When they finally broke away, they stood forehead to forehead, breathless, wrapped in a silence that held them gently now, instead of pulling them apart.

"This isn't a get out of jail free card, Derek," Mia said through her breath.

His smile faded. His hands cupped her face. "I know. I promise. I'll tell you everything."

"You've said that before—"

"I'll tell you the moment I know anything." His voice was steady now. Grounded. "If the voice speaks, you'll hear it too. If it takes me again, I'll bring you with me. And if it ever comes down to choosing between the world and you... I'll choose you."

Tears welled in her eyes, not from pain this time, but from relief. She pressed her lips to his, slow and deep. When she pulled back, her voice was softer, a teasing breath against his cheek.

"We're going to be late for dinner."

He chuckled, dizzy and dazed. "Think it's okay to be fashionably late?"

Chapter 19

Confusion

A sharp knock rattled the heavy door of Derek and Mia's room. "I do not know what you two are up to in there..." Caldera's voice cut through, teasing and impatient. "... but dinner has already started. The party is just waiting on the lovebirds."

Mia groaned, still curled beside Derek beneath the thick linen sheets. Derek just buried his face in the pillow, a sheepish smile creeping across his lips.

"Coming!" Mia called back, rolling out of bed and tugging on her shirt with flushed cheeks and damp hair that refused to behave. Derek followed, grabbing his robes and boots as quickly as dignity would allow.

When they opened the door, Caldera stood with her arms crossed, a knowing smirk tugging at her lips. Her gaze flicked between the two of them, landing on Derek's tousled hair and Mia's unevenly buttoned tunic.

"Well, look at you two," she said, eyebrows arched. "I did not know the rooms came with a mood boost. You might actually be glowing."

Derek cleared his throat. Mia swatted Caldera lightly on the arm.

"Don't start," she said, though her smile betrayed her.

Caldera rolled her eyes fondly. "Just saying... hopefully this dinner does not ruin the good mood. This party smells like danger wrapped in perfume."

The three of them made their way down the hallway, gathering Silas along the way. As they walked through the arch of the dining hall, their outfits all magically changed.

Derek's robes stayed mostly the same, just a snugger fit and a color swap. Silver to match the style of Meridian.

Both Mia and Caldera's garb shifted to elegant dresses. Caldera's green with silver glitter, Mia's an almost fluorescent silver. The dresses hugged their bodies rather tightly, Dallis's idea no doubt.

Silas received a rather strange change. His vest and trousers were replaced with something that resembled a tuxedo. Definitely not something Silas would ever wear.

The grand dining hall of Meridian was everything the group could have imagined from someone as eccentric as Dallis, too much. Chandeliers made of floating crystal orbs glowed above a table carved from pale golden wood that stretched nearly the length of the room. Along the walls, silver-colored tapestries shimmered, shifting with faint illusions of flowers blooming, wilting, and blooming again.

Several smaller tables were sprinkled around the room and balcony. The guests mimicked their host, as if they were puppets on strings.

Dallis stood at the head of the table, draped in a deep burgundy jacket that shimmered like fresh blood, and a silver streak ran from the top to the bottom. His dark hair was swept back in careful waves, and a sharp grin split his face as the three entered.

"Ah! There they are," he said, raising his glass. "The triumphant travelers return. And fashionably late, no less."

His eyes lingered on Mia just a moment too long. Then Caldera. Then back to Mia.

"You clean up wonderfully," he added.

Derek stiffened, his fingers curling lightly around the back of Mia's chair.

Mia gave a tight-lipped smile. Caldera took her seat with an already forming scowl. They hadn't chosen the clothes they wore, so of course he would love them.

The meal was an endless array of decadent dishes: roasted pheasant with honey glaze, violet-root stew, spiced bread with glowing butter, even a pitcher of starfruit wine that shimmered faintly with suspended flecks of gold. And yet, it all felt hollow.

Dallis poked and prodded throughout the evening, but not at the food.

"So, Derek," he said after the first course, resting his chin in one hand. "You are the famous human Semideus, are you not? Tell me, do the rumors exaggerate, or can you actually call lightning from the sky?"

Derek glanced around the table, choosing his words with care. "When the need arises, yes, I can."

"Oh! Show me! Show me!" Dallis exclaimed, his hands clapped with what appeared to be pure joy.

Derek tried to stifle a laugh, but couldn't stop the slight chuckle as he said, "Uh... I don't really perform on command."

"Oh, I would not call it performing," Dallis said smoothly. "Just a flicker, a dazzle... something to stoke the theater of my mind."

Silas interjected, lifting his goblet. "Forgive him. Some of us believe power is best revealed when necessary, not paraded like jewelry."

Dallis waved a dismissive hand, taking a bite of candied fig. "So serious. You must be great at parties. Oh, wait... we are at a party...and you are not!" He erupted in laughter.

Throughout the evening, his attention grew more unsettling. He complimented Mia's earrings, made several comments on Caldera's figure... which almost caused the Chieftain to break character more than once... and referred to Silas as "the ever-brooding shadow prince."

Only Katalynn remained quiet, seated near the end of the table. Her eyes never lifted from her plate. She hadn't spoken since they sat down, not even when Dallis made his usual flamboyant entrance. Her silence felt louder than the laughter around them.

Later that night, the four slipped away from the glowing palace corridors and made their way to the east courtyard, following Katalynn's directions.

Once there, the same servant that led them to their rooms met them. She waved her hand through the air, and their clothes changed back to their normal wear. She motioned again for them to follow her. They walked the streets of Meridian until they came upon what seemed to be the only run down building in the city.

The contrast was immediate. Where the rest of Meridian glistened under the soft magic of ever-light lanterns and clean cobbled streets, this building was a pocket of decay. Cracked stones. Unlit alleys. And the alehouse.

It was a crumbling, vine-choked thing, sitting at the end of a cobblestone street. The wooden sign above the door hung crooked, reading The Cracked Keg.

Derek stared at it, confused. "Why is this place... untouched? Everything else in Meridian is pristine."

Katalynn stepped out from the shadows of the doorway. She was cloaked in midnight blue, hair tucked beneath a scarf.

"Because I made it so," she said, her voice hushed but pleasant. "The illusion around this building is mine. Dallis can not see what he does not know exists."

They exchanged uneasy glances before slipping inside.

The interior was dim and smoky, lit by a few flickering oil lanterns. The walls were lined with aged shelves and peeling paint. Dust clung to the floorboards.

Katalynn led them to a back table, one that bore marks from old blade fights and ale spills.

Once they were seated, she leaned in, "Thank you for coming. I could not risk anything else being included in the note."

"What's going on with Dallis?" Mia asked.

Katalynn exhaled, pressing a hand to her chest. "That is the question. I do not know if it is Dallis anymore."

Silence. Then Derek leaned in. "What do you mean?"

"Before the rumors of Malum's return reached us, Dallis was... well, still Dallis. A womanizer, yes. Arrogant, absolutely. But calculated. Controlled. This... new Dallis? He flirts with anything breathing. His eyes glow sometimes. And the things he knows..." She shuddered. "I think something got to him. Maybe Everan. Maybe worse. He changed almost overnight."

Silas crossed his arms. "You think Everan's involved?"

Katalynn nodded slowly. "Stagran, our older brother, is king of the Shimmering Court in Calistia. He has always warned us about Everan. He believes the old crow made bargains long ago with things we can not understand. And Dallis... Dallis has always been easy to tempt."

Caldera looked down. "So what do we do?"

"You go to Stagran. He will know more. I can stay here and keep an eye on Dallis."

"Won't he notice us leaving?" Derek asked.

Katalynn smirked, the first real smile they'd seen from her.

"Not if he is still recovering from tonight. I slipped something into his final drink. He will sleep like a baby nestled in their mother's arms. You leave at dawn."

Silas tilted his head. "He will be furious when he wakes up and realizes we are gone, will he not?"

"He will not know where you went. He will not even know who told you to leave. And if he suspects me..." she shrugged, eyes hard, "then I will deal with it."

Mia looked around the dusty alehouse again. "So, we run in the morning. To another royal... Another maybe... Another risk."

Derek reached across the table, taking her hand. "At this rate... we will never find the Trinity."

She nodded, squeezing his fingers.

Katalynn stood. "The Trinity... I do not know much, but I have heard of it. It has something to do with the prophecy and the culling." She ran two fingers along her temple. "Dallis would know more, *if* that was the real Dallis. But Stagran will surely know more. Get some rest. You'll need it. The Shimmering Court is a world of secrets, and there are plenty that need to remain that way."

"That is all you can tell us, Katalynn?" Silas asked.

"That is all I know, old friend." She answered.

The rest of the group exchanged confused glances. Silas gave them a look that said, not here... not yet

Katalynn rose from her seat and walked towards the door, "All of you... be careful."

They left the Cracked Keg in silence, the spell around the place sliding over their shoulders like a curtain of shadow. They had one more night in Meridian, and then back into the sun-scorched unknown, chasing answers across a world of lies.

Chapter 20

Shopping

Pale golden light shimmered from a window, spilling softly into the hallway. Derek and Mia stepped out of their room hand in hand, their fingers laced, both wearing sleepy smiles. Almost in sync, Caldera emerged from her own room just a few doors down.

She arched an eyebrow, smirking. "More fun?"

Derek chuckled. "Morning to you, too."

"Where's Silas?" Mia asked, glancing toward the far end of the hall.

"His room is down there. Should we knock?" Derek offered.

The three began walking, but Derek paused a few steps in, lifting a hand to stop them.

"Wait. Before we get him, I should fill you in," he said, turning to Caldera. "There's more to what the voice said last night."

He recounted everything he'd told Mia. The voice and the warning of not trusting the shadow wielder. Caldera listened in silence, arms crossed loosely, her eyes distant.

"I knew something felt off ever since we left Silas's estate," she admitted. "But to be honest... everything has felt off for quite some time now." Her gaze dropped to the floor. "Between losing Codi and Barry being sent to Ignis... nothing has truly felt right. I know that does not pertain to what you have spoken of, but... I suppose I mean to say... I understand."

Derek's lips pulled into a soft, grateful smile. Hearing that—I understand—from the Chieftain meant more than he could say. Most of the time, he didn't even understand what he was going through. But with Mia and Caldera both here, he didn't feel quite so lost anymore.

"One more thing," he said. "Back at the oasis... when I let you hear the voice, did you notice the chirping sound at the end? That trill?"

Caldera nodded without hesitation. "I did. That was the song of the hummingbird."

Derek and Mia locked eyes, both whispering a breathless "aha." That was it. That was the sound. Familiar, comforting, just out of reach... until now.

"But why would the voice let Derek hear a hummingbird?" Mia asked, puzzled.

Caldera folded her arms. "We do not yet know who this voice belongs to, but in ancient fae folklore, the hummingbird is believed to represent the safe crossing of a soul into the afterlife."

Derek raised a brow. "So... does that mean the voice is from the afterlife?"

Caldera chuckled lightly. "Not quite. Hummingbirds are one of the few magical creatures known to exist in every realm."

Mia's eyes widened. "Wait... hummingbirds are magical?"

"Not in the way you might think. They do not cast spells or conjure flames, but consider this, how else do you explain how fast they fly? How they vanish before you can blink?"

Derek leaned forward. "Are you saying they can travel between dimensions? Without a portal?"

Caldera smiled softly. "Precisely. It has been studied, of course, but no one has uncovered exactly how they do it. That is why, in our stories, they are considered caretakers, guides for souls making their way to the after. They can stay beside them the entire journey."

Derek's throat tightened. He wiped at his eyes with his sleeve, voice thick as he murmured, "That's... beautiful."

Mia slipped her arms around him and pulled him close. Derek leaned into the embrace, his heart full. Caldera looked away, biting her lip, trying to blink away her own tears.

Then, with a creak, a door down the hall slowly opened. Not Silas's room.

But it was Silas who stepped out.

Half-dressed, shirt bunched in his hands, he winced as the door clicked shut behind him. A rare, subtle smile curved on his face as he pulled the shirt over his head and turned toward them, only to freeze mid-step.

"...Morning," he said flatly.

He continued walking as if nothing were amiss. "We should leave. Before Dallis wakes."

Caldera smirked. "I do not believe that was your room."

Silas breezed past her, still adjusting his shirt. "Not the time. Nor the place."

The market was alive with motion and magic. Though the city's perfection still loomed in every symmetrical line and glowing lantern, today felt different. People were shopping, really shopping. Fruit and meats floated in lazy spirals above food stalls. Perfume vendors released puffs of scent into the air like aromatic fireworks, catching the noses of passersby and drawing them closer.

"Look, there's a clothing store," Mia pointed toward a stone arch draped in velvet. "Maybe we should get something better suited for desert travel?"

Caldera's eyes lit up like a child spotting the first snow of the season. "I have not shopped since I left the forest to come here!"

Before Derek could respond, Caldera seized Mia's hand and pulled her toward the shop. "I'll find something for you!" Mia shouted over her shoulder with a grin.

Derek just laughed and shook his head. He and Silas stood in an awkward silence for a beat, the noise of the market a soft hum around them.

"So..." Derek began, hands in his pockets. "You wanna talk about whose room you came out of this morning?"

Silas didn't blink. "Katalynn."

Derek blinked twice. "Wait, so when she said 'old friend,' she meant... *friend*?" He threw a wink at the end.

Silas let a humorless chuckle escape. "Yes. Katalynn and I used to be an item. Many... many years ago. After her parents passed, she moved here with her brother, Dallis."

Derek nodded slowly. "You don't have to share if you're not ready, but... you're the one who said we need to trust each other. Communication is a part of that."

Silas exhaled through his nose, opened his mouth to speak, but Derek cut in gently.

"Before you say anything else, I need to tell you something."

Derek repeated everything. The voice. The warning. The hummingbird. He laid it bare again, and even though his chest clenched as he spoke, he knew this was the right path.

Silas's brow furrowed. "Why tell me now?"

Before Derek could answer, a twitchy fae appeared at his side. Thin and spindly, with eyes just a touch too large for his angular head, the stranger buzzed with strange, chaotic energy.

"You... you are the Human Semideus, are you not?" he asked, bouncing slightly on his heels.

Derek hesitated, unsure how to respond.

"No answer? That is fine! I know. I know all about you! I am Romulus!" he exclaimed, his voice far too loud for comfort.

Derek glanced at Silas, silently pleading for help, but just then Mia and Caldera reappeared, arms full of folded garments.

"Hey there!" Mia greeted cheerfully. "What can we do for you?" She handed Derek a fresh outfit, a lightweight, long-sleeved white tunic and sand-colored pants tailored with breathable threads. A pair of white boots, soft yet sturdy, completed the set.

"I want to help! Help the Semideus!" Romulus cried. "I have dreamt of this... literally! I have seen you all. I am there. Helping."

Caldera tossed Silas a clean tunic, a nearly identical replica of the one he wore but pressed and sun-bleached. "We appreciate the offer," she said kindly, "but we must remain small in number for this journey."

Romulus clasped his hands together. "No worry! No worry! Romulus can stay small. I can crawl if I must!"

Silas motioned toward a narrow alley. The group turned to follow, clearly hoping Romulus would take the hint and drift away.

"I will stand guard while you change!" Romulus said, proudly puffing out his chest. "Romulus will protect you! You will see!"

"Hey, buddy," Derek said gently. "Really, we're good. But thank you for offering. That means a lot."

"It is okay!" Romulus chirped. "Romulus will wait right here! I will not peek. Then, we go into the desert!"

Silas's face darkened. His jaw clenched, shadows curling at his wrists like ink in water.

"Enough!" he barked, stepping forward. "We do not need your help. We do not need a tagalong. And we certainly do not need a stray begging at our feet like some desperate pet!"

Romulus recoiled as if slapped. His twitching stopped. His eyes dropped to the dirt.

"...Okay," he whispered, and turned away, vanishing into the crowded street.

A heavy silence followed.

"Did you have to be so mean?" Mia asked quietly, her voice edged with disappointment.

Silas didn't flinch. "Did Derek have to hide what the voice said to him?"

"That's not fair," Derek snapped, his voice low and tight.

Silas's breath hissed through his nose and his shadows receded. "You are right. It is not fair. I let my emotions get the better of me again." He glanced down the alley. "But he would not take no for an answer."

No one replied, but none of them truly disagreed.

They took turns standing guard as the others changed. Derek tugged on his white tunic and tan pants. The boots fit perfectly, cool and snug like they'd been waiting for him all along.

Silas swapped into the fresh tunic, almost identical to his last one. Still elegant, still brooding.

Mia and Caldera had picked matching desert leathers. The tailored outfits were snug and breathable, a soft tan that shimmered slightly in the light. But as the girls tightened the belts around their waists, the fabric glistened. Caldera's outfit now bore vine-like green accents curling along her sides and shoulders, while Mia's glowed with delicate pink trim.

"They're enchanted to adapt to the wearer," Mia whispered with a grin. "Pretty cool, right?"

Derek turned to share the moment with Silas, but the fae warrior still wore a cloud over his expression.

"You okay?" Derek asked.

Silas nodded stiffly. "I am... for now. But once we step beyond those gates, the Murder will be watching."

The mood shifted instantly. They had barely escaped the last encounter. Derek was rested now, but the terrain ahead was unfamiliar. He wouldn't be able to "ride the lightning" there.

"Keep going."

The voice boomed again in Derek's mind, clear and commanding.

He didn't hesitate this time. "The voice spoke again," he told them. "It said... keep going."

No one argued.

Together, they made their way toward the shimmering gate they'd passed through only a day ago.

Derek paused, turning to look back at Meridian. The silver spires caught the sunlight like frozen lightning. Something twisted in his gut.

This is the last time it will look like this, he thought. *I know it.*

Mia touched his arm. "Do you think Romulus was sent by someone? Or... something?"

Derek shook his head. "No idea. But whatever this voice is... it's always watching us. And it wants us to move faster."

And so, they did.

Chapter 21

Beast

The desert stretched endlessly before them. Rippling golden dunes rose and fell like waves in a petrified sea. The sun was merciless overhead, yet the group pressed forward in silence. Only the crunch of sand beneath their boots filled the still air.

After some time, Derek fell into step beside Silas.

"I've been meaning to ask," he said, brushing sand from his hair, "about being a Semideus. What else can you tell me?"

Silas didn't look at him. He kept walking, shadows flickering faintly under his feet despite the blazing sun. "It means you were never going to have a simple life."

Derek chuckled dryly. "Yeah, I kinda figured that out."

For a while, it seemed Silas wouldn't say more. But then, with a sigh, he relented.

"My magic manifested after I turned ten," Silas said. "I was alone when it happened. Thought I was cursed."

"You were ten?" Derek blinked. "So... how old are you now?"

Silas hesitated, then gave a half-smile. "Older than you can imagine... but younger than you would think."

Derek rolled his eyes. "Cryptic as always. Look, I'm not asking to be nosy. We're in this together, right? We have to do the whole trust thing, remember?"

Silas exhaled slowly. "Fair. Alright." He stopped walking, and the others paused too. "There is the Sacred Dimension, right? Some call it the Origin. Beings from there sometimes... step down. They take partners in our realms. Fae, Human, Orc, it does not matter. Sometimes, it is love. Other times, it is... less romantic."

"Let me guess," Derek said, "the kids from those unions are the Semideus?"

Silas nodded. "Powerful. Too powerful. Some burned bright and fast... others simply vanished. Over generations, the bloodline diluted. But it never fully disappeared." Silas rubbed his temple, contemplating how to explain the rest. Finally, he said, "Cults rose, desperate to preserve or awaken the power again. They failed. Like I told you before, the blood only awakens under certain circumstances. When someone accepts their true nature, the truest version of themselves... or when it is the last gasp of the bloodline, trying not to die out. In those cases, it manifests... violently. And the host goes mad."

Derek swallowed. "Which am I?"

"I do not know," Silas admitted. "But your mind is not ill... at least not in this sense. That is more than most."

Before Derek could respond, the ground trembled beneath their feet. It was a familiar shift. Lightning crackled from Derek's fingertips instantly.

Caldera froze, eyes narrowing. "Another drake?"

Silas's eyes narrowed. The sand shifted again, this time with a deeper rumble, closer, hungrier. "No," he said grimly. "Worse."

The desert exploded.

A monstrous roar shattered the quiet as a massive beast burst from the sands, flinging debris high into the air. Sand cascaded from a hulking, sinewed body. A lion-like frame with obsidian-scaled wings and a segmented, scorpion-like tail curling above it. Its fanged maw snarled, revealing rows of serrated teeth. And its eyes, dark, glimmering with sentience, locked instantly on them.

"Manticore!" Silas bellowed, shadows already lashing out from his arms and solidifying into twin scimitars.

"It's enormous..." Mia gasped, stepping backward. "That can't be real. Nothing this big should have survived out here."

"Only the worst of the worst did," Silas snapped. "Stay sharp!"

The manticore lunged.

Silas met it head-on, his shadows slashing in wide arcs. One blade collided with the beast's clawed paw, a burst of dark magic pushing the creature back slightly. Derek extended his arm and fired a ball of white light. It struck the creature's shoulder, burning a smoking hole into its hide. The manticore shrieked and retaliated, lashing out with its tail.

"Move!" Mia cried. She quickly spun her hands in a circle, blue essence swarming around her, and hurled a wave of mystical water between them. It caught the tail mid-swing, freezing over just enough to redirect the attack into the sand.

Derek's heart pounded. He stepped forward, calling blue lightning into his hands. The crackling power danced across his skin before launching skyward, arcing down like divine fury, directly into the manticore's back.

The beast roared, stumbling, but it wasn't done.

Caldera channeled her blue essence into the ground. The sand beneath the monster's hind legs shifted and solidified into jagged thorns of stone and bramble, ensnaring its paws and tightening like claws of nature. She extended her arms, vines sprouting from the oasis brush around them, coiling up to wrap the beast's legs.

"I have got it held!" she shouted.

Mia dashed forward, her essence forming into two spinning water daggers. She leapt, slashing across the manticore's front leg in two fluid strikes before diving aside as the tail struck down. The sand burst where she had been, a crater forming.

Derek saw his opening.

He raised both hands, white light glowing on his arms, blue fire coiling in his fingers.

But the manticore broke free.

With a furious roar, it tore through Caldera's vines and leapt toward Derek. Its wings unfurled, sending out a gust of wind powerful enough to knock him back. He hit the ground hard, skidding across the hot sand.

The manticore pounced.

"Derek!" Mia screamed.

Silas threw himself into the beast's path.

A shadow-forged shield bubble expanded around them as the creature's claws tore through the air. One landed true, piercing through the shadows and raking across Silas's ribs. Blood sprayed.

He grunted, but never wavered. His life force dripped out of him as he launched both of his scimitars toward the beast. It was a desperate attempt, but as the blades drove into the manticore's neck, Silas collapsed.

"No!" Derek shouted, the world going still around him.

He rose to his feet, white light and blue lightning now coalescing in his hands.

The manticore turned its attention back to him.

"Don't touch them," Derek growled.

Mia shouted, "Derek, no! You'll over do it!"

The sky cracked.

Blue lightning surged down from the heavens as Derek called the storm. It struck his body, dancing around him like a second skin. His eyes glowed white. The magic thrummed in his blood. Power like never before.

He ran toward the beast, ducking beneath a tail swipe, then leapt, white light shimmering around his arms, blue lightning threading through his veins. He punched the creature dead in the chest.

A blinding flash erupted as the white light seared into the manticore's heart. The impact split the air. A blue fire ignited deep within the wound. Lightning surged from the sky, engulfing the wretched creature in a symphony of strikes. The beast shrieked, wings thrashing in agony.

And then, it fell. The manticore collapsed, shaking the ground as its monstrous body gave one final convulsion... then, went still. The sand exploded, leaving a cloud of dust.

For a moment, all was quiet, save for the whimpering breath of the wind and the soft shift of sand.

Derek stumbled, but he held it together. He would not pass out this time. He turned to see Silas on the ground, the sand beneath him coated in red. Derek fell to his knees beside him. Blood soaked his side, but he was breathing. Barely.

Mia knelt on the other side, her hands glowing with blue essence as she called healing waters. The liquid formed and flowed over the wound, sealing torn muscle and slowing the bleeding.

"I've got him," she whispered, wiping sweat from her brow.

The manticore's corpse began to sink back into the sand, like the desert was reclaiming it, taking it home. In its place, a single gem remained. It glowed faintly with an iridescent pulse.

Derek nodded, and Caldera approached it. She could feel something emanating from it, "Derek, I think it is best if you come over here."

Derek looked to Mia and Silas, the latter whispering, "I am okay. Go see what it is."

Clasping his hand in Silas's, Derek said, "Thank you. You saved me."

"Trust, right?" Silas coughed.

"Trust." Derek answered.

Derek rose to his feet and approached the gem. Then, he felt it too. There was a power humming through it, a power he had felt before at the... at the barrier!

He leaned down and picked it up. A jolt surged through him. Power, raw and ancient, flooded his senses. He staggered. He had never felt such power inside him.

Silas groaned as he tried to sit up, against Mia's words of caution. He watched as lightning struck from the sky and onto Derek's skin. "I've... never seen anything like it," he rasped.

Like a tsunami, the power faded as quickly as it started. That's when Derek heard the voice again.

"This is the right path. The Trinity awaits."

Again, Derek didn't hide it. Still catching his breath, he met each of their gazes.

"It spoke again."

Caldera knelt beside Silas, helping Mia stabilize him. Derek glanced down at the gem still glowing faintly in his palm, its light sinking into his skin like it had always belonged there, and he placed it in his pocket.

On the horizon, silhouettes shimmered into view, figures cresting the dunes, armor glinting beneath the relentless sun. A small scouting party, moving fast.

Silas groaned and pushed himself upright, leaning heavily on Caldera for support.

"Someone is coming," Derek said, watching them draw closer.

Mia stepped beside him, her fingers slipping into his. She didn't speak, but the quiet pressure of her hand steadied him.

"The Murder?" Caldera asked, squinting against the light.

Silas shook his head slowly. "No. Look at their armor. The Shimmering Court... they are here to see who could have felled the beast."

Mia's eyes lit with hope. "Will they take us to Calistia?"

Before anyone could answer, Derek's knees wobbled. He staggered but refused to fall.

"Let's hope so," he muttered. "I don't think we're ready for another fight."

The scouting party came to a halt just beyond the remains of the battlefield. One armored figure stepped forward, voice echoing across the sand.

"Who has slain the Manticore?"

Silas straightened as much as his battered body allowed. "Derek. The human Semideus."

A beat of silence.

"What does he want in return?" the guard asked.

Derek inhaled slowly, the gem pulsing with quiet power in his pocket. Every muscle in his body ached, but his voice rang clear.

"An audience with Stagran."

Chapter 22

Wrath

The air in Torvania hung heavy, not with smoke, but with silence. That strange, aching kind that comes when devastation no longer howls, but settles.

The ambush had fractured more than shields and bones. It had broken something deeper, and though every survivor still breathed, some of them felt as if they shouldn't.

Mr. Monton knelt in the dirt outside the Fickle Fae, his back curved like a collapsed pillar. His hands sat lifeless on his thighs, palms up, as if still waiting for something... someone... to return. He didn't blink. Didn't move. The stillness of a man who'd stopped existing the moment his son vanished.

Nidalle knelt beside him, her long fingers trembling midair, hovering just above his shoulder. She didn't touch him. Maybe she was afraid it would shatter whatever was left, holding him together. Her eyes were red-rimmed, but no tears fell. It was as if even her grief had dried out in the heat and dust of the desert.

Abhaya crouched beside David's body, gently draping a cloth over his face. The motion was slow. Hollow. Not from lack of care, but from too much experience. There was no spell left to try. No magic to call on. David was gone. Just another soul taken by Malum's endless hunger. She smoothed the cloth once over his chest, then folded her hands and bowed her head. Not in prayer. Just... in surrender.

Tah'quhal had said nothing. Had given no orders. No vows of vengeance. He had simply turned and walked away. His strides were purposeful, but silent. Like a storm cloud slipping off into the horizon, still rumbling, still gathering.

Barry stood alone in the center of it all, arms slack at his sides, boots sinking into the churned-up earth. His heart thudded wildly. Too fast, Too loud. But his body wouldn't move. Wouldn't speak.

This wasn't how it was supposed to go.

He looked to Mr. Monton, still motionless. Then to David, covered now. Cold.

Why? Why John? He thought to himself.

Barry had made the deal. He had spoken to Talissa. He had flirted with the edges of something forbidden, something desperate. So why had Johnathan been the one stolen?

He clenched his fists so tightly his knuckles cracked. He wanted to scream, but the sound was buried beneath guilt and confusion, beneath the kind of ache that doesn't have a name. He just wanted to go back. Back to the first day of senior year. Back to worrying about passing history and catching footballs. Back to laughing too hard at dumb jokes and thinking they had time. So much time.

But time had turned on them. Twisted around them. And now, it was blood and silence and choices.

Then he looked down the path Tah'quhal had taken. Faint footprints marked the dust, but it wasn't that which called to Barry.

It was something deeper. A tether in his chest, pulled taut. Not curiosity. Not fear.

Duty.

Something cracked inside him. Not completely broke...shifted. A decision. Quiet and certain. He started walking.

Tah'quhal's home was dim, more shadow than shelter. The only light came from a dying hearth, its orange glow flickering like a breath on the verge of vanishing. Smoke curled low across the ceiling beams, and the air felt thick with memory and dust.

Barry stepped inside quietly, barely breathing. Every instinct screamed at him to turn around, but he didn't. Not this time.

In the center of the room, Tah'quhal knelt motionless, his back to Barry, spine rigid like a drawn bow. The silence around him felt sacred. Or dangerous. Or both.

Barry hesitated at the threshold. "Tah'quhal?"

No answer.

Then, slowly, the blade on Tah'quhal's back... Orgí... began to glow. Not bright, but dark. A deep purple pulse, like a heartbeat echoing in the void. It wasn't light. It was presence. Malevolent. Alive.

A thick, viscous substance began to drip from the weapon. That same dark violet bled downward like liquified stars. It hit the floor and vanished into the shadows, only to reappear on the blade again, an endless cycle, feeding itself.

Then, the wind began.

It came from nowhere. No open windows. No door ajar. Just a gust from some other realm, scattering jars and scrolls, knocking over vials, sending ancient parchments flying like frightened birds. The storm was building, but it wasn't outside. It was inside of him. Inside Tah'quhal.

Tah'quhal started whispering. A language Barry didn't recognize. Deep, guttural, old. The words vibrated in his chest, not his ears. Words soaked in thunder. Words that didn't ask... they commanded.

And then the blade moved. It ripped from his back as if it had a will of its own, hovering behind him for a moment, waiting, wanting. Then, in a blink, it vanished... only to reappear in Tah'quhal's hand.

He stood. Fast. Precise. Terrifying. His eyes were not the eyes of a strategist anymore. They were wild. They burned with something that had no name, only an edge.

"Let the world tremble," Tah'quhal said, voice low and lethal. "Let all of Luminfae watch my outburst." His gaze snapped to Barry, sharp enough to cut. "I will raise Orgí. I will summon Derek's army once more, hunt Malum across every dimension, every realm… and when I find him…" He took a step forward. "I will unleash everything inside me. I will bury him beneath it. Until he chokes on my *wrath*."

Barry's stomach flipped, but he didn't back down. Not this time.

"I get it," Barry said. His voice was quiet but steady. "I really do. But this? This isn't okay. You're not okay. None of us are."

"They do not play by the rules, so why should we?" Tah'quhal roared, voice splitting the stillness like the crack of a whip.

Barry didn't blink. "I never said we had to play by the rules."

Tah'quhal's shoulders shook. His voice dropped, thick with exhaustion. "I *watched* your first friend die. I *watched* Mia suffer for months when Derek did not return. I *watched* Komipea tell us all the truths we were not ready for. I was captured and tortured by someone I called friend." He swallowed. "And I watched Derek risk everything to end this before it became a wildfire we could not contain."

His voice trembled on the last word. For a second, Barry thought maybe, just maybe, he was breaking through.

Then, it came again. That rage.

"I will not **watch** ever again!" Tah'quhal bellowed. The blade in his hand pulsed, the shadows behind him thickening.

"Then don't watch!" Barry shouted back. "But this?" he motioned to the swirling storm of magic, the chaos around them, "This isn't action. This is destruction. This is grief pretending to be justice."

Tah'quhal flinched.

"I have to do something!" he growled. "Derek would."

Barry stepped forward, voice softening but not weakening. "I know. And I want to bring John back just as bad as you do. Maybe more." He took a breath. "He was my friend before we ever met you. My brother, in all the ways that count."

Tah'quhal's hand trembled.

"I'm not saying what you feel isn't real. Or right. But John? He's tough. He's smart. He's not gone. Not yet. He can hold on until we come for him. But this path?" Barry's voice cracked, just barely. "If we go down this path now, full of fury and no plan... we lose him. We lose us."

The wind slowed. The papers settled. The purple glow dimmed.

Tah'quhal's chest heaved with shallow breaths. "Then what... is the right way?"

Barry took another step forward, closing the space between them. "Put down the sword," he said, gently.

Silence.

For a long moment, neither moved. Neither breathed.

Barry managed a small grin. "Trust me, Taco."

The corner of Tah'quhal's mouth twitched. The name. The memory. The blade dimmed. The storm stilled. And with a quiet exhale, Tah'quhal sheathed Orgí. The fury in his eyes faded to grief.

Barry let out a breath he didn't know he'd been holding. "There's the Chieftain I know."

Tah'quhal shook his head, voice still hoarse. "You must stop calling me Taco."

Barry chuckled, finally stepping beside him and slinging an arm over his shoulders. "But tacos are delicious."

"I have never had one."

Barry blinked. "Seriously?"

"I do not believe they exist here."

"Well, we gotta fix that. It might even be Tuesday."

Tah'quhal raised an eyebrow. "What is the significance of that?"

Barry laughed. "Taco Tuesdays, man. Damn, you've got so much to learn."

As they turned to leave the house behind, a flicker of peace passed between them… thin, but real.

"So," Tah'quhal said, his voice calmer now, "what is the right way to handle this?"

Barry grinned. "Let's get back to the Fickle Fae. If Mr. Monton's up for it, maybe he'll make us some tacos… and I'll tell you exactly what I'm thinking."

Chapter 23

Planning

The Fickle Fae felt quieter than it should have. No clinking glasses. No off-key tunes from the battered piano in the corner. Just the groaning hinges of the front door and the soft scuff of boots against wood as Barry helped Mr. Monton inside.

Johnathan's father leaned heavily on him, his eyes unfocused, his body slack like a marionette with cut strings. His right arm dragged, like it had forgotten how to be a part of him. The bar, usually warm with lantern glow and laughter, felt like a tomb. Silent, still, too aware of itself.

Nidalle appeared without a word and pressed a crystal tumbler into his hands. The dark amber of Nectar swirled inside like smoke in a bottle. Mr. Monton didn't hesitate. He downed it in one long pull, as if chasing a silence deeper than the one already hanging in the air.

"Thank you," he rasped, barely above a whisper.

"You should sit," Barry said gently, guiding him toward a chair by the hearth.

"I should do a lot of things," Mr. Monton muttered. He sank into the chair, shoulders hunched, his hands slack in his lap. "But right now, I can't think clearly. My son... I know he's still alive, but I feel like I've already buried him."

Barry crouched beside him, elbows resting on his knees. "Then don't think about the mission. Not right now. Just... breathe. Maybe keep yourself busy."

Mr. Monton looked up slowly. His eyes were glassy but not empty. Just lost. "Busy?"

Barry offered a faint smile. "Tah'quhal's never had a taco."

That got a blink. Then, miraculously, a tiny snort. Mr. Monton huffed a breath through his nose and rubbed a hand over his face.

"Gods above," he muttered. "I think I saw some vegetables from Terra and spices from the Magia Forest in the back. Let me see what I can whip up."

He pushed himself to his feet with a grunt, the tremble in his legs noticeable but didn't stop him. The kitchen door swung shut behind him with a soft thud.

The moment he was gone, Barry stood slowly and turned to face the others. His gaze swept the room. No one spoke. Even the hearth fire cracked more quietly, as if it, too, was waiting.

"We've been playing right into Malum's hands," Barry said. His voice was quiet, but it carried. "We thought we were ahead of the game after he and Derek faced off, but we're not. Malum wanted Derek to beat him. He needed to lose."

Abhaya leaned forward. "You think Malum *wanted* to lose?"

Barry nodded. "Think about it. Derek wins, but barely. Trey sees that, and maybe it finally breaks something in him. It freaking pushes him to Malum's side for good, because he saw what his friend did to his dad. And Talissa… those people she met with? They might not have been players yet. But Malum needs them for something."

He paced slowly, hands moving as he spoke.

"He loses just enough to seem vulnerable. Not weak, but strategic. Then, Talissa reaches out, gets things moving. Those people see him survive Derek's Semideus onslaught and decide maybe he's the horse to bet on after all."

Nidalle's voice was almost a whisper. "That is dangerous logic. That would mean he played us like chess pieces."

Barry stopped. "Exactly. Which is why I'm done playing the board he set. We don't need any more armies. No more open battles."

Tah'quhal's brow furrowed. "Then, what?"

"We gotta go in silence. All sneaky like," Barry said. "I know those tunnels under Ignis better than most now. If I can get a few of us inside, we wait until they return to their little meeting spot. Then, we strike. Hard and fast."

Nidalle shook her head. "That is unnecessarily reckless. Dangerous."

Abhaya spoke. "It's dangerous, yes," she said, voice soft but certain. "But how many have we lost already? Codi. David. Nearly

Derek. Countless others. If there's even a chance to end this without another full war…" She looked at Barry. "We have to try."

Tah'quhal nodded once, slowly. "Tell us more."

Barry exhaled. "We don't know when they'll be back down there. Could be days. Could be a week. But last time, it seemed like they met about twice a week. So we sneak in and we wait. We ambush. We end this before it spirals again."

A beat passed. Then, Nidalle asked, "And if they do not come back?"

Barry shrugged. "Then, we adjust. Give it a week. If they're not back, we move to Plan B."

Silence again.

Nidalle sat very still, but her fingers tapped against the side of her chair. Tap. Tap. Tap. Her lips pressed together, a crease forming between her brows.

Tah'quhal noticed. "Speak," he said, softer than usual. "If you know something, now is the time."

She flinched, turning to Abhaya, eyes dark with something between guilt and fear.

"I did not want to say anything before because… I did not think it mattered. I thought it was just noise."

"What?" Abhaya asked, voice barely a breath. Her body tensed, every instinct tuned to her Chieftain.

"Talissa," Nidalle admitted. "She has contacted me. More than once. Whispered things in dreams. Left messages through mirrors. I never took her seriously."

The room froze.

"You never mentioned this?" Tah'quhal's voice was low, nearly a growl.

"I thought she was just... sowing doubt. Confusion. You all know what she is."

Barry stepped forward, jaw tight. "But?"

Nidalle's eyes shut. "But... she told me something. Over and over again. She said the rifts... the ones appearing all over Luminfae, they are not just tears. They are going to fuse... Merge. That the process has already started. That nothing we do can stop it now. All realms will become one."

No one moved. Even the air seemed suspended.

Barry's voice came out hoarse. "All of them?"

Nidalle nodded once, gravely. "Every dimension. One world."

The kitchen door creaked open behind them. The scent of roasted vegetables and spices drifted into the silence.

"Tacos are almost ready," Mr. Monton called, cheerily oblivious.

But no one answered. No one smiled.

Not anymore.

Chapter 24

Dinner

The quietness inside the Fickle Fae was suffocating. Painful even. Nidalle's words still echoed in their minds, twisting the air between them. They felt betrayed. They were hurt. But most of all, they were terrified. The merging of realms. The veil between dimensions thinning, like silk stretched out evenly in all four corners.

Barry stood by the cracked hearth, arms crossed tightly over his chest, his expression unreadable. The others sat scattered at the long table, the shadows from the lanterns dancing across their tired, shell-shocked faces. For a moment, no one moved.

Barry spoke, quiet but steady, "We can still do this."

Tah'quhal let out a low scoff but didn't interrupt.

Barry stepped forward. "Malum's set something in motion. Whatever. Maybe we can't stop it. But we can still rip the rot from the ground before it spreads. We can fight. I'm gonna fight."

Barry caught Nidalle's eyes searching the group, as if she hoped for any sign that she didn't ruin everyone's trust in her. She looked at Abhaya, pleading. "I never wanted to hurt you."

Abhaya met her gaze. Her face was hard and unreadable as she stood. Slowly, deliberately, she walked away from Nidalle's side and positioned herself beside Tah'quhal instead. When she spoke, her voice was low but as sharp as a blade, "You did hurt us. I just need some space to think. That's all."

Nidalle nodded, her mouth pressing into a thin, trembling line. She sank back into her chair, looking impossibly small. The tension was unbearable.

And then, from the kitchen, came the unmistakable clatter of a tray and the warm scent of grilled meat and spices.

Mr. Monton pushed through the swinging doors with a massive silver platter balanced in one hand. "Figured you lot needed something real in your stomachs."

He set the tray down in the middle of the table with a flourish. "Grathcow tacos, charred, spiced, and folded in sun-dried chaffleaf."

Tah'quhal eyed the food suspiciously. "Grathcow is meant to be made into patties."

Monton grinned. "Food is meant to be enjoyed in numerous ways. I may have transferred most of my magic to John when I passed my Keeper staff to him, but I promise you, I'm still a wizard in the kitchen. Eat."

With a grunt, Tah'quhal picked one up and took a bite. There was a long pause. Then, his eyes went wide. "By the ancestors. This is divine."

And just like that, the room cracked. First, with a huff of laughter from Barry, then Abhaya, then all of them. Even Nidalle smiled weakly. Tah'quhal devoured three more before anyone could blink, grease glistening in his beard. For a brief, precious moment, the darkness retreated.

At least, even in these uncertain times, they could enjoy a meal together. It wasn't like this was a group you would normally find together. A young man who should only be worried about college starting. A father who only wanted to be with his son. Two Chieftains, one who was destined to lead their village, the other who didn't know how he got into this position. Finally, one Keeper who, in the last two months, had watched two Keepers die, one being kidnapped, and one being forced into a role he did not want.

While they ate, Barry pulled out a crumpled piece of parchment and began scribbling notes. "If we're going to pull this off, we need an actual plan. The tunnels are tight in spots, but we can fit in one at a time. Once we are in the main chamber... we can find our spot to set up."

Tah'quhal nodded, still chewing. "We will need veils. Something to hide our auras."

"I am no master enchantress, but if we have anything that has been in the tunnels before, I can weave it into some cloaks, it will mask your presence with Libra magics." Abhaya added.

Barry nodded and ripped the sleeves from his tunic, handing them to Abhaya, "I was in the tunnels before I got sent here." He stepped back to Tah'quhal, "But we're missing something," Barry said, tapping his pen. "Someone."

They all knew who.

"Derek," he muttered. "We need him. He's the only one who's ever really beaten Malum."

A stillness fell again, though not as heavy as before.

Nidalle set her cup down. "Tah'quhal... when you last saw Derek and Mia... were they still wearing the bracelets Abhaya and I gave them?"

Tah'quhal paused, eyes narrowing in thought. "I believe so. Derek definitely was, and if he was, then Mia was too."

Abhaya looked up. "Then... there might be a way."

Everyone turned toward her.

"There's someone," she said slowly, as if weighing every word. "A fae. Not one who resides in any village in Luminfae. He's called the Tracer."

"Catchy," Barry muttered.

"He specializes in tracking magical objects and creatures across Luminfae. If Derek's still wearing that bracelet, the Tracer might be able to find him. Maybe even open a path to wherever he is."

"But?" Barry asked.

"But he doesn't stay put. The Tracer's always on the move. Last I heard... he was in the Magia Forest. Hunting a Lunabeast."

Tah'quhal's eyebrows narrowed, "Shit."

"What's so bad about that?" Barry asked.

"The Lunabeast is a creature made of shadow and moonlight," Abhaya replied. "Rare. And extremely dangerous."

Barry leaned back, gears clearly turning. "So, we find this Tracer, convince him to help us, and hope to the stars Derek's still got the bracelet."

Abhaya nodded. "It's a long shot, but it would be the fastest way to get to him."

"And it's really our only one," Barry finished.

Tah'quhal and Barry discussed for a moment and planned to leave immediately after dinner. They didn't need to waste any time. Time was a resource they were suddenly very limited in.

Nidalle offered to stay behind and coordinate anyone else willing to join their resistance. Mr. Monton busied himself with preparing rations, making sure there were more tacos among them, at Tah'quhal's insistence.

There was still tension between them all, still bruised trust and frayed bonds. But at least now, there was also direction. They enjoyed the last of the meal together, even passed around a pitcher of nectar. A few laughs were shared, stories were told, memories made.

Tah'quhal fastened the last strap of his pack and grunted. "Let us find the ever elusive tracer."

And then the ground began to shake. It started as a soft rumble beneath their feet, barely more than a whisper.

Then, it deepened... louder... heavier... rattling plates, shaking glasses, swaying the ancient beams of the tavern. Dust rained from the ceiling. Something crashed to the floor behind the bar.

They all froze.

Barry reached instinctively for the hilt of his sword. "What the hell was that?"

No one answered.

Chapter 25

Calistia

The sun bathed Calistia in a soft golden light as Derek, Mia, Silas, and Caldera followed the fae scouting party along a winding stone path into the city. Expecting the glimmering splendor of Meridian, Derek blinked in surprise at the subtler, earthen beauty around him. Calistia wasn't ostentatious. It was humble and ancient, its elegance drawn from nature itself.

Stone buildings nestled between towering trees, their walls veined with soft gold and ivy. Crystal-clear water flowed through channels along the streets, catching the light in shimmering ripples. The air carried the scent of blooming barkrose and sun-warmed cedar. The whole place pulsed with magic, but in a quiet, reverent way.

"*This* is the Shimmering Court?" Caldera murmured beside Derek, her gaze drifting to a canopy of amber leaves dancing overhead. "It reminds me quite a bit of the Magia Forest."

"It shimmers in spirit," Silas said. "Not spectacle."

The scouting party led them to a large, circular structure at the city's heart, the palace, if it could be called that. It rose organically from a colossal tree, its branches arcing over to form natural balconies and corridors. Bioluminescent vines spiraled up the exterior, glowing faintly in the dim morning light. It was a lush oasis in the middle of the barren desert.

Inside, they entered a domed chamber open to the sky, sunlight pooling on the floor's mosaic of constellations. Three fae stood around a dais, waiting at the far end.

The first, a male with a wide grin and flowing golden hair, stepped forward. His robes were bark-brown with threads of gold woven like tapestry. "Welcome," he said. "I am Stagran."

Beside him stood two women. One had golden eyes and long silver hair adorned with morning lilies, her smile wide and welcoming. The other had sharp features, her red hair pinned back with obsidian feathers. Both wore flowing robes that seemed to leave little to the imagination. The silver-haired one's attire was golden, while the other's matched the feathers in her hair.

"Makria," Stagran said, gesturing to the silver-haired woman.

She smiled widely.

"And Konta."

Konta offered a short nod.

Derek took a step forward, hands slightly raised. "We appreciate your hospitality. We're here because—"

Stagran raised a hand. "We already know. You seek the Trinity." His voice was guttural and harsh.

Mia blinked. "How could you know that?"

"Everyone we have talked to has acted like it does not exist." Caldera added.

"Because they knew," Stagran replied, glancing at the two women. "The Oracles of Welderan. One sees the distant future. The other, the near."

Silas tensed beside Mia. "Which is which?"

"That," Stagran said, "is for you to determine."

The room seemed to still. A quiet test. No tricks, no illusions, only reason.

"There are rules," Stagran continued. "You may not ask them questions. You will be given three clues. Decide correctly, and I will help you find what you seek. Fail, and we will not speak of this again."

Derek looked to his friends. Mia bit her bottom lip, her eyes darting between the two Oracles. Caldera confidently nodded. Silas's eyes were locked onto Stagran's.

"We accept." Derek said with his chest puffed.

"The first clue," Stagran said, spreading his arms, "are their names. Makria. Konta."

Mia squinted, whispering, "I think those are Greek. I've heard Makria before," she thought for a moment, her finger running across her temple, "I think it means 'far.'"

Derek's eyes studied the silver-haired fae.

"Second clue," Stagran said. "Makria prefers the sunrise. Konta prefers the sunset."

Caldera tilted her head. "Symbolic. Sunrise could mean beginnings. Distant things. Sunset is endings, the immediate."

Silas crossed his arms. "I noticed something. When Makria was introduced, she smiled like she already knew us."

"Final clue," Stagran said. "The one who sees the distant future has known of your coming for some time."

Silas arched a brow. "So she smiled because she foresaw us."

"That's assuming she did," Mia said. "But it tracks."

"Or... Derek could shoot lightning at Stagran," Caldera offered, her face unbothered. "The one who sees the near future would warn him. Problem solved."

Derek gave her a look. "Let's not electrocute the guy who might help us."

They deliberated for a few more minutes. Everything pointed to the same answer. Derek stepped forward. But for a moment, his mind fought against him.

What if I am wrong? Derek thought to himself. *If I say the wrong thing, then what happens? Is all of this for nothing?* He was at war with himself. Terrified to be correct. That's when he felt it. Not the voice from the void reaching out to him, not his magic coursing through his veins. It was Mia's touch.

She had walked up behind him and placed her hand in the small of his back. *How does she do that?* Derek laughed to himself. He turned around to look at Mia.

"No second guessing yourself, Lavender." She whispered.

The corners of Derek's mouth rose, "You're right."

He turned back to face Stagran and the Oracles, "I know which Oracle is which."

Stagran moved to the side and extended both hands, palms up, one in front of each Oracle.

Derek took a breath. "Makria is the one who sees the distant future."

A silence fell.

Konta looked to her sister. Makria tilted her head, expression unreadable. Stagran said nothing.

The face of the Shimmering Court simply closed both of his hands. A smile bore across his face. His thumbs went up in the air, as he chuckled, "Very good. You are correct!"

Chapter 26

Another Test

The chamber pulsed with soft golden light as the energy of the Oracles faded from the air, leaving behind a quiet stillness. Stagran stood at the center of the stone dais, a satisfied smile tugging at the corners of his lips.

"You chose wisely," he said, nodding toward Derek with something close to reverence. "I knew you could figure it out. Someone who is searching for purpose always finds the right answer."

Derek noticed a strange glint in Stagran's eyes. Something that seemed to speak directly to him. Almost like Stagran was carefully choosing the words he spoke to Derek. Mia's hand drifted from his back and the feeling parted. He turned to her, and was lost in her soft, knowing smile.

Breaking the silence, Caldera muttered, "About time we caught a break."

Stagran raised his hand, and from the floor, smooth stone benches rose in a circle. "Please," he said. "Sit. You have earned more than answers... you have earned clarity."

As they took their seats, sunlight filtered through the crystalline dome above, casting warm beams across the room. The dome seemed to be capped at the opening of the large tree that the palace was carved from.

Stagran and the Oracles stood side by side now, no longer distant judges, but storytellers. Makria stepped forward first, her golden robes trailing behind her like autumn leaves in the wind. Her voice was soft and melodic, like a lullaby wrapped in wisdom.

"When rumors of Malum's return first reached our ears," she began, "my gift... *shifted*. I still saw the future, but reality began to bend around those visions." Her brow creased in thought. "For instance, I once foresaw a merchant caravan bringing honey apples and beef sticks. I was sure of it. But when it arrived, the crates were filled with oats and spearpears instead."

Mia blinked. "That's not exactly catastrophic."

Makria gave a faint smile. "No. Not at first. But imagine that slight wrongness repeated again and again, like cracks in a mirror. Every time I peered forward, the reflection was just a little... off."

Caldera leaned forward, eyes narrowed. "Something was interfering with fate?"

"Yes," Makria said. "Like a thread being pulled from a tapestry."

"But the interference stopped," Derek guessed. "When Malum was defeated."

Makria nodded. "The moment we heard you had won, my visions returned. The world came back into focus. I even foresaw your arrival here."

A hush fell over the chamber until Stagran's expression darkened.

"But balance," he said, "always demands a cost."

Konta stepped forward, arms crossed tightly over her chest. She was the opposite of her sister in every way. Stern where Makria was gentle, sharp where Makria was soft.

"As my sister's clarity returned, mine vanished," she said, her tone clipped. "My visions used to let me see moments before they happened. I could predict movement, emotion, shifts in wind and fate. Then, the beasts arrived."

Silas shifted. "The manticore?"

Konta nodded. "It came from under the sand, and almost overnight, my foresight dulled. I couldn't sense the ambush, the beast's approach, or the danger it brought."

"And now?" Caldera asked. "Is it gone?"

"Since you defeated it," Konta said, "some of my sight has returned, but it is... fuzzy. Fragmented. As though I am looking through fog."

Derek glanced at the others. "You said beasts... like more than one?"

"There is another," Konta said. "South of the city. We do not know what it is yet. Its presence weighs on the land, like the pressure before a storm."

Silas folded his arms. "Why are they here exactly?"

"We believe," Stagran said, "they have been sent to keep some-thing... or someone away." His eyes locked onto Derek's, "We know you come here to seek answers about the Trinity. It seems someone else knew you would as well."

Derek ran a hand through his hair. "But the only people who knew we were coming to the wild... er... Welderan, were people we trusted."

Stagran let out a deep, echoing laugh that bounced off the dome above. He looked at Derek with shining eyes, the weight of centuries behind his gaze.

"No one else knew... or told you to seek out the Trinity?" Stagran finally asked.

Mia interlaced her fingers with Derek's, the latter saying, "No. There is no way you would know about that." Electricity sizzled along his free arm.

Caldera stepped forward, falling beside Derek and Mia. Silas rose to his feet, his shadows coiling around him.

Konta, unamused, spoke up, "I knew I saw electricity."

"Konta, now is not the time." Stagran commanded before look-ing back to Derek, "Easy friends. Do not mistake me for your ene-my."

"If you want our trust, start with the truth. Where is the Trinity?" Derek snapped back.

Stagran raised an eyebrow, "Trust? I have extended you and your friends great trust!" His brow fell back into a straight line. "After you slayed the manticore, I allowed you into the city... *my* city... free of harm and shackles. I did this because I *know* what you need to *know*. There is no need to see me as anything other than on *your* side."

The lightning died down. "Forgive me, but these last few months have been anything but normal. I... I'm just not sure who's really on *my* side anymore," Derek spoke softly, "But how could you know about the voice in the void?"

"The same way I know, that if you were to use your magic here and now against me, you would be depleted and need to rest." Stagran stated, his chin lifted in the air. "The voice in the void? It speaks to me, too. Told me to trust in my Oracles and to aid you whenever you arrive."

Derek looked to the ground, his shoulders relaxing, "But... why? Why does it speak to you?"

"Because, Calistia is home to a grand portal. The magical energy that flows out of that portal is why the city looks like a rainforest in the middle of a desert." Stagran said, almost as if he were running out of breath... or time. "There are two grand portals in this realm. One here and one located in Luminfae. Malum, Torviid, and others... that is what they used to traverse to the Sacred Dimension."

Stagran took a step closer to Derek, prompting Silas to stand in front of the group, his fist clenched. Derek waved Silas off, an unspoken reassurance that everything was okay.

"And the Trinity?" Derek asked.

"What you seek," Stagran said quietly, "can not be found."

The words hit like a stone dropped in still water.

"It must be learned. The Trinity is not a place or an artifact. It is a convergence. A truth waiting to unfold."

He lifted a hand, pointing first to Derek, then Mia, Caldera, and finally Silas.

"You are already walking its path. The threads are tightening. The pattern is forming. But to wield its power, to understand it... you must be taught."

Silas raised an eyebrow, shadow coiling faintly around his feet. "And I am guessing you are the only one who can teach us?"

Stagran's smile returned. "For now. I am sure Derek knows the voice he hears could guide him, *but*... that voice is probably a little less up front with his information than Derek would like."

Derek straightened and nodded his head "Then teach us."

The golden light shifted in tone, as if responding to his voice. Magic hummed faintly beneath their feet.

Stagran's smile faded. "Not yet."

A quiet hush fell over them.

"There is another beast," he said, his eyes flicking southward as if he could see beyond the chamber's walls. "And while it remains, I can not take you to the grand portal. I fear that if the magical energy surges from that room, the beast may attack the city. Until it is gone, the portal's chamber must remain sealed."

"So, we clear the path," Caldera said, cracking her knuckles. "Again."

Stagran nodded solemnly. "Do that, and I will show you what the Trinity truly is."

As they stood, Derek felt the weight of it all settle on his shoulders. Fate, magic, prophecy. And yet, for the first time, it didn't feel overwhelming.

It felt like purpose.

Chapter 27

Custos

"Well, I will say... Stagran's got quite the armory," Caldera quipped as they stepped through the southern gate of Calistia.

Silas didn't break stride. "How can you choose a weapon when you do not even know what we will be facing?"

"I only need a spear," Caldera said with a smirk. She twirled the weapon in her hand. "And this is definitely an upgrade."

The haft had been carved from ancient darkwood. Smooth as river stone, yet etched with time-worn scars like tree rings preserved in battle. Verdant runes twisted along its length, pulsing gently in sync with her breath, like the forest itself had lent its heartbeat to the weapon.

At the tip, a golden spearhead shimmered, not polished, but infused. It caught the sunlight and refracted it like a blade of captured dawn, its edges too perfect, too otherworldly, to be forged by mortal hands.

"It called to me when I saw it," she added softly, reverently.

Derek rolled up the sleeves of his robe. The elixir Makria had given him still coursed through his veins. Raw magic hummed beneath his skin, and lightning threaded through his muscles like a second pulse. He'd been wary at first... Silas's elixir hadn't exactly left fond memories, but Makria's brew had done exactly as promised. Heightened focus. Tighter control.

"But what about your old spear?" Derek asked, nodding toward the ornate weapon.

Caldera shrugged. "A weapon is just a tool. No need to get attached."

"But there's a tool for every job," Mia added, falling into step beside them.

"Enough," Silas snapped, eyes narrowing. "We are not alone."

He flicked his head toward a tower behind them. High above, Stagran and the Oracles stood motionless, cloaked in golden light, their gazes fixed on the desert.

"Spectators," Silas muttered. "Too afraid to fight. But eager to watch."

Derek let out a dry laugh. "Well then... let's give 'em a show."

As if summoned by his words, the desert trembled. Sand shifted and danced beneath their boots. A low rumble rolled beneath their feet, too deep to be wind.

Then, ahead of them, barely a hundred yards out, the ground burst open.

A shriek of ancient stone and cracking desert ripped through the air as an enormous form erupted from below. Wings... massive, leathery, and tattered, unfurled like the sails of a dying god. Each wing alone could have blotted out the sun.

Mia froze, her voice barely a breath. "Guys... that's going to be a huge manticore."

A deafening roar shattered the silence. Magic rippled across the desert like a shockwave, distorting the air and tearing at the sky. Caldera staggered. Mia dropped to her knees, hands clamped over her ears, her face twisted in pain.

Derek dropped beside her. "Mia! Mia, what's wrong?"

She didn't respond, but her eyes widened. Terrified. Transfixed.

A second roar followed, splitting the sky like thunder cracking from the heavens. Caldera fell to one knee beside them, shaking.

Wind surged around them. Derek's robes whipped wildly. Mia's hair danced in the gusts. The ground shook again. Closer this time. The sand recoiled from each footfall.

Then, a voice. Deep. Gravel-thick. Impossible.

"Semideus."

Derek turned slowly, heart pounding, lightning already flickering between his fingers. And there it was. A dragon. No tale, painting, or whispered legend could have prepared him.

It towered above them. Rotting scales clung to a colossal frame of muscle and bone. The creature's hide was deep blue, but dulled with time and rot. Flesh sloughed off in places, revealing sinew, cracked bone, and raw, glowing veins of green ichor. Its wings, if they could still be called that, were ruined sails, stretched and punctured, yet still capable of flight.

Its claws, each one the size of a man, sank into the sand as it stepped forward. Steam hissed from its nostrils, and its jaws parted to reveal jagged fangs dripping with venom.

"Semideus," it rumbled again, voice vibrating the marrow in Derek's bones.

Out of the corner of his eye, Derek saw Silas's shadows coil tighter, preparing for war.

Behind them, Caldera hauled Mia to her feet just as the dragon's voice thundered once more:

"One of you does not belong here."

Derek and Silas exchanged a quick glance, the former clenching his fist as lightning burst across his knuckles.

"From our perspective," Derek said, voice steady, "you're the one who doesn't belong."

Caldera hissed, "Derek, you should not talk to a dragon like that."

The beast let out a growl that rattled their teeth. "I was woken from the ancient slumber." Steam billowed as it exhaled. "I should not be here... and yet, here I am." It lowered its head, green fire burning in its eyes. "Do you know why?"

Derek hesitated, watching Silas out of the corner of his eye. He watched how the fae's magic pulsed, eager for release. Don't trust the shadow wielder, the voice in the void had warned.

Derek pushed the thought down. "All I know is this. Your presence is tearing at the magic here. It is negatively affecting the people who live here."

The dragon laughed. A low, wheezing sound that turned into a hacking cough. A spray of ichor splattered across the sand.

"These mortals know nothing of where they lay their heads," it spat. "I guarded these lands and skies long before their ancestors crawled from their hovels. I do not take orders from children."

Silas stepped forward, his voice ice. "You sound tired, ancient one. Perhaps it is time you returned to sleep." The shadows around him rose like a tide.

The dragon moved with unnatural speed. Derek and Silas barely dove aside in time, the beast's massive head crashing down between them with a thunderous impact that shook the sand beneath their feet.

"You shall have your glorious fight," the dragon growled, its voice like boulders grinding beneath the earth. Its head swayed in a serpent-like motion, each shift shedding more rot and scales that sizzled as they hit the ground. "But first... you will hear my words."

Mia took a tentative step forward.

"Mia, no! What are you doing?" Derek called out, panic flaring in his chest.

She held up a hand, a quiet signal that she would be okay. "What is your name?" she asked the dragon softly.

The dragon lifted its decaying head high, slower now, regal despite its ruin. Its hollow black eyes locked onto hers.

"In life, I was known as *Custos*," the dragon rumbled. "One of the last true protectors of this realm. One of the few dragons permitted to cross the realms unhindered." It turned its head, slowly, deliberately, first toward Silas... then Derek. "And that is how I know... one of you does not belong."

Mia blinked, her voice a whisper. "Custos... That means guardian."

Caldera, quiet until now, stepped up beside her. "If that was your name in life..." she asked, voice cautious, "...what do they call you now?"

Another guttural exhale spilled from the dragon's maw, expelling steam and thick ichor from the open sores along its snout. "In due time," it rasped. Then its great, rotting eyes locked on Derek. "You seek the Trinity."

Lightning stuttered across Derek's skin, but it had slowed. No longer attacking the air, simply humming. He opened his mouth, but Custos cut him off.

"You seek knowledge no human has ever held," the dragon said. "What makes you think yourself worthy?"

Derek held the dragon's gaze. Its pupils were drowned in blackness, like voids of time, but in them swirled flecks of ancient blue. Stars trapped in an abyss. The air felt thick, suspended, like time itself was waiting on his answer.

He knew brute strength wouldn't matter here. This wasn't just a battle of might. It was a judgment. A test. He closed his eyes and dug deep.

He saw Johnathan. His best friend grinning wide, the frayed brim of his old cap shadowing his eyes. That same cap he wore every day.

Then Izzy, and the pain crashed into him. Her laughter, her calm... gone. He missed her in a way that never faded. He thought she was the glue of their group... but now he saw the glue wasn't a person. It was the bond they'd built.

Trey came next. That face at the lunch table, scowling while the others laughed. Derek had ignored the signs, but how could he have known? He hadn't even known magic was real then.

And then the memories softened. Barry, jumping on a chair, reenacting a game-winning touchdown with a dramatic flair that only Barry could pull off. That ridiculous grin. That joy. They weren't just friends. They were his why.

A hand touched the small of his back. Warm, grounding. Mia. He opened his eyes to see hers, deep forest green, shimmering beneath the high sun of the desert.

"Whatever you're thinking," she said, "we're with you, Lavender."

That was all he needed. He turned to face Custos. Lightning returned to his arms, crackling softly, waiting to be called. He lifted his chin and met the dragon's stare.

"I don't think I'm worthy," Derek said. His voice trembled, but only for a moment. "I never really felt like I belonged back home. I had it good, I guess, but... something always felt off. Like I was meant for more. I just didn't know what."

He looked around at those that were with him. Mia, Caldera, even Silas. "Since coming to Luminfae, everything's been insane. Dangerous. Terrifying. But also... it fits. I feel alive here. Like I'm finally becoming who I was meant to be."

He took a breath. "I don't think I'm worthy. But I am searching for purpose."

Then, with the weight of every truth inside him, he said, "There are two important days in a person's life. The day they're born... and the day they find out why. I think I'm standing on the edge of my second day. And I won't let you stop me from reaching it."

Thunder cracked overhead. Clouds churned as if summoned by his conviction. The sun vanished. Forks of lightning split the heavens, tracing jagged lines through roiling black. Derek's arms ignited with radiant white light, sacred and wild, while veins of deep blue lightning surged into the earth, causing the sand to sizzle and shift.

Custos studied him for a long moment. Something ancient stirred behind those ruined eyes. Something almost like approval.

Then the dragon turned his gaze to Caldera. "In life," he intoned, "they called me Custos."

His ruined wings spread. Tattered, holy things. They beat once, slow and seismic, sending up cyclones of sand as the creature began to rise from the earth, its massive claws tearing free of the ground.

"In death..." he thundered, "...they call me *Prodromus*."

Chapter 28

Barry Would NOT Like This

The sky had turned black. A storm of Derek's creation churned above them, painting the desert in strobes of pale blue and white lightning.

Prodromus now towered above them, his wings like torn curtains of shadow and scale. Ichor dripped from his jaws, sizzling where it hit the sand. This was no mindless monster. This was a relic of a forgotten era, turned to ruin by something even older. With a roar that split the air, he launched skyward, vanishing into the clouds like a specter of death.

It was calm for a few heartbeats, but only a few. Derek surveyed his surroundings.. Silas stood nearby, his face etched with pure determination. Caldera gripped her spear until her knuckles turned white, and Mia, no matter what was about to happen, he knew she would have his back.

Then, Prodomus dropped. The ground quaked. Derek rolled to the side, narrowly dodging a crushing claw. Sand exploded outward as the dragon struck, and from the heart of the dust storm came another deafening roar.

"Spread out!" Silas called, already vanishing into a flicker of shadow. He reappeared behind the dragon, twin blades of darkness materializing in his hands.

Derek surged left with lightning spiraling up his arms. He flung a bolt toward the creature's shoulder. The blast struck, sending flakes of rotten scale flying, but the dragon didn't flinch.

Mia raised both hands and let the blue essence pour from her fingers. It twisted and spun until it became sharp, jagged daggers of frozen water. With a whip of her arm, they launched toward the dragon's face. Prodromus turned just in time. Only one dagger nicked his eye, eliciting a roar that cracked the clouds above.

Caldera drove her spear into the ground, and the earth obeyed. Vines burst from the sand, wrapping around one of the dragon's legs. Thorns, thick and pulsing with essence that began blue and shifted to green, constricted.

"Barry would hate this," she muttered, twisting her spear. The vines flared bright and *pulled*.

Prodromus stumbled. That was their opening. Derek darted forward, lightning pulsing up his spine and down his arms. He jumped, high, and slammed both fists into the dragon's snout with a flash of blinding white light. The impact echoed across the battlefield... but again, the beast rose, unfazed. This was a creature of death with no nerves left to feel true pain.

The tail came too fast.

It swatted Derek midair and sent him flying. He hit the sand hard, his breath torn from his lungs.

"Derek!" Mia screamed. She ran to him, sliding to his side as he groaned, clutching his ribs.

"I'm... good," he coughed. It was barely convincing to even himself.

Above them, Silas leapt from the shadows, blades slashing down across the dragon's wing joint. Dark energy crackled from the points of impact. An angry roar followed.

A massive claw swept Silas from the sky like a bug. He landed hard next to Derek and Mia, and didn't get up.

"Silas!" Caldera cried.

Before she could run to him, the dragon inhaled deeply. A wave of corrupted fire and decaying energy came with the exhale–a sickly green blast that twisted the very air.

Caldera raised her spear and slammed it into the ground. A wall of thick bark and thorn rose in front of her and Mia, shielding them from the worst of it, but it splintered under the weight. Caldera flew back, a piece of the splintering bark smashing into her face. Blood ran down her forehead.

Mia screamed as the bark wall collapsed, but a flick of her hand summoned a dome of mist and water. The acid fire hissed as it hit the shield, evaporating in a burst of steam. Still, the force knocked her back to the ground... they were all down.

Derek rolled onto his side, heart pounding, ribs aching. Lightning buzzed uselessly across his hands, his vision swimming.

We can't win. Not like this. He thought to himself.

Prodromus advanced, step by thunderous step, wings curled like death around his shoulders. He opened his mouth, charging a second breath.

Derek crawled toward Mia, his eyes never leaving the massive dragon. He searched for anything– anything that could help them.

The dragon shifted slightly. A subtle twist. A movement that didn't speak of animal instinct, but intention. A cry from something buried beneath scale and shadow. An opening of the chest that exposed the soft, rotted underbelly just beneath the rib cage. No armor. No deflection.

It was too perfect. Too *intentional*. Derek froze.

The dragon's eye glowed the faintest blue, not soulless, not entirely.

Is this... a gift? Or a trap? A warrior would strike. A tactician would retreat. What am I?

Mia stirred behind him. The panic was setting in her eyes. "Derek..."

He looked at her. Then at Silas... three massive gashes in his side, the sand painted with his blood, groaning, but alive. Caldera was using her magic trying to stabilize Silas the best she could.

"Mia, follow my lead." Derek whispered, realization dawning.

Lightning began to hum from within him. He stood, slowly, pain burning through every joint. The wind howled, but the white light within him grew brighter, stronger, until it radiated from his very skin.

He shouted, his voice carrying on the thunder. "Caldera! Pin his leg again!"

Caldera, bloodied but breathing, paused her aid to Silas for a quick moment and lifted her hand. Magic flared green and blue, and the desert floor obeyed. Roots burst forth again, snaring the dragon's leg.

"Mia, go for his eyes!"

Mia's trembling hands rose. The air turned cold as the mist poured out, veiling the dragon's sight in a sudden storm of frost.

"Silas, we're almost there! Don't you go where I can't follow!"

But Silas vanished in a pulse of darkness. He reappeared at the dragon's flank, slashing hard. Prodromus turned. Silas fell to the ground again, his wounds in an even worse state now, but the turn was exactly what Derek needed.

The opening widened. This was it. Derek's feet left the ground as he surged upward, lightning spiraling from his fists, blinding light exploding from his core. The storm above screamed with him.

He *dove*, both arms forward, white light and blue lightning arcing together.

"Over here!"

The strike hit true. His fists slammed into the soft spot beneath the rib cage, and the light exploded outward. Through scale, through ichor, through the decay and darkness that clung to the ancient beast's soul.

There was a roar, not of rage, but release.

The light burned so bright the others had to shield their eyes. The desert was bathed in purity. Cleansing, searing, freeing, and then, silence.

When the light faded, Derek stood in a crater, gasping. Lightning flickered like dying fireflies around him.

Prodromus lay still. His massive body fading... turning to ash, to wind. But in his final moments, he looked at Derek once more. That glow of blue in the black eye. Soft now. Proud.

"Thank you," the dragon whispered, not with sound, but in Derek's mind. "Go forward. Learn the Trinity."

Derek felt the gem in his pocket start to heat. The gem he had found after defeating the manticore. He pulled it from his pocket.

Prodromus's eye opened wide one last time, "A Lazarus gem? Impossible." The dragon huffed a gust of steam. "Forbidden. They said they were all destroyed." His eyes began to close again, "Nevertheless, that must be how they awakened me."

"I found it after the manticore." Derek whispered.

Prodromus closed his eyes completely. Then again, in Derek's head, he heard the beast's voice. "Semideus."

"Wait!" Derek shouted. "You said one of us does not belong here. What did you mean?"

The gem grew even warmer in Derek's hand. He looked at it and noticed the symbol from the wall in the cave. He looked back to the dragon and saw the same symbol in between the beast's eyes.

"Prodomus!" Derek shouted, desperate for answers he would never receive.

The scales of Prodomus's face began to fade away. And with that, the dragon vanished. Gone.

The storm above began to break. The clouds lightened and the sun beat down on their backs once more.

Derek dropped to his knees. Another question left unanswered. Another riddle not solved.

"Derek? Are you okay?" Mia asked as she placed her hand on his shoulder.

Derek looked back to her, but before he could respond, Caldera rushed past them, sprinting for the downed Silas.

"Shit, Silas!" Derek shouted. Leaping to his feet, he ran towards the shadow wielder, but he didn't make it far. The elixir Makria had given him was starting to wear off. The toll of the massive amount of magic he had used was weighing heavy on him. He collapsed back to his knees, and then to his back in the sand.

Mia slid down beside him, "Derek! No, not again. Come on. Stay awake."

A smile ghosted Derek's lips, "I'll be okay in a few hours... help Silas."

Mia looked at him with an eyebrow raised, "Are you sure?"

"Of course." Derek closed his eyes. The faint blue glimmer from Prodromus's eyes danced in his mind. "I'm getting used to this now."

Chapter 29

Nightmares Redux

Grass tickled the back of Derek's neck. Opening his eyes, a fiery sunset steak across the horizon, bathing the honey-colored field in a soft light.

Gentle hills rose and fell like waves in the distance, and the sweet scent of blooming flowers filled the air.

Warily, he stood and appraised his surroundings. Within moments, a vicious heat licked at Derek's skin as the scene around him changed. The once comforting warmth of the sky melted into a burning crimson. His skin continued to heat, but he felt no pain. Derek watched as fires raged through the fields surrounding him. The flames moved closer... closer... closer, until they were underneath his feet. But still no pain.

Sweat slicked Derek's skin. Was it the heat from the flames? Was it the adrenaline running through his veins? He tried to scream for help, but no sound came out. He tasted salt on his lips, whether from his sweat or tears, he wasn't sure, and then he heard it.

An unnerving voice rang out from the skies above him.

"To bridge the gap, unite the world's divide,
With courage, he'll mend what's torn inside.
The realms tremble as the battle nears.
In his hands, the fate of all appears."

Derek ran through the fields. He knew where he was now. It had been so long since the nightmare. He hadn't had it one time since finding Luminfae. But here it was.

He now sprinted through the flaming grass. His eyes darted around looking for an escape. Any escape. *This isn't right.* He thought to himself. *I usually wake up by now.*

The flames inched closer and closer until he had nowhere else to run. Then, suddenly, the flames were gone. The peaceful field was back to beautiful grass swaying in the wind. The clouds danced in the sky.

"What is this?" His words echoed around him as they left his lips. "Just a dream?"

Laughter. That maniacal laughter he knew all too well.

"MALUM!?" Derek shouted.

"To save Luminfae and realms beyond compare, he'll face the trials, his destiny to bear. With magic yet awakened and a brotherhood born, mend the pages from the time once torn." Malum's voice echoed high overhead, but he was nowhere to be seen.

Derek twisted and turned, he looked all around him. he couldn't find the ancient fae anywhere. As far as his eyes could see, there was only grass and sky.

Malum's voice continued, "The scales of fate demand a heavy cost. Balance is needed or all will be lost. Only love can stop the strife and bring in an everlasting light."

"Show yourself!" Derek demanded.

The twisted fae obliged.

Just as the world turned red, he thought he heard it... a whisper, buried in the wind.

"This is..."

Fire swallowed the sky. The clouds ran away, as if called home by their master. The grass wilted and died. A meteor appeared overhead, but it wasn't moving fast. No. More like a rhythmic fall to the ground, a dance that slowly built anticipation for what was to come next.

The ball of fire set down twenty yards from Derek, and out of the blaze, Malum appeared.

Derek clenched his fists, preparing to fight. He willed every fiber of his being to summon the storm within him. He looked at his hands and... nothing. No white light. No lightning.

"What are you doing to me?" Derek screamed.

"We are in your dream, boy. I have done nothing to you." Malum answered, his voice calm, unwavering.

Before he knew what was really happening, Derek's legs were sprinting. Running full force toward Malum, he balled his fist.

Derek's feet pounded the scorched ground, but the sound came a moment after each step. Malum stood impossibly still as the world warped around him.

Fifteen yards.

His knuckles cracked from the pressure. His right palm was bleeding from his nails cutting into them.

Ten yards.

"Let's finish this!" Derek shouted.

Five yards.

Derek rolled his shoulder back, raised his right leg into the air and pushed off the ground with his left foot. With every ounce of strength he had, he delivered a superman punch aimed straight for Malum's face.

Zero yards.

Derek slammed to the ground. He tumbled and rolled as his body slid through the grass. He had gone right through Malum!

The fae straightened his black robes and turned to face the now prone Derek. "Why do you insist on acting so childish?"

"Do not call me a child!!" Derek's eyes burned with rage. "You did this to me! You gave me these nightmares, made me feel like I was losing my mind!"

An unimpressed laugh echoed from Malum, "I did no such thing, you fool."

"Liar!"

"Tell me, Derek, why would *I* want you to know the very prophecy that could stop my plans?" Malum asked.

Derek had no answer.

"Why would I point out the only rock capable of causing a land-slide?"

Derek still couldn't find the words.

Malum shook his head. "I did not send you those nightmares before…" The ancient fae turned away. "But I do visit your dreams now."

"Wh… why?" Derek whispered. "Why now if not before?"

Malum spun on his heel to face Derek again, his robes flowing around him, "Because it seems we are at an impasse. Someone is telling you the path to follow." Malum stepped closer to Derek and then dropped to one knee. "Look in my eyes, boy." His eyes were bright red, with black swirls dancing inside them. "They are telling me my path, too."

"No!" Derek shouted. "You're lying! This is just some game you're playing. Some sick, twisted game to throw me off *my* path."

"Listen to me Derek, we are not friends. I do not even wish for you to be my ally. Our vision of the future is just too far apart for any sort of alliance." Malum rose back to his feet. "But I do feel like you deserve to know what cards you have been dealt. You did best me once, after all. Consider this my acknowledgement of that… you will get no other."

"Malum… why are you here?" Derek paused, looked to his hands still seeing no lightning or white light. "If you really didn't cause the nightmares before, then why would you come to me now?"

The slightest smile grew on Malum's face, "To warn you. You *think* you were chosen to defeat me. Vanquish evil. Eradicate my influence from all the realms?"

Derek nodded hesitantly.

"I *know* I was chosen to unite all the realms under one banner, one rule. We are two sides of the same coin. Two puppets, our strings pulled by the same master." Malum closed his eyes. "The difference is, you want to obey this master... I want to be him. Make the realms a place of order, of rule."

Derek slowly rose to his feet, careful not to startle the ancient fae in hopes he would keep his eyes closed.

Malum continued on, "Torviid thought he was the chosen one of the prophecy. Before him? I am sure there were others. My brother was a fool. He believed the Deus to be some almighty beings." His eyes still shut, Malum chuckled, "They are living things just like you and I, Derek. They were just blessed by where they were born."

"Then what am I, Malum? What does it mean if I am a Semideus?" Derek asked. Then he felt it. A familiar tingle returned to his hands. His lightning was coming back, he just needed to stall a little longer. "You told me that my magic is consuming me from within. What did you mean by that?"

"You really know nothing about what you are? In this time of silence between our factions you really have sought no answers?" The ancient fae asked, his eyes still closed tight, "The blood running in your veins is tied to the ones in the Sacred Dimension. How could you possibly think a human could contain that much power... that much raw magic?"

Derek tried to answer, but Malum's eyes flung open and the twisted fae cut him off, "It can not! Your species is not capable of handling magic, let alone the 'power of the gods' as your stupid human textbooks call it. Think of every story you have heard in school, any piece of your so-called mythology. How many of those 'demigods' ever survived?"

Malum stared at the now standing Derek. He noticed the lighting arcing between his fingers.

"That will not do you much good here, boy." Malum pointed at Derek's hands.

"I just want answers. No one, not even you will be straight up with me. Why?" Derek asked, knowing his surprise attack wouldn't work now.

Malum raised his left hand, rubbing his index finger and thumb together, and red mist sprouted out of his nails. "You are still my enemy, Derek. You still plan to stand in my way, even though I am telling you we are both being led to water by the same shepherd."

Derek couldn't take it anymore. He had tried to stay calm, but he couldn't believe any of this. He couldn't believe Malum. Not now. Not ever. Especially not with what was happening to the dimensions.

"Why the hell would I believe a word you say? You're just a pompous ass who thinks he knows what's best for everyone. You have no problem slaughtering millions so that you can rule how you see fit over every dimension." Derek spouted out, his words laced with poison. "You think I don't know what those rifts that are appearing are? You started something that I can't undo... but I can make damn sure you won't be around to play king!"

A sigh escaped Malum's lips. "Ahhh, yes. Play the righteous card, Derek. You can try to stop me, but we both know how last time went. You gave it your all, and while that slowed me down... I am still here." Malum lowered the hand he had been holding up. "The world needs a hero, right? What is it that the warriors say?" He acted like he was lost in thought for a second, "Oh, that is right. Still I stand, until I fall, I will heed the lonesome call. Do you know what that *really* means, boy?"

The lightning was arcing up and down Derek's arms now. He could strike whenever he wanted, but he held out hope that maybe Malum was about to slip, giving him some kind of information that he could use against him.

"It's a mantra. Something for them to live by. It means they will stand tall on the eve of battle. They will fight until their last breath." Derek quipped.

"No, you fool." Malum laughed. "You search for the Trinity, yet you do not even know that you have spoken it before."

Derek's brow furrowed, his eyes grew wide. "Wh... what? How do you know that's what I'm doing? How is a mantra the Trinity? Why are you here?" Derek rattled off question after question.

"It seems *our* master is only giving you half truths. He could have just told you exactly what it means, instead he makes you search for it, leave your friends behind, go on pointless journeys into forgotten lands, fight massive beasts, just to try to understand it." Malum smiled wickedly.

The sweat was pouring from Derek's skin. His heart beating fiercely in his chest. How did Malum know all of this? There is no way he should know any of this.

"You're lying! The Trinity has to be more than just words!" Derek shouted.

"Oh, it is my boy. It is so much more than words, it is the meaning behind those words, but alas... it seems the voice in your head does not want you to just *have* that information." Malum tilted his head down slightly and peered at Derek through his brows. "Don't worry, the voice will never know about my little visit in your dream. I have learned a thing or two about only letting it see what I want it to."

Derek stumbled backwards. Everything was crashing down. Literally. The sky itself was now littered with meteors falling to the ground. The dead grass was starting to catch flame. Malum was inching closer and closer to him.

"ENOUGH!" Derek shouted as he raised both of his hands to unleash a torrent of lightning right at Malum.

Malum was ready. Malum was fast. He closed the distance between them in less than a heartbeat, his nails stabbing into the scar that was left from when he had stabbed Derek during their battle.

"Stay on the path." Malum whispered into his ear. And then he trilled like a hummingbird.

Derek shot out of bed, lightning surging from his outstretched arms and blasting into the ceiling above him and Mia.

Mia leapt to her feet. Quickly sliding away from the falling debris, she used her magic to put out the small fire that the lightning had started.

Derek was slick with sweat, his heart still racing. Tears formed in his eyes.

"Derek? What the hell?" Mia asked.

Before he could respond, Caldera burst through the door to inspect what was going on. Silas came running in behind her.

"What was that? It sounded like Prodromus was landing on the roof." Caldera panted.

Derek still sat on the bed, taking fast, hard breaths. His eyes darted around the room. *It was just a dream,* he thought to himself, *just a dream.*

Mia approached him cautiously, her hand slowly resting on his shoulder, "Derek?"

Derek turned his head to meet her stare. Her eyes, her beautiful forest green eyes, were his anchor. He pulled her hand to his chest, grounding himself in the present, in her.

A whisper, barely audible, "The nightmares. They are back... I talked to Malum."

Chapter 30

It Has Begun

The sky above Torvania was in turmoil. The normally beautiful hues of blue and purple were rippling violently. A tear formed due north of the city, spewing shades of green, orange, and red. Not only had a new rift opened, it was growing larger with every second.

"What the hell is happening?" Barry shouted, running out the door of the tavern.

Nidalle sprinted past him, "Another rift."

Screams. Shouts. People running in every direction. Fingers pointed skyward. Eyes toward the tear, ever growing.

Parents grabbed their children and rushed them away. Store owners frantically locked up their shops and sprinted for the statue of Torviid, hoping they would be safe there.

A fruit stand crashed to the cobblestone, apples scattering under fleeing feet. Somewhere, a bell tolled in warning. Guards barked commands, but their voices were drowned in the chaos.

Tah'quhal slowed his run to a jog, then to a walk, finally standing still just outside the northern gate of Torvania. Nidalle followed in the same pattern. Barry and the others brought up the rear. All their eyes were locked on the sky, but no words were shared between them.

Barry's hands warmed, and as he looked at his palms, embers were starting to drip from them. He clenched his hands tight, doing his best to hide the sparks of flame. The fire licked his arms again. Hot, hungry. Barry felt his chest tighten. Not from fear, but anticipation. His breath caught. He liked it.

Tah'quhal broke the silence, "It stretches all the way to the Magia Forest."

"This is the largest rift we have documented." Mr. Monton added.

Nidalle pointed toward the sky, one eyebrow raised, "Is it growing... or is it falling?"

The rift did seem to be getting larger, but this one was so high in the sky it was hard to tell if it was because it was taking up more of the sky, or if it was getting closer to them. The colors bursting from the rift intensified, even reaching all the way to the ground.

"I... I think it's falling." Abhaya pointed out.

Tah'quhal squinted his eyes, "Is that...NO!"

The inside of the rift was becoming clearer. No longer just a slurry of colors. Lines. Shapes. Figures.

"Are those tents?" Abhaya asked.

Mr. Monton took a step back, "By the gods." He covered his mouth with his hand, tears forming in his eyes.

The air warped. Barry's skin prickled as hot and cold battled across his arms. A scent... not Torvania's crisp mountain air, but gasoline and smoke, invaded his nose. Earth.

Inside the rift, the group could see the encampment. The humans were screaming and running, similar to the citizens of Torvania. For the first time since the rifts began, the other side was visible.

"So they do not all lead to Mythos." Tah'quhal said.

Mr. Monton gasped out, "Is that my farm?"

Just then, a couple sprinted through the area, snagging Barry's attention.

"Mom... dad?" Barry questioned, squeezing his eyes shut.

Tah'quhal turned to comfort his friend, "Bar... Barry, your hands!" He sprinted to his friend. "You are on fire!"

Barry could feel his muscles twitching. The heat coursed up his arms and licked his face. He held his palms upward and slowly opened his eyes. Tah'quhal wasn't lying.

His hands were fully engulfed in a deep orange flame. He could feel the heat, but there was no pain. It almost felt... good.

"I... I'm fine Tah'quhal." Barry whispered with a shaky voice.

Nidalle cut in, "I would not go so far to say you are fine, Barry. This is Talissa's magic taking hold of you."

"That wouldn't make sense." Abhaya interjected.

Nidalle and Tah'quhal both turned to her, a quizzitive eyebrow raised on both their faces.

"What do you mean by that?" Tah'quhal asked.

Abhaya hurriedly got to Barry's side, "I myself am a Keeper. You should all know this, but magic doesn't just manifest out of nowhere like this. Even with Talissa's archaic way of selecting her Keepers and transferring power, Barry would still need to be trained, he would need to know incantations to start."

"I have seen it happ—" Tah'quhal began to speak.

"We have bigger things to worry about right now!" Nidalle cut him off, her finger pointed towards the rift. "This isn't just a portal opening!"

Mr. Monton dropped to his knees with a choked sob. His hands trembled violently, clawing at the dirt as if grounding himself might stop the sky from tearing. Abhaya turned and walked slowly toward the rift, her hand unknowingly reaching for Nidalle. Tah'quhal instinctively gripped Orgí. Nidalle left her hand outstretched, shaking fiercely.

Barry took several long, slow deep breaths. The flames in his hands ebbed and flowed with each inhale and exhale. He could feel his control over the heat with each breath. A final long breath in. The fire danced up his arms. A finale exhale. The flames extinguished.

The sky overhead roared again. This time accompanied by a surge of blue light that caused everyone to shield their eyes. As the light faded, it took a minute for everyone to be able to see again. The first thing they noticed was the sound.

The cries coming from Torvania seemed to have doubled, like all the citizens were now outside. But it wasn't coming from Torvania; it was coming from where the rift had been.

Tah'quhal was the first to have his eyes begin to focus again. "No. no, no, no." His voice cracked as if it hurt him to speak.

"What have we let happen?" Abhaya choked out as her eyesight returned to normal.

"My... my farm?" Mr. Monton asked through a shaky voice.

Barry squinted as his vision returned to normal and the flames subsided. When he fully opened his eyes, what used to be grass fields, followed by the trees of the Magia Forest, was replaced with rows and rows of tents. They were the same ones that'd been placed on Mr. Monton's farm as a refuge from in the wake of Malum's attack. The city that represented the human spirit.

Running through the encampment, Barry recognized quite a few faces. He saw Derek's parents trying to calm everyone. Izzy's parents by their side. And finally, his eyes landed on his parents. His parents now stood in Luminfae.

"Mom...dad?" He whispered again. The flames flickered in his hands again. "Mom! Dad!" This time he yelled as he sprinted towards them. "MOM! DAD!" His voice grew louder as he continued to shout, sprinting through the tents until he stood in front of both of them.

"Bear!" Glorinda, his mother, exclaimed, looking up to her son.

"How… how are you guys here?" Barry asked.

But there was no time to answer. A howl echoed from the woods still remaining in the area. A sound unlike anything Barry had ever heard. A cacophony like a thousand voices whispering through a winter storm.

A large fae, one that Barry might have mistaken for a viking thanks to his wardrobe and braided gray beard, was flung out of the woods, landing on his back. By now Tah'quhal, Nidalle, Abhaya, and Mr. Monton had joined Barry's side.

"That's the tracer." Abhaya said, nearly out of breath.

The world hushed. Even the wind stilled. A shape moved between the trees. Antlers. Eyes like twin moons. Then, sound returned like a scream.

"And that is the Lunabeast." Nidalle added. Her hand again trembling as she pointed at the eyes.

The Lunabeast emerged like a living shadow against the night sky. The towering four-legged creature was cloaked in silvery fur that shimmered with each movement, as if it was woven from strands of moonlight itself. Standing nearly twelve feet tall at the shoulder, its form was regal and terrifying. It looked like a hybrid of wolf, elk, and something wholly alien. Its elongated limbs ended in obsidian claws that left frost in their wake, and its antlers were vast and gnarled branches. They glowed faintly with a pale, spectral blue hue, pulsing in rhythm with the moon overhead.

Barry gave his mother and father a hug before turning to Tah'quhal, "Well, at least we don't have to search the whole forest."

"What are you talking about, son?" Davis asked.

Barry shot a smile at his father, "Oh, you know, just saving the day again."

Chapter 31

Lunabeast

Barry sprinted towards the beast, behind him he could hear his parents shouting for him to stay with them. He could hear Derek's parents asking Tah'quhal about Derek's whereabouts. None of that mattered. Not right now.

Barry stole one glance back and saw Tah'quhal closing the distance between them. As his ally drew closer he shouted, "What's the plan, Taco man?"

Tah'quhal breezed past him, "Use your sword. Do not tap into the magic. You do not know where it comes from."

Barry watched as Tah'quhal leapt into the air, a massive bound that covered the distance left between him and the Lunabeast.

Tah'quhal unleashed Orgí. A strike of pure wrath aimed for the creature's left antler. But the creature was fast–too fast. It was a blink. One second, Orgí was about to make contact, the next, the creature was ten feet away.

"Damn beast." Tah'quhal grunted.

"Lunabeast." A voice from the edge of the woods echoed. "And a pissed one at that."

The Tracer sprinted from the edge of the woods, throwing a large net toward the creature. Again, the creature moved faster than their eyes could comprehend.

Barry joined the engagement, "Okay, are you killin' this thing or catching it?"

"Either is fine. I just need one of the bloody things antlers." The Tracer answered.

That was answer enough for him. As the words left the Tracer's mouth, Barry drew the sword from his back. He flicked his wrist for Braven, his shield to appear.

"Everflame!" Barry shouted and watched as flames danced up the sword's blade.

"Now, that is one fancy tool you got there, human." The Tracer added. "I might even know the fae that mad—"

The Lunabeast charged towards them. It's head slammed into the Tracer's chest sending him flying yet again. Luckily, Tah'quhal and Barry dove out of the way just in time.

A screech cut through air above. This time it didn't draw panic. Barry knew that screech, and he knew the roar that followed it.

"Eriene!" Barry shouted as the griffin descended from the skies, landing right next to him."Where have you been, girl?"

"Ask questions later, Barry!" Tah'quhal demanded as he flicked his hand in the air. Blue essence swarmed around him, formed into a tendril of solidified blue mist and launched toward the Lunabeast. "*Hastam*." Tah'quhal whispered, not needing the incantation to conjure, but willing it to move fast enough to strike the creature.

This time the blow landed. It drove deep into the beast's left front leg, and it slammed to the ground.

Dirt and debris filled the air. It was silent again.

"Damn, did you get it before I could even swing my sword?" Barry asked.

Then, a noise that could make their ears bleed came from the cloud of dust. A low hum vibrated in the air, as the seconds ticked by, the pitch grew higher.

"Shit. Run." Tracer mumbled as he darted for the trees.

Barry leapt onto Eriene's back and clicked his heels into her hide. The griffin took off in a sprint, but not before Barry reached out his hand for Tah'quhal. He pulled the Chieftain up onto the back of his mount, and Eriene went skyward with one powerful thrust of her wings.

Below them, the Lunabeast standing back to its feet. Its antlers were glowing with bright white light.

"That looks like what Derek does with his arms." Barry pointed out.

Tah'quhal leaned over to look, "Get us higher!"

Eriene beat her wings harder, and they rose further into the sky. The pitch of the humming got higher and louder.

"What the hell is about to happen, Tackle Box?" Barry's voice cracked, trying to steady himself with humor.

There was no time for a response. The light erupted from the Lunabeast's antlers. A stream of bright white light exploded into the woods where the Tracer had run. It completely eviscerated the trees in its path. The hum, an unbearable pitch.

As the glow faded, the Lunabeast stalked towards the now eviscerated woods. Where there was lush forest, there was now nothing but dirt. A straight line of complete desolation. It was like the trees and bushes within a five foot wide, twenty foot deep line, just vanished. No scorch marks. No fires. Just gone.

Then there was movement, two legs sprinting as fast as they could, just outside of the damaged area of the Magia Forest. The Tracer survived; he was just outside the blast radius.

"Hell yeah!" Barry shouted from the back of his griffin.

Not a good idea. The Lunabeast jerked its mighty head up toward them. For a moment, it seemed like it was staring directly into Barry's eyes, and the hum started again. The antlers began to shine again.

"Hell no!" Barry shouted as he motioned for Eriene to bank left, and then right.

They zigzagged through the sky, hoping the Lunabeast would not be able to zero in on them. But the humming only continued to pierce their ears as its intensity grew again.

"Turn us around, Barry." Tah'quhal demanded.

"Naw, man. You saw what that thing did to the forest." Barry rebutted.

Tah'quhal placed his hand on Barry's shoulder, "Turn us around. You need to find Derek. You both need to save Johnathan." Tah'quhal's breath hitched. "Let me save you."

Barry's eyes stung before his mind could catch up. Tah'quhal's words echoed, heavy with finality. His body instinctively rolled, and Eriene banked, turning back around.

The griffin hesitated, but ultimately gave in to Barry's command. The turn and descent were quiet. Barry didn't know what to say. For the first time in his short life he was actually speechless. He could taste the salt in his mouth from the tears falling from his eyes. He could even almost feel the honor and pride emanating from his friend behind him– his friend who was willing to make the sacrifice play.

One hundred yards. He had one hundred yards to try and say something to Tah'quhal, but nothing would come out. Part of him knew something had to be done. It wasn't just that he needed to find Derek and save Johnathan, part of Earth was here now, and that beast was rampaging right on the edge of the tent city. Some of his friends were there. Some of his coaches. His friend's parents. His parents...

Heat. His hands began to heat. Heat turned to flame. Barry lifted both hands off of Eriene's back, careful not to burn her. He closed one fist and the flames went out, but they intensified in the other. Open. Close. Open. Close.

Twenty five yards. It wouldn't be long now. Tah'quhal would leap from Eriene's back and strike down the Lunabeast. Barry turned to finally speak to his friend.

"Don't move, Taco."

Barry leapt to his feet on the back of the griffin.

"Eirene, hard left!"

She turned to the left and Barry pushed off her back, leaving Tah'quhal riding alone on Eirene. The fae's eyes were wider than the beast Barry was now going to slay. Barry leapt into open air, the wind howling in his ears. For a heartbeat, he flew. Not on Eriene's wings, but by sheer force of will.

Barry cut through the air in a direct path toward the Lunabeast, a human missile. He drew his sword, whispering its name, and pointed it out in front of him.

Tah'quhal watched in absolute horror. A knot in his stomach tightened harder than anything he had ever felt. He watched as Barry flew through the air, his sword outstretched. One might have even thought Barry was a large javelin thrown by a giant. But, no. It was Barry, a human. A human that until just a few short hours ago, could not use magic in any way whatsoever.

Tah'quhal gripped the reigns on Eriene to steer has back as she banked a hard left. He forced himself to look away, afraid of what might happen next, but it was woefully unfair to make Barry face this alone. Tah'quhal pulled on the reigns in a moment of bravery to face the scene before him. Barry deserved to have someone bear witness to the events that would unfold, regardless of the outcome, and there was no one more suited for the job.

When they were facing towards Barry again, Tah'quhal's jaw hung open. Red hot fire spun toward the Lunabeast, but Barry was nowhere in sight. He was only able to see it for a second before an explosion tore through the air, light flaring so intensely that Tah'quhal instinctively squeezed his eyes shut, but the heat... there was no escaping that.

It slammed against him in waves, a scorching force that burned against his exposed skin, searing his face like the breath of a sun-god. The wind, usually cool and crisp at this altitude, had twisted into something molten, each gust dragging fingers of fire across his arms, his neck. Sweat slicked his brow, only to evaporate in the oppressive furnace surrounding him. The griffin's feathers flared hot beneath his grip. The creature let out a shrill cry, its wings faltering for a heartbeat before pushing forward through the fiery vortex that was still spinning. His lungs had fought against the suffocating warmth, the air thick with the scent of burning. Char, ash, something unnameable, yet unmistakably destructive. Even as they surged away, the heat lingered, clinging to him like a phantom of the blast, refusing to be forgotten.

Eriene landed on the other side, in the clearing that was made by the Lunabeast. Tah'quhal leapt from the griffin's back, his skin still scorching hot, and ran towards where Barry should be.

The dust, debris, and fire slowly settled.

"Barry! Barry, where are you?" Tah'quhal shouted.

He hadn't noticed it before, but his ears were ringing. He could just barely make out the shouts coming from the others who were sprinting over from the tent city.

"What did he do!" Nidalle cried out.

That's when Tah'quhal saw the massive paw of the Lunabeast. It was unmoving and sprawled on the ground. Underneath it, he could see Barry's sword. Tah'quhal sprinted towards him, fighting the pain from his singed skin as he moved the paw out of the way.

There was Barry. On the ground. The grass around him all burned away. The dirt that remained charred black.

"Barry..." Tah'quhal whispered. "Barry!" He was shouting now. "Someone help! Over here!"

Tah'quhal slid his arms under Barry's legs and neck. The coarse dirt peeled his burnt skin off his arms as he did, but he gritted his teeth and fought through the pain. Tah'quhal lifted Barry and sprinted with him towards the tent city.

He saw Nidalle, Abhaya, Mr. Monton, Derek's parents, and... Barry's parents... all sprinting towards him.

"Bear! No!" Glorinda shouted.

Tah'quhal fell to the ground, laying Barry out in front of him. "I do not think he is breathing!"

Nidalle and Abhaya slid to their knees in front of him. The latter started chest compressions as soon as she confirmed the worst. Nidalle began weaving magic.

"No, this was not supposed to happen." Nidalle muttered.

Abhaya looked back her way for just a second, but never broke her routine.

"Please! He's just a boy! He's just my boy! Please save him... save my Bear!" Glorinda cried out. Tears streamed down her face as Davis did his best to stay strong, keeping her on her feet.

Barry lay motionless, his chest unnaturally still, his face drained of life's warmth. Abhaya worked in a frantic rhythm, pressing down on Barry's chest, each compression a silent command. A demand that he return.

Tah'quhal's fists curled, nails digging into his palms, but he did not move, did not speak. His breath was measured, his stance unshaken, but the storm inside him was a roaring tempest. A sharp, foreign tightness coiled in his throat, a weight in his gut that no blade or armor could ease. Tah'quhal didn't notice the blood from his own arms. He didn't feel the heat anymore. All he saw was Barry. Not breathing, not moving. And all he could think was, *it should have been me*.

"It was *supposed* to be me." He whispered.

Chapter 32

Enough

The ceiling above was still singed from the lightning. Bits of debris trickled down every so often as Derek stared through the hole he had made. A chill ran up his spine as the breeze cooled the sweat on his back. The only thing to break him from his trance was the sound of Mia's voice.

"What do you mean you talked to Malum?" Mia asked.

Derek slowly turned his head towards her, locking onto her forest green eyes. No words came from his mouth. He just stared at her. He wanted to speak, but his mind was moving too fast for him to form words.

"Lavender..." Mia placed her hand on his. "How did you talk to Malum?"

Caldera inched closer to him as she said, "Semideus... we need to know what is going on."

He took a deep breath. His mind finally settled enough for him to speak. "It was the same nightmare again." He closed his eyes and shook his head. "But this time, Malum showed up... he was there. Really there... but not really."

Silas leaned against the wall, arms crossed. "Oh, sure. Totally makes sense. A dream demon giving cryptic advice? Happens every day."

Derek cut his eyes at the shadow wielder, but steadied himself before turning back to Mia. "I tried to attack him." He looked down to his hands, studying every inch of them. "But my magic wouldn't work. I tried to punch him, but I just flew through him."

He went on to tell them everything Malum had said in his nightmare. Every single detail. When he was finished, Mia wrapped him in a reassuring hug.

Mia pulled back to meet Derek's eyes as she gently asked, "Do you think it was just a dream, or do you *truly* believe Malum found a way into your mind?"

Derek tried to answer, but Silas butted in, "Dreams can be doors. If I was a betting fae, I would wager three elixirs that he was really in your mind."

A crinkle of the nose, a twitch above Derek's cheekbone. His jaw clenched. He could feel the familiar crackle under his skin. The electricity that always danced closest when his heart raced.

He glared at Silas, and his voice dropped an octave. "Riddle me this 'Shadow Wielder.' Why did the voice in the void tell me not to trust you?"

Silas's eyes widened, "Well, I am no—"

Derek cut him off this time, "Why the hell did Prodomus tell us that one of us does not belong here?"

Silas again tried to answer, but Derek continued. "What are you not telling us, Silas?

It was quiet for just a moment before Silas opened his mouth. Once again, he was prevented from speaking as Stagran and the Oracles entered the room.

"I may be able to help answer these questions." Stagran smiled as he approached Derek. "It is time you learn the secrets of the Trinity."

The lighting in the room seemed to dim subtly, and for just a second Derek thought he could hear the trill of a hummingbird.

Derek wasn't done though. His blood was at the boiling point. Electricity crackled along his arms. He wanted to strike someone, but thanks to Mia's hand on his back, he was able to keep his cool. He turned his anger toward Stagran, but at least it was only his words. "Malum told me the same voice that speaks to me... to you... speaks to *him*! How do I know this isn't all some elaborate setup?"

Stagran raised his hands in front of him, palms facing Derek. "Easy, friend. I am only a messenger."

"Well then, get to delivering the message. I have been to hell and back over the past few months, and I'm getting tired of not having the full story!" Derek demanded.

"I understand." Stagran replied. "I do not believe for one second that the voice I have heard... the voice you have heard... is the voice guiding Malum."

Silas finally spoke up, "Then, tell us Stagran, when did the voice first speak to you?"

Stagran's eyes glared at Silas for just a second longer than necessary. "Derek, Malum's appearance in your dream could have been just that... a dream. Your subconscious giving life to things you try to keep buried. A fear giving shape." Stagran motioned for the group to follow him. "I have something I would like to show you."

Derek and Mia rose from the bed. Derek noticed he was not in his normal robes. He was wearing some kind of linen shirt and lounge pants. He quickly patted his pockets and realized that the Lazarus stone was not on him.

His eyes darted around the room, frantically searching for his robes. He saw them laying on a chair across the room. He marched over to grab them, but still there was no stone. His mind began to reel again. A flash of dread rushed over him. *Did Malum take it from my dream?*

"How long have I been asleep?" He managed to blurt out, not wanting to sound completely insane.

Makria answered him with her calm voice, "You have slumbered for nearly two days."

"Two days!" Derek exclaimed. His mind focused back on the missing gem. "And where is the rock that was in my pocket?"

Mia walked to him, "It was in your robes when we changed you into the clothes you have on."

"We?" Derek's eyebrow raised.

"Oh stop, nobody saw a thing." Mia chuckled.

But Derek wasn't looking for a chuckle. He had been asleep for almost two days, visited by Malum in a nightmare, someone helped Mia change his clothes, and now the Lazarus stone is missing.

Stagran spoke up, "Derek, my friend… why are you so worried about the gem? Something so powerful… so dangerous… should be sealed away, not carried in your pocket."

Derek's blood was beginning to boil again. "I've faced beasts older than this realm. I've bled for Luminfae. I didn't find that gem by accident."

The air went stale for a moment. Stagran eventually relented, "Very well." He motioned for Konta to retrieve the stone.

After a few awkward minutes of waiting, Konta returned. She handed the stone to Stagran, who held it into the air.

"This Lazarus stone is something no mortal should ever possess. The power confined in this gem is enough to raise a drag—"

In one quick motion, Caldera stepped forward, swatted with the blunt end of her spear, and knocked the gem out of Stagran's hands. Derek caught it with a quick outstretched palm.

"It was not yours to take." Caldera sneered.

There was a long silence. Stagran's jaw ticked. The smile that returned to his face didn't quite reach his eyes.

"Very well. Are you ready to learn the truth about the Trinity?"

Chapter 33

The Trinity

Silence. Derek and company followed Stagran and the Oracles down several long corridors, leading deeper into the palace. No words were spoken. Too many accusations were being thrown around, and not a single person felt like now was the time to speak.

The only sound was the echo of footsteps off the cobblestone ground. Each staircase they descended brought a new feeling of ancientness. Before the first descent, the palace still seemed to be worked around the inside of the hollowed out tree it was built inside of.

After the second staircase, the walls were lined with fading murals of battles long past. Curiously, there was a new mural at the edge of the next staircase. It was Derek and his friends facing off against the Manticore and Dragon. Derek found it strange that this mural was at the end of the hallway. It felt like it was placed there because the artist or the designer knew there would not be another battle recorded in these halls.

The next corridor was even stranger. There was no art on the walls, but sigils had been carved into the walls. As they passed, some lit up while others remained unbothered. Derek couldn't decipher what that meant, but he paused every time Mia stopped to examine one.

They were led down yet another stone staircase and another long corridor. This one was covered with tracings of constellations. Derek recognized some of these this time. Especially his father's favorite. The Little Dipper. His dad told him that he loved it so much because it reminded him of Derek. His very own little dipper.

When they made it to the final corridor, Derek noticed there was nothing on the walls except the torches that lit the path. The temperature dropped as they walked along the cobblestone. Shadows danced along the walls, some of them lengthening unnaturally. Derek assumed, or hoped, that it was Silas growing bored with the quiet walk.

Whatever it was, Derek couldn't shake the feeling of being watched. Every step seemed like a judgment being made as he walked down this hallway. He knew he wasn't alone in feeling that either. He felt Mia's breath on his arm as she drew closer to him, clearly suffering the same symptoms of a wandering imagination.

At the end of the hallway, Stagran came to a stop. He motioned to the two Oracles. Each of them went to opposite sides of the wall in front of them. Together with Stagran, they placed both palms on its surface. There was a flicker of light, and the wall began to slide into the floor.

On the other side of the wall was a large square chamber, and at its center, were three floating orbs. One orange, one blue, and one red. Each seemed to be made of obsidian with veins of rich color running through them.

At the far end of the chamber, a large stone arch stood with what could only be described as melted stone in the middle.

Stagran stepped toward the center of the room. He approached the orange orb first, "Still I stand." He looked back at Derek. "This represents Steadfastness," he took a breath. "The kind of strength that does not roar but endures. This Pillar... person... they remain upright, not because they have never been hit... but because they *always* rise again."

Stagran stepped toward the blue orb, not giving anyone time to speak, "Until I fall." His eyes fell to the ground. "This orb honors vulnerability. The fall... the fall is inevitable. Pain, loss, and failure. But falling reminds us that we are alive. It teaches us *humility*... and this Pillar understands that."

He moved slower towards the red orb, but still none of the others spoke. This time he asked a question, "Do you know what this one is?"

Derek understood now. His head tilted slightly down as he said, "I will heed the lonesome call."

"Correct." Stagran admitted. "It is the flame within. The courage to stand, even when no one else does. The voice that whispers truth when the world screams otherwise. This Pillar is the one that can shut everything else out and make the hard decisions on their own."

Derek thought for a long moment. Still, no one else spoke up. He looked to Mia, hoping to find some kind of answer in her eyes, but he only saw the same confusion that he was sure was reflected in his eyes.

Finally, he turned back to Stagran, "But how does understanding what these orbs mean help us stop Malum?"

"The voice from the void has already told you that you can not stop Malum, no?" Stagran said, his face expressionless. "His plan is a river already flowing. All we can do... all you can do now is remove his evil from the universe."

Derek knew that response was coming. Of course, he did. The voice did tell him exactly that, but a small part of him still held out hope that there would be some way to stop these rifts. Stop the merging. His fists clenched, almost hard enough for his nails to draw blood from his palms. His anxiety was building again, turning to anger uncharacteristically fast. It was all just so much. His shoulders sagged, the weight pulling him down as if the gravity of the room had intensified.

Then he felt it. Mia's hand spread wide on his chest. It slid up to his chin and pulled his eyes to hers. Her voice was the calm breeze after a storm.

"Then, we'll find the banks of that river. We'll build a dam. You, me, and all of our friends. We'll do everything we can, Lavender."

His fists unclenched, and a spark of smile danced along his lips.

Stagran continued his explanation, "The Trinity you see, it is not a prophecy. It is a mechanism. A *cosmic* key. The Sacred Dimension, and many like it, respect balance, and this threefold truth is part of that balance."

Stagran pointed back to the orbs. He told them how each one was a living archetype, the words of the fae mantra breathing life into each of them. With his left hand, he pointed at the stone arch on the back wall. "That is the Grand Portal of Welderan. It was sealed long ago thanks to the pact Torviid made with the beings of the Sacred Dimension."

"Then, how do we open it?" Silas spouted out.

Stagran smiled. "Understand this well. The Grand Portal is not like any other portal you have seen before. It is not bound to a single realm or plane. With just one Pillar of the Trinity present... *one* soul who embodies *one* of the three truths... it can open a door to *almost* anywhere. Any dimension. Any plane of existence. Possibly even... other times, if the stories are true."

Stagran let the words hang. "A single Pillar bends reality. But not all doors open willingly." His eyes flicked to the archway. "The Sacred Dimension is... different."

"So one Pillar is like a key, but the portal is actually three doors?" Derek asked.

"And with all three keys, we can go to the Sacred Dimension, and do what exactly?" Mia added.

Stagran responded to Mia first, "That is not for me to decide. That is a decision only for those who travel that *path*."

There it was again. Path. *Everything has been about his path. That's what the voice in the void told him. That's what Malum said. It's all about the path he is taking.*

Stagran continued, "To reach the Sacred Dimension, the Trinity must be whole. All three pillars must be represented. Steadfastness, humility, and inner truth. Only then will the portal allow passage into that place. No substitutions. No tricks. The Sacred Beings who dwell there demand balance, and balance cannot be faked."

A pause. The air seemed to hum with the weight of the words spoken.

"With only one Pillar," Makria added gently, "You may open doors... but not *that* one."

Caldera stepped forward, "Helian reached the Sacred Dimension without your 'Trinity' after Torviid's pact. That is a fact."

Makria rebutted, "There are... *other* ways. The Grand Portals are the *right* way. The sanctioned way."

"The Grand Portals were crafted to lead not just to *any* dimension... but to any point in any dimension. Some believe they can even access time itself." Konta chimed in.

A knot formed in Derek's stomach. As if everything he had been through wasn't already crazy enough, now he was being told there was a possibility for actual time travel with these portals. *Why does the voice in the void want him to know all of this? Does it want him to travel back and stop everything from happening?*

Makria spoke again, "But not all doors are *meant* to be opened."

"The other paths? They demand sacrifice. Blood, or worse. They are not welcomed by the beings who dwell in the Sacred Dimension." Konta added, her voice hardened.

Makria's voice filled the air again, "There is a reason Helian was cursed to carry out the will of the Hellfire Queen. His passage was not granted. It was stolen."

Derek's stomach was churning as fast as his thoughts were swirling. This isn't what he thought the Trinity would be. He'd hoped for a tool. A weapon. Anything to help him fight Malum. Instead, it was just another puzzle to solve.

Mia's voice was barely audible, "What if... what if none of us are part of the Trinity."

"Sounds like we are all screwed then." Silas answered in kind. Still sarcastic, but this time, he meant the words.

Derek closed his eyes again. He could feel each orb in the room calling out to him. His thoughts fought against him.

Is it even possible for one person to bear all three truths? Oh, of course. I'm the Semideus. The miracle boy. I'll just be all three. I'll unlock the Sacred Dimension, rewrite fate, stop Malum, and save the universe. Easy.

Don't be an idiot, Derek.

This isn't about you... is it? Then, why is no one else hearing the voice in the void? If Stagran and Malum are listening to the same whispers, why not Mia? Caldera? Silas? Tah'quhal? Barry? Why not Johnathan!?

Why just me?

Derek's thought derailed when he heard Stagran chant in some long forgotten tongue.

Stagran touched the archway, it gave off faint pulses of light. First, red. Then, blue. Finally, orange. Then, in the common tongue, he spoke, "When the three stand as one," his voice lowered, "This door will truly open. And beyond it... answers to all your questions."

Chapter 34

More

Derek's eyes were unmoving. The three orbs danced in the air in front of him. The events of the last few months blurred together in his mind. Everything that had happened to bring him here. The nightmares. The chaos at Riverrun. The showdown at Johnathan's family farm. Being stuck in Mythos. Learning he was a Semideus. The voice in the void. Mia's confession of love. The manticore. The dragon. It all led to this. This very moment.

Then, a touch, warmth spreading to his skin from hers. Mia's fingers on both hands interlaced with both of his. A quiet reassurance that she was still there. But his mind did not move. She was with him, but he did not truly *feel* her.

The memories relayed like moves in his mind. Two stood out above all others. His eyes stung from unfailing tears. Izzy's death replayed in the theater of his mind.The moment the light left her eyes while he stood there, powerless. Well, not entirely powerless, just... ignorant. He had no idea what he was capable of at the time.

Trey's death came next. This one was worse, not because it was more brutal, but because this time, he'd known. He'd known what he was capable of. And it still wasn't enough..

Another pulse of warmth radiated into his hands as Mia squeezed tighter. This time he heard her voice, "Lavender? Are you still here with me?"

Derek's eyes shifted from the orbs to Mia's face. One of her faded pink highlights clung to her cheek. A small smile tugged at the corner of his lips. He brushed the hair away, sliding it behind her ear with the rest of her brunette locks.

"I'm still here." He said with as much emotion as he could muster.

Right on cue, Silas impatiently blurted, "How do we figure out who represents each orb?"

Caldera's eyes danced between each orb, she whispered, "I do not know how to explain it, but I can feel that I represent none of these."

Stagran's lips formed a thin line as he looked at Silas. "The orbs are not the solution. They are only tools, meant to respond to those who embody their truth. It will react when the Pillar that embodies its truth speaks the line of the mantra associated with it." He walked to the east wall and pressed a loose stone. "But there is a way to speed up this process. To truly know if someone represents one of the three truths."

Stagran turned and walked to the west wall. Another loose stone was pressed. A low rumbling came from the floor, and in the center of the chamber, a stone pedestal rose from the opening. A new orb sat atop it, glassy and white, shimmering faintly with rainbow hues like oil on water. Even from here, it felt... alive.

Derek's trance was now fully broken. He stared at the new orb in front of them, one eyebrow raised.

Stagran picked up the sphere, "This is the Veritas... the orb of truth. It can reveal hidden truths, answer impossible questions, and most importantly... reveal one's true nature."

Mia asked, "Is this why you know so much?"

"In part, yes." Stagran answered. "When the Oracles told me of the Veritas, I peered into it myself. The voice in the void spoke to me for the first time when I let go."

Silas marched toward the sphere, but Stagran held up his hand telling him to stop, "Not so fast. Seeing one's true nature can break your mind. Especially if what you see on the inside is not what you believed yourself to be." He placed the orb back on the pedestal. "If you look inside and can not accept what you see, the Veritas will consume you... your mind. It was once transparent," Stagran said. "But now it is shrouded in that white haze. That is what remains of the minds it has consumed."

Derek forced the lump down that was holding in his throat. "How do we use it?" He asked with a shaky voice.

"There are two ways that I know of." Stagran explained. "If two people hold the Veritas, one can ask a question. Both holding it will receive the answer in their mind's eye."

"Mind's eye?" Caldera questioned.

Mia offered up, "It's when you visualize something in your mind. Usually, it's voluntary. This... wouldn't be."

"The mind's eye is where magic enters your body, child." Makria added.

Konta chimed in, "Every being possesses it. But not every being can access it."

"And the other way to use the orb?" Derek asked.

Stagran nodded and continued, "If you wish to see your true nature, then you only need to hold the orb and recite the Trinity. The Veritas will then show you your true nature."

Mia raised an eyebrow, "But the portal... if it opens to one or more of the Pillars being present, then couldn't we each just approach the arch and see if it reacts."

"You are welcome to try it." Stagran motioned toward the portal. "But if the Pillar does not know which truth they represent, the portal may react... erratically."

"Stagran. How do you know all of this?" Silas asked.

Stagran began to reply, but Derek cut him off, "The voice told him."

The group turned to look at Derek. The confidence in his voice suggested that he was stating a fact, not a guess or shot in the dark.

"You would be correct, Derek." Stagran admitted.

Mia jumped in again, "So how do we decide who should try and see their true nature without endangering anyone?"

"Again, that is a decision you must make. I have had my time, my decisions. It takes a leap of faith." Stagran shifted his focus to

Derek. "I truly believe you to represent one of these three truths, not because the voice has told me so, but because of the actions and decisions you have made. I could see a part of you aligning with any of these truths, but it is up to you to decide which one you truly represent."

Derek's voice came out shaky, nowhere near as confident as before, "If I'm one of them... one of the Pillars, and the voice really spoke to you and to Malum... is it not possible... that the two of you are the other two Pillars?"

A hearty laugh escaped from Stagran as he shook his head, "Stay with us here, Semideus. I already said I have peered into the Veritas. I know I am not a Pillar. The portal has never opened while I am in this room. Hearing the voice from the void does not mean you embody the truth of the Trinity."

Softly, almost as if he was afraid to speak, Derek asked, "But... Malum?"

Stagran's lips pressed back into his straight line. "I told you that I do not believe Malum truly visited your dreams, Derek, but... It could be possible that he represents one of the truths. He could be a Pillar."

Silence.

Derek's eyes again locked on the Veritas. Almost like he knew what it would reveal to him if he peered into it.

Stagran's voice, almost a whisper, broke the quiet. "The truth is waiting. The question is... are you ready to face it?"

Chapter 35

Confrontation

Derek shifted his focus between the Veritas and Silas. Something still wasn't sitting right. The burn in his stomach had returned. Hot, warning, undeniable. He needed answers. He was done with secrets.

"Why do they have a problem with you?" Derek demanded as he turned toward Silas.

Silas raised an eyebrow. "What are you on about now?"

"The voice told me not to trust you." Derek began, his voice growing in intensity. "I should have listened. I don't know what, but something is off with you... and I'm not talking about your piss poor attitude."

Silas took a step toward Derek, but Derek cut him off, "And the dragon, Prodromus... he said one of us did not belong. Why do you not belong here, Silas?"

Lightning crackled along Derek's arms. Shadows coiled around Silas in response. The two stared at each other, but seemingly ready to strike.

Silas spoke, "Prodromus did not single me out. He said 'one of you.' Maybe he was talking about *you*."

Silas pointed his finger at Derek and shadows began to dance around him.

But Derek did not back down. "Maybe he was," Derek replied, "but I haven't hidden who I am. I feel like you are constantly hiding something from us. What else haven't you told us?"

Derek raised his own hand, small jolts of lightning zapped at the shadows, fighting them back.

"I'm not afraid to find out if I belong." Derek said with his chin held high.

Silas called his shadows back. He paused for a moment before replying, "Neither am I."

Without hesitation, they both approached the Veritas. Stagran tried to speak, but both Derek and Silas cut their eyes toward him, a silent instruction to let them settle this once and for all.

Mia's voice rang out, "Derek? Are you sure about this?"

Derek's thoughts zipped through his head. *Does this really matter? Why should he trust a voice that has never truly revealed itself over someone who has bled for him? Why trust a dragon who was trying to kill them? We've come this far. We're together.* He began to lift his hand from the Veritas, but Silas was quicker.

"Which of us do not belong here?" Silas asked.

The Veritas vibrated under their hands. Derek heard a familiar noise–the hummingbird trill. He still tried to lift his hands, but they were unmoving, like a magnet under his skin was drawn to the Veritas. A second later, both Derek and Silas's eyes went solid white.

The ground below Derek whipped past at breakneck speed. He desperately tried to pull at his magic... a last ditch effort to slow himself down, but it was no use. His stomach turned as if he was on a roller coaster. He was floating in the air, a weightless sensation ran all through his body. It felt like some horrific version of a VR game he'd played back on Earth. It was unsettling to say the least.

He calmed his mind, remembering that this was the result of asking the Veritas a question. A few deep breaths and he felt centered once again.

This place was vaguely familiar. On the edge of the fields, he could see city walls that he recognized. It was Torvania. *Why is the Veritas showing me this?*

He hovered over the statue of Torviid towering over the city. *Wait. That statue doesn't look right.* He was correct. The statue of Torviid he knew had its arms crossed over its chest. This one? It was holding a sword and a shield.

A white flash obscured his vision until he was hovering in the Cresidia Library. *At least this looks right... actually... where are all of the books?* Derek recalled that when Johnathan ranted on and on about the library, he told him how the day it was finished being built, scholars filled the shelves with all the knowledge they could find. The shelves were almost empty. *Something is wrong.*

The library doors burst open behind him. A young couple ran into the middle of the library. The man moved like Silas. Same frame, same determined stride. Even the way he clenched his jaw was familiar. The women's eyes? A perfect match for Silas. The woman was carrying a baby in her arms.

They rushed over to the fireplace inside the library. *Well, that looks the same. Even the same suits of armor sit on each side of the fireplace.* The man removed the helmet from the left suit and the sword from the right.

He tossed them both into the fireplace as he said, "*Verum domi.*" The flames in the firebox erupted in a bright blue hue.

That... definitely wasn't in the tour.

BOOM! BANG! BOOM!

Knocks and shouts came form the library doors. "Let us in!" One voice shouted.

Another coldly screamed, "The abomination must be killed!"

The flames in the fireplace died down, and as the last flame flickered out, the ground shifted. Pieces of stone on the floor slid open to reveal a staircase. The family rushed down them, Derek's disembodied form followed.

Beneath this section of the library was a vault-like chamber, almost identical to the one Derek and Silas were standing in, in Calistia before this vision began. The only notable difference? There were no orbs. But there was a portal... and it was open.

The father kissed the child. Then, his lips met the mother's. As he pulled back he whispered, "You will see a new world. One where he will not be hunted. I will not let them pursue you... I love you."

The mother wiped a tear from her eye, "I love you, too." She stepped through the portal, the child's cries echoing as they disappeared.

The man turned back to face the staircase. He drew his sword from his hilt, and his voice trembled as he whispered, "Our story will not end with my last breath. My son carries the rest of it now."

The portal closed behind him.

Three fae appeared from the staircase. Each with a weapon drawn. The first lunged fast with a sword, the father parrying the attack and knocking the fae back.

The second used a spear, sweeping the father's legs. He was fast, but not fast enough. The father jumped into the air, and slammed his foot back down upon the spear, snapping it in half.

The father swung his sword at the fae that had been knocked back. His swing stopped just shy of the fae's neck, and his sword fell from his hands.

The father looked toward the staircase where the third fae still stood. They were holding a bow, but the string was not pulled taut.

The father looked down to his chest, the arrow pierced through his heart.

The father's blade clanged against the floor as he staggered. His hand went to his chest, now blooming red.

He dropped to his knees, blood on his lips. His eyes didn't leave the portal, now sealed shut.

"Find peace... my love."

His body hit the stone floor, still facing the path he'd sent them down.

Another flash of white and Derek and Silas both flew backwards from the Veritas. Silas rolled over onto his stomach, burying his face into his arm. Derek tried to stand, but his knees were weak.

Mia rushed to help Derek up, but he motioned for her to stop. He slowly crawled toward Silas, his arms shaking. When he made it to him, he placed a hand on his back.

"Si...Silas?" Derek asked.

Soft sniffles came from the shadow wielder.

"Silas, was that chi—"

Silas cut him off. "Yes. I think that child was me."

Derek finally got to his feet, and offered to help him up. Silas placed his hand in Derek's. The latter asked, "What does that mean?"

Silas wiped the tears from his eyes. "I think it means Prodromus was right. One of us does not belong here." Silas turned his head away at an angle, his eyes looking at the floor. "I do not belong *here*."

Chapter 36

Reunited

The air in the chamber hung still. No one spoke. Silas was still staring at the floor. Derek's heartbeat was alarmingly slow, considering this was the exact situation that should have his heart racing. At the very least, he should be sweating or have a knot in his stomach, but he remained calm. It was like he was somehow meant to see this moment, and his body knew it.

Mia slowly stepped towards Derek, her hand finding that familiar spot in the middle of his back. Her voice broke the stillness, "Wha... what did you see?"

Derek slowly placed his arm around Mia and pulled her into a half of a hug. His mind might not have been fighting him at this moment, but he still wanted... no, needed her touch. She was still *his* constant. Still *his* anchor.

He rested his head atop hers, his voice calm and steady, "It's not my story to tell."

There was an accepting silence again. The only sound was the faint nasally breaths coming from Silas... faint but persistent. Everyone understood whatever the two had seen, it had left its mark. Silas most of all. His eyes were still locked onto the ground beside Derek's feet. Almost as if he was searching for something in the stone.

Silas's breathing hitched, and a tear escaped the corner of his eye as he pressed his sleeve to his nose. "I will tell you, but I will need Derek's help."

Derek touched Silas's shoulder, letting his friend know he was there for him. The next few minutes felt like hours as Silas and Derek recounted everything from the vision the Veritas had given them.

Mia never left Derek's side, if anything she'd gotten closer. Derek could tell when she realized what they were describing. Her hand gripped his robes at his stomach when realization set in. Her utter shock was visceral without her needing to say a single word.

Silas got choked up at the part where his father died and his mother escaped through the portal, and Derek stepped in to help.

Caldera, the Chieftain of the Magia Forest. One of the generals in Derek's army against Malum. Most likely the toughest, and at times the scariest member of the Enchanted Circle. The fae who competed for the gold medal of never showing emotion with Tah'quhal... unless she was alone with Barry, stepped towards Silas.

Derek stopped talking, afraid of what Caldera was going to say to him. A smile ghosted Derek's lips when he watched her place her hand on his shoulder and then brought him into a hug.

"No one should have to witness a loss like that." Caldera whispered to Silas.

Derek finished up his tale, even though there wasn't much more to say. "And then we were back here."

Silas leaned away from Caldera. He shared a short unspoken thank you and rubbed his knuckle across his eyes, wiping away the tears. "I... I had no idea."

A small frown formed on Caldera's face, "But what does that mean exactly? Was it a different time? How old are you, Silas?"

"It sounds like you have discovered two truths for the price of one." Konta spoke up. "You discovered the likely location of the Grand Portal in Luminfae, and that our friend Silas here is not from this dimension."

Mia's nose crinkled and her brow furrowed, "Well, neither am I. Neither is Derek. Are you saying there could be another dimension that is extremely similar to Luminfae?"

"My sister says dimension, but the word she is looking for is *universe*." Makria added. "Silas may not be from this *universe*."

Makria gave an almost playful smile to her sister. Konta returned one in kind.

There it was again. Another silence. After all he had witnessed, this was the same conclusion he'd come to. Mia was close, but not close enough. Caldera splayed her fingers through her hair and scratched her head.

Stagran took a step towards them, stroking his chin, he said, "Some scholars have spoken of parallel universes before. It, of course, has never been proven... but Silas here... he may be proof."

Silas stepped completely away from Caldera. His eyes wide with horror as the realization set in. "What does that make me? Am I not Semideus?"

Stagran raised an eyebrow, "Well, what would make you think that? Is it not possible that *if* you do come from another universe, they also have a Sacred Dimension there?"

Caldera interjected, "I know you have been through a lot, Silas, but I must ask... how did you learn that you were a Semideus?"

His voice trembled as he answered, "My... my mother. Sh... she told me stories. Stories that I remember from being a little boy." His eyes fell back to that same spot on the floor. "But she never told me this."

"You are Semideus." Derek's voice rang out. "The one chas..." Derek stopped for a second but pressed on. "The ones that were chasing your family. They called you an abomination."

Stagran joined, "It sounds to me that Semideus or maybe even the beings of your home's Sacred Dimension, are not held in a high regard."

"I... I just do not understand." Silas whispered.

"You do not have to." Stagran stepped to Silas, placing his hand on his shoulder. "Not right now. All that matters is that you are here now."

Derek smiled at Mia before turning back towards Silas, and placing his hand on his other shoulder again.

"You are here now for a reason. Whatever happened... it led you to this moment. It led you to us, and something tells me... we *need* you."

Silas bit the inside of his cheek. One more sniffle. One more wipe at his eyes. "You are right. I am here. Let us finish this."

Derek pulled him in for a quick hug and Mia and Caldera joined them. For the first time in a long time, they felt like a true group.

Derek looked back over his shoulder. His eyes landed on the Veritas once again. "Time to find out what part I play in this."

He turned from the group and took a step towards the orb. Before his fingers could graze the surface, Mia's hand tugged him back.

"Wait." Mia's voice shook.

Derek slowly turned to face her, his eyebrow now raised, "What is it?"

Mia looked to Stagran, "Before, you said a Pillar may be able to open the portal without knowing their truth, it just may respond erratically. What did you mean by that?"

Stagran's head cocked to the side, his brows furrowed, "It may not open to exactly where you want to go. Why do you ask?"

Derek's shoulders sagged, "Why don't you want me to learn my truth, Mia?"

"It's not that I don't want you to learn." Mia's eyes were glistening with unspent tears. "But what if you look into that thing, and you aren't a Pillar? Or worse... what if you are, but it isn't what you believe yourself to be and it *breaks* your mind?" Her hand was still tight around his. She closed her eyes as her head angled down to the ground. "I can't lose you to that orb, Lavender."

A regular cadence, the whisper of the heart's song, the beat rang in his ears. Still calm. Still no rising anxiety. He pulled Mia to him. Looking down into her forest eyes, he whispered, "You won't."

Their lips met in a deep kiss. In that moment, nothing else mattered. He knew his truth. He knew he was a Pillar. He may not have been sure which truth he truly embodied, but he knew he was here for a reason. Just like Silas, he knew he had purpose.

Derek pulled away from her and a goofy smile tugged at his lips. He turned to Stagran, who gave him a slight bow.

Derek's chest rose as he took in a deep breath. It fell as he exhaled and took a step towards the dormant Grand Portal.

His hand traced along the smooth surface inside the arch. "Still I Stand." His voice was barely above a whisper. "Until I fall." The stone began to shift, almost as if it were becoming liquid. "I will heed the lonesome call."

The trill of hummingbirds erupted from the stone arch. Derek staggered back, Mia joining his side again. Silas and Caldera stepped forward to be alongside them.

The stones shifted and swirled, the center becoming a gray liquid, and then the colors danced. First orange, ethereal hummingbirds fluttered out of the liquid. Then blue, ghostly flower petals appeared in the air around them. Finally, red. Nothing poured from the portal, but it was a beautiful sight.

Stagran's smile was wide. The Oracle sisters embraced. This was a moment they had waited far too long to see.

Silas broke the silence, "Where does it go?"

"The portal responds to intention. Derek must tell it where to lead." Stagran instructed.

Derek glanced at Mia and Caldera, "Ready to go home?"

Before either of them could answer, Derek heard the voice from the void in his head.

"This is the path."

The voice spoke again. Same as before. Same cold certainty. He still didn't know if he trusted it, but he trusted the path it led him on. Derek's spine stiffened, "The voice seems to think so."

"I'm not sure if that is reassuring or not, but I could sure use a tall glass of nectar from the Fickle Fae right about now." Mia added.

Stagran interrupted, "Before you go. Take the orbs with you. When you decide to decipher the Pillars. You will need them."

Derek watched as Mia opened her backpack and let Stagran place each of the obsidian orbs inside. The red veins of the first orb looked like blood. The blue veins of the second orb, like a river constantly flowing. But when Stagran placed the orb with orange veins inside her bag, Derek noticed a faint glow in its veins.

He opened his mouth to speak, but thought better of it for now.

"You should keep the Veritas separate. I was not told why, but the voice did instruct me to never let them touch." Stagran added as he held up the solid white orb.

Caldera stepped forward and opened her satchel. Stagran nodded and placed the orb inside.

"Take these, just be careful not to use too much too fast." Makria added.

She handed Derek ten small vials of the elixir he had taken before fighting Prodromus.

"Thank you." He said as he tucked them away in the small satchel he was carrying.

Derek turned to the portal and commanded, "Torvania."

The portal shimmered in response, its blend of colors swirling until just orange was visible.

"Let's hope we got this right." Derek added.

Mia interlaced her fingers with his as they stepped towards the portal.

The air inside the chamber turned violent. A sudden gust of wind spiraled around them. A voice called from the far side of the chamber Familiar, stunned, and unmistakably human.

"Dude! Where the hell are we?"

Chapter 37

Tears

Only Abhaya and Nidalle moved. Everyone else was painfully still. Even the birds overhead seemed to have landed out of respect, or maybe they could just feel the grief.

Abhaya continued her frantic chest compressions. Her palms were bruised, her breaths shallow and desperate. Tears fell from her chin and splattered across Barry's unmoving chest.

"Barry... please... not another." Abhaya whispered.

For a moment... just a breath, Abhaya thought she felt warmth beneath his sternum, but it vanished. She shook her head and kept pressing.

Tah'quhal was only a few feet away, his shoulders slumped, his soul beaten. His usually imposing frame looked small, fragile even.

Mr. Monton was locked in an embrace with Glorinda. Her cries cracked open the skies, and Tah'quhal's heart alongside it. They echoed across the valley, a plea to the Gods who had turned their backs on them. Phillip, Derek's dad, held Davis up, acting as a human crutch for the man who'd just lost his son.

The Tracer slowly approached Tah'quhal. He placed his hand on his shoulder, offering comfort in any way possible, but Tah'quhal did not respond.

Nidalle's rhythmic motions came to a halt as her blue essence faded around her. She grasped Barry's hand and her gaze met Tah'quhal's. Barry was gone. She tried to hold in the tears, but they betrayed her when they cascaded down her cheeks.

Tah'quhal rose to his feet. He pushed the Tracer's hand off his shoulder, turning toward the Magia Forest. Without a word, he walked away. The emptiness settling into his chest his only companion.

It should have been me.

His jaw muscles clenched with every step that he took.

Nidalle rested her hand on Abhaya's shoulder, giving a gentle pull. She said, "He is gone, Abhaya. There is no need to continue."

The dirt from the ground rose to the air as dust when Abhaya fell backwards off of Barry. Her tears now becoming sobs.

Erien slowly inched toward her rider. Her paws softly nudged him. When he did not respond, she let out a low hum from her throat. Still no response. She laid her head down next to his, her body in a curl around him.

Tah'quhal stopped in front of the first tree he came to at the edge of the forest. He stared at the ancient bark, his jaw still clenched.

"What happened up there?" Missy's voice rang from behind him.

Tah'quhal turned back to see Derek's mother who had followed him to the treeline. His voice was low, shaky, painful, "It was supposed to be me. I am the protector. I am the Chieftain of Torvania. I am supposed to keep everyone safe."

He turned and drove his fist into the tree he had been staring at. The bark cracked beneath his knuckles, the tree splintering all the way to the sapwood. Blood covered three of his knuckles.

"Barry came to this world knowing nothing about it! He had no training. He had no magic, not until today. He had NO REASON TO STAND BESIDE US!" Tah'quhal's chest heaved as his breaths grew more ragged. "... and yet he never wavered. He made the hard choices. He... he protected *us*." His voice trembled, "He was better than me. Braver."

Missy placed her hand at the top of Tah'quhal's back. "He did it because he believed in you. He believed in Derek. Barry put his trust in his friends, in you. You have done so much more than anyone could have expected."

Tah'quhal's lip trembled, "I never told him how brave he really was."

Missy's reply was gentle, but firm, "Tell him now. Let it out."

The sun was beginning to dip behind the hills of Torvania. Tah'quhal slowly made his way back to Barry's side. He watched as Glorinda and Davis were led away by Mr. Monton and Phillip. He gave a nod to Nidalle who was guiding Abhaya, who was nearly limp with grief. He could see the honor guard heading towards Barry's body with a stretcher made of wood and cloth. A simple hand motion and they stopped in their tracks, allowing him his moment.

Tah'quhal took a knee beside Barry. Eirene lifted her head, but did not move her body.

His voice was still low, but now more steady, "Barry... you were braver than any of us. You fought without power. You bled for land that was not yours. You *chose* us." His voice cracked. "I always thought I had to be fearless, but watching you taught me that true courage is being afraid and doing it anyway." He swallowed hard, forcing down the lump in his throat. "When Tarik and... Sarika betrayed me... it changed me. I have always been cold, but it only made me colder, harder. I thought I would stay that way forever, destined to exact my wrath on the world. But you... you showed me how to move forward."

A tear dropped from Tah'quhal's face and landed in the dust beside Barry's hand. He placed his hand on top of Barry's. "Life feels like a bunch of tiny moments... built up, only to be taken away. But at least there is purpose. The key is a long memory for the sweet, and a short one for the bitter."

Tah'quhal rose to his feet. He didn't know if the pain in his eyes was from the salty tears, or if dirt made its way into them as he brushed them away with the back of his hand.

"Farewell, my friend. Until we meet again."

Tah'quhal turned to face the honor guard who had been waiting for him to finish up. He gave them a nod, signaling for them to retrieve Barry's body, and took a step towards Torvania.

Eriene's wings flared wide. Her ears pinned back as she let out a shriek that split the air like lightning. Everyone turned. Her golden eyes locked on Barry's chest. Then... she roared, not in pain... but in alarm.

Tah'quhal whipped on his heels and his eyes widened as he brows rose on his forehead.

Up...down...up...down.

Barry's chest rose and fell. Slow. Shallow.

His eyes fluttered open, flames dancing in his irises. A soft gasp escaped his lips as he drew his *first* breath.

Chapter 38

Phoenix

Embers rose from Barry's body. He left out a cough, and flames flared from his fingertips. His arms rose and danced like he was reaching for help. Eriene cocked her head sideways as she looked down at her rider. She leapt to her feet and put herself between Tah'quhal and Barry.

What is this beast doing, can she not see what is happening? Tah'quhal thought to himself. Anger started to creep in. He couldn't understand why the griffin would want to stop him. What were her intentions?

"Eirene, out of the way! Barry needs help!" Tah'quhal shouted.

The griffin was persistent. She pressed her eagle head into Tah'quhal's chest. Shoving him back with every step. Tah'quhal tried to get around her, he could only catch glimpses of the embers rising into the sky... more and more by the second.

The anger melted away to confusion, and then to sadness. He wanted to help his friend while he had the chance. He needed to, but Eirene just wasn't listening.

"Eirene, please!" Tah'quhal begged. "He needs my help."

Eirene answered with a mighty roar. One so loud, Tah'quhal had to cover his ears. He could feel the vibration in his chest. He stepped back, hands over his ears, and bowed to Eirene, letting her know he would obey.

Eirene pushed him one last time with her head, this time hard enough to knock him on his ass. She turned back to look at Barry just in time.

The ground trembled beneath them. A swirling vortex of flame erupted from Barry's chest. It covered a ten foot radius around him, the heat distorting the air.

Tah'quhal shuffled back, his hands digging into the dirt and pulling, his feet pushing off the ground. The honor guard that had come to collect Barry's body rushed to guard him and Eirene from the heat.

One of the honor guards shouted, "Sir! Behind us!"

"What the hell is that?" Another asked as they watched in terror. Their feet never moved into position with the rest of the guard, instead falling to their knees in shock.

The other guards held the line. It didn't do much, the heat seemed to reach much farther than what was normal.

The vortex of fire shrieked and howled as it spun violently. Tah'quhal could feel a drying sensation on his skin from the heat. It stung his already burned skin. He watched as the flames caused the shadows around them to dance unnaturally.

The group that was headed back into Torvania turned around at the sight of the fiery tornado. Glorinda and Davis pushed off their escort and ran as fast as they could. His mother's feet stumbled as she ran with her arms outstretched. "What is happening? What's happening to my baby!?"

The only response she received was the roar of the vortex, the fire crackling like a storm of fury and rebirth.

Eirene reared onto her hindlegs, and let out another ear-piercing screech. Her wings were spread wide. Her eyes were locked on the center of the vortex, rhythmic screeches escaped her beak as she danced back and forth.

Nidalle and Abhaya made their way back, the latter still supporting by the other. Abhaya stared wide-eyed at the vortex. Her expression was not of fear, but recognition.

Missy approached Tah'quhal behind the honor guard. Her voice was quick and frantic, "Do you know what this is?"

"I. Have. Zero. Idea." Tah'quhal responded, his voice breathless.

Another screech emanated from Eirene, this one a different tone. It was much softer, almost reverent

The firestorm started to collapse on itself. As the flames shrank, they moved like threads being woven. It wasn't chaotic, it was purposeful.

The griffin bowed her head as the final embers began to flicker. Abhaya fell to her knees, the tears streaming down her face again.

With the flames completely discarded, Barry stood at the center of the scorched earth. His shirt torn and singed, his body covered in soot and bruises. His breathing was labored. Flames engulfed his hands and danced up his arms, the fire licking up to his shoulders in ribbons of red, orange, and even bursts of white. The irises in his eyes still danced with fire, the flame wanting to feed.

Glorinda tried to run to her son, her arms reaching out for Barry, tears falling like a midnight rain, but Nidalle grabbed her arm.

Glorinda's face contorted as she demanded, "Let go of me! I'm going to see my boy!"

Nidalle kept her hold firm, "I will let you… just not yet. That is not just your boy, and if you go to him now, you will be hurt."

"What do you mean?" Davis asked, panic laced in his voice. "He's right there, of course that's our son."

Abhaya slowly rose back to her feet. Her voice was barely audible, "He has become a Phoenix."

Glorinda collapsed into Nidalle's grip, and Davis reached to hold his wife. Their eyes were locked on their son and the fire that danced around him.

Not a single human, fae, or griffin moved. They watched in awe as the flames pulsed. Barry, standing tall, looked at his hands as if seeing them for the first time.

He opened his mouth to speak, but the fire on his arms pulsed and he shut it.

He wasn't sure if he was burning or breathing. The fire didn't hurt, but it felt ancient. Like it had always been a part of him, waiting. Watching. Barry blinked, and the world shimmered with heat and color.

Barry was silhouetted by the last light of the sunset, the flames reflected in every stunned eye around him. A small whisper finally escaped his lips, "What are y'all staring at?"

The fire pulled in slightly, almost as if it reacted to his words. His knees began to weaken. He clutched at his chest, but quickly removed his hand as the flames danced towards his face. His eyes searched the crowd again, wide, worried.

His knees buckled again. Not from pain, but from the sheer weight of it all. His heart beat like a drum against a cage of ash and bone. And for a terrifying moment, he wasn't sure if he was entirely human anymore.

"What is going on?"

Eirene approached her rider. Her head bowed low. Slowly, she put one paw in front of the other until she was just inches away from him. A low hum came from the griffin's throat, and she touched her head to his chest.

Chapter 39

Tell Me

The flames on Barry's arms completely extinguished. Eirene's head was still pressed to his chest as he lifted a his hand and ran it through the feathers on her head.

"Hey, girl." He said, his voice raspy.

Barry looked past Eirene to Nidalle and his mother. Nidalle let go of Glorinda's arm and his mom ran to him. Her arms were stretched out in front of her, and he could see the tears streaming down her face as she got closer.

Eirene backed away, allowing Barry's mother to hold him. Barry's knees buckled, but Glorinda kept him upright. He hugged his mom, a tight, loving embrace.

Still unsteady, Barry managed a half-smile. "Damn, I knew I was hot, but not that hot."

Relief. Glorinda chuckled hearing her son's voice. Her hand lightly smacked the back of Barry's head. "Language, son!" Her eyes met his and the moment grew serious. "Don't you *ever* scare me like that again."

Barry's half smile turned into a full grin. He could still feel the heat inside him, but it wasn't something that scared him. It felt like it was helping him. He felt his strength returning. His back straightened, and he was able to stand without the aid of his mother.

The bruises and scorch marks on his body began to heal. Not just heal, but disappear. His eyes widened as the long scratch on his forearm closed up and left no sign of any damage or scarring.

Davis joined his wife and son, giving his son a proud, wordless nod. He didn't wait for a second before he wrapped an arm around each of their necks and pulled them into an embrace. It wasn't just a "glad to see you" hug. It was a long-overdue, "I'm sorry I've been gone so long" kind of hug.

Barry could see Tah'quhal approach behind his parents. He lifted from the hug, his eyes meeting his father's first. "I know you aren't gonna like this, Pops." He shifted his gaze to his mother, "You either, Momma... but whatever just happened... I think it's only the beginning."

Tah'quhal spoke in a low, calm voice, "He is right. There is muc—"

Davis cut the warrior Chieftain off, "My son has done enough. Let someone else carry this weight."

"Pops, I know you mean well, but this is bigger than all of us. I'm not carrying the weight alone." Barry pointed to everyone around them. "Every person here has a role to play. Derek has one of the biggest, and I need to help find him."

"Dammit, son, you've already given us one heart attack to—"

Glorinda raised her hand in protest, stopping Davis mid-sentence. "That's enough, Davis." She reached up and placed both of her hands on Barry's face and said, "Our boy knows his path. He's just gonna be a tad more careful now. Ain't that right, son?"

Barry's eyes stung from the tears forming in them. His cheeks lifted as his smile grew, "That's exactly right, Momma. I'll have a cooler head next time... no pun intended."

Glorinda wiped her own tears from her face and hugged her son tightly once again. Davis was hesitant, but something in him understood. He joined the hug with his family. When he let go, Barry told both of them he loved them and went to talk with Tah'quhal.

"Glad to see you are okay." Tah'quhal stated, his voice slightly shaky.

Barry raised an eyebrow, "Okay? Bro... what do you mean okay? What the hell just happened?"

Tah'quhal's shoulders shrugged, "I am not quite sure, but Nidalle and Abhaya seem to have an idea." He motioned for the Chieftain and Keeper of Nuetrale to join them.

Abhaya's eyes bore into Barry. She stared at him, almost in awe of what she witnessed, but Nidalle immediately explained what the others were doing.

"Mr. Monton is going to take Derek's parents, your parents, and the Tracer to the Fickle Fae." Nidalle said while looking at Barry. She turned her attention to Tah'quhal, "They are going to try and decide how to manage the wave of humans that have just come through the rift."

Tah'quhal's face contorted. It was like a realization had just hit him, or at least he just remembered what happened before the Lunabeast arrived. "The rift... what if this was not the only one to merge into Luminfae?"

"That is what I am afraid of." Nidalle spoke softly. "If others have not merged, it is likely only a matter of time before they do so."

Tah'quhal asked, "But why did this one move so swiftly? It had only arrived seconds before the lands shifted."

"Perhaps because this one was from Earth." Nidalle stated a little too confidently. "We know the one above Terra led to Mythos. But all the others... we have no idea. Magic is not very prominent on Earth, maybe that is why it happened so fast."

Barry noticed Abhaya's eyes lingering on him. He gave her a nod, but she did not respond. Finally, he spoke up, "Okay... I get the rifts and all." He waved at Abhaya again, who still did not move, "I know I am a good looking dude, too, but she is scaring me a little. What just happened?" He turned to Nidalle, "One second, I'm on the back of Eirene... the next, I'm covered in flames and everyone is staring at me like I grew a second head."

Nidalle's voice was unwavering, "Barry, have you heard of a Phoenix?"

"Like the firebird thing?" Barry asked.

Abhaya finally broke her silence with a laugh, "Yes, the 'firebird' thing."

Nidalle continued, "You were reborn in the fire. Risen from the ashes just like a—"

"Phoenix!" Abhaya interjected.

Barry swallowed. The air was suddenly thicker, heavier. He whispered, "Wait... I was dead?"

The others looked at him in confusion, like they didn't hear what he asked.

Barry's eyes darted back and forth between the Chieftain and Keeper, "Reborn? Wait, wait, wait, you mean I was DEAD!? Like *dead* dead?"

Tah'quhal slapped his hand on Barry's shoulder, "That is why we were all staring at you. You were gone, and gave us quite a scare. Abhaya tried to bring you back to us, but... your heart stopped. Your heart no longer pumped your lifeblood, your lungs no longer drew breath."

"Do not terrify the boy, Tah'quhal." Her eyes glared at the warrior, and then she turned to Barry, her gaze much softer, "You did die, Barry, but that does not matter anymore." She leaned in close, voice just above a whisper and with a light laugh, "Tah'quhal even cried for you."

Tah'quhal grunted, "No, I got dirt in my eye when I rubbed my hand across my face."

Abhaya nudged him in the ribs, "And why did you rub your eyes?" Her face twisted in a smirk.

"That is neither here nor there." Tah'quhal whispered.

Barry's eyes continued to bounce between the bickering group, "But how!? How did I come back? I'm not attuned, I have no magic... and don't say because of Talissa, cause Abhaya said that Keeper magic doesn't just manifest like this." Barry scratched the side of his head. "This was cool when it was just some small flames in my hands, but full on DYING is a whole different ball game."

There was silence for a moment. Tah'quhal was the one to finally speak, "Derek's magic awakened all at once, too."

Nidalle asked, "Do you think Barry is a Semideus?"

"Hell no. There ain't no way I am a *Semidude*. It just isn't possible." Barry demanded.

Abhaya's wise eyes softened again, another laugh escaped her as she corrected, "You may be a 'firebird.' A being blessed, or *cursed*, to rise again from your ashes. Or... you might be a Semideus." She made sure to say the word loudly and the correct way. "I guess you could even be something we have never seen, but one thing is for certain... it was beautiful to watch such raw power, such pure magic, bring you back to us."

Nidalle raised an eyebrow, "Barry, do you think you could summon the fire again? Control it?"

Barry looked down to his hands. Without a word, he turned and walked toward a clearing. With his eyes closed, he searched his mind for anything. Any clue. Then, he could see it... feel it. The embers were still inside him, waiting for his command.

He focused that energy into his left palm. A spark. A flicker. Then... WHOOSH. Fire bloomed in his hand.

"Oh yeah!" Barry shouted. "Hot stuff just got a *whole* new meaning."

He thrusted his hand forward. A fireball swirling with oranges, reds, and occasional bursts of white flew through the air. It landed roughly twenty yards away in a fiery bloom.

Tah'quhal whispered an incantation that Barry didn't understand and waved his hand. Blue essence poured from his fingertips and smothered the small fire. "Easy. How about we try not to burn down anymore of the forest."

Barry laughed and turned back to the group with his smile wider than it had been in quite some time. He shook his left hand and the fire fizzled out in his palm.

"At least he can control it." Nidalle admitted.

Abhaya nodded in agreement.

Barry rejoined the group, and asked, "So, what now?"

"Now, we should figure out how to find Derek." Tah'quhal spoke up.

Abhaya added, "Then, we should head to the Fickle Fae and talk with the Tracer."

The group agreed. Nidalle and Abhaya turned and walked in front. Tah'quhal and Barry brought up the rear.

Barry elbowed his friend, a grin on his face, as he said, "So... big bad warrior cried over me, huh?"

Tah'quhal only looked ahead, "Do you think Mr. Monton will have more tacos ready when we arrive?"

Chapter 40

No Way Back

The Fickle Fae pulsed with life. The weight of the day's events clung to the air, but those inside chose laughter over grief, if only for a little while.

Barry looked around the room. He saw Mr. Monton talking with his own parents. Missy brought Tah'quhal a few tacos from the kitchen. He laughed, watching the warrior scarf them down. The Tracer sat at a table by himself, contently working on whatever would help them find Derek.

When Missy and Tah'quhal walked towards the Tracer, Barry followed. They all took a seat at the table, an awkward silence filled the air.

Tah'quhal broke the quiet first, "Missy. When I saw you on Earth and I entered the rift, it sent me to Ignis. Why do you think the rift opened and deposited your tent city here instead?"

"Well, just before it happened, the rift back home started spazzing out. The colors inside all started blending together." She paused for a moment, as if remembering it caused her pain. "The rift started falling down on us. It was probably only twenty feet away, and we were all certain it was the end, the colors smoothed and showed us the green field we all ended up in."

Trace added, "It sounds to me that something or someone changed your destination."

Silence fell again. This time it wasn't an awkward silence, but an eerie one.

Barry finally spoke up, trying to change the subject, "Soooo."

The Tracer raised his head from the branch he had wrapped with cloth, one eyebrow lifted.

Barry continued, "Can you do it? Can you get us to Derek?"

"I can." The Tracer admitted. "But..."

"There is always a but." Barry cut in.

The Tracer stared at Barry, his right eye twitching ever so slightly, "But... It can only send one of you, and it will be a one-way trip."

Missy shook her head, "No. That is unacceptable. There has to be a way to get them back." She turned to Tah'quhal, "How long is it to my son on horseback," She looked at Barry, "Or by griffin, maybe?"

"Without his precise location, it is impossible to estimate. The Wilds are vast and untamed, but to the edge of the Wilds, it is three days on foot." Tah'quhal admitted.

As the others talked, the heat rose within Barry. Power thrummed just beneath his skin. It wasn't violent. It was willing. Urging. It wanted to help. Then, it clicked. It was telling him to go.

"Give it to me." Barry demanded. "I'll go."

Tah'quhal started to object, but Barry cut him off, "Like I told you after Johnathan was taken... you may feel responsible and we may be your friends now, too, but they were mine first."

Tah'quhal searched Barry's eyes, looking for whatever was driving this decision. Barry let the flame flicker in his irises, a silent gesture reminding his friend he had this.

The Tracer chimed in, almost teasingly, "Now, as far as I can remember, I have never seen someone fight to the death, get reborn, and then sign up for a one-way mission with no return date without a damn good reason. So tell me, who is with them that you love, lad?"

Barry laughed, "Okay the Tracer, yo..." Barry paused. "Wait, what's your name? I feel kinda weird calling you 'the Tracer' all the time."

"Trace." He answered with a wide smile, showing off his crooked teeth.

Barry exhaled a soft laugh, shaking his head. "Of course, it is." He looked to Tah'quhal, "Trace is right, though. Caldera should be with them. And after... everything... I need to see her."

Tah'quhal motioned for Barry to join him alone. They walked to the far end of the tavern, the conversations around them dying down like they wanted to hear what was going to be said.

There was silence for a moment, but Tah'quhal finally spoke up, "When you..." A lump was in his throat, he forced it down with a gulp. "...when you di—"

"When I died. It's okay to say it." Barry placed a hand on Tah'quhal's shoulder to reassure him.

Tah'quhal nodded. "When you died... I thought Torvania lost one of her strongest allies."

"What does that mean?" Barry asked.

"From the moment you arrived in our world, you have never backed down. You have shown resilience that is not present in most fae, let alone a human." Tah'quhal took a deep breath. "But it would not have just been a loss for Torvania... I would have lost one of my closest friends."

Barry didn't respond immediately. His chest felt a little heavy. The tears stung his eyes. It was him forcing down a lump in his throat now as he gestured to himself, "You ain't getting rid of all *this* that easily." Barry joked to try and keep from crying.

Tah'quhal put one hand on his friend's shoulder, and reached the other out for a handshake. "You and your friends are some of the best humanity has to offer. It is an honor to call all of you *my* friends."

Barry couldn't quite hold the tears in anymore, he pulled his hand from Tah'quhal and wiped it across his face, saying, "Dammit, I think I got one of them magical mosquitoes in my eye."

When Barry could see through the tears again, he noticed Tah'quhal's outstretched hand. He placed his hand on Tah'quhal's shoulder mirroring the Chieftain's stance. It was a warriors handshake, a heartfelt moment fueled by brotherhood.

They broke apart with everyone in the tavern looking at them. By the time they turned to rejoin Trace, they'd returned to their conversations.

Nidalle and Abhaya were now at the table with Missy and Trace. Trace held part of the antler of the Lunabeast in his hand. He used a knife from his waist holster to slice a thin piece of it off.

"My family has hunted the Lunabeast for generations. They only appear near the end of their life cycle, knowing their time is nearing, they search out a noble death." Trace began. "My father's father discovered their antlers magical properties when one almost took his life, luckily my grandpa got the better of the creature." Trace held the thin sliced piece up to the twig he had wrapped in cloth. "We can imbue items with magical essence with pieces of this antler."

Barry watched in awe as Trace whispered something ancient and low. The antler sliver shimmered, melting into the bark like wax to a flame. When Trace peeled the cloth away, the wood gleamed like polished silver with two glowing runes now etched into its surface.

"My father made the very sword you are carrying, Barry." Trace admitted.

Barry touched the hilt of Everflame, his expression giving away his shock.

Trace continued, "He made it for a very good friend of his. That man was brave... incredibly brave. You actually remind me of him. But that... is a story for another day." Trace handed the trinket to

Barry. "When you are ready, throw it on the ground and speak the words *hic ultra*. You will be teleported to the Bracelet of Sorrow."

Barry's brows furrowed, "Bracelet of Sorrow?"

Trace explained, "The jewelry your friends wear have a name. The "Bracelet of Honor" was made for a soldier in the First Fae Wars. It was crafted so that if the wearer perished in battle, their partner—wearing the "Bracelet of Sorrow"—would be notified." A smile crossed Trace's face, one only those who'd lost true love would recognize. "It offered a final goodbye. If the Sorrow's wearer ripped the bracelet from their arm, they would be teleported to Honor." Trace's smile brightened, "Luckily, it seems from what I have heard, your friends have found other uses for these bracelets. Since Sorrow can already track Honor, this trinket will track Sorrow."

Barry stared down at the trinket. Part of him was ready, but he knew he needed to at least say goodbye first. He turned to look around the tavern again. There were a few faces he did not recognize that had come in to order a drink. His parents were laughing at a table with Mr. Monton. He smiled, knowing it couldn't be easy for any of them to laugh after the events that had happened, but here they were.

He turned to Missy, his voice full of confidence, flames starting to flicker in his eyes, "I'm gonna go get Derek now."

"Do you not want to say goodbye to your parents?" She asked.

Barry shook his head. "They'll just try and talk me out of it, but this is okay. I'm not leaving forever. I'll be back."

Missy gave him a tight "be careful" hug, patted his back, and said, "Bring my boy back."

Barry nodded and turned his attention to Tah'quhal, "Don't let any more crazy shit happen while I'm gone." He glanced out the window towards the stables where Eirene was eating, "And don't ride my griffin." He widened one eye and cocked his head giving a goofy faux intimidating stare, "She will tell me if you do."

Without waiting for a reply, Barry slammed the trinket into the floor, whispering, "*Hic ultra.*"

Magic answered in a rush of wind and whispering light. When it faded, Barry was gone. Only a swirl of glowing blue essence hung in the air where he'd stood.

Chapter 41

It's Time To Go

The wind tore through the chamber underneath Calistia's palace. Derek was ready to step through the portal when he heard that familiar voice.

"Dude! Where the hell are we?"

Derek spun on his heels. His eyes lit up with joy as he rushed toward his friend. Barry was standing at the back of the chamber, a grin across his face. Barry stumbled when Derek plowed into him, nearly tackling him, and wrapped him in a tight hug.

"How are you here?" Derek asked.

Barry squeezed out, "It... long... story."

Realizing he was hugging a tad too tight, he loosened his hold and leaned back. His hands moved to Barry's shoulders as he looked him in the eyes. He didn't care how Barry was there, he was just ecstatic that he was.

Mia joined them, giving Barry a quick hug as she said, "It's so good to see you."

"Whew." Barry gulped in, getting some air back in his lungs. "It's good to see you, too."

That's when Barry saw her. Caldera. She was standing just behind Derek. Her left foot crossed over her right. Her hands in front of her, clasped together and fidgeting.

Derek and Mia parted and Barry walked straight to her. Slow. Deliberate. Eyes locked onto Caldera's. When he got to her, he didn't say a word. His hands cupped her face and he kissed her. It was deep, hungry, desperate... but sure.

He pulled back for just a moment to say, "I need to tell you something."

"It can wait." Caldera whispered softly.

Barry's brow knotted, "No, it can't. If I wait, I might not get the chance..."

Caldera's face tightened, a worried expression fell over her for just a beat.

"I love you." Barry confessed.

Caldera lunged back into him. Her lips met his again. And again. And again. In between kisses, she whispered, "I love you, too."

Derek and Mia exchanged a tender glance, their hands intertwined as they watched their friends' love bloom.

Derek got lost in thought. It had been roughly seven months since all of this began. A day he wanted to forget quickly turned to a day he would always remember. He was so embarrassed about his first words to Mia. He felt so out of place in his world. Even with everything that had happened since, he cherished moments like these.

Silas had made his way over to them, nudging Derek in the side, which caught the Semideus off guard, "So... she's dating a human huh?"

Derek jumped from the surprise, but once he realized it was just Silas, he laughed as he said, "Don't be that guy, Silas."

Silas gave him a genuinely confused look. Derek could hear him talking, but was no longer paying attention to what he said. His eyes and all his focus shifted to the embers floating through the air. Tiny sparks of flame drifted upward from Barry, swirling like fireflies caught in a breeze. Brief, brilliant, and gone before they touched the ceiling.

"Barry?" Derek managed to speak. "What's going on with you?"

Barry pulled back from Caldera. Derek's gaze was locked on the air above him. The embers still danced about, and his eyes followed one up just as it burned away.

Barry rubbed the back of his neck, "Yeah... about that. A lot's happened since you left. I'd love to fill you in now, but we really need to find a way back..." Barry's face hardened. "Johnathan's been taken."

Derek nearly lashed out in confusion, but Stagran held up his hand and pointed to the portal, "Look, the Grand Portal... it is *changing*."

His mind was still focused on Johnathan as he looked past Barry to witness the portal's erratic behavior. Sure enough, the once fluid-like movements of the portal were now erratic. The colors darkened and spun too quickly, like twin whirlpools spiraling in opposite directions. They crashed into the center, tearing through the current of magic that once flowed smoothly.

Konta slowly approached Barry while everyone else was studying the portal, her eyes looked him up and down. She mumbled, "I... I did not see you coming"

Barry leaned back ever so slightly, his head turned to the side, an eyebrow raised. He talked out the side of his mouth to Caldera, "What's she talking about?"

Caldera whispered in response, "She is an Oracle. She can see the near future. Her sister over there." She pointed to Makria, "She can see the distant future."

Glancing between the two Oracles, Barry asked, "So... what? Both of you missed me coming? I guess I'm just too sly." He smiled wide to Caldera, who couldn't help but smile back at the awful joke.

Silas's eyebrows formed an arch, "She is dating *that* human?"

Derek laughed in response, but before he could speak, the voice in the void brushed through his mind again.

"The path has changed!"

Derek's breath caught in his chest. His eyes darted to Mia. Before he could vocalize what he heard, Satgran rushed to him. The Leader of the shimmering court grabbed Derek's arms and shook him.

"Did you hear it, too?" Stagran shouted, his voice laced with urgency.

Derek nodded, "Yes. I heard it too."

Barry's face might as well have been in a state of constant confusion at this point, he reluctantly asked, "What the hell is going on here?"

A small spiral of shadow appeared in Silas's palm, he nonchalantly answered Barry, "The same voice that speaks to Derek? It apparently whispers in Stagran's mind, too."

Barry's eyes blinked as he watched the spiral spin in Silas's hand, "Oh... okay." His tone started nonchalant to match Silas, but then his voice rose an octave, "Forgive me, but who the *hell* are you?" This was all just too much for him to process.

A wide smile formed on Silas's face, his shadow spiral melted away and new shadows coiled around his body, "Silas, such a pleasure to meet you."

"We have quite a bit to catch you up on as well, Bear." Caldera whispered to him.

"We don't have time. We can catch him up when we get home. Something is happening... the voice said that the path has changed." Derek admitted.

Mia squeezed Derek's hand, "Changed... how?"

Derek's stare locked on to the portal, 'I'm not sure, but we need to go. I hope whatever that portal is doing hasn't ruined our way back."

Derek looked to Stargan, and the fae leader gave him a nod. There wasn't time for many goodbyes, but Stagran did wish them well and good luck on their next journey.

Derek and Mia walked hand-in-hand to the portal first. He was just about to step through when Barry's hand rested on his shoulder.

Barry's voice was barely over a whisper as he said, "Hey, man. Before we go… I just wanted to say, I am *really* happy you've got a way for us to get back. Because the one I took? Yeaaa… that was a one-way ticket."

Derek's eyes narrowed as he looked over his shoulder, "Barry, is this really the time?"

"Probably not… but I wanted to make you laugh." Barry whispered.

"Why?" Derek asked.

"It's your parents… my parents. They're in Torvania." Barry admitted.

Derek's jaw tightened, "What? Why would they—"

His heart thudded. The breath caught in his throat. The implications hit him like a truck. Something terrible must have happened. Why else would they risk coming here?

Derek turned back to the portal. His chest rose and fell slowly as he took a deep breath. With Mia's hand in his, he stepped through the Grand Portal.

Barry and Caldera followed, their fingers laced together as well.

Finally, Silas stepped up. He paused before entering the portal. His shadows clung to him, forming a cloak. "Until we meet again, Stagran."

Chapter 42

Crash Out

The Grand Portal didn't deliver them where Derek had hoped. The instant he and Mia stepped through, his stomach dropped. They were falling.

With Mia's hand still locked in his, Derek reacted fast. He wrapped his arms around her mid-fall and twisted his body just in time. It was only about a ten-foot drop, but it still knocked the breath from him.

Derek looked up at Mia sprawled on top of him. For a heartbeat, he just smiled. She was laughing, breathless at the absurdity of it all. Then, he remembered, Barry and Caldera were next. He rolled hard to the left.

Right on cue, Barry and Caldera came falling out of the air next. Barry did the exact same thing Derek had done. Another thud on the ground. Followed by more laughter. Caldera smiled down at Barry.

She leaned for a kiss, before she remembered Silas was next. She leapt off Barry and rolled to the right.

"Well dang, girl, I thought you—"

THUD

Silas slammed down on top of Barry. Barry opened his eyes, laughing when he saw the confused fae laying on top of him now.

"Listen, if you wanna lay on me... you gotta take me to dinner first." Barry joked.

Silas's face was expressionless. He rolled his shoulders and shadows lifted him off of Barry. He brushed himself off with quick swipes down his tunic, clearly irritated, maybe even slightly embarrassed.

Derek got to his feet, and helped Mia do the same. He asked everyone, "I figured the portal would have sent us through the Anchor, didn't y'all?"

Barry stood with a wince, "I wish it did. That kinda sucked."

Silas looked around at the city he was now standing in. Nowhere near as grand as Meridian or Calistia, he asked, "Where are we?"

"This is Torvania." Derek answered. He pointed his finger towards the tavern, "And that is the Fickle Fae."

The tavern doors swung open. The first to walk out was Tah'quhal. Nidalle and Abhaya were right behind him.

The next person to walk through the doors was one of the largest fae Derek had ever seen. His beard was white and gray, braided, and just as long as the hair on his head.

"When did a viking find their way to Torvania?" Derek asked.

"Oh that's Trace! He made the trinket that got me to you guys." Barry answered.

Trace looked like he was going to follow Tah'quhal, but leaned against the Fickle Fae, keen to let everyone else have their moment.

Then, Glorinda and Davis walked out. Barry smiled wide. He reached for Caldera's hand and led her to meet his parents.

Finally, Missy and Phillip emerged. Derek's eyes began to sing. The tears were coming and there was nothing he could do about it. He reached for Mia's hand, and when he found it, she squeezed gently.

His parents closed the distance between them, and Missy opened her mouth to speak, but Derek cut her off. He threw his arms around her, and buried his face in her shoulder. "I've missed you so much."

Phillip joined the hug, his voice a warm reminder of home. "Heard you've been doing some pretty amazing things, champ."

The hug lasted a few minutes. Nothing was said while they embraced. Even though it had only been two months for him thanks to the time dilation he experienced in Mythos, he had never been away from his parents for this long. It healed his heart being able to see them, feel them, hear them again.

As he pulled away from them, he let out a light sob. "How... why are you guys here?"

Missy looked to Phillip, and then back to her son, "There's a reason we didn't have you return to Earth, a reason outside of you needing to be here. The rifts... they've gotten worse."

"How bad?" Derek asked with a raised eyebrow.

A defeated sigh escaped Phillip's mouth. "It's probably best if we just show you."

Derek looked to Mia, "I'll be right back."

Mia nodded. "I'll go check in with Abhaya and Nidalle, catch them up on everything and try to get caught up."

A smile ghosted Derek's face. He turned to Silas, "That's Tah'quhal over there." He pointed to the warrior fae. "He is the Chieftain of Torvania, and a good friend. He can show you around."

Derek and his parents made their way towards the city gates.

Barry led Caldera to his parents. His hand was slightly slick. It wasn't his sweat. It was Caldera's. It was comical, really. Of all the people to be nervous, he never imagined it would be the badass Chieftain of the Magia Forest.

"Mom, Pops, I want you to meet Caldera, my girlfriend." His smile was as wide as it had ever been.

Glorinda stuck her hand out to shake Caldera's, and Barry could tell something wasn't right. He studied his parent's faces for a moment, his eyes narrowing.

He said, "Momma, you're a hugger... why are you trying to shake her hand? What's wrong?"

Glorinda looked at Davis and she jerked her head towards Barry, prompting him to respond.

"Are you two sure this is a good idea?" Davis asked.

Caldera's shoulders lowered, and Barry's mouth opened.

Regaining his composure, Barry asked, "What's that supposed to mean?"

Davis continued, "It's not like that, son. It's that you two are *literally* from two different worlds. Think about it, once all of this is over, what happens?"

Barry didn't respond.

Glorinda cut in, "Baby, you'll need to come home. Come back to Earth once this is finished. And Caldera here seems very sweet, but she is a *Chieftain*. She has responsibilities of her own."

Barry whispered, "I guess I never thought of that.

His hand was much slicker now, but he was pretty sure it was some of his sweat, too. He looked to Caldera for answers. She only wore a soft smile.

Caldera squeezed his hand and said, "You are right. I will not be leaving Luminfae."

Barry's face crinkled in surprise.

She continued, both of her hands wrapped around one of his, "I love your son. He has shown me more kindness than any male from my realm. He is gentle. He is brave. And he is honorable."

Barry's surprised face faded as he realized she was building to something deeper.

"But... we learned things in Welderan. At least, I did. I believe Derek has known for sometime, just not to the full extent."

An eyebrow arched on Glorinda's face, "And what does that mean, dear?"

Caldera's voice became solemn, "It is not my story to tell. But... I do not believe there is going to be a home for you to return to."

Tah'quhal and Silas faced each other near the Tavern's wall. Nidalle, Abhaya, and Trace were behind them.

Neither of the two brooding men would speak. The air around them grew tighter. Abhaya tapped Nidalle on the shoulder and started to walk away. Trace followed behind them.

Silas decided to break the quiet first. 'Silas. Semideus of Shadows." He reached out his hand.

"Tah'quhal. Chieftain of Torvania." Tah'quhal replied with a dark expression, but did not return the gesture.

Silas tried to step past Tah'quhal, clearly annoyed at the mockery, but Tah'quhal blocked his path, placing a firm hand on his chest.

"What do you mean 'Semideus of Shadows.' I only know one Semiedeus, and you are not him." Tah'quhal demanded.

A smirk popped on Silas's face, "Of course, A small-minded Luminfaeinite thinks there can only be one."

The hair on Tah'quhal's neck bristled, but he remained silent.

Silas leaned towards his ear, "You do not know, do you?" He leaned back and laughed. "Wow! I thought maybe Caldera was just kept in the dark, and the humans... well they are new to this anyways. But it seems this entire half of the realm has been shut out."

Tah'quhal shoved Silas back with the hand still planted in his chest. "Explain." A one word demand was all he needed.

Shadows coiled around Silas. It wasn't an attack, more of a statement. A show that he could hold his own. Begrudgingly, Silas divulged everything that he had showed Derek and the others while in Welderan.

Fear and curiosity, mostly the latter, crept into Tah'quhal's mind. The sky above them began to darken.

Tah'quhal's nose twitched, "Are you doing that, too?"

Before Silas could answer, a clap of thunder roared through the sky.

And then.

Derek's voice cut through the air, full of heartbreak and laced with fury, "WHY DID NO ONE TELL ME!?"

Chapter 43

Tension

For the first time in a long time, there were more conversations happening than anyone could keep track of. The air was thick with tension, laced with magic and barely contained rage, like a spell waiting to explode. Thunder roared overhead and the buzz of magic hummed faintly in the air, sitting on the razor's edge.

Derek stood in the middle of the yard in front of the Fickle Fae. His chest heaved as if he were out of breath, but it was his anger boiling inside him. He looked at Barry, whose face was one of pure shock. Derek knew Caldera must have just finished filling him in on everything. His gaze shifted to Mia, she was still talking with Nidalle and Abhaya, and by now, they knew as well. He looked out into the street where Tah'quhal was walking towards him. Each of his footsteps sparked faint tremors, shimmering lines of energy spreading across the ground in his wake. His wrath was barely restrained.

"WHY DID NO—" He began to shout again, but Tah'quhal cut him off.

"No. Derek, why did you not send word the moment you discovered the Wilds were a whole damn land of their own? Their own governance, their own traditions... a part of Luminfae." His tone wasn't cruel, but it was frustrated, burdened.

Derek sneered at the Chieftain, "Oh, that's rich. Real damn rich, Tah'quhal. Why didn't we send word? Maybe because we were trying to figure out what the HELL WAS GOING ON?" He paused for half of a second, "It seems you were keen on keeping the tent city on Earth, in MY hometown a secret." He motioned his hands around, pointing at each of the group. "Malum has hurt all of us, and you, and who the hell knows who else, didn't even bother to tell me what was really happening back home."

Tah'quhal tried to speak, but Derek didn't let him, "You didn't think I should know about *that* chaos?"

Barry stepped in, "Bro... I get it. But you could've told all of us about this whole dimension-merging crap way before now. Don't act like you're clean in this."

"I was GOING TO, BARRY." Derek lashed out at his friend. "Mia showed me why it was wrong to keep it from all of you. I was going to tell everyone as soon as I saw them. But *that*." He pointed to the tent city outside of Torvania's gate, "That was hidden from me for at least a month."

Caldera tugged on Barry's hand, her voice calm but commanding, "Derek... when Mr. Monton told us what was happening, you were still in a dark place. You had been through too much. We did not want to burden you." She glanced down. "Even Johnathan agreed."

Derek's body trembled. His core buzzed with unspent power. He couldn't believe what he was hearing. The truths hit like hammers, each one shattering a piece of the trust he thought he had built. Everything had been going so good for him. His magic was under control for the most part. The anxiety? Almost never a problem. And when it was? Mia was there to help him.

Thunder cracked overhead. White light began to shine from his hands. The lightning that normally crackled on his arms, spun into mesmerizing bands that rotated around his arms, small arcs lurching off at random intervals.

"Johnathan *knew*." He bellowed. "WHO ELSE KNEW?"

It took a minute for anyone to react. But Tah'quhal raised his hand first. Then, one by one, more hands went into the air.

Nidalle and Abhaya. Derek nodded, them he could almost understand.

Mr. Monton. That one made sense. He is the one who told everyone else apparently. Derek was still pissed that he didn't tell him, though.

Barry's parents and his own parents. Again. He was angry, but they were there, so of course they knew.

Caldera and... Barry. Derek bit the side of his cheek and his nose crinkled. Caldera, again he almost understood it, but Barry? No. He couldn't accept that.

Then, his eyes landed on Mia.

She looked right at him. No hiding. No excuse.

And then… slowly… her hand rose.

Derek felt the air punch from his lungs, not from the storm above, but from the one inside his chest.

The thunder stopped roaring. In its place, rain began to fall. Derek's chest felt heavy now, like was fighting to breath.

His voice softened, "Yo…you *knew*?"

"I was going to tell you. I just didn't know the right—"

"How about when you were lecturing me for not telling you everything I saw?" Derek cut her off.

Mia reached for his hand, but he pulled away. "You told me to trust you… but you didn't ever *trust* me." A tear fell. Just one. "I need to be alone." His voice cracked like the sky above him.

"Derek." Tah'quhal's voice cut through the air.

Derek didn't stop. Another step.

"Derek Stratum!"

Still, another step.

"You bled for this world. As did I. From warrior to warrior, I call out to you. Hear what I have to say." Tah'quhal demanded.

Derek stopped. He didn't turn around.

Tah'quhal continued, "We all have secrets. Whether it is out of fear, guilt… or trying to protect the people we care about, we keep those secrets close to the heart." Tah'quhal looked to Barry, and then back to Derek. "Not so long ago, someone showed me that anger, revenge… wrath, is not the only path. I promise, you will have time to be mad at us, maybe even hate us for a time, but right now... we need a plan to save Johnathan."

Derek turned back around, his eyes were red and stung from unshed tears. His voice was hoarse as he said, "I *was* mad. Mad that you all kept this from me. Who knows, maybe I could have helped figure something out?" He turned to Mia, "But now... I'm hurt. I don't underst—"

Derek froze. His breath caught. The world had gone... quiet. The buzz of magic that was present, familiar... had shifted. Not vanished. Warped. Wrong. He turned, eyes scanning the sky. And then, he saw it. Blood-red clouds. The storm he had summoned had changed, and it wasn't his doing.

Panic laced his voice as he turned to Silas, "Is this you?"

Silas's eyes searched the sky, "That... that is not of *my* doing."

Barry turned around, "Oh shit. Not this again."

A massive meteor emerged from behind one of the clouds, a long tail streaking through the sky. It was aiming right for them.

Derek yelled, "Anyone who can fight, get behind me! Everyone else, get inside!"

Chaos erupted again. The parents ran inside the Fickle Fae and peered out the windows. Civilians panicked in the streets, scrambling to get as far away as possible. The rain turned to steam as the heat of the meteor drew closer and closer.

Just feet above the ground, the meteor halted. A burst of blinding orange light flooded the yard. The heat licked everyone's skin. Derek and the others raised their arms to shield their eyes.

As the light dimmed, Malum stood center stage, his face twisted in an awful, hungry grin. Sarika was to his left, Trey to his right. Beside Sarika stood a raven-haired woman whose gaze cut deeper than any blade. Something ancient and venomous simmered behind her smile. Beside Trey, was a hooded man with an ominous and unreadable aura.

"Do you like the show?" Malum sneered at Derek. His voice slithered. "I thought it would be... *poetic* to arrive the same way I entered your dream."

Chapter 44

Out Of Time

"Poetic?" Derek spat at the ground, eyes locked on Malum. "Why show your face now, after hiding for over a month?"

Malum looked at the spit in the dirt. His grin grew wider. "Oh, my boy. I have already told you everything you need to know."

"Yeah? Well let me tell you everything that *you* need to know." Derek took a step forward. His stomach was a knot, his anger boiling back up. The lightning coiled around his arms again. "We are going to put an end to all of this. Right here. Right now."

Malum laughed hysterically, "Oh, really?" he stopped to catch his breath. "I do not think so. Our story is *far* from over."

Tah'quhal interjected, "If not to fight, then why are you here?"

"My, my. So impatient. You really are more like Torviid than you realize." Malum taunted. "He never was one for... *theatrics.*"

"Give us back our friend," Barry growled, "and maybe we won't bury you right here."

Malum cackled again, this time his entourage joined him, all of them except Trey.

Malum made eye contact with Barry, "If it is not the one that escaped Talissa's... *adventurous* claws."

"Where is the succubus anyways?" Abhaya asked.

"I was hoping someone would ask." Malum responded. "She is tending to the little Johnathan as we speak... hopefully she keeps him alive." He cut his eyes back to Derek, "I have such *big* plans for him."

The door to the Fickle Fae swung open. Mr. Monton sprinted out of the Tavern, tears already starting to drip down his face.

"Just give me my son back! This isn't right, he did nothing to you!"

Abhaya grabbed Mr. Monton's arm, desperately trying to keep him from putting himself in danger.

"Did *nothing* to me!?" Malum looked at Mr. Monton with pure disgust in his eyes. "Your son helped Derek raise an army in a matter of a few days. He uncovered an ancient spell to try and stop my plans. He helped Derek strike me down! And they almost succeeded."

The raven-haired female joined Malum's side, she laced her fingers into his as Malum continued, "That was *almost* the end of it." He shifted his focus to Tah'quhal, "Torviid is not the only one capable of striking a deal with certain *beings*. Time will tell who made the better choice."

Thunder roared overhead. Lightning sparked from Derek's arms. He squeezed his knuckles into his palm hard enough for them to pop. "Just tell me why you are here."

Malum smiled at Derek. With his free hand, he made a flicking motion in the air. Red essence poured from his fingertips and rained down to form an image. It curled into three spinning orbs. "Because you have something that *I* need." His hand moved to point at Mia, "Well, *she* does."

Derek's eyes grew wide. That knot in his stomach started spinning. The lightning around his arms arced out even further. He shifted his feet like he was getting into a fighting stance.

Malum clicked his tongue. "Tsk. Tsk. You can try, Derek. You can try to stop me, but I believe you will find that some things have... *changed.*"

Changed, Derek thought. *Is this what the voice meant by the path had changed? The voice in the void... had it warned him about this moment and he was too blind to see?*

Trey stepped forward. His eyes bore into Derek's. No words came out of his mouth, but there was a begging in his stare, a call for Derek to stand down. Trey didn't want any part of what was about to happen, but he would play his role if necessary.

Trey's nose crinkled when Derek didn't move. One long inhale. One long exhale. His veins popped, neon green visible from beneath his skin. Green flames flickered to life along his fingertips.

Malum spoke again, "Would you like a demonstration? Or will you make this easy and give me the orbs?"

Derek clenched his fist. He never looked back to Malum. He stared into Trey's. *Just give me something*, he thought. He just needed a sign that his friend was still there.

I don't want to do this again. His thoughts were spiraling. Trey had already *died* once because of Derek, or at least he thought he did. It all seemed so real. The muscles around his throat contracted. He swallowed hard, forcing down the lump.

That's when he saw it. Trey's eyes glanced back toward Malum, just for a second. Derek darted his own eyes, he noticed the raven-haired woman whispering something to Malum. Her eyes... they were the same neon green as the fire dancing along Trey's fingertips. Trey flicked his head towards Malum. It was a quick flick, hardly noticeable, but Derek saw it.

Trey was standing directly in front of Malum. Derek didn't hesitate. Already in a fighting stance, his left arm in front of his right, his right foot balancing on its ball, he threw a quick jab in the air towards Trey. The lightning rings around his arm fired off of him like a shot from a gun.

Thunder cracked overhead, the loudest that Derek had ever heard. Trey dodged. He saw Derek's move and turned to the right just in time. The fist was nowhere near him, but he watched as the lightning zipped past him.

It raced toward Malum, but the hooded man was too fast. Just as Derek swung, the hooded man disappeared in a burst of feathers, reappearing in front of Malum, blocking the lightning's path. The magical electricity should have pulverized the man, but he got his hands up just in time. A wall of red essence shielded him from the blast, the force of the hit knocking his hood off.

Beneath the garment, eyes darker than the void Derek had traveled to were revealed. A too long and pointed nose sat in the middle of his face. Feathers crowned his head in place of hair.

Silas gasped, "Everan!"

There wasn't any time to question Silas. Everything next happened so quickly.

Malum chuckled as he looked at the raven-haired woman first, "My sweet Circe... it seems that they would prefer a demonstration." He turned to Sarika next, "Retrieve the damned orbs!" He demanded.

A twisted smile formed on Sarika's face, her red hair dangling in front of her eyes, as if she had been waiting to be released. Waiting to cause chaos. She moved faster than Derek or Tah'quhal had ever seen her move. She had always had great magical control over the wind, but now she was the wind itself. One second, she was standing beside Malum, the next... she was behind Mia.

There was no dagger to Mia's throat this time, not like when Sarika had captured her and brought her to the top of Malum's tower as he and Derek faced off. No. She only ripped the backpack off Mia's back.

"Derek!" Mia screamed, her voice cracking through the air.

When Mia screamed, Derek turned to see the horror. He knew the panic she must have been facing. He took a step towards her.

Snap

Derek couldn't move. It was like every muscle in his body had frozen. Paralyzed.

"Not so fast, young Semideus." Malum's voice hissed behind him. "I told you some things have changed."

Tah'quhal had seen enough. He drew Orgí from his back. The blade rippled with purple energy and he charged at Malum.

Snap

Tah'quhal was frozen now as well.

Barry shouted, "Oh, to hell with this!" He flicked his hands towards the ground and they ignited with flames.

Trey looked to Barry, pure confusion in his eyes.

"Oh, you have some new tricks as well I see." Malum taunted.

Barry started towards Trey, "Come on, Trey. We've got shit to sett—" he felt a searing pain in the back of his head as he fell to the ground. His ears rang in a high pitched tone as he lost consciousness.

Caldera screamed, 'Traitor!" As Nidalle walked past Barry's unconscious body, a large, bloody rock in hand. Caldera swung her spear in a large arching motion, ready to strike Nidalle down.

Clap

The clap reverberated through the still air. It was so loud it could have been mistaken for Derek's thunder. Caldera was frozen, and everyone who was not aligned with Malum was stuck in place.

Malum's voice rang out again, "Nidalle, Sarika, it is almost time for us to take our leave."

Nidalle walked past Abhaya. She took a moment to look at her friend, there was even a hint of sorrow in her eyes. But they were not met with the same emotion. Abhaya's eyes only showed hatred for the fae.

"Bii…" Abhaya struggled to move her lips. Her breaths came ragged, fighting against Malum's spell. "Bit…Bitch." She finally managed to get a single word out.

Nidalle looked away and took her place next to Malum's entourage.

Sarika twirled a section of Mia's pink highlights on her finger. Her eyes met Derek's and she slowly walked to him. "For old times sake." she gloated. Her lips pressed against his. With a wink, she walked away. As she sauntered past Tah'quhal, Mia's backpack in hand, she stopped. She turned slowly and stared at him. Her finger ran down his chest, "If only you would have stayed with me. You could have been on the right side of history." Her giggle filled the air and she joined Malum's side once again.

Malum held his hand in the shape of a claw and rotated it counter-clockwise. As he did, Derek's paralyzed form spun to face him.

"I would just end you now, but the voice that speaks to me…" the right corner of his mouth lifted in a smirk, "To *us*… I want it to watch as I tear you limb from limb. And Derek," His smirk vanished as his lips formed a straight line. "The next time we meet. I *will* destroy you."

Derek watched, unable to move, as Circe began to move her hands through the air.It would have been mesmerizing if these were different circumstances. He felt his nose twitch. The muscles in his body gave an inkling of response as he tried to move them. This was his chance.

He fought with everything he had. He felt it. The bicep on his left arm twitched. His fingers wiggled. The hair on his arms stood up, the lightning was ready to surge. He strained to open his mouth, but when he did, he released an almost animalistic roar, "MALUM!!"

Time seemed to slow.

A green ring of hellfire sprouted from the ground around Malum and his allies. It was no taller than a couple of inches when Derek shouted. His heart pounded against a prison of still flesh. A thousand pins pierced every joint. The air tasted like copper. Still, he pushed and yelled again, "MALUM!" The scream tore from his throat like a wounded animal.

The hellfire circle was a little over a foot tall now. When he extended his left arm fully, lightning lurched from his fingertips. Not rings like before, the lightning formed a bow of electricity in front of him. He forced his right hand forward, and two arrows of lightning appeared. With everything Derek had, he pulled his right hand back just past his ear and opened his grip. Thunder boomed as the two projectiles raced toward Malum.

Malum wasn't as fast as Everan or Sarika, but he still managed to turn. Unluckily for him, he didn't turn far enough. One of the arrows struck their target. Electricity erupted inside the ring of hellfire. It danced in the air above them, cracked with blue and golden sparks.

A smirk curled at Trey's mouth when Malum yelled out in pain. Derek pushed his right hand forward again, two more bolts appearing, but the hellfire circle grew too fast, completely engulfing Malum and his lackeys. Derek loosed the bolts into the sky, the thunder roaring once more.

Just as fast as it appeared, the dome of green flames vanished. Only the echo of Malum's scream could be heard through the thunder.

Chapter 45

It Never Ends

The silence fell all at once. Like a cut string.

Bodies that were frozen mid-motion, collapsed to the dirt with sickening thuds. Human and fae alike, crumpling like puppets whose strings had been severed. A groan echoed somewhere in the haze, followed by coughing, the rustle of gravel, and the soft sobs of someone realizing they were able to move again.

Caldera was the first to react. She dropped beside Barry, already rolling him onto his back with trembling hands. His face was pale and bruised, but when his eyes fluttered open, that familiar grin pulled at his lips.

"Am I dreaming?" he croaked, voice thick and dazed. "Cause I'm seeing the most beautiful girl in the world."

She let out a choked laugh and leaned down to kiss him, her fingers in his hair. It was quick, desperate, but when she pulled back, Barry blinked up at her again.

"Oh damn," he whispered. "There's two of you."

Caldera snorted, wiping at her eyes. "Let me get you inside and get you looked at."

"Girl," Barry mumbled as she helped him sit up, "you can look at me anytime."

Mia ran past them, heart hammering in her chest. She found Derek on his back in the dirt, white dust clinging to his dark clothes, his face half-buried in a patch of trampled grass.

"Derek!" she gasped, dropping to her knees. She cradled the back of his head, and reached for his hand. He didn't move at first, but slowly... slowly... his fingers curled and laced into hers.

His eyes opened, just barely. He looked up at her like she was far away.

"I'm so sorry," Mia whispered. Her voice cracked. "I'm so, so sorry."

Derek's voice was quiet, raspy. "I know. I'm just... hurt."

He didn't mean the bruises. Not the magic. Not the fight.

"You wanted me to trust you," he continued, "but you couldn't trust me."

Tears gathered in Mia's eyes. "I love you, Lavender," she whispered. Her thumb brushed his temple. "I love you."

Derek didn't answer. Not right away. He turned his head slightly, looking around.

Silas was helping Tah'quhal to his feet, shadowy wisps still curling from his arm. Caldera supported Barry as they limped toward the door of the Fickle Fae. Mr. Monton was at Abhaya's side, trying to coax her up, but her face was slack with grief. The betrayal in her eyes mirrored what they all felt. Nidalle had cut deep.

Derek turned back to Mia. Her forest green eyes shimmered like trembling leaves. He could see every detail of them now, see the way her lips trembled and her hand held firm despite her shaking.

This isn't the time for pettiness, he thought. *We've already lost so much. I don't want to lose anymore.*

Maybe, just maybe, if they'd trusted each other a little more... if they hadn't spent so much time arguing, they could've seen the warning signs. They might have stopped Nidalle before Malum ever showed his face.

"I love you, too," he whispered.

Mia let out a soft, shaky breath, and kissed him. Not desperately. Not to prove anything. Just full of truth.

Then, she helped him up, wrapping one arm around him as they walked together toward the tavern.

Inside, the Fickle Fae was a wreck. Tables overturned, chairs smashed, glass glinting in the corners of the room. But everyone's eyes were on him as Derek entered. Silence spread like fog.

His parents rushed forward. Missy gripped her son's arm tightly, while Phillip looked him over.

"Are you okay?" Phillip asked, his voice thick with worry.

Derek gave a tired nod. "Trust me. We've been through worse."

The crowd was a beautiful blend. Fae and humans, warriors and rebels, townsfolk and leaders. They were all waiting. Waiting for him.

He took a breath. Mia placed a hand in the small of his back, grounding him.

"I'm sorry," he began, voice loud enough for all to hear. "I don't know what to do now. I thought... I thought when we got here, we'd have time to form a plan. Time to prepare before Malum showed up again. But that wasn't in the cards."

No one spoke.

"The things we learned in Welderan... they might not matter now. Stagran said the orbs were meant for something... and now Malum has all of 'em."

A beat passed.

Caldera stood, pulling her satchel off her shoulder, and pulled something from within.

"Not all of them," she said, holding up the glowing Veritas Orb. "They never checked me."

Gasps rippled through the tavern.

Derek's eyes widened. "The Veritas?"

"What does that mean?" Tah'quhal asked, his voice still hoarse.

"It means," Silas said, stepping forward, "we can still confirm who the three Pillars are."

"And then, we can open the portal," Caldera added. "To the Sacred Dimension."

"We just might not know what to do once we get there," Mia said.

Derek added, "But if we can get there. We still have a chance."

Barry, who'd slumped in his chair, raised a hand. "How do we even find the portal?"

Derek turned to Silas, then back to the group. A small, knowing smile tugged at his lips. "I think me and Silas know exactly where that is."

Missy stepped closer, eyes filled with concern. "Derek... what's going on?"

He looked at his mother, and his expression softened. "It'll be easier to show you."

Turning toward the tavern door, a bright flash of light swallowed him, and he was gone in an instant.

Mia's heart dropped. "Derek?" She spun, her fingers fumbling toward the bracelet on her wrist, panic blooming fast. "Where did he go?!"

She pulled at the bracelet.

"Hold on there, dear," Trace said, suddenly at her side.

Mia blinked. "Who the hell do you think you are?"

Before Trace could answer, Mr. Monton stepped in. "He's Trace. And he's the one who might have figured something out... why Derek couldn't see the voice in the void last time."

Mia turned to him, breath catching. "What do you mean?"

Mr. Monton's voice was low, measured. "He believes... it's because you followed Derek. That the void, the voice... wasn't meant for your eyes. Only his."

Mia's face fell. "So I'm just supposed to stand here? Do nothing? Take this stranger at his word?"

Tah'quhal spoke up, "He may be a stranger to you, but Trace is the one who crafted the bracelets you and Derek wear."

"And, he got me to you guys, remember?" Barry added.

Derek's parents gently embraced Mia from either side. Missy whispered something comforting, but it barely registered.

Mia stared at the spot where Derek had vanished, her fingers still trembling.

Barry leaned on Caldera like a crutch, a fresh bandage on his temple. He glanced down at her, her eyes meeting his.

"There just isn't an easy day in Luminfae," he muttered.

Caldera gave him a tired smile and tucked the Veritas back into her bag. "No," she said softly. "There never is."

Outside the tavern, the thunder rumbled. But this time? It felt more like an echo than a warning.

Chapter 46

The Void

White light seared behind Derek's eyelids. He blinked rapidly, expecting to see the ceiling of the Fickle Fae, or maybe the sun filtering through its windows. Instead, all he saw was darkness. It was not an empty void like before. This was something else. The air around him buzzed faintly with life.

Then, came the sound. Soft at first, like tiny flutes... and then, louder. A chorus of trills and chirps that echoed through the stillness like water over stone.

Hummingbirds? Derek thought.

He sat up, heart pounding. The ground beneath him felt like moss, cool and damp, though no dew touched his fingers. With a breath, he summoned the white light into his palm. The orb pulsed, casting its glow out in trembling waves, and the forest revealed itself.

It was beautiful. Tall trees with glistening leaves swayed as if underwater. The air shimmered with iridescent mist. Dozens... maybe hundreds of hummingbirds made of smoke and light darted through the trees, trilling with impossible harmony. They were almost translucent, yet more vivid than anything he'd ever seen. Reds, purples, blues. Each one left a soft glowing trail in the air, like they were being drawn in real time by some celestial painter.

Derek rose to his feet slowly, unsure whether he was dreaming. His boots made no sound on the mossy floor. The forest felt... ancient, like it had been waiting.

And then, in the distance, a voice. It was faint at first. Someone was mumbling, talking to themselves.

He moved toward it cautiously, weaving between glowing tree trunks, the birds zipping past his head. The voice grew clearer, weathered and soft, but somehow familiar.

Derek slowed as the trees opened into a small clearing.

There, hunched and barefoot, was a frail old man with silver hair and skin like crumpled paper. He wore no robe or crown, just tattered clothes and bare arms. He placed a wrinkled hand on a nearby tree. The second his fingers touched the bark, the entire trunk burst into flame. It didn't burn naturally. It withered, crumbling into ash in seconds. As the trunk disintegrated, several of the hummingbirds dove down into the ash and vanished.

Derek's breath caught. He took a step back, a twig snapping beneath his boot.

The old man turned. His eyes were peculiar, one gold, one clouded white. They met Derek's with an impossible weight.

"Derek Stratum," he said gently. "It is time we met."

Derek opened his mouth, unsure if he should speak, or run, or scream. He hadn't just heard this voice before. He had felt it in his bones, in his dreams, in his moments of crisis. It was the voice in the void.

Before he could react, the old man snapped his fingers, and in a blink, Derek found himself seated on a mossy log across from him. No transition. No motion. Just... here.

"Welcome," the old man said. "To the Forest of Life."

The words hung in the air like mist. Derek stared at him, unsure what to say.

The old man turned, gazing at the distant trees. "Tell me, Derek. Do you know why you are here?"

Derek shook his head slowly.

The man's expression remained calm, but his voice took on a gentle command. "Use your words, son."

Derek narrowed his eyes. The tone... there was something oddly familiar in it, like a father, or a teacher, or someone older than either.

"No," Derek said. "I have no idea why I'm here. And honestly?" He leaned forward. "If you could bring me here all along, why not just do that from the beginning? Why the riddles? Why the voice in my head? Why the cryptic crap and wild goose chases?"

The old man gave a tired sigh. "Why give someone answers... when what they truly need is understanding?"

Derek didn't respond.

The man went on. "When I reached out to you over a month ago, I tried to bring you here. I tried to let you see me. But *someone* followed you." His eyes narrowed. "*She* was not meant to see this place."

Derek's jaw tightened. Mia.

"Where am I, really?" he asked.

"Somewhere outside of time."

"The Sacred Dimension?" Derek guessed.

The old man laughed, the sound like wind rustling dead leaves. "Oh no. You must venture there on your own. All in due time."

"Out of time..." Derek muttered. Then, his eyes widened. "We must be in Mythos."

The old man recoiled, his expression twisted in revulsion. "Heavens no. That place is a rotting limb. A foul thing I have yet to burn."

Derek ran a hand through his hair. "You've been talking to me this whole time. You've shown me glimpses, pushed me to act... why not just tell me what I need to do?"

"I needed to be sure you were ready," the man said. "Truth is... I'm *still* not sure. But we are running out of time."

He looked into Derek's eyes, and something cold passed between them.

"The Culling is upon us."

Derek's stomach turned. "The path has changed. You told me that. What does it mean?"

The man's expression froze. His next words were sharp. "I said no such thing."

Derek's throat dried. "Yes, you did. I heard it in *your* voice, in *my* head. You said the path had changed."

The old man stood, face grim. "The path you walk is the only path that can end this. There is no other."

Derek's pulse quickened. "Then, who said it?"

But the old man closed his eyes instead of answering. He began to hum. It was a low, haunting note that seemed to shake the trees. The hummingbirds reacted immediately. Their trills changed pitch. They darted in frantic spirals.

Derek stood, too. "The Trinity," he said quickly. "What does it mean? What am I supposed to do? Who are the Pillars? Why do you speak to Stagran... and to Malum?" The questions flooded out of him.

The old man's eyes snapped open. The color had drained from his face.

"Stagran was a guide. A necessary one. He could show you what I could not. Be there while I am stuck here. I have spoken to him for years... preparing for this." He paused. "But *Malum*?" The name left his lips like a curse. "I would *never* speak to that *thing*."

Derek clenched his fists. "He told me you did. Twice. He knows things he shouldn't. Things only you have said."

The hummingbirds shrieked. Smoke curled in on itself.

The old man gripped Derek's shoulder tightly. "You know what the Trinity is," he said. "You feel it in your bones. You know Malum's plan can't be undone... but he can be removed from the world. He's going to attempt the Trials in the Sacred Dimension. If he succeeds... if he passes through that gate... no force in the realms will stop him."

Derek's voice was shaking. "But the voice that told me the path changed, if it wasn't you... who the hell was it?"

The old man didn't answer. Behind him, the forest began to shimmer. One by one, the trees combusted into flame, collapsing into ash.

"I do not have time to explain," the man said. "Use the Veritas. Find your Pillars. Stop him before he reaches the gate."

The forest trembled. Smoke rolled like thunderclouds.

"Take the night. Rest. You are no good if you can not stay awake, or if your energy is drained."

The old man stared deeply into Derek's eyes.

"The culling is near."

And then, with both hands, the old man shoved Derek backward.

He hit the ground hard, flat on his back. Wooden beams. Warm torchlight. Voices. He was back in the Fickle Fae. Everyone turned to stare.

Mia was already kneeling beside him, eyes wide, reaching for his hand. "Derek?!"

He sat up slowly. The scent of smoke clung to his clothes. He didn't say a word. But in his mind, the flames still burned.

Chapter 47

The New Plan

Derek blinked, disoriented, his breath catching in his throat.

The Fickle Fae came back into focus. Warm firelight, creaking wood, the scent of honeyed bread and scorched magic hanging in the air. His friends were frozen exactly where they had been before the flash. Not a single body had shifted. Not a single breath seemed to have passed.

He stared at them, stunned. "How long was I gone?"

Mia wiped a tear from her eye. She laid her head on his chest, her breaths ragged, "Only a few seconds," she whispered.

Silas stepped forward, shadow coiling at his feet. "Where did you go?"

Derek tightened his grip on Mia before speaking, like he needed her warmth to stay grounded. "It felt longer than a few seconds... It felt like at least half an hour. I was with *him*. The Voice in the Void. Somewhere called the Forest of Life."

Tah'quhal's ears perked up and he crossed the room, calm but alert. "Could you see anything this time?"

Derek nodded slowly. "Yeah. I saw him. He looked like... a withered old man. He said he hadn't shown himself before because..." He hesitated, then looked at Mia. "Because you followed me."

Mia's embrace faltered. Her eyes met his, wide with guilt. "I'm so sorry," she whispered. "I didn't know. I just—"

"You couldn't have known," Derek said softly. "You were just trying to find me."

Missy stepped forward next. "Well, son," she said in her steady, Southern drawl. "What did the Voice say?"

Derek took a deep breath. "Malum's going to the Sacred Dimension. There are challenges there... trials that will make him unstoppable if he completes them. We need to use the Veritas, open the Grand Portal, and stop him before he can finish them."

At the mention of the orb, everyone turned to Caldera. She still held the Veritas delicately in her hands, the soft white light pulsing like a heartbeat within.

Mia looked back to Derek. "Are you sure?"

He nodded. "I am." His eyes surveyed everyone else in the tavern. "But that doesn't mean y'all have to be. If you choose to use it... you risk losing your mind. Stagran told us about the risk, you have to be willing to accept that."

Mia gave him a small, bittersweet smile. One that said she'd follow him anywhere, even if it cost them everything.

"I'll take the orb, Caldera. We can all meet back here in the morning. I think we all deserve a good sleep before we lose the chance." Derek added.

Tah'quhal asked Derek, "Can we have a moment?"

Derek raised an eyebrow, unsure of why anything would need to be said in private, "Uh, sure."

He followed Tah'quhal to the corner of the tavern.

Tah'quhal let out a long breath and explained, "When I left Barry in Ignis, I was stuck somewhere."

Derek studied his friend's face. A sense of worry spread through him

Tah'quhal continued, "I was in a place I had only heard of in bedtime stories. A place called the 'Between.' I spoke with Torviid again."

"Why are you just now telling me this?" Derek asked, his face distraught.

"Because I did not know what it meant until just now. You said you were in the Forest of Life?" Tah'quhal asked.

Derek nodded, unsure of what was happening.

"Torviid told me, 'The Forest of Life has many that tend to its trees.' Did you see anyone else there?"

Derek shook his head, but admitted, "There were hummingbirds made of colorful smoke, trees burning..." It hit him. Maybe there was someone else. "Before the voice sent me back, trees in the distance started to burn. He acted like he was scared of something... maybe he was scared of someone else seeing me?"

Tah'quhal added, "I am not sure. These are the only words Torvid gave me, and they made little sense at the time."

"The voice told me he didn't speak to Malum like Malum claims. Maybe there is another being there? Maybe they are the ones whispering to Malum?" Derek asked.

"If that is the case, then we do not need to waste any more time. We need to stop whatever Malum is about to do." Tah'quhal looked at the Veritas in Caldera's arms.

"We will find the Pillars, but first we need to rest. Even the old man knows we are gonna need our full strength for whatever we are about to face." Derek took a step toward Caldera, extending his hand for the orb. He never made it.

A blur of motion. A sharp gasp. And suddenly, Derek was yanked off the floor, his back slammed into the wooden wall of the tavern. His feet dangled inches above the ground, one of Trace's hands crushing his throat while the other held a narrow, shimmering dagger against his neck.

All hell broke loose.

Tah'quhal roared, drawing Orgí in a fluid motion. The blade crackled with blue essence.

Barry's hands ignited in a roar of flame.

Caldera tossed the orb to Mr. Monton, then kicked her spear into her waiting hand.

Mia's fingers flicked downward. Two gleaming ice daggers burst from her essence, ready to strike.

Trace only laughed, calm and infuriating. "Now, now. Everyone just take it nice and easy." His grip tightened. "If any of you move... so much as flinch before I say so, I will bury this dagger into Derek's throat."

Barry shouted, "What the hell are you doing?!"

Trace cocked his head. "Take a look at the tip, Barry. Do not be shy."

Barry stepped forward warily, eyes narrowing, then widening in horror. "Shit. That's a piece of the Lunabeast's antler."

Gasps spread through the room.

"Do any of you know what happens when this pierces Derek's skin?" Trace asked, voice calm. "No? Neither do I. But *Helian* was very... specific about what it might do."

Caldera's voice cracked through the tension like a whip. "Helian? You are that vile creature's lackey?"

Trace didn't flinch. "Helian is a visionary! He was robbed of his true destiny! With the Veritas, he will return to the Sacred Dimension. He will slay the Hellfire Queen. He will—"

A blast of purple essence slammed into his wrist with a sickening crack, pinning it against the wall.

"Now, Derek!" Abhaya's voice echoed through the tavern like thunder.

Trace turned, stunned, but it was already too late.

Derek's eyes blazed pure white. Lightning surged along his arms, crackling with barely contained rage.

"Looks like you flinched," he said.

Lightning exploded from Derek's chest and arms, blasting Trace off his feet. He hit the opposite wall with a heavy thud and crumpled to the floor.

Tah'quhal sprinted over, his stigmata glowing with furious light. He knelt by Trace's stunned body and whispered, "*Ligatus.*"

Blue essence spiraled from his palm, wrapping Trace's wrists and ankles in glowing bands of pure energy.

"He will not be moving anytime soon," Tah'quhal said.

Barry broke the tension with a sharp laugh. "Okay, seriously... anyone else wanna stab us in the back?"

Silence fell over the tavern like a curtain. All eyes shifted. Everyone waited for someone to speak, waited for someone to confess.

Abhaya's voice rang out. "The next person to try that won't get a disarming blast. They'll get a kill shot."

Tah'quhal crossed his arms. "Are we sure it will not be you, Keeper of Neutrale?"

Abhaya's expression twisted in offense. "Why in the realms would you say that?"

"You were Nidalle's second-in-command, and we just saw where her allegiances lie. Who is to say you were not conspiring with her?"

"I didn't know," she growled. "You think I would stand by while she betrayed everything I—"

Caldera stepped between them, firm and unshaken. "That is enough. I have known Abhaya longer than most of you have known the truth about this realm. She has earned more trust than you are giving her."

Silas smirked, arms crossed. "And none of you knew anything about Welderan before we got here. So maybe we should hold off on the accusations."

The room fractured. Arguments burst out like cracks in glass. Voices overlapping. Accusations, defenses, anger. Everyone speaking, no one listening. Except Derek.

He stood in the middle of the storm, silent. Thoughts racing. Heart thundering. The Voice's warning echoing in his skull.

He scanned the tavern and spotted the Veritas resting on the bar where Mr. Monton had set it down. He walked toward it slowly. No one noticed. He picked it up.

"Enough," Derek whispered. No one heard. "ENOUGH!" he shouted.

The orb pulsed with light in his hands. Everyone froze.

"Derek?" Mia asked, voice trembling. "What are you doing?"

"There's only one path forward," Derek said, voice cracking. "We need answers... I need answers."

His eyes locked onto Mia's. She understood immediately. If the orb consumed him, if this was the end, he wanted her to know that he forgave her.

"In the morning, Lavender." Mia pleaded. "You said it yourself. One night of good rest, and then we proceed."

His eyes met hers. She was right and he knew it. The old man even told him to wait until morning. Maybe that meant something.

He opened his own satchel, looking at the elixirs inside, he placed the Veritas on top of them and folded the flap back over.

"Then, in the morning, I'll find my answers." His voice rang through the air in the Tavern.

Mia walked to him, placing each of her hands in his. "No. *We* find *our* answers."

Chapter 48

In The Air

Derek sat cross-legged on the wooden floor of the bedroom he shared with Mia. The flicker of the enchanted lantern warmed the space, casting slow-moving shadows against the walls. His eyes were distant, fixed on the floorboards in front of him, but his thoughts were elsewhere—the portal, Malum, and what came next.

Behind him, a door creaked open. Steam rolled out in waves as Mia stepped from the bathing room, a soft towel wrapped around her body, her hair damp and curling near the ends.

"It never amazes me how magic keeps the water warm," she said with a light laugh, crossing the room to grab her nightclothes, an oversized T-shirt and a pair of cotton shorts. She paused, looking at him. "Are you going to take a bath?"

Derek stood slowly, his joints aching more from exhaustion than pain. "Even better," he replied, walking toward the steam-filled room. "The water even stays clean. Never have to drain the tub."

Mia snorted. "Laziness disguised as convenience."

He stepped into the bath and sank beneath the surface. Warmth enveloped him. With a small flick of his finger, a layer of shimmering bubbles rose over the water's surface. "And the bubbles are pretty cool," he added.

Mia returned, this time dressed for bed, and perched herself on the edge of the tub. She dipped her hand into the water, trailing her fingers through his hair. "Derek, I really am sorry," she murmured. "I never meant to—"

He stopped her with a shake of his head, sliding a bar of soap along his arm. "It doesn't matter anymore. I can't go into all of this mad at you. Or upset. I kept things from you, too."

Her hand stilled. She leaned down and kissed him, slow and lingering. The silence afterward was soft and forgiving.

"Can I ask you something?" he asked, running the soap across his chest.

"Of course."

"Is there anything else?" His voice was steady, but his eyes held quiet pleading.

Mia met his gaze without flinching. "No. Nothing else. I promise."

Derek studied her face, letting the silence linger. He didn't just hear the truth, he felt it in the way her shoulders relaxed, in the way her breath remained steady. The tension he hadn't realized he carried melted into the warmth of the water.

"I know I said one thing, but…" he hesitated. "I've got one more."

"Go ahead."

"Our parents are here, mine… Barry's… Mr. Monton." he said carefully. "Are you… worried about where yours might be?"

Mia stood from the edge of the tub. Turning her back to him, she was quiet for a moment too long. When she finally spoke, her voice was barely above a whisper. "I think about it all the time," she said. "But if Dad thought something was wrong, he'd have brought as many people as he could to Oceanus. Or maybe… maybe they got caught in a rift and ended up somewhere else in Luminfae. There's no way to know."

He stepped from the tub, wrapped himself in a towel, and walked to her. His arms slipped around her waist from behind.

"I didn't mean to upset you—"

"You didn't," she said. "We just… we keep moving forward. That's how we make it matter. That's how we make it worth it."

Derek kissed the back of her head, then turned to grab a pair of shorts and tugged them on. When he turned back, Mia was slipping beneath the covers.

He joined her, laying beside her as she nestled her head on his chest, her hand tracing lazy shapes along his stomach.

"I'm sorry," he whispered. "For how I acted… overreacted."

"We're allowed to have emotions, Derek. You don't have to be perfect."

He smiled as her hand began to trace hearts on him now. "I love you." He whispered.

Mia tilted her head up and kissed him gently. "I love you, too."

In the next room over, laughter echoed as Barry wrestled with Caldera, both of them locked in a playful scuffle that had tipped over a stool, sent a pair of boots flying, and nearly cracked the bedpost.

"This isn't what I thought you meant by 'have some fun,'" Barry huffed, narrowly avoiding a palm strike to the chest.

Caldera ducked under his arm with catlike grace. "Is this not fun?," she asked, breathless with laughter. "And I need to know what I am working with now that you have got this whole fire magic thing. Last thing I want is to have to drag your unconscious body off a battlefield."

Barry caught her wrist mid-spin and twisted it gently until she spun into his arms, facing him. "Didn't Derek say we're supposed to be resting before tomorrow?"

"I am resting. Just... dynamically." She leaned into him, smirking. "I need to know if I can trust you to hold your ground."

"You can trust me," Barry said, leaning down to press his forehead to hers. "I may not be some chosen warrior or fae commander, but I'm not the same guy I was a few weeks ago."

She stepped back, assessing him with an unreadable look. "No," she said softly, "you are not."

Barry turned his head, catching the edge of seriousness in her tone. "You okay?"

Caldera walked toward the bed and flopped onto it, stretching across the mattress like a lounging cat. "I keep thinking about tomorrow. About what we are walking into. I have seen a lot of battles. I have watched people I care about fall. But this? This feels... final."

Barry crossed the room and climbed onto the bed beside her. "Then, we just have to make sure it's not."

She rolled over and looked up at him. "Are you scared?"

He nodded. "Yeah. But I think that's what makes us brave, right? We're not supposed to be fearless... we just do it anyway."

She stared at him for a long second, her expression unreadable. Then, she suddenly swung her leg over his lap, straddling him. "You are smarter than you let on, Bear."

"Gotta keep expectations low. It's part of the charm."

She leaned in and kissed him deeply, her fingers threading into his hair. When she pulled back, she rested her forehead against his. "Whatever happens, I meant what I said to your parents. I want us."

Barry smiled, brushing a thumb across her cheek. "Well, if Derek does find a way to reverse what Malum has done, then I have some good news."

Caldera grinned, "Oh, really? Please tell me."

"Portals!" Barry said. "Long distance has never looked so doable."

Caldera laughed, her tension easing. "Do you realize we could literally have breakfast in Magia Forest and dinner on Earth?"

"Only if I get to cook," he said.

Her brow arched. "I am not eating anything you char."

He grinned and flipped her onto her back, pinning her down with faux seriousness. "One grilled cheese and suddenly I'm unfit for kitchen duty?"

"Barry," she said, smiling under him, "Whoever invented melted cheese on bread should be imprisoned. There is no sustenance in that." She poked up at his chest, "And according to Johnathan, you almost burned down his family home."

"Which is still better than Derek, who once tried to boil water in a wooden bowl."

Caldera blinked. "Wait, what?"

"Exactly." He leaned down and kissed her again. "See? Low bar."

They stayed there a moment longer, tangled together in soft warmth and breathless affection. The lantern light danced along the walls. Outside, the wind shifted through the trees.

"Do you think we'll get a quiet life after this?" Barry asked.

"I think we will have to fight for it," she answered. "But I also think it will be worth it."

Barry's jaw tightened as he whispered, "Better to be a warrior in a garden than a gardner in a war."

Caldera's brow knitted, "Bear... is everything okay?"

His face returned to normal. He leaned down to kiss her, saying on the way, "Just a saying I've heard."

A hush settled over the room. Barry reached to turn down the lantern. The light faded slowly, casting them in a cocoon of shadows and whispered dreams.

Tomorrow would bring another war. But for tonight, they rested, together.

Chapter 49

The Truth

The next morning, everyone was gathered back in the tavern. For the first time in a long time, a smile was on everyone's faces, each of them relaxed from the night before. Derek wasted no time.

He pulled the Veritas from his satchel, "Is everyone ready?"

Nods and agreement spread through the room. Derek placed both hands around the Veritas. His eyes met Mia's for just a moment before he took a deep breath.

His voice dropped to a whisper. "Still I stand. Until I fall. I will heed the lonesome call."

His eyes turned white.

The room held its breath.

And the Veritas answered.

Derek opened his eyes. He wasn't in the Fickle Fae.

He was standing in the parking lot of Riverrun High School. The morning sky above him was heavy with mist, tinged in gray and gold. Cars were parked haphazardly, a few kids milled around with backpacks slung over their shoulders. There was no sound. No wind, no voices. Just silence.

He turned slowly and spotted his younger self.

He and Johnathan were getting out of the latter's truck. His hair was a mess. He fidgeted with his sleeves. And then Mia got out of her own car and walked towards the school... towards him. A tiny, awkward smile played across the younger Derek's lips as he approached her, fumbling through their first ever conversation.

Lavender, He thought to himself. *Such a goofy thing to say, and I still can't escape it*. He laughed out loud, and then covered his mouth, afraid someone would be able to hear him. But, of course, no one did.

Derek watched with a bittersweet ache. He remembered the nerves, the way his heart pounded in his chest... and the blue streak that shot across the sky that morning, right before everything changed.

But something was wrong. A faint orange glow surrounded his younger self. It was barely visible at first, like a halo, or a warning flare no one noticed.

His breath caught. He blinked and the memory shifted.

Now, he hovered inside the school hallway, ghostlike. Ivan slammed his fist into the locker beside Derek's head. Younger Derek flinched, lips pressed into a thin line, trying not to give Ivan the satisfaction of fear.

The orange aura was still there—subtle, but constant.

Another blink.

He was in the school auditorium, sitting among a sea of students as the assembly dragged on. Mia placed her hand on Derek's knee. He remembered how happy that made him. Younger Derek was tense, shoulders hunched, clearly elsewhere in his mind. The glow hadn't dimmed.

"Why do I keep seeing it?" Derek whispered aloud to no one. "Was it always there, or...?"

Another blink.

Now, he was at the Monton family farm. The air was thick with grief. Izzy's death hung like a veil over the room. He saw himself sitting on the steps outside, staring at the field, jaw clenched, eyes burning.

The orange aura pulsed brighter.

He took a step closer, heart heavy, memories resurfacing. It wasn't strength, not entirely. It was something quieter, something rooted deeper than pain or rage.

Steadfastness. That word filled his mind like thunder.

Another blink.

Darkness. Mythos. He watched himself battle the harpy alongside Sarika. Shadows slashed through the air, claws raking across stone, Derek's white light crackling through the dark. And still, the orange glow lit his silhouette like a fire within.

Only now did it strike him. He never saw this aura back then. The Veritas was showing him something hidden, something essential. It wasn't real light, it was the truth.

And truth had a color. He closed his eyes and focused. Three orbs. Three colors. Still I stand... orange. Steadfastness. Until I fall... blue. Vulnerability. The lonesome call... red. Courage.

He blinked.

Torvania. Outside the Cressida Library. Caldera and Barry were rushing inside, carrying Johnathan's unconscious body. Derek's past self stayed outside. He didn't move an inch. Not even a muscle flinched.

He looked for the orange glow again, but it wasn't there. Blue light shimmered faintly around him, a softer, colder glow. It wrapped him in silence.

His chest tightened. Blue. Until I fall. Vulnerability. He remembered what Stagran said, "Each Pillar represents one truth." Then, why was he seeing multiple truths?

Blink.

The top of the twisted tower in Oblivion. Malum stood across from him, monstrous and gnarled. Lightning crackled around

Derek's arms. Izzy... her spirit or vision or memory, spoke to him in the chaos, surrounded by an unfamiliar pink aura that pulsed like a heartbeat.

But Derek's own glow had changed again. Red. Burning. Relentless. Uncompromising. The lonesome call. Courage.

He fell to one knee as pain lanced through his skull. The vision blurred, then vanished. Darkness closed around him. No colors. No memories. Just black.

And then, the field, the same field from his nightmares before all of this began. Endless grass. Soft wind. The sun was somewhere far above but cast no warmth. He knew this place, and he hated it.

The anxiety that once paralyzed him after every nightmare returned like opening an old wound. The sky dimmed. His vision narrowed. He was fading. The Veritas was taking his mind.

He gasped, struggling to breathe, to remember who he was. Everything blurred. Mia, Barry, Caldera, Silas, Tah'quhal. Gone. Even his name felt foreign.

The corners of his vision curled inward like burning paper. He was dissolving. No. *No.*

His family needed him. His friends needed him. Luminfae needed him. Earth needed him.

He didn't survive his panic attacks to die like this. He didn't raise an army just to fall now. He didn't watch friends betray him to be undone by a whisper of light.

This was his destiny, his path, and he wasn't giving it up.

"STAND."

The word exploded in his mind, and his vision snapped into clarity. The field vanished. In its place stood a surreal landscape–three terrains, each with a silhouette of himself.

Straight ahead, stood a massive mountain, towering and eternal. At its base was Derek, glowing in vibrant orange.

To the right, a wide river flowed gently through the valley. Another Derek stood there, surrounded in blue.

Behind him was a roaring inferno, flames licking skyward. There, a third Derek waited, shrouded in red.

Three Pillars. Three truths. Three paths.

But only one glowed the brightest. Only one had followed him from the very beginning. Only one had shown up in every scene, every quiet moment when no one else stood with him.

The mountain. He turned toward it, heart pounding. Each step forward made the silhouette sharper, more defined. His own face. His own scars. A mirror, waiting for him to decide.

He raised a trembling hand. It glowed with orange light. He touched the hand of his mirrored self and the world went black.

Derek opened his eyes again, he was back in the Fickle Fae. No one had moved. Every face stared at him, breath held.

Derek exhaled. His eyes fell on the Veritas orb. The glass shimmered faintly, as if it had just recorded a sacred vow.

Then, he looked at Mia. His voice was steady. Quiet. Unshakable.

"Still I stand."

Chapter 50

The Path

The tavern was quiet—too quiet. Derek blinked, disoriented, his breath shaky in his chest. The Veritas orb was warm in his hand. All eyes were still on him.

Mia stepped forward first. "What did you see?" she asked, voice barely above a whisper. "Tell me everything."

He hesitated, not because he didn't want to, but because he didn't know where to begin. "It was... overwhelming," he finally said. "Like I was walking through a movie made from my own memories. But it felt real. Too real."

He recounted it all. The parking lot at Riverrun High, the first awkward morning with Mia, the orange aura flickering faintly around his younger self. The jump to the Monton family farm, to the Mythos battle, to the tower in Oblivion where Izzy had whispered through death. Each scene, each shift, came with a new color. Orange. Blue. Red. Steadfastness. Vulnerability. Courage.

"Then, it took me to a field," he said, his voice faltering. "The same one from my old nightmares. Before all of this began. And for a moment... I thought I wasn't coming back."

The words hung in the air, but inside, Derek was unraveling. Just remembering it brought the panic crawling back. Cold fingers clutched at his lungs, that suffocating pressure folding his body inward like it had in the dream. He felt the phantom pull again, the slow collapse of light, like the edges of his mind were curling into smoke. He swallowed hard, but it did nothing to clear the tightness in his throat.

His hands trembled at his sides not with fear. No, this was something deeper, a kind of mental exhaustion that felt like it had aged him years in the span of minutes. The Veritas hadn't just shown him truths. It stripped him down to the very fiber of his being and showed him who he truly was.

He clenched his jaw, his shoulders tense, like he was bracing for it to happen again.

And that's when Mia stepped forward.

Mia's eyes filled with tears. "We could see you twitching," she admitted. "Your eyes turned white, like you weren't even here anymore."

Barry stepped up beside her. "At first, there was this orange glow coming off of you. Then, it turned blue. Then, red."

Silas nodded. "And just before you came back, all three colors were swirling around you."

Tah'quhal folded his arms and added, "It was like a storm of light, like the orb was deciding."

Silence fell in the wooden walled room.

Derek's breath hitched in his throat. He hadn't realized he was still holding it. His hands, though steady now, remembered the tremor. The silence in the tavern faded to a distant hum as his thoughts pulled inward.

He had been drowning... no, unraveling, inside that vision. His mind split apart by memories, doubts, and truths too heavy to bear. That field... that darkness... it hadn't just been a nightmare. It had been the brink, the end of him.

And yet, he came back.

He blinked, grounding himself in the familiar flicker of candlelight and the quiet shifting of his friends nearby. The Veritas hadn't broken him. He'd walked through fire, through grief and fear and the lure of surrender, and emerged whole. Scarred, maybe. Changed, definitely. But still here.

The orb hadn't chosen for him. He had chosen himself.

A weight lifted in his chest, not fully, but enough. He had faced something that wanted to erase him, and he'd said no. Somehow, impossibly... he'd won.

Derek held the Veritas closer, its surface dull now, inert. "I don't think it means I'm all three," he said. "I think the Veritas shows you what you could be. The truths you might hold. But you have to choose one. I chose Steadfastness because it stayed with me through every memory. It burned the brightest." Derek let a smile show on his face. "It felt... right."

He looked down at the orb. "I think if you lie to yourself, if you choose the wrong truth... that's when it takes your mind. I barely held on." The grief tried to creep back in. "I wouldn't wish that feeling on anyone."

Another stillness followed. The tavern held its breath.

"I will not look," Caldera said, breaking the silence.

Barry turned to her, brows pinching. "What?"

She didn't hesitate. "I already know who I am. The Veritas does not need to tell me. It was never meant for me." She reached for Barry's hand. "But I think... I think it *is* meant for *you*."

Barry's face grew serious. He gave a small nod. He understood what she meant, so much had changed for him in the last year, but really... he had grown the most in the last few days.

Caldera leaned in and kissed him.

Barry stepped toward Derek, reaching for the orb, but Derek held out a hand, stopping him.

"Not here," he said. "We should do this in the Grand Portal chamber."

Barry blinked. "Man, I done hyped myself up. Caldera done hyped me up. Why you gonna make me wait?"

Derek's gaze swept across the room. "Because this next step needs to be immediate. We need to be ready to go as soon as we know the other two Pillars." Derek paused and looked around the room once more. "Anyone who wants to come with me... follow. But know this... once we enter that chamber, there's no turning back. If you come with me down there, that means you're walking through that portal with me, too."

Murmurs filled the room.

"You don't have to look into the Veritas to stand with me," Derek continued. "But we'll need all three Pillars to open the right portal."

His parents approached him. Missy wrapped him in a fierce hug. "We'll hold things down here," she whispered. "We always do."

Phillip clapped a hand on his back, his grin tired but proud. "Go kick his ass, son."

Glorinda and Davis found Barry and embraced him tightly. "We're better put to work here," Davis said. "They'll need help in the tent cities."

"Be careful," Glorinda added. "You've always been brave. Just don't be reckless."

Mr. Monton stepped up last, his hand trembling slightly as he placed it on Derek's shoulder. His eyes glistened.

"I'm sorry we didn't tell you about the tents sooner," he said, voice thick with regret. "That was my mistake." He swallowed hard. "Please... bring my son back."

"I will," Derek promised, but a seed of doubt nestled deep in his chest. He didn't know if Johnathan was still alive, but he'd move heaven and hell to try.

He tucked the Veritas beneath his arm. Mia's hand found his, their fingers interlocking like puzzle pieces worn smooth by time.

Barry looked at him. "So... where exactly is this portal chamber, my guy?"

Derek glanced over his shoulder. The group was assembled. Mia. Barry and Caldera. Tah'quhal. Silas. Abhaya.

He smiled. "The Cressedia Library."

And with that, they walked out the door.

Chapter 51

Finish Them

The castle at the edge of Oblivion stood alone, shrouded in a haze that refused to lift, as if the realm itself rejected the light. It was carved into black stone, ancient and jagged, the towers rising like fingers desperate to claw the sky. No birds sang here. No wind stirred. Only the quiet hum of dark magic reminded the world that something lived within.

"Dammit!" Malum roared, his voice echoing off the cold walls of the throne room. His clawed hand slammed into the arm of the obsidian throne, splitting the stone.

The wound from Derek still throbbed. Blue lightning had kissed his face, burning a jagged scar into his cheek that refused to heal.

Sarika stood beside him, conjuring red essence into her fingertips. Her movements were careful, surgical, as she brushed the essence over his torn skin. "It will scar," she said calmly. "But you will live."

"I do not care about scars," he hissed. "He needs to die. I want something sent after him... anything. I want it done. Over."

Footsteps echoed through the chamber as Circe entered. She moved like a queen—regal, sharp, untouchable. She was draped in a black velvet gown embroidered with threads that shimmered like emerald.

"Do not be so crass," she said coolly. "You know as well as I do, for the convergence to complete, Derek must perish in the Sacred Dimension. Leonidas must see it. That is part of the balance."

"I could care less what that fossil sees," Malum spat. He rose from his throne with a grunt, rotating his shoulders. "Derek is a thorn in my side. A blight. If Torviid could not stop me, why does this child think he can?"

Sarika snorted under her breath. "He has kicked your ass a few times."

Malum's head snapped toward her. His crimson-irised eyes swirled with power. "He was your mess to start with. Speak out of turn again," his voice dropped, venomous, "and I will let Talissa have her fun with you next."

Sarika lowered her gaze and knelt in silence. Circe moved to her side, gently lifting her back to her feet.

Malum turned to the massive arched window that overlooked Oblivion's jagged cliffs. The dark sea churned below, hungry.

"Why can he not see it?" Malum murmured. "My vision would bring balance. Equality. One realm. One people. No gods, no gates, no separation. No suffering!" His voice only got angrier as he went on.

No one replied.

He continued, voice gentler now, as if reciting a sermon to ghosts. "It is peace. The only peace that is real. One ruler to keep it all in order."

Still silence.

Everan stepped from the shadows, bowing his head. "And then, my liege?"

Malum didn't turn to face him. "Then, we move to the next. And the next. And the next."

Circe placed a hand on her hip. "Until you rule them all."

Malum's smile was all teeth and madness. "Exactly, my queen. With you behind me, anything is possible."

"Beside you," Circe corrected gently.

"I spoke correctly," he said without looking back. "You may be the dread *Hellfire Queen*, but this was my vision long before you tied your name to it."

Circe's smile flickered.

"If not for me," she said slowly, "you would be—"

"Dead?" Malum cut her off. "Yes. And my plan would have proceeded. Someone would have taken my name, my will. My legacy. I do not need to be alive to be immortal."

Circe glanced at Sarika, who met her eyes and quickly looked away. That look did not go unnoticed.

Malum turned back, eyes narrowing. "You resent me," he said. "Good. Let it fuel your fire the next time you face Derek."

He stepped toward Sarika, his gaze now only for her. "And maybe you will keep your lips off him next time. Use your blade instead."

Without waiting for a reply, Malum strode from the room.

Circe's mask of calm faltered for only a moment.

"Where are you going, my king?" she asked, her voice too smooth.

"To check on our prisoners," he said over his shoulder. "Both of them."

The dungeon reeked of blood, rust, and magic.

Johnathan hung from the ceiling by chains that bit into his wrists. His boots barely scraped the cobbled floor, surrounded by dried blood and strange neon-green puddles, the serum Talissa injected regularly. His arms ached, his body trembled, and his voice cracked as he shouted into the dark.

"Dadgummit, would you just wake up already? I know you can hear me!"

Only eerie stillness.

"I thought you were our friend..." Johnathan's voice faltered.

Across the hallway, the shadows shifted.

"Trey?" he pleaded. "I couldn't stop them from hurting Izzy. But this ain't on me. Be mad at ya daddy!"

Fists slammed into iron bars with a metallic clang.

"Don't you think I am!?" came the hoarse reply.

Trey stood, ragged and pale. His eyes were bloodshot, his breath uneven. "He's got me locked up the same as you. He only lets me out when he's drugged me to the brink. Only when I am not in control."

Johnathan let out a laugh, dry and broken. "At least you're talkin' again."

Trey smirked. "Malum told me and Ivan everything. Ivan loved it. Me? I've been stalling, waiting. Figuring out how to stop it from the inside."

Johnathan grunted as he struggled against his chains. "Why not just tell us? Tell Derek?"

"If I did," Trey said, "he would've killed Derek outright. He wanted the moment... the drama. That's how he works. Wanted it to be *poetic*."

There was a pause. Then, Trey added, "But I did fight back. Last time I was out there, I fought through whatever they drugged me with just long enough to signal Derek. Cut my eyes to Malum and let him throw lightning at me. Dodged it just in time. Got dear old dad electro-blasted in the face."

Johnathan chuckled. "You played the long game, huh?" But the pain returned, deep and sharp. He coughed, blood flecking his lip. "Don't know how long I can last, man."

"You have to," Trey said firmly. "They need a Keeper. They won't let you die, not yet."

"But what for?" Johnathan gasped. "Why me?"

"Because of the Kee—"

"Tsk, tsk, tsk," Malum clicked his tongue as he entered the corridor. "How talkative we have become."

Neither man replied.

"Talissa," Malum called, "put them both to sleep. I do not need them conscious anymore."

Talissa emerged from the shadows with Nidalle at her side.

Johnathan whimpered as Nidalle entered his cell. "Please. Don't do this."

She didn't speak. Her eyes were calm, unreadable.

Trey said nothing. His silence was unnerving.

Nidalle slid a needle into the IV, injecting a dark purple liquid. Johnathan's vision began to swim, his limbs going limp. As the drug pulled him under, he saw her raise a finger to her lips.

Shhh.

She tapped her ear.

Listen.

He could barely nod. His heart pounded, then slowed.

From somewhere far away, he heard Malum's voice. "Everan, are Cerberus and the Hellfire legions ready?"

"Of course, my lord. As is the hydra."

"Good," Malum said. "Send them all to Torvania. When I return, I want to hear how bright the city burned."

And then... nothing.
Only darkness. Only silence.

423

Chapter 52

Not Again

The fire in the Cressida Library's hearth burned low, casting long, flickering shadows against the spines of ancient tomes. Derek stood before it, eyes fixed on the ornate frame above the mantle. It was an exact match to the one he and Silas had seen in their shared vision. He reached up and gently placed the Veritas atop the mantle, its glow muted and waiting.

Without hesitation, he removed the helmet from one of the suits of armor that flanked the fireplace and took the other's sword. With purpose, he tossed both into the flames. The fire roared to life, shifting into a brilliant, ethereal blue.

A rumble beneath their feet followed. Stone grated against stone. The floor in front of the fireplace trembled, then slowly opened, revealing a spiraling staircase leading down into darkness.

Derek retrieved the Veritas, tucking it under one arm. Mia slid her fingers into his, and together, they stepped into the shadows.

Silas followed close behind.

Then came Barry and Caldera, shoulder to shoulder.

Abhaya moved to step forward, but paused as she noticed Tah'quhal hadn't moved. "Is everything okay?" she asked, voice quiet amid the settling stone.

Tah'quhal's gaze swept the walls, then the flickering blue fire. "It seems there is something new to learn about my home every day."

Abhaya approached him, placing a gentle hand on his shoulder. "True stillness," she said, "comes from embracing the moment."

He blinked, his brows knitted tightly together. "What does that mean?"

"You've endured more than most," she said, her blue eyes almost violet in the shifting light. "You keep moving, keep pushing forward. But sometimes, stillness isn't weakness. It's grace."

Tah'quhal stared at her, unreadable. For a brief second, the tension in his shoulders softened, but then he turned away.

"When this is over," he muttered, stepping past her, "I will embrace the moment. Until then, I will keep moving."

The staircase led into a vast stone chamber, lit by the eerie hum of arcane crystals embedded in the walls. The Grand Portal stood at the far end. A monumental arch carved into the stone, identical to the one in Welderan. The magic in the air hummed like thunder in the bones.

Barry whistled. "This damn library has more secrets than the tunnels under Ignis."

Mia laughed in response, and looking over her shoulder, she said, "At least there isn't a Succubus chasing us through the library, right?"

Barry made an overly dramatic face, the corner of his lips spread wide, his eyebrows raised up on his forehead, and his eyes completely open, "Don't remind me."

Just inside the chamber, Derek turned, and glanced at the group. Tah'quhal and Abhaya had descended last, but Silas lingered near the steps, eyes wary. Derek approached him quietly. "You okay?" he asked.

Shadows flickered along Silas's arms, crawling like nervous thoughts. "I am. It is just... this chamber... it looks identic—"

Derek's voice was low, reassuring, "Identical to the one where your father was killed."

Silas nodded his head. The shadows dancing around him stilled.

Derek placed a hand on his shoulder. "I know I said whoever came down here was in it for the long haul, but you don't have to be here if you don't wanna be.."

"I do," Silas said after a beat. "I want to be. I want answers. And I will not find any if we do not finish this."

Derek gave his shoulder a firm pat. "Then, let's finish it."

He walked to the front of the group and turned to face the others. Behind him, the portal loomed, inactive.

"The Veritas showed me who I am," Derek said. He pressed his hand to the stone arch, and the portal pulsed awake. Stone became fluid, swirling with molten orange light. "Right now, this portal can take us almost anywhere. But not to the Sacred Dimension. Not unless all three Pillars are present."

He looked across the faces of his friends. "We don't *have* to use the Veritas. But if we don't, we might not know if we're truly ready." Derek paused for a second. "I can't stress enough how terrifying looking into the Veritas was. If you don't think you are strong enough to open your eyes on the other side of it, then don't risk it."

Silence hung for a breath.

"I will use it," Tah'quhal said.

"I will as well," Silas added.

Barry stepped forward. "I damn sure ain't being left out. I already tried to use it and you just keep building up the anticipation. Count me in."

Mia, always at Derek's side, gave his hand a reassuring squeeze. "I'll try too."

Everyone turned to Abhaya. She bowed her head and whispered a quiet prayer, her lips barely moving. Then, she raised her eyes and said, "I will look into the Veritas."

The portal behind them pulsed again. The orange light drained out, turning solid white, like milk rushing through stone. It was still moving, but all color had vanished.

"What's happening?" Mia asked, eyes wide, her voice shaky.

"I think we're running out of time," Derek said with conviction.

Barry stepped forward without hesitation. "Looks like we better get to it then."

Derek handed him the Veritas. "Be careful." He looked into his friend's eyes. He could see the flames starting to come alive in his irises.

Barry nodded and cradled the orb in both hands. He smiled back to Caldera, "Be right back, babe."

Caldera returned the expression, "Make it quick, Bear."

Barry looked down at the Veritas in his hand and whispered, "Still I stand... Until I fall... I will heed the lonesome call."

His eyes turned white. Time seemed to stop.

His body twitched, just like Derek's had. Seconds stretched unbearably. Caldera looked as though she might speak, but then... a faint glow appeared around Barry's body.

"Blue." Derek whispered. "Vulnerability."

Everyone let out a breath. The aura changed to red.

"Courage." Derek added.

Tah'quhal grinned, "That sounds like Barry."

Then, it changed again. Blue. Red. It swapped faster. Blue. Red. Blue. Red. The auras swapped back and forth so rapidly, it was hard to tell which color lingered longer.

"Bear? What is happening?" Caldera called out.

Derek answered, his voice low, but panic tried to creep in, "The Veritas is giving him the choice."

Barry's body convulsed, but he stayed standing. Every visible muscle was fighting against itself. When his neck started to shake uncontrollably, Tah'quhal began to worry.

"Dammit, Barry," Tah'quhal muttered, stepping forward.

Derek raised a hand. "Don't touch him! We don't know what could happen."

The light vanished. Barry's body stilled. Then, he opened his eyes. "Until I Fall," he said with a weary grin.

Derek smiled in relief and opened his arm, motioning for Barry to hug him. Barry marched to his friend, his smile wide. Caldera joined, her arms wrapped around Barry's waist from the back.

"I knew it, Bear, I knew you would make it." Caldera whispered.

"Two Pillars," Derek said. "Only one more to—"

A hand shot through the white portal and gripped the collar of Derek's robes. He had no time to react. In a flash, he was yanked through it.

Mia, still holding his hand, screamed as she was pulled in too.

"Derek!" Barry shouted, dropping the Veritas as he dove into the portal head first after them.

The edges of the portal were already turning back to stone. Barry had jumped in plenty of time.

Caldera didn't hesitate, she leapt as well. The portal was only still slightly large enough for her to fit through.

Tah'quhal lunged forward, but by the time his foot touched the edge of the portal, it had turned completely back to stone again. Solid. Sealed.

"No!" he bellowed, slamming his fist against the portal. Again. And again. Blood smeared the surface, but it didn't budge. His knuckles ached, but he continued slamming his fist into the stone wall.

Silas knelt and gently picked up the Veritas. Its glow had dimmed, but its weight felt heavier than ever.

Abhaya stepped to Tah'quhal, placing her hand on his shoulder again. "Tah'quhal?"

He didn't answer.

His fists were raw, blood dripping to the stone floor. He turned and slammed his back into the wall. The pain meant nothing. The stone wall clawed at his back as he slid down it, falling to a seated position on the floor. The pain in his eyes finally broke free, spilling tears down his cheeks.

He was supposed to be their shield.

Ever since he was named Chieftain, he had tried to be wise, to be steady, to be strong enough for all of them. But no matter how fiercely he fought or how far he traveled, someone else was always one step ahead. Derek with his lightning. This new guy, Silas with his shadows. Barry with his laughter that somehow held them all together. He didn't resent them, not for a second, but gods, he just wanted to carry something that mattered, to lead and have it *mean* something.

And now, when it finally came time to stand between his people and the unknown... he had failed. Again. He hadn't been fast enough. Hadn't seen it coming. Hadn't saved them.

He clenched his jaw, knuckles trembling against the floor. He didn't want glory. He didn't want praise. He just wanted to help. To be the reason someone else made it home.

He reached up and touched the stone wall behind him. Defeat settled over him, something he had grown all too familiar with.

His voice was hoarse, nearly broken.

"Not again..."

Acknowledgements

Thank you for reading my book! I truly hope you had as much fun exploring Luminfae as I did writing this adventure. If so, please leave a wonderful review. Reviews are the lifeblood of indie authors like me. The more positive reviews we have, the more likely it is that others will pick up the book as well.

A lot went into this book, and I've had some great encouragement and love from folks along the way. But I would be remiss if I didn't thank a few very specific people for helping me on this journey.

First and foremost, I would like to thank God. He has given me strength and encouragement throughout all the challenging moments of completing this novel. I am truly grateful for his endless love, mercy, and grace.

I want to thank all my family and friends that encouraged me every step of the way. Even when this was just a "I bet I could write a book" you kept me motivated. I would love to name all of you, but I would need a whole chapter to do so.

Travis and Morgan, guess what? You're here again. Thanks for being you and always pushing me!

Alexis at Oak and Dagger Editing. Thank you for coming in mid-series and helping me get this where it needs to be. Thank you for everything!

HulaLotus Design, you did it again! You continue to blow me away with your artwork. Your magic in bringing my jumbled words to life will never cease to amaze me.

The BookTok crew! #Tom4Lyfe

And finally, my amazing wife Kendell and my son Zeke. You encouraged me and inspired me to chase this crazy dream. You have sacrificed time on countless days to allow me to blaze trails in this crazy fantasy world. I love you both to the moon and back.

About the author

T.M. Ford is a husband, father, and author. His debut novel *Still I Stand* is the result of his love for the fantastical and a good story. His background is in telecommunications, having been in the industry for over 10 years, he has quite the love for technology. When he isn't spending time with his family, he is either rooting on the Tennessee Titans or playing a good RPG. He and his wife reside in Tennessee with their son where they enjoy playing disc golf and spending time with family.

Review

Good reviews are vital for Indie Authors. The importance of reviews in helping others find and take a chance on an indie author's book is impossible to overstate.

If you enjoyed this book, would you help me get it in front of more people by taking a minute to give it a good review?

I can't tell you how thankful I'd be.

Check out this link. It will take you to T.M. Ford's website, where you can find the best places to review this book and help me get it to more readers who love good books just like you and me! You can also find all of T.M. Ford's social media and newsletter at the same link, just in case you want to stay in the know for what is next.

T.M. FORD